Rough Exile

Sorcha Black

Belfry Publishing

This book contains dark themes and rough scenes that may be disturbing to some readers. Visit www.sorchablack.com for more information. This book contains scenarios that should not be attempted or emulated.

Sign up for my newsletter here!

Cover

Designs by Morningstar

www.morningstarashley.com

Editor

Nerine Dorman

Proofreader

Donna Jay

Contents

Chapter One

My left shoe was missing.

I groped around for it in the dark, then shrugged. The cleaning staff would find it and return it to the stylists. After a moment's consideration, I put down my right shoe near the nightstand. It would probably be easier for them if I left both shoes in the same room.

Yawning, I glanced back at the bed. The impressive pile of muscle looked like it was asleep, but he might just be ignoring me.

It wasn't like I was expecting flowers.

I'd already forgotten his name. He was pretty but had nothing else going for him other than being rich. It was like that with some of these guys—their money was their entire personality.

Despite the late hour, the sound of sex still filled the halls. I wouldn't be the only woman asking medical for some of their miracle cream to take the edge off her soreness in the morning.

As I passed through the cavernous ballroom that linked the predator's wing to the prey's, the wall of windows showcased the breathtaking night sky. I'd grown up in the city with parents who were always working, so I'd never been camping. My first tour on the Island had been my very first vacation, and the sight of so many stars had transfixed me and had me gazing out at them every night, always hungry to see more.

Maybe an astronomer could look up at those stars and tell us approximately where we were in the world, but none of the women I'd met on my four tours here had known how to navigate that way. I'd tried looking it up once, back home, but I'd never figured it out.

I'd been heading to my room, but there was no rush.

The terrace was magical at night. It was a shame they never held events out here in the dark. The wind had picked up, carrying fresh ocean air. Sometimes, when I was home—especially in winter—I lay in bed and dreamed about this place. I couldn't afford a resort vacation, but this? Food, drinks, and hot, dominant men. How could a resort compare?

Sure, I couldn't always choose my sex partners, and sometimes things got too rough, even for me, but I actually liked it here. Not that I could tell people that. My strategy of sleeping with men on my free days meant that most of them took it easy on me when they could make my life a living hell.

Poor Lane couldn't bring herself to do it, and the target on her back was only getting bigger. I'd rolled out of my sex partner's bed to go check on her, but something told me to wait until morning. The last thing I wanted to do was interrupt her and her two shadows. The poor girl probably thought she was going home after this tour scot-free, but if those guys didn't follow her home and sweep her off her feet, I'd eat my missing shoe.

Freaking Lane. She thought of herself as less attractive than the taller girls here, and yet Ajax and Calder wouldn't leave her alone. I always had to wait my turn to hang out with her.

It never would have crossed my mind to look for a best friend in this place, and it had only been a few weeks, but sometimes you could just tell when someone was going to be important in your life.

I leaned on the stone wall, looking out at the astronomical miracle shining on the jungle below.

A nearby movement caught my eye, and my prey instincts made me stumble back.

Two shadowy figures stood so close I wasn't sure how I hadn't noticed them. Both men, judging by their height and bulk.

"What do you want?" I demanded.

One man chuckled. "Only to continue the conversation we were having before you interrupted."

Oops.

I studied them, trying to place the voice, the accent, and the general size and shape.

"Sorry. I didn't realize anyone was out here."

"We thought everyone else was asleep. I suppose whores don't always get to choose their own hours."

Ugh. Asshole.

Of course, it was Bronislav, and therefore probably Ilya. I had no idea what to make of these two. They kept to themselves, but always seemed to be watching me. I'd never even seen them with a woman. What was the point of coming here if they weren't into hunting down women like prey? It was the only reason rich men paid to be here.

"I thought the two of you only spoke Russian."

"There's no point in making conversation with a woman you can simply take and use when you wish."

"Some women are worth having a conversation with."

"Here? Doubtful." There was the flash of white teeth in the darkness, splitting the impressive beard I knew was there. I had a difficult time telling them apart, but only Bron ever seemed to speak, and only he was covered in tattoos. I'd heard they weren't related, but they could have been twins—same height, similar builds, same long hair and beards. If someone told me they were lumberjacks I might believe them, except lumberjacks could never afford to come here.

There was no point in getting offended. Many of the men here were misogynists, so it wasn't like coming across this in the real world, where it was still a surprise, sometimes.

"So, you didn't come to the Island to make conversation. What *did* you come here for?"

"Our business here is none of your concern, woman."

I had to swallow my pride. It would be easy to walk away from this conversation and go to bed, but every scary man I could sleep with voluntarily might stop short of really hurting me during a hunt.

"You know, if the two of you are looking for some company, I'm free for the rest of the night."

"The last thing I want is a cunt already dripping another man's seed."

I didn't let his disgust hurt my feelings. It was hardly the first time someone insinuated I was a slut. Hell, he hadn't even said the words aloud. If he wanted to slut shame me, he'd have to get more creative, and maybe build a time machine. My entire high school had called me Dirty Delilah for two years because of something done to me without my consent. It had made me bulletproof in the shame department.

You can't hurt me with your words, you big Russian ox.

He pushed away from the wall he'd been leaning on and stalked toward the door. Ilya followed him, more like a menacing shadow than a man.

I expected one of them to turn back and say something cutting, but they only spoke to each other in what I assumed was Russian, as though I really had interrupted something important. Once they were in the ballroom, I could see them more clearly as they headed for the predator wing. They looked like they'd recently raided a village with bloody axes in hand.

Why did they stare at me all the time, then avoid speaking to me? If I couldn't even get them into a conversation, how was I going to get them into bed? My complete inability to engage with them made me nervous.

I understood how the other men here ticked. Those two were a complete mystery.

Chapter Two

L aughing with Lane was my new favorite pastime, and hanging out on a beach with her was even better. The sun was bright, but her smile was brighter.

Something about her always made me feel like I was back in middle school, but the way I wish it had been. I had a good friend, and I had time to spend with her, gossiping about boys and dreaming about the future. It wasn't that she was immature—it was that I could be myself with her and relax. I didn't feel that way about many people. It was a gift she had, and I doubted she realized it.

And she'd just agreed to be friends with me once we went home.

She claimed she'd been trying to think of a way to ask me to stay friends, too, but I wasn't sure if she was only trying to make me feel better about being such a dork. Either way, things had turned out in my favor.

Riding that high, I was imagining going to her place for movie night, or her coming to my place to read books together. We seemed to have a good time, no matter what we were doing, and suddenly my future was looking a lot less lonely.

I wasn't alone often, but there was a difference between having people around versus having an actual friend.

We were grinning at each other, and I felt bright and hopeful for the first time in a long while. Maybe she could even help me figure out what I wanted to do with my life.

I opened my mouth to tell her where I lived, but sudden clouds obscured the sun, and the breeze picked up.

Lane looked at the sky. "Umm—do you think this is one of those storms they warned us about?"

We were alone on the beach, and then we weren't. Men seemed to appear miraculously out of the ether, moving fast, surrounding us. I opened my mouth to scream as they tugged a black cloth bag over Lane's head. No matter what I'd told her about this place being every woman for herself, I lunged, trying to get them off her.

Then my world went dark, too.

I fought like hell, afraid for her even more than I was afraid for myself. I wasn't anything special, but Lanie?

I sucked the fabric of the loose bag into my mouth and bit the next piece of person that came near my face. A man howled and jerked away, hurting my teeth. He said something sharp, swore, and a blow connected with the side of my head, sending me sprawling into the sand.

There was so much shouting—some of it was me.

A man howled in rage, and I could feel the chaos around us growing. Rough hands hauled me away and my feet dragged along the sand. I dug in, trying to slow their progress, but what kind of rescue would come? Even if security saw something strange happening on the cameras, they couldn't get someone here fast enough to put a stop to this.

It felt like a hunt, but no one had told *us,* and there was nothing scheduled for today. Usually, they gave us a bit of warning. This felt completely unsanctioned.

"Leave her alone!" I was screaming, but the wind and crash of waves were so loud in my ears I wasn't sure anyone could hear me. Men were shouting, but none of the voices were making sense, except for a few that were fading.

They hefted me up and passed me from one man to the next until someone put me down. The ground felt man-made and lurched underfoot.

A boat?

"Who are you people?" I demanded, as though their identities would somehow help me make sense of this. Was it even possible to be kidnapped from an island like this? It made no sense. Who even knew this place existed? Why wouldn't kidnappers choose someone off the street in any convenient town rather than take us from a place with so much security?

There was the roar of a motor and then the feeling of traveling on water. It felt like we were going fast.

"Lanie! Lane, can you hear me?"

I strained my ears, listening for her. There was no answer. No one objected to me calling out, either. No one would hear me except for my kidnappers and Lane, I supposed. But where was she?

I struggled but managed to sit on what was probably the deck of the boat. When I tried to pull the bag off my head, someone slapped my hand away and muttered in a language I didn't know. Hands took my arms again, twisting them behind my back and lacing them together with rope. I tried to get to my feet, and someone cuffed my head.

"Be good and we won't hurt you." His accent made him difficult for me to understand.

"Who are you people?"

"Hired men."

The boat skipped along the water, jarring me, the thrum of it buzzing my teeth together.

"Where's Lanie?" I hadn't heard her since they had transferred me into the vessel, and I was wondering if they'd left her behind.

"Your friend was rescued. You were not."

Rescued? Those angry voices must have been Ajax and Calder. Why wasn't I surprised they'd been spying on us?

It was a relief knowing she was safe—at least comparably safe. Ajax and Calder weren't Boy Scouts by any stretch of the imagination, but at least they were the devil we knew instead of whoever these people were.

Eventually, the boat slowed and then idled. The cries of gulls were far off, almost muted by the wind and the slosh of water against the hull.

Someone jerked the bag off my head, along with several strands of my hair. My eyes struggled to adjust to the comparative brightness. The sky seemed ominous now, along with the endless expanse of sea. I focused on the dour, bearded face of one of my two nemeses on this tour.

"Bron," I growled. "Why the fuck would you kidnap me off the beach?"

He shrugged. "I suppose we could have kidnapped you from anywhere, but we were trying to take your friend Lane as well."

"What do you want with us?"

He sucked his teeth. "We'd only planned on taking her to improve your likelihood of cooperation."

I swallowed, scrutinizing his fierce, dark eyes. "Well, what do you want with me, then?"

"To offer you a choice. Do you want to do this the easy way or the hard way?"

"Tell me my options, and I'll give you my decision."

We stared each other down.

"Accept the contract I'm offering you."

"Or what?" An 'or' was definitely hanging over his statement.

"Or don't, and we'll take you anyway."

Of course. Fucking misogynist assholes.

My anger made me feel overly warm, although I was only wearing a bikini.

I looked around to see if any help might be forthcoming. The other men had all disappeared, leaving me alone with Bron and Ilya. On closer inspection, in the light of day, they looked less like twins. The shape of their eyes and the line of their noses were different. Cousins? Close friends? It was hard to say.

I worked hard to contain my disgust.

"You couldn't just ask me? Why the kidnapping? Why the theatrics?"

Bron smoothed back my hair, a cruel smile forming on his lips.

"We couldn't take the chance that you would refuse and walk away. Think on it. For now, we will treat you like a paid captive. If you do what we say, things won't be any more unpleasant than they can get on the Island. If you are difficult..."

"The entire point of the Island is that we consented to be there—to do those things. This is a real kidnapping."

He shrugged at my accusations. "Only if you don't agree to our terms."

"Why me? Why not grab some random woman off the street?"

"Most other women are not able to provide what we need."

This didn't sound like it would be a good time. "And what exactly do you need?"

"You. Specifically, you."

I glared at him, and he narrowed his eyes, as though in warning.

"How much are you offering?"

His gaze was black ice. "Why would I bother to negotiate with you?"

"Obviously, you'd prefer if I was voluntary, otherwise you wouldn't have made the offer." I tried to work at the rope holding my arms, but whoever had tied me knew what he was doing.

He grunted. "I've overheard things. I understand you plan to return to the Island for a scholarship for yourself."

"Yes."

"We'll offer you that, plus what—say, half a million?"

I swallowed. An education and enough money to buy a nice house, at least where I was from. How was a girl supposed to say no to that?

"For what? For how long?"

"In exchange, you'll be our captive for the next four months."

"Four months! I can't abandon my family for that long."

"Your family is busy with their own affairs. Your siblings are in school, or will be after this contract with the Island. You planned on coming right back here for yourself anyway, so what is the issue?"

"There's a big difference between coming back for a month and being gone for four more months."

He sighed, as though I was being emotional and unreasonable. "We'll allow you to make a few phone calls to settle your affairs."

"What about Lane? I don't have her number."

"What about her? We don't want her, and we suspect the men currently courting her will hunt us down if we try to take her again."

"I don't want you to take her. I need to write her a note or something. I can't let her think I've disappeared."

He rolled his eyes heavenward and crossed his arms over his broad chest. "I'm sure we can make some sort of arrangement for the Island to tell her you're safe."

"What exactly will you expect me to do for you?"

"Nothing you would not be doing here."

"But with the two of you rather than an island full of men?"

He gave a curt nod, but I wasn't sure whether we were really on the same page or if he was just trying to shut me up. I considered the offer. It was bold of him to assume I would cooperate just because of the money he was willing to splash around, but the Island didn't pay anyone in cash. As far as I knew, if a woman dropped out of her program of study or didn't pass, they didn't fork over money instead.

It was true what he'd said—my siblings were all busy with school. My parents would be shorthanded at the store, and there would be no one around to clean the house and cook meals, but they wouldn't miss me, specifically.

I considered it, looking down at my lap. It was difficult to sit demurely in a bikini with my arms bound so tightly behind me, but I'd balanced myself with my legs folded off to one side.

Mulling over the offer and wondering if I should ask for more money, I studied the two men. Both were the rugged, outdoorsy type I'd always been attracted to, but why had they chosen me for this? I hadn't thought they were interested.

It didn't really matter why they'd chosen me. They were offering me the money.

"What kind of guarantee do I have that you'll let me go after the contract is done?"

His dark eyes flashed in annoyance. He was even hotter when he was annoyed, which was a bad thing for me. I really didn't need to be leering at assholes who were coercing me into taking their contract.

What proclivities did they have? Both of them had been on a free-for-all sex Island for three weeks and hadn't slutted around like the rest of us. It made me more than a little curious.

He crossed his arms. They were heavily muscled, tanned, and tattooed. "What kind of guarantee do you get from the Island?"

I shrugged. "The Island is an established business. A friend referred me there. There were official contracts to sign. They are professionals. Taking your contract would be more of a risk for me."

"I'm sure we could write up a contract, if it would make you feel better," he said sardonically.

"That wouldn't make any difference. Without seeing your Yelp reviews, there's no way to know what I'm getting myself into." I smiled a little, trying to make a joke out of it, but he only scowled. So cranky, this man. Then again, a celibate month on a sex island might be more than most men could tolerate.

I glanced over at Ilya. His dark eyes were following our conversation, but he still hadn't said anything. He hadn't even spoken to Bron.

"I can't offer you more assurances than I have, other than possibly to get Island management to cosign the agreement."

"Where are you taking me?"

"Another island."

"And you promise not to kill me or maim me in any way?"

"That wasn't our intention. However, you are testing my patience."

I snorted, assuming it was a joke, until I saw his expression.

Of course, it wasn't a joke.

Great. Four months with two men who had no sense of humor? This was going to suck, but money was money.

My head was still swimming from the piña coladas we'd been drinking. It was strange to think my glass might still be sitting on the beach next to the thermos we'd borrowed, unless it had gotten knocked over or broken in the struggle.

"I wish you'd asked me and given me time to tell people, rather than scaring the hell out of everyone."

"And how would that be any fun for us?"

"You took a big risk by doing this. The Island might have come after you for it."

Bron turned his head and spat over the side of the boat as if that was his opinion of the Island. If I craned my neck, I could see land in the distance, but there was no way for me to guess how far it was.

"You think this place is so good, but they don't care about you. Where do you think your little friend Clover ended up? She isn't at home looking at schools on the internet. She's alone with dangerous men, and probably with no extra money to show for it. The Island isn't hunting those men down to have her returned. All of you are replaceable to them. They gave us access to your files with no hesitation, as though it was a simple extra charge."

I swallowed, my chest hurting with his with the information he'd dropped in my lap. I wanted to say it couldn't be true, and yet why couldn't it be true? Maybe I was too trusting, but I wasn't an idiot. Poor Clover.

"We have to help Clover," I said desperately.

"How?" he said with a snort. "Do you think the men exchange phone numbers, or are friends on that...Facebook? I doubt the Island cares. They took her away so there was no mess to clean up. And her family? Well, girls go missing all the time."

"Is that supposed to make me more comfortable about leaving with you?"

"Like I said, you're coming with us either way. You're a silly little girl if you think you're safer on the Island than you would be with us. Stupid risks are stupid risks."

He had a point. They had me anyway. Agreeing to their proposal was merely a formality.

Slowly, I nodded. "I'll do it."

The gleam in his eye suggested this wouldn't be easy money.

Chapter Three

If I'd known about having to wear the fabric hood that covered my face the entire time we were traveling, I might have turned down the offer.

Not really, but the hood was dark and stuffy, and made me feel claustrophobic.

I'd thought the boat had been bad, but the turbulence in the plane was terrible. The ship in between had been better. The plane felt small, but I doubted we were on a commercial aircraft, considering they were traveling with a woman who was hooded and usually bound.

For the first leg of our journey, they hadn't tied my hands, but when they discovered I'd taken off my hood—so I could breathe better, not to be nosy—they'd tied my wrists behind my back again. Someone checked on my arms and hands periodically, but it made me regret having done anything I hadn't had permission to do.

At least they'd put a shirt on me. It felt like a very large man's button-up—almost cozy if I pulled my knees up inside it with me.

I lay on what felt like a carpeted floor. No light filtered through the opaque bag. I'd slept so long my head hurt, but there was nothing else to do but sleep and wait.

How long would the trip there be? No one would say.

What if this 'deal' I'd been offered was no more than a sly way to keep me quiet while they transported me for trafficking? Sure, I liked rough sex more than most girls, but the idea of being trapped in a life where I'd be used until I died kept edging into my mind, keeping me scared. I had no reason to trust that Bronislav was on the level.

I wasn't even sure who was tending to me, since they never spoke.

The Island had been so busy. To go from that to a complete lack of stimuli was jarring, but I was no stranger to boredom. I made up stories in my head to pass the time, remembering bits of my favorite books and movies and patching ideas together. I tried not to think of what would happen once we arrived at our destination. Too many unknowns twisted my stomach when I let my mind stray in that direction.

I woke from a doze with the feeling I was not alone.

There was the scent of heated food—something processed. It reminded me of the chicken nuggets that were a staple in our house when I was growing up, before I learned to actually cook. My stomach growled, and I struggled to sit up.

Strong hands helped me to my feet and mercifully freed my arms. I worked at the pins and needles as he walked me to the bathroom, then returned me to my spot, which was still warm. Unfortunately, he tied my hands again.

Damn it.

He rolled the bag up over my nose, and a forkful of food touched my lips.

"If you untie my hands, I can feed myself."

There was no answer, only the tap of food against my lips.

Grumbling inwardly, I accepted the bite, chewing for a while, savoring having something to do and interacting with another human being, even in such a small way. I swallowed and opened my mouth to say something, but he shoved more food in before I could get any words out. I wasn't sure what he was feeding me—maybe breaded chicken? Fish? It was terrible, like a microwaved TV dinner. They were always better in the oven, but they probably didn't have an oven on the plane.

"How much longer?" I blurted before being assaulted with another mouthful.

He didn't answer.

When I was full, I told him so, and he held a bottle to my lips and tipped it up so fast I almost made a mess. I expected water or soda, but beer was a welcome surprise.

I chugged it.

The man chuckled, his deep voice such a welcome input of sound that I smiled back. The slight buzz that came with the alcohol was almost immediate, and I didn't fight when he put the bag back over my head.

A few moments later, lethargy swamped me. Was it a food coma, or the effects of the modest amount of beer I'd drank? Both seemed unlikely. Maybe I was worn out from being tied up and bored for so long?

Soon, the sensation became all too familiar, dragging at my limbs, making my body feel heavy and pliant.

"No," I whispered into the close darkness of the bag.

Memories flicked past.

Sleepover night on the Island.

My date with Brandon after the game.

I tried to push that thought away, along with the sea of faces I remembered all too well. They'd starred in my nightmares long enough. Their names rattled off in my head. Their expressions as they'd each taken a turn with my limp body, jarring me, coming inside me.

The hospital the next day and the medication they'd given me. The bedside light turning on in the middle of the night as the doctor groped my breasts and told me it was normal to do more than one exam after an assault. I didn't know any better at sixteen, but the anger still burned in me at twenty-two.

You couldn't trust your high school boyfriend or the doctor.

You couldn't trust your science teacher after he'd heard the rumor you'd fucked the entire team.

I knew I hadn't failed that test, but who would take my word over his? I needed to pass and get the hell out of that school, so I did what I had to do, kneeling under his desk.

Mom and Dad were busy running the store. They didn't need my problems. It was my job to take care of the kids, so I made sure they were bathed, fed, got to practice, and got their homework done. I kept quiet and didn't make any more trouble.

Tears leaked from my eyes—pride for the siblings I'd raised and the good, hard-working people they'd turned out to be.

Fuck, I hated these drugs. They slowed me and slowed time, and made me feel helpless. I could take whatever these men wanted to do to me, but I wanted to be lucid for it. How was I supposed to brace or protect myself if they drugged me to the gills or I was out cold?

When he came for me, I was exhausted and dizzy. He picked me up like a doll and sat, pulling me into his lap. Large hands played with the ties on the bag over my head and tugged the bottom of it up, exposing my mouth again. I was glad for the fresh air, but it did nothing to clear my head.

The muscles cradling me were hard rather than comforting.

What do you want from me? I would have demanded if I'd been able to speak.

I felt his breath on my lips.

The longer we sat there breathing each other's air, the farther my bad memories receded. I didn't expect this to be fun, but I'd only expected violence from these men.

When his lips brushed mine, they were gentle, along with the prickle of facial hair. He didn't deepen the kiss.

Instead, he pulled the bag back down and secured it. The darkness was thick in the bag, and it was hard to remember I wouldn't suffocate in here—that I'd stayed alive fine with a bag over my head for what had to be a day or maybe two at that point. Time was meaningless, and I'd stopped trying to keep track.

I felt boneless when he put me back on the carpet and arranged my limbs for me.

The feel of the barely-there kiss lingered on my lips.

Which of them had that been?

Loud, angry male voices cut into my thoughts, but the words weren't English.

What was the problem? Had it been a crew member taking liberties with me?

My mind drifted, and my thoughts grew more disjointed.

Sleep stole me away.

I woke to the feel of buttons being undone. Where was I? Who was touching me?

It took some effort, but I forced my eyes to open. Was my bed sheet pulled over my head? I could see pinpricks of light, but there was cloth touching my face.

The fabric of my shirt parted, and the cups of my bra—was it a bra?—got pushed down and hooked under my breasts. There was a rumble of male appreciation.

A man said something I couldn't understand. Was it Russian? I didn't know enough of the language to guess.

Another man replied, then the first raised his in irritation. The depth of their voices made me think of animals growling at one another, but the one who'd partially undressed me was definitely the most annoyed of the two.

I was too exhausted to care why they were disagreeing.

Hands groped my breasts, kneading them with enjoyment. He rolled my nipples between cruel fingers, tugged, then crushed and twisted, making me wish I could at least protest.

Please, no. Stop. It hurts.

The whining words in my head wouldn't come, and I panted for breath.

The Island—was this sleepover night?

No, this was the other contract I'd signed. The Russians.

Heat flooded my pussy as my body reacted to what it liked—rough handling and my wishes being ignored. I hated that I enjoyed being treated this way.

Why couldn't I like gentleness?

The other times I'd been drugged, it had felt creepy and taboo, but this time it felt matter of fact, as if I were being handled by a man who took command and wouldn't hesitate to hold me down and do what he wanted, even if I wasn't drugged. I didn't know why that difference made this more acceptable to my twisted brain, but soon he had me writhing on the inside, all the more frustrated because I couldn't respond.

He let go of my poor, tortured nipples, and I whimpered in relief so intense, a sound escaped me.

Hands skimmed down my body, and the man who was farther away said something that sounded like a warning.

"Watch," the man touching me commanded.

A finger hooked under the edge of the crotch of my panties and pulled them aside. The air was cold on the heat of my core, and I felt my body respond to being exposed.

"So pretty here." He caressed my pussy as though he owned it, spreading me wide to brush a fingertip over my throbbing clit's hood, then pushing the tip of a thick finger into my entrance and spreading the slickness upward to torture my clit.

The man touching me kept speaking in another language, but the other man had stopped responding. Was he really having a casual conversation while he played with my exposed, helpless body?

A few harsh words were followed by the thunk of a door closing.

He sighed, as though he'd lost an argument. Slowly, he stripped me naked, exploring me. He picked me up, cradling me against his chest. Was this the man who'd kissed me earlier? Would he take it easy on me?

He put me belly down on something hard. A table? It was cold, except for my bag. My face was warm. Unfortunately, so was my pussy.

"You act like a queen, with your chin high and your disdainful eyes, but look at you now. Nothing but a beautiful body for me to use. No face. No pretty hair. No haughty words. Just holes for my entertainment."

What was he talking about? Haughty? When had I ever been haughty?

"I would take my time and torment you, but I haven't had a woman in so long I find myself impatient." The purr of a metallic zipper opening was almost lost in the thrum of what I was pretty sure was a plane.

I braced myself mentally, unable to do anything else to defend myself.

Not wasting any time, he rubbed the tip of his cock up and down my pussy, coating himself with the slickness my body had made to protect itself. It had nothing to do with my weakness for rough-looking men with rough hands.

Rather than plunging into me, he slid in with smooth, slow thrusts that made me want to groan as he convinced my body to take him. He was thick and long, and I reveled in the feel of him inside me, even though I hated that he'd waited for me to be incapacitated.

"Fuck...how did I forget what pussy felt like?" he growled, but it was pleasure rather than irritation. "I watched them fuck you like a rag doll at that sick sleepover party. That seriously fucked me up. I couldn't get the idea of drugging you out of my head. Are you even awake? Do you even know I'm balls deep in your slutty little cunt?"

Damn, he felt amazing.

Why did toxic men always have the best dick?

He fucked me slow and hard, jarring me against the table, trapping my thighs against the edge to hold me in place. The table must have been bolted down because the force behind each thrust should have slid it incrementally across the floor.

"Your body loves my cock. Such a nasty, gorgeous little whore. Even unconscious, you're hot for me and dripping down my balls." He kept muttering to himself in Russian, and whatever he was saying sounded filthy and possibly degrading, and so fucking hot. My toes dragged against the carpeting, and I tried to focus on that, but his hard cock, the wet sounds my body was making, and the sexy roll of his hips left me with too much stimulation. He was bare inside me, and the silky, hot slide of him made me glad I couldn't make a sound. If I'd groaned for this man the way my body urged me to, it would have probably gone to his head.

The last thing this man needed was an ego boost.

The tension in my lower belly made me desperate for the orgasm I knew he could choose to provide, but he didn't touch my clit or do anything to make things good for me. He could have been using his hand for all the interest he paid me. For some reason, that made this hotter.

"This beautiful body is my toy now, *De-li-lah*," he grumbled, his voice deliciously dark. "Any hole, anytime I please. Mine."

His rhythm stuttered, but he pulled out and lowered me back to the carpet, lying me flat on my back. It was a lot more comfortable on the floor, but the need he'd created in me was making me want to squirm. Seconds later, hot liquid hit my breasts. Damn it. He might be done with me, but I wasn't done with him.

Men.

His rumble of satisfaction was humiliating enough, but I felt him crouch down next to me, and then he rubbed his cum into my tits, thumbing my nipples, and I wished I could arch or gasp. He loosened the bag around my neck and rolled it up, exposing my mouth the way the other man had—at least, I assumed it had been the other man.

He parted my lips and rubbed two fingers over my tongue, making me taste his satisfaction while I had none of my own.

"Did he kiss you, Queen of Whores?" he demanded, rubbing his thumb mockingly over my bottom lip. "Are you going to make him love you?" He spat, and it hit the corner of my mouth and slid inside. "I read your file—watched the videos of your medical exams. How do you stay so regal after everything men have done to you? I think your secret is that you enjoy it."

If it was anyone else, I might have been humiliated at the idea of him reading my psych profile and watching those videos, but he'd been on the Island for the past three weeks. He'd already seen me get abused by several different men.

He left me that way—used, naked, with the bottom of my face hanging out of the bag.

I was too groggy and tired to care.

Chapter Four

"Up." Someone smacked me.

Was I late getting my siblings up for school?

Exhaustion and nausea dragged me down, but the hands wouldn't let sleep reclaim me. They forced me upright. My legs were unsteady, and the floor beneath my feet lurched, but the hands kept me from falling.

"You stink."

I do?

Why couldn't I see? I blinked, but it didn't help. I tried to push back my hair, but there was fabric in the way that prevented me from reaching the strands that obscured my vision and tickled my face. The air was stale and humid with my breath. Something was over my face and when I tried to pull it off, he pushed away my hands.

"Leave it."

Oh, right. The bag.

I stumbled again, but the man caught me before I went down. His chuckle was unpleasant and triggered a cascade of memories—hands, mouth, a too-big dick. He smelled like fresh air, even through the cloth over my face. My body ached from hard use and bruises that felt like they went down to my bones.

He stripped off the shirt and undergarments I wore—or was it a bathing suit?—then lowered me to a toilet. I peed for what felt like twenty minutes.

"Done?"

"Yes," I croaked. My stomach was empty and clenching, but at least there was nothing for me to throw up.

Water turned on somewhere, and he picked me up off the toilet and shoved me into a shower. I gasped at the cold, but it soon warmed and thawed out my cold limbs. He removed the bag from my head, but the darkness in the shower was complete, as though we were in a basement room with no windows. The floor pitched again, and I banged into a plastic wall.

"Wash." He pushed a bar of mildly scented soap into my hand, and I washed, eager to get the smell of his cum and my fear off me.

Apparently, there was no shampoo, so I lathered the bar between my hands and washed my hair with it, too. I rinsed my mouth with water and brushed my teeth the best I could with my finger. My eyes stung from the soap, but the burning gave me the illusion of being cleaner, at least. I cleaned my pussy and ass gingerly, both of them aching from vigorous overuse. I only remembered bits and pieces of things, but my body remembered it all. Even as I washed, cum dripped from me.

I must have made a sound of discomfort because he tsked. "Poor little princess. Did I make you sore?"

"Yes," I admitted.

"A whore like you should have a tough pussy by now."

I didn't answer, since there was nothing to say. His accent was thick. Was his voice familiar?

Time had blurred into a confusing series of sex, small meals, and assisted trips to the toilet. He didn't usually speak to me, but he'd pumped me so full of drugs I hadn't been well enough to even wonder who'd taken me and why, until now.

Maybe it didn't require a genius to figure out why.

Wait. The Russians. Bron.

"Does the Island really know you have me?" I whispered. "They'll track you down."

He shut off the water, depriving me of the heat I'd been enjoying.

"They know who has you."

"And they let you take me?" I asked, doubtful.

Lane had her suspicions about the Island's possible side businesses, but I hadn't really believed it. Maybe I'd been naïve in thinking the Island was forthright in what they were about. It didn't make sense to have girls sign up to be there voluntarily, then to let them get involuntarily kidnapped. Why bother having a middleman when it would be just as easy for rich men to kidnap a woman off the street? Maybe because no one would report me missing from the Island?

God—Lane must be out of her head with worry. First Clover and now me? It wasn't like there was anything she could do to rescue me, even if she knew who had me and where I'd gone.

"Is Lane okay?"

"Yes." He toweled me off with impatient movements, chafing my skin with the rough cloth.

He sounded exasperated. Had I asked him that before?

"Drink this." He put a glass in my hand and pushed it toward my mouth.

"Is it drugged?" I asked, wanting to cry. Fuck, I hated being drugged, but this guy seemed to be a big fucking fan.

"Last dose." The hand over mine was unrelenting.

Maybe I didn't want to deal with his excessive use without the drugs.

Reluctantly, I downed the mixture. He led me back into a room that smelled like stale air and too much sex.

"I'll bring your clothing back when it's clean." He shoved something at me—a blanket? It was scratchy wool, but warmer than what I'd been wearing for however long I'd been with him.

The floor was still shifting underfoot. It had to be a boat this time.

He left, and I wrapped myself in the blanket before the lethargy tugged me back down into its clutches.

*

I woke to someone over me—in me. Grunting. Stabbing into me with his body. Every thrust was a hot poker. My pussy stung, and my ass ached. How long had he been on top of me?

My limbs wouldn't obey, so there was no pushing him away. I tried to complain, but speaking was beyond me.

He shuddered and went still, then withdrew with a rush of fluid.

Sleep closed in over my head, suffocating.

*

Hands were on me.

Everything hurt.

Again? So soon?

Not that I knew how long it had been. How had I ever thought servicing only two men would be easier?

Slowly, carefully, the blanket was peeled away. Whoever was unwrapping me was making an effort to not wake me.

My mind drifted.

Cool air washed over my skin, but I'd been overheated this time. Someone had dressed me—or had I dressed myself? I couldn't remember.

The drug still had me in its grip. My limbs felt leaden and foreign, and the dark dreamlike.

Was it dark, though? If I concentrated, was that light I could see through the bag, or was it my imagination?

Did he think I was asleep? Probably.

I felt a ghost of something. Breath? Fingertips?

Carefully, he unbuttoned my shirt until the fabric hung open, exposing the bikini beneath. More touching. Sensation glided along my skin, making me shiver, although I wasn't sure I moved.

I kept waiting for him to say something, but the room was silent, other than the distant hum of a motor. It was like being stuck in sensory deprivation with the only input I received being from this person.

This was so different from the other times. It had to be someone else. Hell, it could be anyone. I had the impression we were on a ship, but they might have moved me several times. For all I knew, it could be a member of the crew.

I could almost feel the person's gaze on my skin. My nipples were tight, and my body responded to the anticipation, even though I hated not being able to move and not having any choice.

It was probably Ilya. Bron wouldn't have left me lying around where some strange man might climb on top of me, right? Or maybe this was Bron playing a different game?

My whimper of dread caught in my throat and died there.

Something soft touched my belly. Inwardly, I quivered. What was he doing? An exhalation puffed along my skin, skating across my navel. Soft lips, facial hair. He tasted me, his tongue barely grazing my skin. Gradually, he became bolder. His fingertips explored me, tickling without meaning to, his touch gentle, as though he was afraid to wake me.

Being explored like this felt more pervy than Bron simply stripping me down and fucking me. I tried not to let myself get turned on by what he was doing, but it had been so long since anyone had been so careful with me that my body couldn't help but respond. My nipples tightened to painful peaks. The tension in my pussy grew and made me wish I could press my thighs together to ease my frustration.

He traced around my bathing suit as though he were enjoying the feel of my skin. Once, his finger strayed over the stiff peak of my fabric-covered nipple, and along with the twinge of heat, I felt my body lubricating itself, ready for more. I waited almost breathlessly for him to pull aside the small cups of my bikini top to expose my breasts, or to slide down my bottoms. Instead, his touch moved to my collarbone, to my neck, and to the swell of my breasts where they showed over the top of my swimsuit.

My breathing grew more halting. Could he tell from the movements of my chest or the flutter of the fabric of the bag over my face? Was I basically a faceless sex doll to him, or did he know who I was?

He slid a finger under the outer edge of my bikini top, exploring the curve of my breast. The finger quested, found my nipple. A short nail scraped the hard bud, and the jolt of pleasure spiked to my pussy, and made it pulse once. Liquid heat dripped from me.

Something softer touched me then, rubbing over my stomach close to where his mouth had explored. My entire body tensed, and even though I wasn't able to move, my arousal was almost painful.

The man groaned, and hot liquid splashed across my bare skin, scalding, pooling in my navel. He said something I didn't catch, his voice a low murmured growl that made my insides quiver. With quick, impersonal movements, he wiped me down with a soft cloth. His fingers strayed again to the mounds of my breasts, to my throat, his touch gentle before it disappeared, leaving me in a drugged, needy fog.

Dark dreamlessness beckoned, and although I fought, it sucked me under.

Chapter Five

I hated the island before we even got there, enduring days upon days of traveling, treated like cargo rather than a person. We arrived at a place that was cold. It had never occurred to me that the island they were taking me to wouldn't be lovely and tropical. Instead, there were only trees and more trees—a lot of them evergreens. The deciduous trees were just starting to bud. The forest seemed to be holding its breath, waiting for warmer weather before trading the drab browns of dead foliage for shades of green.

The cold powered through the button-down shirt I was wearing. I had no shoes and no coat. I trudged from the SUV to the house, my feet freezing on the bare ground, with Ilya in front of me and Bron behind, as though I might make a run for it. There was nowhere to go, but with the bag off my head, at least I could see and breathe clean air.

I'd been expecting nothing more than a cabin in the woods with a bucket to piss in, but a ramshackle house sprang up out of the ground before us. It was an odd place and made me think of a fairy-tale castle belonging to an unhinged evil sorcerer. It appeared to have been built over several decades, mostly using rock and concrete. The dull gray of the structure blended into the landscape, despite the strange tower at the back of it.

There was no question these men belonged here. The place looked as rough as they were.

At least the walls would keep the wind out.

"I guess I never asked if this place was warm," I said wryly.

"It's nice to be home. That island was too hot," Bron grumbled.

Ilya watched me the way he always did, like he wasn't sure what to make of me.

It was easy to tell the two of them were close, but I still hadn't had the guts to ask who they were to each other. From their dynamic, Ilya was Bron's servant, or possibly his little brother.

"Does anyone else live here?"

"Who were you hoping for?"

"A housekeeper?" From the looks of the place, I doubted there was enough to keep a housekeeper busy other than cooking. It wasn't like these men had possessions to tidy up. They took the term minimalist to a whole new, sad level.

There was no way I could fool myself into believing I was on vacation in this place.

I sighed. "Let me guess—I'm going to have to sleep at the foot of your bed or something, aren't I?"

"Of course not, Queen of Whores. We would never treat you with less than the utmost respect," he mocked. "Ilya, I have arrangements to make. Take her to the tower."

The tower? As fairy tales went, this one sucked.

Ilya nodded, his eyes wary, as though he would need to keep his wits about him when he was alone with me.

He led me through the massive house. The stone corridor opened onto Spartan, often furniture-less rooms. There was very little in the way of comfort, and the flagstones were cold under my feet. Almost every stick of furniture I saw looked homemade and serviceable rather than pretty. The few pieces of art were of trees or melancholy landscapes that lacked color. There were no photos, family or otherwise.

I plodded along after him, grumbling inwardly. It had never occurred to me I might miss all the times I'd had to run barefoot during hunts, but at least then my feet had been warm. Now they ached with cold. I was tired, sore, and angry.

We entered a wide open space that held nothing except a gigantic spiral staircase with no handrail.

Yikes.

This must be the tower. The staircase followed along the inside of the tower's stone walls. Narrow windows brought in just enough light to see the worn steps.

Was he really going to make me climb up the spiral staircase of doom?

Apparently yes.

I had to stick to the wall to avoid feeling like one misstep might topple into the void, and to my death. The place was definitely not up to code. I was so tired I snorted at the idea of calling my OSHA rep to complain.

I looked back at Ilya, who didn't seem worried about falling. Then again, it might feel like a good option compared to living on this godforsaken island.

When I tried to meet his gaze, I realized he was staring at my legs. Now that we were alone, was he going to make a move? He caught me looking at him, and he shifted away his gaze, as though I wasn't already bought and paid for.

Interesting.

At the top of the stairs was a large wooden door with steel reinforcements. He opened the wrought iron latch and gestured me in.

Compared to the parts of the house I'd seen, the room was unexpected. It had two walls of windows, and was bright and cheery, and was furnished with a double bed, a dresser, and a desk. A bookcase jammed with paperbacks and movies took up a whole wall. The carpeting was soft underfoot and there were enough textiles to cut the cold of the building. There was a lot of dust, but that was easily fixed.

"Is the heat on?"

His brows lifted. He shrugged, but I wasn't sure if that was a response or if he didn't speak English. He gave me a moment to take in the magnificent view of the ocean. Jagged rocks lined the shore between the base of the tower and the water, making escape that way impossible. Besides, even if I could sneak out, where would I go? The water had to be frigid, and I had no idea where the mainland was.

As I perused shelves filled with books, baubles, and trinkets, he pushed open a pocket door I'd assumed was a painting to reveal a large, full bathroom with windows that looked out over the roof far, far below and forest beyond. I doubted the bathroom had been updated since the 1970s, but Ilya twisted the taps to show me everything was in working order, despite the impressive layer of dust.

Not the Hilton, but at least everything was functional.

The suspense of what might happen next was too much for me. Just like on the Island, I wanted to do a preemptive strike and get ahead of the situation.

I took a step toward him as soon as we left the bathroom, and he looked at me curiously. As far as I knew, only Bron had used me on the trip over. Although I was exhausted from traveling and from the aftereffects of the drugs Bron had kept feeding me, trying to seduce Ilya was probably the smartest next move.

Standing toe to toe, I needed to look pretty far up at him, despite how tall I was. It was an interesting height difference. Most men were similar in height to me or a bit shorter, but Ilya and Bron both made me feel the way Lanie probably felt most of the time.

He raised his brows at me as though surprised to find me in his personal space, but he didn't move away. His jaw tightened, as though he was gritting his teeth. I pulled him down and pressed my lips against his and he inhaled, freezing in place like a startled deer. He didn't move other than a slight flare to his nostrils. I tried to lure him into participating in the kiss, but he pulled away, not looking upset so much as uneasy.

Did he not like women?

Confused, I stepped back. Maybe he was used to being the aggressor? Not sure what to do, I watched him edge away. He gave me a shy smile. I swallowed, feeling guilty.

Was I only here for Bron?

He retreated to the door but turned before leaving.

"The closet is full of my sister's things. Use whatever you like."

I watched him in bemusement.

He could speak English?

Such a strange man. Such a strange place.

"This used to be the lighthouse. They built the main house onto it later."

Now that made a lot more sense than this place having a random turret for no reason.

I went to the closet and found it filled with every type of clothing I could imagine. It was all out of date by at least ten to fifteen years, but it looked serviceable and warm, even though there were far too many dresses. Hopefully, there were leggings to go with them, or at least some long socks.

I shook out a dress that might fit. Dust coated most of the room, but at least the closet doors had cut down on how many cobwebs clung to the clothing.

Back in the bathroom, I ran myself a bath with water that steamed in the cold air. I stripped off Bron's borrowed button-up shirt and the bikini I would gladly burn at the first opportunity, gratefully used the toilet, and stepped into the bath with more relief than I normally had after any orgasm.

The water scalded my skin although I doubted it was really that hot, and my limbs prickled like I was being swarmed by ants. The tub was big enough that the water covered me to my chin and didn't leave any part of me poking above the surface. There wasn't much I wouldn't have done for this luxury.

I nodded off. By the time I woke, my bath was cooling. I pulled the plug and showered, grateful for the thick towel I found within arm's reach, since I hadn't thought to check for one earlier.

This entire suite was a time capsule, as though the woman who belonged here had walked out over a decade ago and never returned.

I contemplated the dress I'd chosen, then slipped into a fluffy robe instead. There were relatively clean linens on the shelf in the closet, so I changed the bed, hoping the folded set of sheets would have less dust than the set already making up the bed.

As I settled in, I noticed a romance novel set on the bedside table, the bookmark a little past the halfway point. Was it a book she had read multiple times, or had she never reached the end?

Where had she gone? Was she dead?

It would be awful to die in the middle of a good book and never have the chance to see how it ended.

I thought about reading the first chapter, but to my chagrin, it wasn't English.

Suddenly worried about my supply of reading material over the next few months, I checked the rest of the bookshelves, relieved to find an entire section of English titles. Too bad I couldn't go through them with Lane, but sharing books with her would have to wait until I got home. Hopefully, she wouldn't be too angry at me for agreeing to take this contract. Knowing my friend, she'd understand.

Bron had said Clover had been taken off the Island, too, but that she wasn't getting paid for whatever was happening to her. Anxiety for her tightened my stomach. She was such a sweet kid—brave and smart and determined. She was also gorgeous, vivacious, and a flirt. Would whoever had her eventually let her go, or would they keep her forever?

God, I hoped they wouldn't kill her.

Despite my morbid musings, my stomach reminded me I was hungry. I dressed, discovering Ilya's sister's shoes fit relatively well, too. They were a bit too big, but that was better than too small.

I made my way downstairs, still wondering about Clover, but also wondering about Ilya's sister. It was like she'd abandoned her entire life and run off.

I wandered around the rambling old house, finding several other barren rooms, then a large living room with newer furniture and, shockingly, a flat screen TV.

Eventually, I ended up in the cavernous kitchen, which had a rough hewn table and six chairs. After searching the cupboards and fridge, I realized there wasn't much snack food on hand. There was plenty of fresh food, as though someone had stocked the house before we arrived, but not so much as a potato chip. Then again, from the looks of Bron and Ilya, they didn't indulge in junk food.

"I will cook." Ilya stood behind me, watching me warily. Was he worried I'd try to kiss him again?

"I don't want to be a bother."

"We all need to eat."

Couldn't argue with that.

He moved around the kitchen, as though he was comfortable in it.

"Why does a man with so much money do his own cooking?" I asked. "I thought most rich people had cooks and servants."

"Better to do it myself." He spoke to me without looking directly at me, as if one of us was in danger of having hysterics.

After days of sensory deprivation, I was starving for interaction, even if the guy was grumpy and stand-offish. At least he wasn't as bad as Bron.

"Have you lived here long?"

He sighed, as though I was being a nuisance. "Since I was small. The others lived here, too, until they got married and moved to the mainland." His English was stilted, as though he didn't use it much, but he didn't seem to struggle to find words.

"The others? Like your sister?"

"All of us lived here as children. One of my sisters is married, but the one whose room you are using—" He shrugged. "One night she was gone."

I inhaled, feeling guilty for touching her things. Jeez, I was wearing her dress! Not that I had other options, but still.

"What happened?"

"Probably Vas." He shrugged.

Why was this like pulling teeth?

"What is Vas?"

"Vas is our father. He is a very important man in Moscow."

My idea that Ilya might be Bron's servant was wrong, obviously.

"Is Bron one of your brothers?"

He laughed, the flash of straight white teeth and the delight in his eyes turning him from good looking to gorgeous. Wow.

"The Queen of Whores is making you laugh?" Bron said, appearing in the doorway, freshly showered and looking far too delectable for my own good.

Ilya sobered as he mixed seasonings together in a large bowl. "She thought we were brothers."

Bron snorted rudely. "If I was Ilya's brother, I would jump from the tower like poor Yana."

"Yana didn't jump," Ilya snapped, pointing at him with the mixing spoon. "If she had jumped, we would have found her body."

I grimaced, thinking of how far down the ground was from Yana's tower, and the rocks beneath it.

Ilya went to the fridge and used its door to shove Bron out of the way.

Bron frowned at him. "The only escape from your family is death."

"Unless you're like me and your father is ashamed of you."

"That will change soon enough."

Ilya sent a glance my way, arching one skeptical eyebrow, then got back to breading fish. "She's perfect, but her perfection won't hide my flaws."

"We shall see." Bron lifted a lock of my hair and rubbed it between his fingers. He sniffed it, then dropped it like produce that hadn't quite met his approval.

Asshole.

Chapter Six

I was deep into a book when my growling stomach sent me back downstairs in search of food.

Leaving the sanctuary of Yana's room was always difficult, and not only because the staircase gave me wicked vertigo. The longer I spent with Bron and Ilya, the stranger things became. I couldn't complain about the easy money, but the fact that neither of them came to my room to have their way with me felt like danger lurking. It would be easier if they got it over with instead of making me wait and wonder.

It was late—probably somewhere between eleven and twelve. The two of them always disappeared after dinner, and I would retreat to my room to read and watch old movies on Yana's VHS player, which I'd had to figure out how to use. She had a bookcase full of cartoons, teen comedies, and several romcoms from around when I was born. Luckily, many of them were in English.

Why had Yana and Ilya been exiled here, away from the rest of the family?

The kitchen was at the side of the house, near the stairwell to the other bedrooms. If I wasn't quiet, I'd wake someone. They always went to bed early. It didn't matter what time I got up in the morning, the two of them were awake and busy taking care of the small farm attached to the property.

I sorted through the cupboards and fridge, then decided to make myself a grilled cheese. I got the pan onto the stove without clanging it and was in the middle of buttering a slice of bread when I heard Bron's voice. Considering he was upstairs, and it sounded like behind a closed door, the strident, berating tone made me cringe, as though I'd done something wrong. I was glad I couldn't understand Russian.

He punctuated his statements with grunts.

Was he working out? Maybe coaching Ilya through push-ups or something?

Curious, but not wanting them to know I was snooping, I snuck up the stairs.

As I neared the room with the closed door, I could hear whispered, almost whimpered responses to Bron's questions that I hadn't been able to hear from downstairs. Whatever Ilya was saying, though, Bron apparently wasn't satisfied.

There was a loud gasp.

What on earth?

The doorknob turned before I could find somewhere to hide, and then I was staring at Bron's bare, sweat-slicked chest.

"What do you want, woman?"

My gaze couldn't help but dip down to his jeans, which were unfastened. His black leather belt was folded in one hand. His mouth kicked up in a jaded smile.

"You come looking for dick?"

"No, I just..." My gaze slid past him to Ilya, who was pushing up from where he'd been sprawled on the floor. He was naked, moving stiffly, and welts covered his back and legs. I jerked my gaze away. "I was making a grilled cheese sandwich and was going to ask if either of you wanted one."

Bron had seen me looking at Ilya. His dark eyes were like flint.

He made a spitting sound, although nothing came out of his mouth, then stalked past me and headed across the hall into another bedroom. He shut the door behind him.

I almost turned and went downstairs, but pretending none of this had happened would probably make it more awkward, considering I'd be with these men for weeks.

When I turned back to Ilya, he was tugging on a pair of track pants and not meeting my gaze. His face was scarlet where his facial hair didn't hide it.

"Are you okay?" I whispered.

"Yes, it was my..." He gestured in the direction Bron had gone. "Penance?"

"Your penance?" I repeated. "You're Catholic?"

"Maybe it's not the right word. I've done wrong, so Bron corrects me."

"He punishes you?"

"Yes. Punish. That's the word."

I looked up at the tall, broad-shouldered man. If I didn't know how big Bron was, I wouldn't have believed someone could physically dominate him.

"Why do you let him?"

"It is his place to correct me, my place to learn," he explained slowly.

"By beating you with his belt?"

"Hard lessons are remembered best."

"What did you do wrong?"

He shrugged, smiling. It was impossible to tell whether he was in pain, but the raised welts all over his back had to hurt. "Many things."

"Are you hungry?"

The change of subject made him relax. He stretched carefully, then nodded.

"I was about to make a sandwich. Want one?"

We went down to the kitchen together, and I continued buttering bread where I'd left off, but added four more slices to my stack. He ducked out to use the bathroom.

When he came back, he settled on a chair carefully enough that it made me wonder if the beating wasn't the only thing that had happened. Why else would Bron's pants have been undone?

"You and Bron look so much alike it surprised me when you said he wasn't your brother."

"We keep our hair and beards the same, but we are not the same under that."

I found the cheese in the fridge and sliced some off the brick.

"How did you meet?"

"He was one of my father's men, but my father sent him here to teach me."

"To teach you what?"

"To be strong." He flexed one of his biceps and the rock-like bulge was impressive. "To be a man."

I swallowed. "So, he's older than you are?"

"Yes. He's thirty-four. I am twenty-nine."

And I was twenty-two, going on a hundred.

"Has he been your teacher for long?"

"Since I was eighteen. He came when my father began to worry."

I figured out how to turn on the stove. Ilya watched me with curiosity. He'd been the one cooking since we'd arrived.

"So, he teaches you to be strong by beating you?"

"When he has to. By the time we go to see my family, I'll be like him."

I flipped the sandwich over, surprised at how quickly it had browned. He watched with amusement, as though I were an inferior cook. He wasn't wrong, even though I'd been cooking for my family for years.

"What does Vas think was wrong with you?"

"I'm too soft. Men don't want sons who are soft. He says it's because Yana and our nanny didn't raise me to be tough."

It was an interesting statement coming from a man who looked like the logo for a chain of hunting and fishing stores.

"You don't look soft to me."

"I cut a lot of firewood."

All those muscles from cutting firewood? Men back home were wasting their time at the gym. "So why am I here?"

I plated the sandwich and cut it diagonally to be fancy, then handed it off to him.

"Thank you." He took a bite and smiled at me, as though grilled cheese was a treat. Maybe the treat was having someone else make food for him.

I started frying the next sandwich and didn't fill the silence between us, hoping he'd eventually answer.

"Bron brought me to the Island where we met you to teach me how to take pleasure with women and not get attached to them."

"Yes?"

"I...could not. I watched, but I could not take part."

Out of habit, I pressed down on the top slice of bread with the back of the spatula. "Sexual aggression isn't the same as being a man. Men don't have to be hard and violent."

"Yana always said that, but our father disagrees."

"You have to be a man the way your father says? He keeps you away from the rest of the family for that?"

"He also holds the family's money. If I can't prove myself by the time I'm thirty, my father will send me away."

I nodded, then flipped the sandwich in the pan.

"So…Bron is here as a manliness tutor?" I bit my lips together, trying not to laugh. The situation wasn't funny—especially if Ilya lost his family and his source of income, but the idea that a manliness tutor even existed was hilarious.

"Yes, and you're here so I can learn how to be with a woman."

Oh, shit. He'd never been with a woman? No wonder he'd acted so weird when I'd kissed him.

"Do you even like women?"

"Yes, but I need to learn how to treat them."

"You've treated me fine."

"My father and Bron would disagree. I must take command."

I scooped the sandwich up onto the spatula and carried it to him, sliding it onto his plate, where I cut it for him. The first sandwich was already gone. He'd eaten it so quickly, I wasn't sure I'd seen him chewing.

"Thank you."

"It's nothing fancy, just a sandwich. I made it from your food."

I built my sandwich in the pan. My stomach was anticipating the snack, and it growled with impatience.

"What do you mean by learning to take command of a woman?"

"You know—the way Bron does."

"The way he does with you?"

He swallowed and looked down at the half sandwich in his hand. "Yes."

"Do you like it when he takes command of you?"

"He shames me." He bit into the sandwich, not meeting my gaze. "I'm not in control of my own body. He punishes me and I…" He glanced at the doorway as though afraid he might find Bron listening.

"I feel ashamed, but I also want more. He uses my body because I can't stop him. I'm weak for him."

Finding that hot was probably wrong, but my mind flashed back to the sight of him naked on the floor, and was eager to fill in the blanks. How was Bron dominating him supposed to make him tougher?

"You don't want to stop him." I sat across the table from him and took a bite of my sandwich.

"No." He chewed slowly. "Is that wrong? I only wish he used me because he wanted me, and not because there are no women here to use." His smile was self-deprecating. "I've heard that in America, a man can lie with a man and not be ashamed."

"Well, we're not a perfect society by any means, but I hope most fathers wouldn't hire a man to beat you and fuck you to make you 'tougher.'"

"I think Bron wants me to grow stronger and fight him off, but instead I dream of him. I sketch his nude body and write him poetry. We're alone here too much, maybe. Since Yana disappeared, I have only Bron."

I sucked some butter from my finger and glanced up to find his gaze arrested by my mouth. "You know, if Bron brought me here to teach you about being with women, you don't have to wait for him to give me orders. You could ask me for what you want."

"And you would do it because I asked?"

"I would."

He glanced away from me and got up and went to the fridge. He came back to his spot and sat, plunking a soda down in front of each of us.

"If you weren't being paid, how would a man convince you to have sex with him?"

I took another bite of my sandwich and chewed, thinking and watching him watch me. His unwavering attention was heady. I'd never had a teaching kink, but he was hot, and his inexperience was adorable.

"Do you want to know how most men seduce women, or how to get me into bed, specifically?"

"Either."

"Well, different women like different things. Assuming a woman is interested in men at all, the next part would be whether she found the man attractive."

"Am I attractive?"

"To me, physically? Yes. You wouldn't be some women's type—they might want you to cut your hair and shave, or they might like their men shorter, or less...well-muscled."

"Okay. And what else?"

"Some women like men who pay attention to them and make them happy, or who can make them laugh. Some women like men who will dominate them and boss them around, or men who want to be dominated, or who will treat them like a queen. Most of them want a man who is nice to them and makes them feel special in his own way, at least sometimes."

He nodded. It felt like he was taking a mental note.

"Does Bron make you feel that way?"

"No," he admitted. "Sometimes he seems to like me a little. It makes me want to please him more, but that's difficult to do."

Yikes.

"If you're in love with him, why do you want to learn about women?"

"I need to learn what I can to convince my father to let us move to the mainland. It's what Bron wants, and what I should want, too.

Until then, it's only me and Bron, and my soft, useless feelings. I can't live like a pathetic *durak* forever, having him but not having him."

His eyes were shining with amused self-deprecation.

The two of us stared at each other for what felt like a long time, his expression growing serious. He'd taken a significant risk confiding in me the way he had. Maybe I was supposed to be teaching him how to be more manly, but there was nothing hotter than a man who let me into his head. He deserved some positive reinforcement for that.

I pushed away from the table and went to him. He looked like he might bolt.

Boldly, I slid onto his lap. He froze beneath me.

"Are you okay with this?" I asked.

"Um...yes."

I took the hand he'd been eating with, popped one of his fingers into my mouth, and then sucked the melted butter from it. His lips parted and his gaze grew shuttered.

"Why are you doing this?" he rumbled, voice low, making me shiver.

I didn't answer. I cleaned that finger, then the next, then his thumb. The pads of his fingers were rough against my tongue, as though he spent a lot of time working with his hands. When I was done, I kissed his palm and guided it lower, sliding it into the neckline of my borrowed dress to cradle my bare breast.

He was holding his breath.

This was fun.

"Have you ever been with a woman?" I asked as he explored my skin. He coaxed my nipple to an aching point, taking his time, making me squirm.

"I've only ever been with a man I'm not allowed to touch."

"Oh."

"You like this," he said, watching my expression intently.

I was holding onto his arm, feeling the flex of muscle as he toyed with me. I exhaled shakily.

"You must have slept with a woman before."

"No."

"Then where did you learn to do this?"

"The Island was an interesting place to learn by watching."

"Most of the men there didn't care if the women had a good time."

"It is easy to see if a woman is merely tolerating something or enjoying it, if one bothers to look."

"You've never kissed anyone?"

"I kissed you when we were on our way here. I doubt you remember. The drugs..." He looked guilty. "I touched you, too. Your skin is so soft."

"I thought that might have been you."

"I thought you were asleep."

I tilted my head back and leaned into him, gazing into his dark eyes. "You should do it again."

He frowned. "I don't want you to feel obligated to do this when we're alone."

"This isn't about obligation. I've never met an adult male virgin before."

"I'm not a virgin."

"You might as well be."

He lowered his head and brushed his lips across mine. Before he could pull away, I dragged him down to me again, and prolonged the contact. Tentatively, I licked the seam of his lips. He gasped, and heat flushed through me.

"Open your mouth a little," I whispered.

He obeyed, and I licked his bottom lip, then caught it gently between my teeth. His tongue shyly came out to meet mine, then retreated, luring me to be bolder.

Although his hand still cradled my breast, his entire focus was on my mouth, and what my lips and tongue were doing. The small gasps and moans that escaped him were heady, and I could feel him hardening against my thigh.

I turned toward him and hauled my skirts up so I could straddle his lap.

He looked stunned. "What are you doing?"

"Getting comfortable." I wrapped my legs around the back of his chair, pushing myself right up against the bulge in his track pants.

His eyes widened, and his breathing became unsteady. "Delilah, maybe Bron won't like this."

"Do you care?"

"I should, but no."

I ground against his erection, and he groaned and let go of my breast in favor of grabbing my ass and pressing me more firmly against him. I kissed him again, and soon we were making out like teenagers, grinding against each other and panting into each other's mouths.

"Please, woman," he whispered between kisses. "Please don't stop."

"Shh, he's going to hear us."

He kept up an almost silent litany of Russian that sounded like a combination of swearing and praise, as though he was getting close to coming. The idea of making a grown man come in his pants was powerful incentive, but he was also sexy, and a quick study.

There was something to be said for a man who paid attention to what you liked.

My clit was aching, and I rolled my hips, getting frustrated by the layers of cloth between us. It didn't help that I had no panties to wear.

His fingertips dug into my ass with eager, bruising force. I nibbled on his neck, and he whimpered. The sound sent a charged thrill through me.

A loud bang almost made me levitate off his lap.

We split apart, my dress gaping at the neck, his track pants tented by his big dick, with a wet splotch of pre-cum at the tip.

Bron poured himself water from the pitcher in the fridge. He leaned back against the counter and took a sip.

His lips curved. Asshole.

"Pathetic."

Ilya got to his feet and kissed my forehead, then turned and disappeared up the stairs, leaving me hanging and alone with Bron.

"Let me guess—we were having fun, so you just had to interrupt."

"I wanted water. How was I to know you would be trying to seduce my charge already?"

"What happens between two consenting adults is none of your business."

"You don't even know why you're here," he said harshly.

"He told me."

He grumbled something in Russian and paced the kitchen.

I put the dishes in the sink and ran the water, expecting him to stomp off. Instead, he grabbed the counter on either side of me, trapping me. My body was still frustrated and responded to him even though I didn't want it to.

"Fuck off, Bron," I snapped, dousing a plate in soapy water and scrubbing it harder than I needed to. The dish water was too hot, but adding cold felt like it would be a display of weakness.

He grabbed my hair and leaned me forward, making me hover over the hot water. I dropped the plate into the sink, and it clanked against the bottom. Hopefully, it hadn't broken.

"Bron, no."

With his free hand he tugged up my dress to expose my bare ass. He smacked it hard enough to rattle my teeth.

"No touching each other without my permission."

"What?"

He speared a finger into me, finding me wet and frustrated. When had he even let go of the countertop? He trapped me, his body crushing me against the counter's stone.

"You heard me. The two of you need supervision."

"Why?"

He spat. I thought it was a commentary on what he'd seen us do.

"Were you watching us, you fucking pervert?"

His hand moved between us, and he bared himself.

"No!"

"Shut up." He'd slicked his fingers with spit and moved them to my ass.

I tried to get away, but he was far, far bigger than me. I wasn't used to feeling so small and helpless, even after so many tours on the Island.

His fingers were too sure of themselves, and he convinced my body to accept one. I should have taken my own advice to Lanie and kept my ass prepped, but we'd been here for days without anyone paying attention to me. It had never crossed my mind that things might change so suddenly.

"Do you like getting fucked in the ass, woman?"

"Only if the man I'm with knows what he's doing."

He barked an ugly laugh. "It's all I've had for so long, I've become proficient."

"Lube?" I requested.

"How about you brace yourself?"

I gritted my teeth when he spat again. At least he was thoughtful enough to do that much. He pressed the broad head of his cock against my asshole and pushed, forcing his way in. I grunted and screeched, but he got into my ass, making my belly cramp and my asshole burn.

"You're too small." He pulled partway out and shoved back in, making me feel like I'd split in two. He hadn't given my body time to adjust.

I squeezed my eyes shut and braced against the wall behind the sink. Heat singed my breast, and I jerked up, arching my back. Hot wash water soaked the fabric over one breast, adding to my discomfort.

He growled into the back of my hair, slamming into me over and over, bruising my hips against the counter. My feet dangled as he angled my hips higher. There was nothing I could do against his onslaught except try not to give him the satisfaction of screaming like he was murdering me. I'd taken men up the ass when they were in this kind of mood plenty of times, but I'd started to feel safe here.

Stupid, stupid girl.

I hated it, but he dug his fingers into my hair, twisting exactly right, turning my head until my neck was bared to him. He bit down, and I shuddered, not wanting to enjoy it, but hating it less despite myself.

It had been years since I'd beaten myself up for liking what I did, but why did I have to enjoy this man being a heinous jerk? Maybe because he was too fucking good at it.

"Were you really going to let him wet his little prick in you?" he snarled. "Two thrusts and he would have been done."

Ilya's cock was anything but little, considering how it had felt, but Bron didn't seem to be in the mood for a friendly debate.

He used me for a long time until my ass screamed for mercy and my legs cramped from the unnatural position. When he came, gasping,

I shuddered, feeling like the slightest touch might send me over with him, even though I was hurting.

Without warning, he pulled out and turned me around. Cum dripped from my ass, rolling down the back of my thighs.

"Spread your legs."

I did, too rattled to disobey. He slapped my pussy through my dress, which had fallen back into place, connecting hard enough to make me squeal. Movement caught my eye, and I saw Ilya watching from the doorway. Of course, he hadn't left.

Fuck.

I wasn't sure whether it was worse that Bron had seen me with Ilya or that Ilya had seen me with Bron.

He hit me there again, hurting me, making me feel good.

Ilya was stroking himself through his pants, his gaze hungry.

Desire shuddered through me, mixing with the pain in my ass, and the pain he was inflicting between my thighs.

He grabbed my throat, holding it only tight enough to make my head swim.

"Come for me, little bitch. I know you need to."

Bron stared into my eyes, and with the next slap I came apart, crying out, shaking, my knees weak as I caught myself on the counter with my elbows.

Across the room from us, Ilya's jaw set, and he came too, spurts of cum leaving wet lashes down the front of his pants.

"Like I said—both of you are pathetic." Bron gazed down his nose at me and let go of my throat. He crossed the room to Ilya and slapped him in the balls, then caught him by the hair and dragged him up the stairs behind him.

I stood there, blinking after him.

Unfortunately, smitten.

Chapter Seven

The knock at Yana's door surprised me. We'd already eaten, and usually the two of them took off for the evening. Now that I knew what was going on between them, I assumed they were usually together.

I tightened the tie on Yana's fuzzy white robe and answered. It had to be Ilya because I highly doubted Bron would be polite enough to knock.

When I opened the door, Ilya was standing there, looking uncomfortable. "Hello."

"Hi."

"May I come in?"

I stepped back to admit him, and he moved into the room. His jeans and T-shirt were clean, as though he'd just put them on, and his hair was damp.

"If you're looking for some fun, Bron has expressly forbidden us from fooling around when he's not with us."

"That's not why I'm here," he said, his cheeks reddening. It was so odd to see a guy who looked like a lumberjack blushing.

"Oh."

"He told you that?" He was clearly trying to hide his eagerness. God, he was so in love with Bron, and Bron so didn't deserve it.

"Yes, yesterday, when he...took over."

"I missed that part."

I nodded.

"Did he force you?"

I shrugged. "I came here knowing it was part of the deal."

He wandered closer to the dresser and stroked a glass pony on a dusty doily in front of the mirror. I'd been working on cleaning the room, but the bookshelves had been my priority, along with vacuuming the wall-to-wall carpeting, and washing the bedding, towels, and clothes to get the dust off them. The laundry room was in the basement, so it took forever to carry things down there and back up again.

"Is there anything you need? I know you've been wearing Yana's things—I should take you shopping on the mainland."

There was nothing wrong with Yana's clothing, considering most of them were neutral classics, but having something new might be nice. Underwear was definitely on my wish list.

"I don't need much, but some underwear and bras would be nice."

His gaze drifted from my face to my chest, then he glanced away, as though he were being rude. The robe I had on was thick enough that unless he got excited by a bare neck or ankles, or had x-ray vision, he wasn't going to get much of a thrill from checking me out. Most of Yana's clothing was downright prudish.

"I didn't even think of that. I'm sure you don't want to borrow those."

"Yeah, it's a little too weird, even for me."

He sifted through a heart-shaped bowl of trinkets and took out a ring. He slid it onto his little finger, but it wouldn't go past the first knuckle. He turned it around and around with his thumb, looking lost in thought. Eventually, he took off the ring and put it back.

"Do you come up here a lot?" I asked.

"Before, yes. Not often since she's been gone."

"Where did she go?"

He shrugged his thick shoulders, his face somber. "There are rumors."

"Rumors?"

"That she was taken by one of my father's enemies. That she's captive, or maybe married to one of them."

"Like...against-her-will married?"

"Maybe she was in love. If she was, she didn't tell me. One morning, she was gone. The cook and nanny did not see her leave. I was eight. She was twenty-two."

"Were the two of you close?"

"As close as a child can be to an adult sibling. She was the daughter of my father's first wife. She was...imperfect. Father kept her here."

"Imperfect?"

"That is how father tells it, but she was perfect to me. I think maybe she preferred women, or maybe she didn't like men who were cruel."

I shuddered at the idea of poor Yana being forced to marry someone.

"Maybe she ran away, but I don't know how she would have reached the mainland without help. None of the boats were missing."

His concern for her even now was moving.

"You miss her." I wasn't sure what else to say.

"She was the last sibling here with me, and my favorite."

"How many siblings do you have?"

"Nine, last count."

"Wow. That must have been fun growing up."

"I'm the only child of my father's third wife. I was much younger, and...not popular with the others."

Did my twin sisters feel the same way? Bianca and Brody had been hell on wheels, but I hoped they'd never felt like the rest of us disliked them.

"And here I thought I came from a big family."

"Five children from the same mother and father?"

"Yes," I said, having forgotten they'd looked at my file. It was a strange thing for him to remember. He was sweet, unlike Bron.

No doubt the only part of my file that had interested Bron had been how I'd reacted to the initial medical. The first time I'd gone, I hadn't realized there'd be a video of it that served as an audition. I thought about the men—a different pair each time I'd been assessed. Hopefully, they were all rotting in hell instead of putting new girls through their paces. I knew the job needed doing, but it took a special kind of sadist to surprise a girl like that and pit her desperation for a scholarship against her common sense.

If it hadn't been for my stupid ankle, I could have gotten a full scholarship instead of doing this kind of work. Even so, that wouldn't have helped my siblings—not when they were all so close to my age. I could have gone to college, but then what about them? They would have been stuck working at our parents' general store for eternity.

"Would you like to come downstairs and watch a movie with me?"

"Are they newer than these ones? These are so old I always think an ad for an adjustable bed is going to play, or that the swears will be bleeped out."

He looked at me blankly. "I haven't seen many commercials, so I'm not sure what you mean, but the movies down there are newer than these."

"Give me a sec." I stripped off the robe and didn't miss the way his eyes widened at my nudity.

He turned his back to me, but not before he had scanned me from head to toe.

"I would have waited outside your door."

"I'm sure you saw me naked on the Island, and you saw me naked in the audition videos and the pictures in my file." I opened a drawer and grabbed a clean nightgown and some thick socks.

"I didn't look!" he objected.

"Why? Am I not your type?"

He made a sound of distress, and it was hard not to laugh.

"You are..." He made some frantic gestures, still not looking at me as I pulled on the nightgown and sat on the bed to put on the socks. "Very, very beautiful." He rattled off some words in Russian that had me giggling to myself.

"Are you going to write me poetry, too?" I asked innocently.

He rubbed the back of his neck. "Do you like poetry?"

The door burst open and Bron stormed in. Ilya jumped, and I swore creatively enough to make a sailor blush and possibly get excommunicated from a religion I didn't belong to.

Bron was in a towering rage, his eyes flashing with malice.

"What the fuck are you two doing?"

"Ilya is giving me privacy while I put on socks," I said caustically. "You should avert your eyes, too. You might see my ankles."

Bron's gaze went to the robe on the bed, but as far as he knew, it had been there for days.

"Why are you up here, *suka*?"

"I asked her if she wanted to watch a movie with me."

He stalked into the room, and Ilya backed away, his eyes huge—afraid and maybe also aroused. Damn, I knew that feeling. I'd seen this dynamic a billion times between men and women, but it was different seeing it between two men. Ilya was big enough to hold his own against Bronislav, but the way he averted his gaze and ducked his head spoke of a deeply rooted submission. Was he submissive by nature, or had Bron just trained him well?

Bron had moved in when Ilya was only eighteen, and from the way this place was, I assumed he'd always been relatively sheltered. He would have had no way to stand up to Bron's bullying if his caregivers hadn't raised him to stick up for himself.

I adjusted my second sock, wondering if I should intervene.

Bron's harsh Russian tirade felt out of place in this room, like arguing in a mausoleum.

Cranky now, I strode up behind Bron, who now had Ilya cornered, his hand on the submissive man's throat. I tapped Bron on the shoulder.

"What?" he snapped, pausing his rant.

"If you're going to do this in my room, at least do it in English so it's not as boring for me."

Bron let go of Ilya, who had a reddened grab mark on his neck—and a telltale bulge in his pants.

"Nosy little bitch."

"You came into my space. I have every right to be nosy. What's wrong with him asking me to watch a movie?"

"I thought I told the two of you to stay away from each other if I wasn't around."

"You told us no fooling around. Watching a movie isn't the same thing."

He paced between us like a father who'd caught his virginal daughter making out with the high school quarterback. In this scenario, I wasn't confident about which of us was the virginal daughter, but I was pretty sure it was Ilya.

"Ilya is not supposed to moon after you like this, like a stupid puppy—kissing you and asking you on a date. He needs to be a man!"

"What does that even mean? There's nothing wrong with kissing. Wanting to spend time with someone outside of having sex with them isn't being weak. It's lonely here. He was being polite and checking on me."

"Don't coddle him! He needs to be tough, not sighing over the thought of holding your hand."

"And jamming your cock up his ass is supposed to make him tough?"

His jaw worked, looking like granite under his beard.

"Tell anyone about that, and we'll all be dead—us for doing it, and you for knowing."

Shocked, I made a sound of disbelief, but when I looked at Ilya, his eyes said Bron was serious.

"Is it that illegal here?"

"Forget the law. Vas would kill us." He mimed a gun with his hand, and I flinched when he put his finger against his head and pulled the imaginary trigger.

Oh god—how was that level of homophobia still a thing? Would Vas really kill them rather than have a bisexual son?

"Even if Vas were to spare you, which I doubt he would, you wouldn't get paid. Maybe he would keep you and use you in one of his clubs. Maybe cut out your tongue."

I shuddered. "Point made."

"It's why you're here. We need to make him harder."

Bron seemed to make Ilya plenty hard, but it was probably a bad time to point that out.

"Come here." He beckoned to me with one hand.

Warily, I went.

"Kneel at his feet."

I hesitated a moment.

"Now!" he barked. He slapped my face—not hard enough to hurt, but hard enough to get my attention.

Ilya gasped, and Bron rounded on him, cuffing him much harder than he'd smacked me.

"You don't make that noise. Ever. Understand me?"

"Don't hit her!" Ilya snapped, surprising the hell out of me, and Bron, too, apparently.

"She needs to learn to obey immediately and without hesitation when she's given a command."

"Then I'll teach her. You only teach me." He glared at Bron, standing up straight and squaring his broad shoulders.

"You don't tell me what to do, you little shit."

"You don't hit her like that." His hands curled into fists. "Hitting women is cowardly."

"Too many years raised by a woman and a nursemaid," Bron grumbled. "Not enough time with men. No wonder you're soft."

"She was going to obey. There was no need."

"She was too slow. If she behaves like this in front of your family, and she doesn't comply with orders immediately..."

"There's time to learn that."

Bring me in front of his family? What the fuck were they talking about?

Bron grunted. "Not long enough. I told her to kneel, and she's just standing there watching us talk."

"She probably didn't want to get stepped on by big boots."

I went to Ilya and knelt in front of him, tired of listening to them argue.

"She doesn't even know how to kneel properly!"

"We didn't choose her because she knew what to do, Bron. My family will never see her kneel, anyway."

Bron raised a fist at Ilya, as though he planned to punch him, but Ilya only jutted his chin in defiance.

"The woman is here for less than a week and you're already disagreeing with me."

"Isn't that the point of having her here?"

They stared at each other, saying silent things, their large chests heaving with emotion. I was an interloper, between two men who'd been together for almost a dozen years. No matter how toxic their relationship seemed to be, it was strong.

"Take her by the hair and fuck her face."

Ilya swallowed. "I won't."

"What will you do when you visit your family? Ask her things nicely? Neither of you will act right if you don't learn how to act with each other in private. Pretending won't fool anyone."

"You're bringing me to visit your family?"

Ilya sighed. "Yes."

"But why?"

"You're proof I'm a man. That I can attract and keep a woman of your quality."

"Bossing women around doesn't make you a man."

Bron let out a breath like a malfunctioning steam engine. "Your Western ethics don't mean anything to these people, woman. You're our best hope for Ilya to be accepted by his family, and for him not to lose access to the allowance he and his siblings get."

"If he can't prove he can boss a woman around, his family will turn him out and he won't have a dime?"

"You are only part of it, but basically yes. The rest is how he interacts with the others. He needs to show some spine."

It felt strange looking way up at him like this while I was on my knees, but I doubted he'd be pleased if I got up again without asking.

"What am I supposed to do there? Play the part of the devoted submissive?"

"Play the part of the devoted girlfriend," Ilya corrected.

"Now shut up and suck his cock."

Glancing up at Ilya, I saw his look of disquiet.

"Is that what you want, Ilya?" I asked.

Bron grabbed Ilya and moved him closer to me, then unfastened his jeans and pushed them down, as though he had every right to manhandle Ilya and his clothing. Ilya sucked in a breath and glanced at Bron. His throat bobbed.

"Let her see you," he commanded gruffly.

Ilya shoved down his underwear. His dick was even bigger than it had felt when I was straddling him, and he was only half hard. I wasn't a girl to get poetic about cocks, but wow...and also, yikes. My jaw was sore just contemplating him.

"Now tell her what you want."

"I want to go watch a movie," Ilya said through gritted teeth.

Bron got behind him and wrapped his arms around him, keeping him from retreating from me. He grabbed Ilya's cock and stroked it mere inches from my mouth.

Ilya's eyes were wide, apparently surprised Bron was touching him.

"Don't you want to feel a mouth on your cock?"

"No, I—" he objected, but groaned as Bron jerked cruelly at his dick. "Please, Bron."

"It's time for you to know how it feels receiving instead of just having your mouth used as punishment."

"I don't need to know," he said uncertainly, but his gaze was on my lips, and their proximity to the head of his cock.

He'd never had sex with a woman before, never gotten head before, and knowing Bron, I highly doubted he'd let him top before. It was a waste of such a big, beautiful cock.

"Your hand feels so different from mine," Ilya said with quiet amazement.

God, he'd never even given the poor guy a reach-around? The man was a damned monster.

I moved closer, and Bron took Ilya's hand and moved it to my hair. "Now grip her hair close to the scalp," he whispered, his voice like warm honey, making me shiver. "Do it how you like it."

Ilya's gaze was molten, and he slid his fingers through my hair, then took a firm grip of it.

"Tell her what you want."

"Touch your tongue to me," he whispered. A bead of precum formed. Through his grip on my hair, I could feel him trembling with excitement. "Please."

Being his first was a lot of pressure. I tried to remember what it was like being a beginner, but I'd skipped a lot of steps, and had never really had the chance to experiment.

Gently, I licked the very tip of his cock, barely enough to taste him on my tongue.

He drew a strangled breath, then exhaled a plaintive, needy whine.

I kissed the tip, running my tongue along the slit, cleaning the drop from his skin entirely, but there was more where that had come from. How were the most basic vanilla things so hot with him? Probably his reactions. Most men prided themselves on being stoic and not letting on when they were enjoying something, but apparently Ilya had missed the memo. I opened my mouth and leaned forward, taking the tip of his cock into my mouth and sucking, swirling my tongue around the thick head.

He gasped, and the sound of his pleasure jolted straight through me to my already throbbing pussy.

"Don't you fucking come, boy," Bron grumbled. "You come too soon, and we will mock you."

His cock twitched so hard in my mouth I thought for sure it was too late, but he managed not to come. He whimpered as though we were torturing him.

Bron stripped off Ilya's T-shirt, and then his own, leaving an entire mountain of well-muscled flesh towering above me.

"Control her with your grip on her hair, the way I do with you. When you need her to stop, make her stop."

"Does it always feel so good?"

"Yes, but you get used to it, so it's not so...shocking."

"I thought it was just a punishment for me, but you..."

"You were a very eager pupil, Ilyusha. I doubt anyone else will ever satisfy me as well." His hand closed more tightly around Ilya's, and he pulled me toward them while pushing Ilya's hips closer to me with his own. I did my best to accommodate his girth, and his length, but Bron insisted on pushing him deep into my mouth and holding him there. Ilya gasped, his hand convulsing on my hair. I tried to hold my breath, but eventually gagged and tried to retreat. They allowed it, and I gasped for air and tried to wipe at my eyes.

"God, she's beautiful."

"Isn't she? We chose the most beautiful one, and they were all beauties."

"Using her this way is so crude. It feels wrong."

"And does it make you feel guilty?"

"Yes."

"And?"

"It makes my dick hard."

"Good. Use her mouth. Show her how to please you."

"Can I sit down? My legs are shaking."

"No. You need to learn how to stand over her—to show her how much bigger you are and make her feel small."

Ilya groaned but pulled me closer on his own this time, pushing the head of his cock between my lips. "Suck me with that pretty mouth, Delilah."

The sound of his low, rough voice saying my name made me shudder. My eyelids fluttered as I took him deeper into my mouth, sucking, licking, showing him what I could do to give him pleasure. Moments later, he pulled out of my mouth and held me away from him as he gasped for breath.

"I swear she's going to suck out my soul."

"Do you care?"

"I'm trying to make it last."

"Ignore what I said before. Everyone finishes too soon the first few times. You last longer when you get used to it."

"How could a man ever get used to this?"

He watched in fascination as I stuck out my tongue and tried to reach him, his cock bobbing impatiently.

"Witch," he growled, tightening his grip on my hair. "Your evil mouth makes me ache."

There was power in the feeling of him being so close to the edge. Had any man ever wanted me so badly before? Maybe it was only because I was his first woman, but damn, it was the hottest thing.

His wild eyes said he was struggling even though we'd paused.

I squirmed where he held me, still trying to get to him while he held me away. Slowly, he pulled me closer. When I reached for him, he gave my head a gentle shake.

"No hands. Give me your mouth."

His gentle bossiness made me shiver. Where had it come from? This wasn't something Bron was coaching him into doing.

"If you are sweet to her, she will get demanding. It's a woman's nature," Bron said. "If you are weak or hesitant, she will sense it and take advantage. She needs a firm hand."

"If you treat people with kindness, won't they be more willing to serve you?" He gave me an amused glance. "And why should I force her if she's cooperating?"

He let me get close enough to reach him with my mouth, and I ran my lips along his length, then dragged my tongue back to the tip. His grip on my hair relaxed as I sucked him into my mouth a bit at a time, varying the pressure. I felt him lean back, and I gazed up to find Bron supporting him. I bobbed up and down on his cock, playing with him as he combed his fingers through my hair. Bron had a grip on Ilya's hair and had pulled his head to the side and was biting his neck. Between the two of us, Ilya was breathing hard, his eyes unfocused, his cock throbbing in my mouth.

Fuck, they were sexy to watch—both of them cut and perfect, skin against skin, Bron covered with tattoos and Ilya without. I pressed my thighs together, the heaviness in my lower belly disconcerting. Ilya hadn't been wrong. I was hot for him. For both of them, actually, and for different reasons.

"Are you going to come in her mouth, *suka*?"

Ilya didn't answer, but I could feel him struggling for control. I forced him deeper into my mouth, gagging, and his body went rigid. He choked on a breath, and his cock bucked in my mouth, then flooded it with cum. I swallowed and sucked, with Ilya groaning as though he would die while Bron laughed softly. When his knees buckled, Bron lowered Ilya to the floor. I followed him down, not stopping until he gently pulled me up to lie on his chest. His heart drummed under my ear, and his labored breathing made it sound like he'd won an uphill race.

I nuzzled his chest, and he twisted his hand in my hair, hugging my head to him.

Bron cleared his throat, and Ilya's eyes popped open. He urged me off him, then knelt at Bron's feet.

"Did you like that?"

"Yes, Bron. Thank you."

He was thanking Bron? I was the one with the sore jaw.

"Show me how grateful you are."

Ilya unbuttoned Bron's jeans with shaking hands, then drew down his zipper with reverence. Bron freed his cock. Ilya clasped his hands behind his back and took Bron deep into his mouth, closing his eyes and concentrating on his work. Bron grunted and threaded his fingers into Ilya's long hair, gripping it but letting the younger man service him without direction. Obviously, he knew exactly what Bron liked.

Of course he did. Bron had trained him. They'd been doing this for years.

I watched, hiking up my nightgown to creep closer, noticing when Ilya's cheeks hollowed, and when his tongue peeped out. Bron watched Ilya, but his eyes also slid my way.

"Maybe you can ask your intended to help you," Bron said. It didn't sound like a request.

When I moved to get up and join them, Bron's dark eyes froze me on the spot.

"Crawl."

Our gazes clashed. Sure, they were paying me to be here, but obeying because they commanded me to do something felt different from being thrown around and used like a doll. I wasn't a great submissive. It had gotten me in trouble a lot in my last relationship and would have ended things between me and Michael if I hadn't needed to break up so I could do another tour on the Island.

Still. Did I want to make a big deal out of something so trivial?

I stripped and threw the nightgown and socks in a pile. Ilya's eyes were on me, studying me with the thoroughness of an artist but the interest of a man who hadn't seen many naked women. Would he sketch me in his book, the way he'd said he did with Bron?

When I lowered myself to the floor, the carpet cushioned my knees. I crawled the few paces to them and knelt beside Ilya, not sure what to do. I'd been tag-teamed several times over the years even before going to the Island, but I'd never gone down on a guy with someone else helping.

Ilya pulled his mouth off Bron's cock and shifted over, giving me space.

I moved in, running my lips along Bron's thick, smooth shaft. He had a beautiful cock, too, even if it felt like hell in my unprepared ass. Ilya followed my lead, mirroring my movements on the other side. Between the two of us we found a rhythm, lips and tongue meeting over and around Bron's cock, almost like it was a toy we played with while we made out. Ilya's fingers stayed firmly entwined behind his back, but I wasn't going to keep my hands to myself. I ran my nails over Bron's balls, glided my hands over his stomach, and moved on to explore Ilya's body, too. Neither of them stopped me, and soon Ilya was gasping on Bron's cock and against my mouth. Where I had trouble going down far on Bron's big dick, Ilya's larger jaw could accommodate him. I worked on whatever I could reach, enjoying it more than I should have.

He pushed Ilya back and dragged my mouth onto him instead. Ilya leaned his head against Bron's leg and watched me struggle to take him, encouraging me with his gaze.

When he came, I swallowed, grateful he wasn't as unaccustomed to blowjobs as Ilya, who'd almost drowned me. If Bron controlled Ilya's orgasms though, who knew how long Ilya had been saving up his load?

Bron pulled free of my mouth, and I knelt patiently, even though I was the only one in the room who hadn't gotten off. On the Island, I'd rarely needed to masturbate—there were enough men there willing to help a girl out. As soon as these two got out of my room, though, I'd be taking care of myself.

Ilya put a hand on my stomach, giving me a half grin. "Our cum is mixed together in there."

Raising my brows, I looked at Bron, whose mouth twitched in the faintest sign of amusement.

"Good thing you can't get a girl pregnant that way," I teased.

His face reddened.

Bron pushed him at me. "Kiss her with your tongue, and taste us both in her mouth."

Shyly, he brushed his mouth over mine. Rather than taking control of things this time, I let him deepen the kiss. His tongue teased at mine, and I stayed passive until he twined them together. It was like a rekindling of making out in the kitchen—picking up where we'd left off. He lowered me to the carpeting and lay down beside me, propping his head in one hand and exploring my nakedness with the other. His fingers were so gentle on my skin that it tickled, giving me goosebumps.

"Enough." Bron kicked Ilya with his heavy boot, making him grunt in pain. "Get up. Both of you."

Ilya got immediately to his feet, hanging onto his jeans so they didn't fall down the rest of the way.

"Go watch your movie. We'll do more of this tomorrow." His eyes were alight with sadistic amusement as Ilya grimaced. His cock was a bulge in his jeans. "No pleasuring each other or yourselves until I give you permission. Understand?"

Ilya swore but zipped and buttoned his jeans.

"How would you even know?" I countered. When I got to my feet, I snatched my nightgown and socks from the floor.

"I have my ways. If I even suspect you've broken my rule, you'll regret it."

"Promises, promises."

Bron shot me a look that should have scared the hell out of me, but I only found it thrilling.

Unfortunately.

My pussy was so needy it was making my IQ drop. Of course, he'd have no way of knowing, but arguing with him was going to get me into hot water.

The movie was good, but I had trouble concentrating.

I went to bed later, determined to break Bron's rule, but when I closed my eyes to fantasize, his fierce expression popped into my head, along with his warning.

Freaking jerk.

Chapter Eight

I shielded my eyes against the day's stabbing brilliance. The house had a decent number of windows, but aside from in Yana's room, most of them didn't get much sun. It would be a pleasant house for vampires, but a terrible one for cats.

Captivated, I watched the two men work. Despite the cold, they had both shed their shirts and were splitting and stacking firewood. It was a shame there were no other women here to appreciate the sight with. Even with the welts and bruises on Ilya, and the scars on Bron, they were definitely eye candy. If I'd had a phone with me, I would have taken some video to share with Lane when I saw her again.

Hopefully, she'd found a way to co-exist with Ajax and Calder, at least until the tour was done, but something told me they wouldn't be content with never seeing her again. It had been about two weeks since Bron had stolen me from the beach. He'd assured me Lane knew I'd been offered a shit-ton of money to take the contract with them, but I was worried that she was worried, or that maybe he was lying and hadn't made sure she was told.

And what about poor Clover? I hoped Bron was wrong, and she'd ended up with nicer men than the ones who'd chewed her up and spat her out during the first hunt.

I had tried helping Bron and Ilya with the firewood, but they'd shooed me away. Instead, I was alternating between sitting on a stump and wandering along the edge of the trees, picking up kindling and stacking it in the box they kept for it.

The garden's greenery kept luring me near, and I examined the plants, not sure which were going to be vegetables and which were weeds. Nearby, penned goats and chickens did their thing, their noises keeping the silence from feeling weird or uncomfortable. It was odd spending so much time outside, but it was an interesting change from my regular, very indoorsy life.

"I can pile wood, too, you know," I said again, when I'd gotten bored with investigating the garden and gone back to watching huge stumps get turned into firewood. They'd used the two-person saw to cut the logs earlier. That also would have ended up in my Russian men-of-the-year calendar, if I'd had a phone.

"Firewood is a man's job. My wifey does not do my work," Ilya said sternly, surprising me.

Wifey? Such a flirt.

"What's wifey work?"

Bron raised a brow. "Cook. Give him pussy. Push out babies."

Ilya shot Bron a quelling look, but Bron barked a laugh.

"I know you're impatient to get your holes filled, woman, but there's work to be done. Ilya can't spend all day panting after you, or we'll freeze and starve this winter."

"What am I supposed to do while you're busy?"

"Read a book? Daydream about dick?"

I daydreamed about their dicks far too much as it was, but I wasn't about to admit that to Bron.

This was far easier money than working on the Island had been, but I was missing the action. After our movie night, Bron hadn't approved of any sexual contact again. I'd fantasized about one, the other, or both sneaking into my room in the middle of the night and having their way with me, but it hadn't happened. I'd gone walking around the house at night a few times when I was trying to sleep, only to hear the telling sounds of Bron using Ilya.

Why weren't they using me for sex? Hell, they were paying for me to be here.

A dark shadow dove from a nearby tree, and I gasped as it alighted on the woodpile. Either the raven was huge, or I hadn't seen one close up. Either way, Ilya's comfort with its nearness freaked me out. Wasn't he afraid it would peck out his eyeballs with its huge, curved beak?

"Where have you been, beauty?" Ilya chided. He stretched his arm out to the beast, and it hopped along the woodpile and onto his hand.

"Tell your girlfriend we have work to do."

"You're only jealous because she doesn't like you."

"Who wants to be friends with a big, ugly bird?"

"Probably the same type of person who spends their time with a big, ugly man."

Bron chuckled and shook his head, as though he approved of the jibe rather than being offended by it. I'd watched my brothers interact that way, but the hierarchy was a lot stricter here.

"Look," Ilya said, turning to show her to me. Her black feathers were lovely in the bright sunshine, but that beak made me want to guard my eyes.

"Yes, I see her," I said uneasily, hoping he didn't plan on introducing us.

"Did you bring me a gift, beauty?" He held out his hand. Sure enough, there was something shiny clutched in her beak that she dropped almost in his hand. He crouched down slowly and retrieved it, turning the item over in his palm.

"More garbage?" Bron grumbled.

"An old coin."

Bron peered at the silver-toned coin in Ilya's hand, leaning far closer to the bird than I would ever dare to.

"A trillion more of those and you might have enough to buy a box of nails."

"Maybe it's worth something to a collector."

"Of course. Then you can forget about needing to win your father's approval and simply live off the coins Verni brings you," Bron said flatly. "You and your silly bird."

"He's jealous of your big brain, Verni. Don't listen to the sour old goat."

"Five years isn't so much older than you, boy. It only feels that way."

The bird eventually hopped down and picked at grubs in the garden.

About a half hour later, they stopped working and rinsed off in a bucket they kept nearby. It wasn't warm out, but they'd both worked up a sweat. Menial labor looked good on them.

I tugged up the shoulder of my T-shirt. It had a wide neckline that kept sliding off.

When I glanced up, they were both watching.

"What?"

"Work is over," Bron said.

"And?"

"I think it's time for the boy's next lesson."

It took a moment to process what he'd said, but Ilya's gaze focused on me. He looked hopefully to Bron, then back my way.

"Can I have her now?" Ilya said eagerly.

"If you can catch her—and if I don't find her first."

"What happens if you find her first?"

"I will use her myself, and you will wait another week to come."

I didn't like the glint in Ilya's gaze. Had days of denial made him more aggressive?

"If I find her first, no more punishments at night?"

Bron tilted his head, considering. "I'll give you two nights free of the belt."

"Thank you, Bron."

"What about me?" I demanded. "If neither of you finds me, what do I get?"

He chuckled. "Both of us have been hunting since we were boys. Do you really think you can hide from us both until dark?"

"I've done several tours on the Island."

"You did well there because you played politics. You found the strongest, most vicious men and made them eat out of your hand."

It hadn't been as easy as he made it sound, but he wasn't entirely wrong.

"What do I get?" I demanded again, propping my hands on my hips and raising my chin.

Both men looked me over with interest. I was pretty sure one of them growled.

"If you can avoid us both until dark, you get a financial bonus."

"I get a bonus and I get to boss you both around for the rest of the night."

Bron barked a laugh, his perfect teeth flashing.

"Boss me around? To do what?"

Oh, the things I'd do with that kind of power. I wouldn't only make him serve me hand and foot, I'd make him bottom for Ilya and give the jerk a taste of his own medicine.

"Anything I say."

He glared at me. Could he read my evil thoughts?

"If the two of you are such expert hunters, then what I might make you do shouldn't worry you."

His head came up. I'd stung his massive male ego.

"Done. You'd better pray it's not me who finds you, *De-li-lah*." When he was feeling aggressive, he always said my name like it was three separate words and possibly the most ridiculous name he'd ever heard.

I gave a toss of my head and ran into the woods, wishing I hadn't chosen a long skirt to wear today. Luckily, my boots fit well enough and protected my feet. Hopefully, they'd support my ankle too—I'd fucked it up running track in high school and it had never been the same since. They'd never given us decent footwear on the Island, and it had always felt like cheating to me. Giving men who were already bigger and stronger than we were an extra advantage seemed unnecessarily cruel.

The forest on this island felt very different. The green was a different shade, and the ground was damp rather than sandy. It was harder going, too, without as many paths winding through the undergrowth.

My heart was pounding. If Ilya caught me, he might hurt me just because he'd be keyed up and didn't know what he was doing. If Bron caught me, he'd definitely let his sadism loose after the bargain we'd struck.

At least there were only two of them on this island.

"Watch out for the wolves." Bron's voice came to me from a distance.

Wolves? He was fucking with me, right?

I hiked up my skirt and kept running, wishing I knew how to tie my skirt high the way Lanie had told me she'd done during one hunt. I'd never gotten around to finding out how and didn't have time to stop and figure it out.

At least my clothes were neutral. The gray was close enough to green that I didn't stick out the way we did when they'd made us wear florescent colors during the Island hunts.

In a way, this was harder. I wanted to win because I wanted to claim temporary mastery over Bron, but my libido wanted me to get caught.

I struggled through some bracken, making a god-awful racket. Damn it, I wasn't used to the terrain here. I spooked a rabbit who spooked me, too, and my scream of surprise rent the air.

The woods held the same mysterious shadows they did in the jungle, but not knowing what might be lurking made it scarier. Needing to worry about other men was one thing, but worrying about animals that might attack and rip me apart was a different kind of fear. As badass as it might sound, getting eaten by wolves wasn't even in my top ten of ways I'd prefer to die.

Eventually, the stitch in my side made me slow to a walk. I'd tripped and almost fallen so many times that I felt punch drunk. My legs shook.

Did I dare find somewhere to hide and sit down for a few minutes?

I looked around, but the forest was an impenetrable wall. If I evaded them until nightfall, then what? I'd never be able to find my way back in the dark. I'd have to wait until morning and find the shore, then follow it around the island to the dock so I could find the road to the house. I wasn't even sure how big this island was. Were there neighbors on it? I didn't think so, but I'd never asked.

I stopped and tried to catch my breath, the fresh damp green smell welcome. Budding leaves had unfurled in the short time I'd been on Ilya's island, making everything fresh and new.

Was the island on an ocean or was this a lake? I hadn't asked, and I hadn't brought anything to eat or drink with me. Drinking ocean water wouldn't help my thirst.

Did I really want to sleep alone in the woods tonight with no shelter when there were wolves, and maybe other predators around?

Maybe I should go back?

I turned in a full circle, not even sure which way I'd come from.

This island felt much more dangerous and isolated than the other had. I wasn't going to stumble across other female prey here, and no other predators would find me.

Not human ones, anyway.

My choice was Ilya, Bron, or spending the night alone in the forest. I shuddered, not knowing which of those options I dreaded more.

An eerie howl filled the air—not close, but then again, what did I know?

Another answered.

Fuck.

Oh, fuck.

I'd hoped like hell Bron was shitting me, but that sound hadn't come from a human throat.

I ducked down behind a clump of ferns.

Could wolves smell how afraid I was?

If I'd been religious, I would have prayed, but all I could think about was how shitty it was that no one would miss me. Maybe Lane, but she'd get over it, especially if she'd hooked up with Ajax and Calder.

My siblings would get their scholarships, at least.

I stopped to pee, even though I didn't really need to. My bladder hadn't liked the sound of those wolves either.

Afraid, I kept moving, trying to find the shore. I wasn't sure if I wanted to head back already and admit I was chickenshit, but at least it gave me a goal. Using the sun as a reference, I walked and walked until I reached a clearing. An old, squat cabin crouched in the middle of it, logs thick with moss.

Did someone live here?

It looked abandoned, but it was also in good enough shape that I couldn't believe it had been empty long.

"Hello?" I called, knocking timidly on the door. I should have passed it and kept going, but the idea of being indoors, away from ravenous beasts, was too tempting.

No answer. Then again, if someone lived here, they were unlikely to speak English. The windows were too grimy to see through.

Another howl came, but it seemed farther away. I tried the rusty door latch. It gave way when I used both thumbs, then I had to put my shoulder to it to get the door to swing inward.

Debris littered the floor. Dust coated the table, and the chairs were broken. The bed was a mouse-chewed, stained mattress on a rusted frame. Rope and dead leaves made untidy heaps on the floor, along with a huge, old-fashioned fishing net.

The place looked like a serial killer hangout.

Even so, I pulled the door firmly closed and made sure the latch engaged. There was no lock, but wolves couldn't open a latch, right?

I felt like one of the three little pigs, waiting for a wolf to blow my house down.

There was nowhere to hide.

Taking refuge in what seemed like the only other structure on the island, other than the house and its out buildings, seemed too obvious if I was still trying to get away from Ilya and Bron, but I was so nervous about the wolves I was almost hoping the men would find me. Rough sex wasn't a big deal compared to getting eaten alive.

I cleared a spot on the floor beside the empty hearth and sat down, leaning on the stone. It was cold in the cabin. The sun was far too weak to reach through the dirt-caked glass to warm the space. I wrapped my arms around myself, wishing I'd had some warning so I could have brought a sweater.

Men. Always springing these things on a girl at the last minute. Bron was probably the kind of guy who told his girlfriends that black tie events were business casual. Hell, he was probably the kind of guy who brought his girlfriends to black tie events completely naked and on a leash.

My ass wasn't even prepped.

Stupid. I'd found lube in one of the downstairs bathrooms. I really needed to start prepping myself, just in case.

Should I go back? If I got back to the house before they did, would that mean I'd won?

When I was about to get up, the door burst open.

I screamed bloody murder and launched to my feet, grabbing a broken chair and holding it out in front of me.

Bron grinned. His shaggy hair had leaves in it, and his eyes—dear god, they were terrifying.

He looked completely unhinged.

"I thought you might be here, stupid cunt."

I brandished the chair at him, as if I were a lion tamer at the circus and had lost my whip.

"Get back!" I shouted, jabbing the legs at him.

He jumped backward to avoid catching the wood in the ribs. Then, as I edged toward the open doorway, he grabbed the chair and yanked it from my hands.

I turned and fled, hearing the chair clatter, and feeling him following close behind.

"Come on, De-li-lah," he mocked. "I'll only hurt you a little."

I shrieked in fear. The look on his face was one I knew all too well—the beast had taken over, and the man had been pushed so far down he might never see light again, at least not until it was too late. It was the face of the soccer team, and of men during hunts. The face of my high school teacher.

I ran and ran, dodging through the trees, my face and bare arms getting whipped with branches, underbrush tangling in my skirt.

Something caught in my hair, and I was jerked to a halt. I screamed in pain, my hands flying up to cover my sore scalp.

"No more flying, pretty bird," he growled.

"No, no, no!" I begged, smacking at him, trying to claw at his eyes.

He wrestled me to the ground, but I kept fighting him. When he pinned my arms, I tried to kick, twisting beneath him to stop him from getting between my legs.

I was getting tired, but desperation made me strong. I got a knee up between us and shoved him off, flipping over to scramble away. He caught my ankle, and I lashed back at him, my nails connecting with skin.

He was swearing now, cursing me in Russian.

"Take her arms," he spat.

Then Ilya was there, grabbing my wrists. Two against one. This wasn't part of the game.

"Let me go. You can't gang up on me!"

"Why? That wasn't in the rules." Ilya was grinning down at me, face flushed, eyes bright with excitement.

"One or the other! It wasn't supposed to be both of you!"

"Pin her with your legs."

Ilya rearranged his hold, and Bron helped trap my hips between Ilya's thighs. Of course, I was face down in the leaf mold. With my arms twisted behind my back I could still kick, and I tried to land something, but my struggles had flipped up my skirt and a cold steel blade sliced through the new granny panties Bron had ordered me with the grocery delivery.

Bron got behind me, pushing my thighs wide, making my attempts to kick him fruitless.

He spat, and warm saliva hit the crack of my ass and slid down to my asshole.

"Please no," I begged.

He didn't listen, spearing a thick finger into my ass with ruthless determination.

"Fuck you, Bron! This isn't fair!"

"Is life usually fair?"

A second finger coaxed its way in with the first, and Ilya's thigh shifted beneath me.

"Enjoying the show, Ilya?" I gasped in discomfort. For some reason, I felt betrayed. I'd thought we were sort of friends—or at least friendly. Why was he helping Bron instead of me?

"Very much."

"You fucking jerk. I wouldn't fake-date you if you were the last man on earth!"

Bron pulled his fingers out of me and spat again, then lined himself up with my asshole.

"No, no!" I pressed my forehead against the ground, bracing for Bron's favorite brand of torment.

"Mmm. Yes, yes." Bron pushed into me with a series of short, breathtaking thrusts. He covered me with his body, bracing against the ground, pressing Ilya's bottom leg harder against my hips, and top leg into my lower back.

I shrieked, and tried to struggle, but they had me so thoroughly pinned there was nothing I could do except cry.

"Shh, little wifey. I know he's big. It will feel better if you stop fighting," Ilya assured me as our tormentor rearranged my guts to suit himself.

Tears leaked out of my eyes, a combination of frustrated helplessness and the feeling that he should have helped me instead of Bron. He knew what it was like to be Bron's victim.

Being tangled with them was a strange sensation. I clung to my anger. Ilya was stroking my hair with his free hand, soothing me like he might do with one of his goats, while Bron fucked me with his monster dick, which felt a lot like a wooden club someone had set on fire before quenching it in my ass.

I clawed at the ground, grunting in pain at every thrust, trying not to link this with my fantasies about mountain men roughing me up and taking what they wanted.

Eventually, Bron growled in satisfaction, filling me with liquid heat that felt like it all rushed out as he withdrew.

Laughing, he slapped Ilya's leg and pulled out of me. Ilya let me go and Bron flipped me face up, and more cum dribbled out of my sore, stinging ass.

"Come here," he said gruffly to Ilya.

He yanked my skirt out of the way and pushed my legs apart, pointing between them, as if Ilya wouldn't even know that much. I closed my legs and tried to fight, but I was tired and knew they'd never let me get away—especially not now, when Ilya was showing the aggression Bron wanted from him.

Ilya stretched out on top of me, catching my wrists and stretching my arms above my head. He tried to kiss me, but I jerked my head away, so his mouth connected with my ear. His knee pressed between mine, and he made room for himself, settling between my thighs. He smelled like fresh air, hard work, and wood. Under that was the smell of soap and sweat...of him.

His cock was hard, and he ground against me—his jeans against my bare pussy. The rough fabric of his pants chafed my clit, and I realized it already ached with a need for release.

Why was my body so stupid? I should hate these men, not find them and their crude handling arousing.

"I've dreamt of pushing my cock into your sweet pussy since the first day I saw you," Ilya murmured, reaching between us to unfasten his pants. His erection was hard and hot, and he rocked it against my slit, the underside of his cock rubbing my clit.

He tried to kiss me again, but I didn't allow it.

"You fight and complain, but I know you lie in bed at night, thinking of us touching you."

"You're delusional!"

He took advantage of my mouth being open and claimed my lips, pushing his tongue between them and trying to force me to reciprocate. Bron tapped Ilya's hip, and he pulled away from me slightly, gasping as Bron took him in hand and positioned him at my entrance. I tried to flex my hips so he couldn't push into me so easily, but the hot velvet of his cock felt too good to refuse.

Maybe I could let this happen, even if I was mad at him. Maybe I could submit to him, at least this one time. The head of his cock was slick, and he slid the tip into me, stopping long enough to gasp in amazement.

"Why would a man ever leave a woman's body after feeling this?" He kissed me again, and his hips moved jerkily, unnaturally. Bron was behind him, controlling his hips with a firm grip. Ilya panted in frustration.

"Let him go, Bron. He'll figure it out," I muttered, trying to stay upset, but wanting him deeper inside me. My brain was frazzled, but the feel of him invading my body was exactly what I needed. Pleasure to blot out the pain, even if he only lasted a minute or two.

Bron let him go, and he pushed harder, with no cruelty but also no finesse. He pulled his mouth from mine and stared into my eyes, slowing down when he saw my discomfort. I wriggled beneath him until he was sheathed, balls deep.

He breathed through the sensation like a woman in labor while I did my best not to writhe beneath him. I needed to be fucked hard, and he was taking the scenic route.

"I'm inside you," he said in amazement.

"You are," I confirmed, in case it was actually a question. It was hard not to laugh at his expression of wonder.

"This is—my bare cock is—"

"Don't think about that yet," Bron warned.

Ilya nodded at him, then gazed into my eyes again. His hips stirred, and he partially withdrew, then slid back in.

"What's wrong?" he asked me immediately. "Am I hurting you?"

"You're probably putting her to sleep. She's used to getting it rough, like you are."

"Oh." He checked my face for confirmation, and I leaned up and kissed him.

"If I need you to stop, I'll say the word, rutabaga."

He gave me a lopsided grin. "Good."

"You can fuck me harder. I won't break."

"I'm fucking a girl," he whispered under his breath.

When I laughed, he let out a tortured groan.

"I need to make you laugh more often."

Bron grumbled and stripped a branch from a tree, picking off the smaller twigs and leaves, and making so much noise that it distracted me from Ilya.

Without warning, Bron brought the branch down, whistling, and hit Ilya with it.

He hissed in pain, plunging into me so hard I gasped.

"Good, now fuck her so we can go home. Harder. Faster." He whipped Ilya three or four more times, until instinct took over and he pounded me hard and fast, stealing my breath. I angled my hips until he was rubbing against my clit, and lifted myself to meet each thrust, not complaining that it was almost too much, and it hurt.

He was good for a beginner, keeping a decent rhythm, paying attention to what my body told him, as well as he could, even though he was going too deep, too hard.

Days upon days of no relief had caught up with me, and I wanted an orgasm so badly I was ready to take any pain to get it.

I was almost at my own orgasm when he came, his eyes shutting so tightly I thought he was going to cry. God, he was gorgeous. Had any man ever looked at me with this much wonder? He dropped his forehead to mine and kissed me again.

"Thank you. I'm sorry it was over so fast." He shuddered and gave a few last thrusts.

My clit was aching so much I wanted to scream.

"It's like that for most guys their first few times," I said, trying not to whine as he withdrew.

He sat back and pulled me into his lap.

"What are you doing?" I demanded.

"Using my hands."

"For what?"

"Slap her here," Bron said, pointing to my clit.

"What? No!"

"Shh. Let me take care of you."

Before I could object, he smacked me harder than I would have expected, connecting with my needy clit. My pussy made a wet sound, which I chose to believe was mostly from boys filling me with their bodily fluids, and not from me being a needy bitch.

"Bend her backward over your leg and pinch her nipples hard as you do it," Bron directed.

"Ilya, no."

But he listened to Bron and bent me backward, catching one of my nipples between two fingers and crushing it. My mouth opened in pain, and my eyes rolled back as he smashed his hand against my pussy again.

Days of built-up tension hovered, waiting for the next smack, and I rode the high, filthy, covered in sweat and cum and dirt. His next slap landed squarely on my pussy, stinging, and my body practically levitated off his leg. I opened my mouth in a silent wail as I glided along the sharp edge of my orgasm, and with the next tug at my nipple came another slap, and I was screaming, convulsing in his arms, feeling like he was exorcising a stubborn demon from my body.

The next smack was lighter, and then he stroked my pussy, almost in apology. I lay across his lap, my back arched over his leg and the back of my head in the dirt. He gathered me in his arms and cradled me against his bare chest.

He kissed my forehead, and I completely forgave his prior betrayal. Had I really expected him to choose me over Bron? I knew where his loyalty would always lie, and I was just temporary in their lives.

"I'm sorry I didn't know what to do. I'll try to be better at it next time."

I blurted a wild laugh. My body felt like it was a bundle of over-cooked noodles tied loosely together. Maybe some of it had been the days of denial, and the adrenaline from the hunt, but I hadn't expected to come so hard.

"Don't feel bad. She's being paid," Bron said, sounding odd.

We both looked up at him. Bron was hovering over us, looking uncomfortable. He ruffled Ilya's hair with awkward affection.

"You did well. We'll have your family convinced, I think. You only need a bit more practice."

Ilya brightened like a Golden Retriever who'd been told he was a good boy. "Do you think so?"

Bron didn't answer. He brushed dirt from his pants and nodded once.

He walked off on his own, not waiting for us.

Ilya held my hand on the long walk back to the house, his elation buoying up my mood.

The wolves, if they were near, kept silent.

Chapter Nine

"Are you sure you two aren't cheating?" I demanded, flinging my shirt onto the pile on the floor that already included my skirt and wooly socks.

Ilya grinned. "You're very bad at playing Durak."

"I've played strip poker before, but is stripping even part of this game?"

"Only if you are good at Durak and want to see your opponent naked," Bron said, topping up everyone's drinks.

It was a good thing I had a high tolerance for alcohol. These two weren't lightweights.

"You've already seen me naked. If you want my clothes off, all you have to do is hold me down and strip me. That's what you usually do."

"We kept her naked for one day, and she's still complaining." Ilya threw down his cards and stretched.

"It was cold!" I wrapped my arms around myself, trying to keep my body heat in, but Yana's old sports bra and my granny panties were no help.

"This isn't cold. Wait until winter."

"I'll be gone by then, thank god. I'd freeze to death."

They both took a drink then and didn't reply.

I narrowed my eyes. "I *am* going home in twelve weeks or so."

Bron thumped down his glass on the wooden table. "That's what it says in your contract."

The statement should have been reassuring, but it wasn't.

"You do look cold," Ilya noted. "You could sit on my lap."

"If I sit on your lap, you'll see my cards!"

"I promise not to cheat."

"You mean, you promise not to cheat *anymore?*"

"He won't cheat any less." Bron's normally dour expression seemed lighter tonight. The alcohol was doing the trick. "Maybe we should stop playing. You keep forgetting the rules."

So much for impressing them with my card playing. I hadn't impressed them with my chess skills a few nights ago, either.

"I thought Russians drank vodka." I swirled the brownish amber alcohol in the glass tumbler.

"They do, but that is like saying Americans always drink lite beer. Not all of them do, and most don't drink only that." He raised his glass to me. "You don't like cognac?"

"It's different from what I'm used to, but it does the job." I laughed, and then stopped, realizing they were both inspecting me. Although I hadn't been shy or innocent in years, I felt myself blushing.

Bron looked away first. He gathered the cards and set them aside, then downed his drink and poured himself more.

"What was the game you played with the other women the night they gave you stuffed toys and had you watch cartoons?" Ilya asked.

"Which game?" Memories of that night were fuzzy, which was probably for the best.

"The one where you were all shouting and laughing. There were no cards, but you asked each other questions or made each other do strange things. It was hard to hear from where we were watching."

"Oh. Truth or dare." I explained the idea of the game, and by the time I was done, they both looked perplexed.

"And this is fun?" Bron asked, unconvinced. "Why not simply refuse to do these dares?"

"A lot of kids won't turn down dares because they're afraid of looking afraid or weak."

"It would be a sign of intelligence to turn down a dangerous dare," Ilya pointed out.

"Well, yes, but is that really how things work here?"

"I was raised with siblings much older than me, so I do not know. They mostly tried to keep me from bothering them."

I grimaced, remembering doing that to my own siblings sometimes, and feeling guilty about it now.

"That must have been lonely for you."

He shrugged. "It was what it was."

"Should we play?" I smirked at Bron. What were the chances a grown man with a serious disposition would agree to play something so silly?

"Why not?" He crossed his arms.

"Okay. Bron, truth or dare."

"I need to pick one or the other without knowing what the challenge will be?"

"That's what makes the game interesting."

He studied me. "Do you have ideas for both?"

"I do, but I'm not telling you what they are."

He grunted. "Ilya will go first."

"Chicken."

His scowl made me giggle. I wasn't a big giggler, but between the alcohol and his expression, I wasn't able to restrain it.

"Truth," Ilya said immediately.

I straightened my face, trying to look serious. Might as well start off with something easy that I already knew the answer to, just to get them used to the game. "How many people have you slept with?"

"Slept with?" he asked, frowning.

"Had sex with?"

"Ah. Well, you know the answer, I think. Two."

"Including me?"

"Of course."

Living here wouldn't have given him many opportunities to find partners, but it was strange to think he was almost thirty and his number was so low. I was probably a terrible judge of what was 'normal,' considering what my life had been like.

"Your turn to ask a question or dare us to do something," I told him, not really remembering if there were rules about turn-taking. "You can pick either of us."

"Do you like when men are rough with you?"

"You're supposed to ask if I want truth or dare."

"Oh."

"I'll answer that, though." I gave the question some thought, wondering if this question was going to land me in a world of hurt later. "It depends on the man, I think. Sometimes it's hot, and I get off on it—on feeling helpless and used—but some men are crueler than others. I absolutely hate it when I haven't consented to it."

Ilya swallowed and took my hand. It was warm around mine. "I'm sorry men have done that to you."

"Thank you." I smiled and squeezed his hand. I took another sip of my drink. The cognac had a complicated flavor, and it cleared away the taste of the bad memories.

"My turn again?" I looked back and forth between them. Bron was staring into his glass. Was he bored or trying to remove himself from the game without leaving the table? "Bron."

He raised his head and met my gaze, looking far too forbidding to take a turn at this silly game.

"What?"

"Truth or dare."

"Truth."

"Have you ever been married?"

Ilya's mouth opened, and his gaze darted to Bron, who rested his forearms on the table and leaned toward me.

"Twice." He gave a short, humorless laugh. "Women like hard men but hate when they don't go soft for them."

"You were married?" Ilya looked crushed.

"Did you think I was a little virgin like you when I got here, boy?"

"Well, no, but..."

"But?"

"Was I your first man?"

"I'd hardly call you a man."

Ilya pulled his hand away from mine, and he turned his glass tumbler in a slow circle. "Answer the question."

"It's not your turn," Bron replied smugly, raising his own glass to his lips.

"This is a stupid game," Ilya grumbled.

Bron actually laughed. "I like it."

Prick. He knew poor Ilya was jealous, and he was laughing at him instead of giving him reassurance.

"Truth or dare, *De-li-lah*."

"Truth."

"What does your family think you do when you're gone to the Island? What do they think you're doing now?"

I pressed my lips together. "They know I'm a sex worker. They don't know the details."

Bron's brow rose. "They have no objections?"

I rolled a sip of cognac around my mouth, savoring the burn and appreciating that it didn't have the same kick whisky did. When I swallowed, the warmth gave me the courage to tell the unvarnished truth. "They're ashamed of me, but not so ashamed that they refuse the scholarships."

Wow, apparently I was feeling catty tonight. I wasn't usually one to air my family's dirty laundry in public.

"You work hard and suffer for them, and they're ashamed of you?" Ilya snapped. "How dare they? The ungrateful shits. How many sisters would do what you're doing for them?"

I had the urge to defend them, now that he'd passed judgment. They were all sick of me parenting them, and 'meddling,' but I'd gotten them through high school with good-enough grades to go to college, but not quite enough to get the scholarships we'd hoped for. If they were going to get out of Mom and Dad's world, which revolved around the store, and only the store, I'd needed to do something to get the money. Of course, they didn't understand—it wasn't something they'd ever thought about except to either judge or pity the people who had to do it to get by.

"And your parents? They couldn't help?"

I snorted. "If our parents had their way, we would have worked at their store in exchange for room and board for the rest of our lives."

People always talked about multi-generational family businesses like they were the best, but sometimes they only stayed afloat by exploiting their children's labor. As their only employees, they hadn't paid us, and we'd gotten no say about our schedules. I'd missed my graduation raising the next generation of labor for my parents.

Such a hardworking, friendly family. Pillars of their community.

Sure, our parents were those things, but they also hadn't set aside a penny for our education and would only let us work other jobs if they didn't cut into schoolwork or our hours at the store. It had felt so claustrophobic.

My whole life had. It still did.

"Your family should make a shrine to you." Ilya raised his glass to me.

"I'll be sure to tell them that the next time I see them."

I was glad Ilya had gotten over his shock at Bron's revelation about his ex-wives. I'd had a hunch, but I hadn't wanted to upset Ilya. How had they lived under the same roof for so long and never discussed it?

"My turn. Truth or dare, Bron."

"Dare." His eyes were at half-mast. Was the man drunk or was the alcohol just helping him relax?

Time to shake things up.

"I dare you to kiss Ilya."

He frowned at me. There was a line there, and after spending so much time with them, I'd noticed it, but I didn't understand it. Was he trying to keep Ilya from falling in love with him? Because if that was the case, he'd failed spectacularly.

"It's a kiss," I teased. "What's the big deal?"

"I'm not gay," he snapped.

"You'll fuck him, but you won't kiss him, and that boundary means you're straight?"

"I do these things to teach him to be harder, not because I like it."

I nodded, biting my cheek so I didn't laugh. "But if you don't like it, why do you get hard? Why do you come?"

He shrugged irritably. At least he wasn't seriously pissed off. If he hadn't been drinking, it might have been a different story.

"It's like using my hand. It feels good, but it means nothing." He gestured dismissively. "I'm not hiding tender feelings for the boy, if that's what you're hoping to hear."

Ilya ducked his head, but the tips of his ears were red. I really shouldn't be stirring up trouble between them, but I was curious to see if his denial was as true as he seemed to think it was.

"So, what's the big deal about kissing him, then?" I prodded. "It's a dare. It doesn't mean anything. A man with two ex-wives shouldn't be threatened by the idea of kissing another man as part of a game."

Bron glared at me but gave a careless shrug.

"Fine. Ilya, come here."

"No," he replied sullenly, meeting Bron's gaze. "It's not my dare."

Bron got up so fast his chair tipped over and hit the floor with a loud bang that made me and Ilya jump. He stalked to Ilya, who leaned back in his chair to get farther away from him.

"Do you get to refuse me anything, *suka*?" He grabbed Ilya by the front of the shirt and hauled him to his feet.

"I don't want you to kiss me," Ilya begged, his eyes wide.

"I don't want to kiss you either, but I won't lose the woman's stupid game." He brought his mouth down hard on Ilya's.

I was expecting a grudging peck on the lips.

Apparently, Bron was serious about not wanting to lose.

The kiss was violent, deep. Bron's grip on Ilya's hair wouldn't allow him to get away, and he forced him to submit, to open his mouth, to accept Bron's invading tongue. Slowly, Bron walked him backward, not stopping until Ilya's back was against the wall. Bron pressed his body against Ilya's, angling his head for better access to his mouth. Between one heaving breath and the next, the kiss went from violent to passionate. Ilya's whimpered, submitting, and the quiet sound of their tongues sliding together made me squirm.

Fuck, watching them together was...

My alcohol haze lifted slightly. Shit. What if this fucked up things between them? They'd been living in a careful balance for years, and I'd just tipped them into what? Admitting their feelings for each other? Unlikely. But this was...something.

Hot. It was fucking hot.

One of Bron's legs pressed between Ilya's, and he grabbed his crotch through his jeans, making him gasp into Bron's mouth.

Ilya's hand crept to the bottom of Bron's shirt and slowly made its way under the thin layer to explore the skin under the fabric's edge, as though it were forbidden fruit.

What was it like to get fucked by the same man for years and never be shown any affection? To never touch him or be touched in any way that wasn't violent?

Ilya's eyes were shining, wet.

Oh fuck. What had I done?

Bron eased back, and his kisses became softer, yearning.

Was he in love with Ilya, too?

No. It had to be the cognac, right?

When Bron broke the kiss, his gaze slid over Ilya's face, then went stiff and stoic.

"There," he said, his voice as steady as if he'd completed some meaningless chore. "My turn."

He righted his fallen chair and sat down, then took a sip of his drink. His hand shook, but it steadied when he saw me looking.

Ilya came back to sit with us, moving like a vigilant hare who could already see the coyote headed his way.

"Truth or dare, *suka*."

Ilya glared at him. "Dare."

Bron's brows rose, as though he'd expected Ilya to choose truth. It took him a moment before he came up with something.

"I dare you to strip the woman naked and pleasure her with your mouth."

"But I don't know how!"

"You didn't know how to suck a dick when I came here, either. You can learn."

I could almost see all the words Ilya wanted to say but was holding back. Doubtlessly, Bron could, too.

Why did he have to be such an ass? If he wasn't into Ilya, I'd eat my cognac glass, but he was either refusing to let it show, or was shoving it down so hard he didn't even realize he was doing it.

Ilya got up again, and Bron's dare registered.

He wanted to teach Ilya to go down on me? Yeah, this didn't bode well.

Taking my hand, Ilya drew me up. He turned me, and I could almost feel the concentration as he studied my bra clasp. I probably should have bailed him out and taken it off myself, but it could be a valuable skill to have.

He fumbled with it, but figured it out, then drew the straps down my arms and watched over my shoulder as he revealed my breasts, as though the sight of naked tits still amazed him. His breath was warm on my neck, and I instinctually tipped my head. He nuzzled my neck and kissed right behind my ear, making me shiver with the delicious sensation. For a guy who hadn't had a lot of reciprocal sex, he was pretty intuitive.

He hooked his fingers into the band of my panties and drew them down my legs, helping me step out of them, my hand resting on his shoulder for balance.

When I was completely naked, he turned me toward him and stepped back, his appreciative gaze sliding over me.

"A woman as beautiful as you would never look to a man like me without money as an incentive." He chuckled, and traced his fingers down my bare skin, stroking lightly, making me feel all gooey and warm. "I'm lucky to have something you want."

The man seriously didn't know how gorgeous he was. It was nice to be with someone who didn't think he was doing me a favor by paying attention to me. Spending time with Bron had made him humble.

"The dare is to lick her pussy, not feed her vanity."

"What harm is there in telling the truth? We chose her because she was the most regal, the most beautiful. Do you think she doesn't know what she looks like?"

"You must always act like any woman is lucky to have you. Telling them how beautiful they are only makes them demanding and full of conceit."

"When has Delilah ever been demanding or conceited? She wears my sister's old clothes and puts up with our groping without complaint. The food here isn't elegant. There are no parties or entertainments the way there are on the mainland, only drinking with two shabby men who spend too much time alone together in the woods."

They frowned at each other.

Ilya kissed me, his lips still warm from Bron's kiss. It felt...like retribution. Was he trying to use me to make Bron jealous? I doubted that would work for him, but I wasn't against the idea.

He'd gotten more confident in his technique, and the warm buzz of liquor in my veins made me melt into him as though he were a guy I was into, and not someone who was paying for my company. The truth was, now that I knew them and was marginally less afraid—at least of Ilya—I'd have done almost anything they wanted for free. The way his tongue teased mine made me sigh and rub against him like a contented cat.

Behind us somewhere, Bron clapped his hands with impatience. "Enough of that. Put her on the table."

I put my arms around Ilya's neck and hopped up, wrapping my legs around his waist.

"Eager little slut," Bron accused.

"I love the way he kisses," I shot back. "I can only imagine what else he can do with this mouth."

Bron grumbled something in Russian, and Ilya smiled against my lips as he resumed our kiss. As soon as Bron had cleared away our glasses, Ilya laid me carefully across the kitchen table. Even though the room was warm, the wood was cold against my back. Ilya straightened and looked to Bron for direction.

Instead, Bron pressed his lips to mine.

He wanted to kiss me?

Okay...

I relaxed into it, and he spat cognac into my mouth. I choked, coughed, and Bron's level of satisfaction led me to believe he'd gladly drown me in cognac right then.

Ilya leaned over me and kissed my navel, making my belly tremble. He nuzzled lower, shy, and I put my hand to his hair to encourage him.

"Hands to yourself, woman. He doesn't need the distraction." We had a war of gazes, and I let my hands fall to my sides. "Spread her legs."

Ilya kissed the tops of my thighs and used his hands to coax me to part them.

I felt very...inspected as the two of them looked me over.

"Pull her ass closer to the edge of the table. It'll be easier." Bron set up two chairs at the end—one between my legs and the other beside it, like he planned to micromanage.

Ilya pulled me closer to the edge, and Bron bent my legs and propped my feet on either corner of the table, leaving me spread wide.

"Did you do this with your wives?" Ilya demanded.

"No. My wives were nice girls."

"Delilah is a nice girl," Ilya objected.

"Delilah is an incorrigible slut. She doesn't complain when a man shoves his dick up her pretty arse. She deserves to be treated like a whore."

"Do I deserve to be treated like a whore, too?"

"If you didn't, I wouldn't need to beat you every night for your disrespect." He shoved Ilya down to sit in the chair between my legs, and he took the chair next to him.

"He never did these things with his wives because he didn't want to admit what kind of pervert he was," I told Ilya. "With us, he can be himself."

The man shot me an inscrutable look, and I stuck out my tongue at him.

Bron turned his attention to Ilya and gestured between my legs. "This is a pussy."

I couldn't hold back a small laugh.

"Thank you. I had no idea," Ilya replied dryly.

"Shut up and look closely at it." Bron reached past my leg and parted my labia with his finger and thumb. "This hole you already know." He tapped my entrance.

Were we really doing an anatomy class on the kitchen table in the middle of a game of drunken Truth or Dare?

"Everything down here is sensitive, and you can play with whatever you want, but the thing that will please most women is here. You don't always need to be rough with it." He stroked my clit hood, and I stiffened at the jolt of pleasure that shot through me. My cold-tightened nipples only got harder.

I felt like an on-the-job training prop, and damn, it was hot. The psychology behind it was baffling.

Ilya leaned closer, and I could feel his breath caressing me. He bit my inner thigh, making me yelp, then bit me again, then again, like he meant to devour me. Why was the man so intuitively sexy?

When he reached my pussy, he bit my mons, making me gasp. A sheen of sweat broke out along my skin. He looked up at me, his smile cocky rather than his usual anxious one. Considering how good he was at blowjobs, he probably felt more confident in this than he did at sex.

I could already feel how wet I was. His tongue dipped, tasting me, and he savored my taste for a moment, as though it were a luxury rather than a chore.

Fuuuck.

Why did I feel like I was in trouble?

He teased me, exploring me with his mouth, his tongue, his curious fingers—tasting and prodding, cataloguing my responses. He eased a thick finger into me and turned it, feeling me. I could almost see the information processing, getting sorted, stored for later.

When he decided to learn about my clit, I had to wrap my hands around the edges of the table to stop myself from writhing. I whimpered, his tongue investigating so gently that it tickled. I panted, trying to distract myself from the velvet feel of his lips. It had been a long time since anyone had bothered going down on me, and his mouth was making me feel like I might levitate off the table.

Bron was watching and giving intermittent direction, but mostly staying silent and sipping at his cognac.

"Suck that little bud into your mouth and fuck her slow with your fingers," Bron suggested.

Ilya ignored him for a moment, but then his pretty mouth fastened onto my clit. My toes curled. His mouth was heavenly torture, and I gasped so loud the sound echoed in the room.

"Not like that with your finger," Bron said, pressing closer to him, whispering directions in his ear.

Ilya turned his hand a little, making me grit my teeth at the angle he was trying.

"No, no. Let me show you."

Instead of switching places with Ilya, Bron wrapped his hand around Ilya's and pushed his finger into me, too, guiding him. I only lasted a minute longer, my orgasm spreading the tightness from my belly to my thighs and up my body. I arched into the impending orgasm, my whole body tingling.

Bron pushed Ilya's mouth off me and withdrew their fingers. My orgasm hovered, buzzing, then nosedived into a throbbing, itching, impatient feeling throughout my body.

"Why?" I asked, my voice pathetic.

"He's already done more than I dared him to," Bron replied. "It's late. Time for bed. Goodnight Delilah."

Ilya looked like he was going to argue, but Bron hauled him up by the front of the shirt and steered him out of the kitchen and up the stairs.

I sat up on the table, looking around, feeling ridiculous and abandoned.

Irritably, I found my glass and downed the rest of the alcohol in it. I emptied the guy's glasses, too, my hands trembling, then pulled my clothes on rather than walk naked all the way back to my room.

Just as I shut off the kitchen light, the slap of leather hitting skin and Ilya's gasps of distress cut off their murmured words.

I crept up the stairs to the floor with their bedrooms and sat there, listening in the dark as Bron beat him and used him, wishing I was brave enough to intervene.

Chapter Ten

"I never thought I would see anyone use that swing again," Ilya said, tugging weeds out of the row he was working on. He was finally close enough to speak to, so I laid my book in my lap and watched him, while keeping a wary eye on Verni, who perched on Ilya's back and was giving me a look I couldn't interpret. She probably wanted to peck out my eyeballs.

"I really wish you'd let me help."

"There are two of us to do this, so there's no need for you to get your hands dirty."

I looked down the row at Bron. Both men were shirtless and tanned from working in the sun. Ilya had welts, some of which were scabbed over. Bron had several old scars—raised, red, white, indented. At thirty-four, he seemed young to have so many.

"You know, you don't have to let him beat you like that every night," I murmured. "You two are practically the same size. You could hold your own in a fight."

He shrugged, the muscles in his shoulders flexing distractingly under his tan skin.

"Things have been this way between us since he came here. It's just how we are."

"But it doesn't have to be. You could stand up to him."

"If he feels like I'm not cooperating with his teaching, maybe he will leave."

"And that would be bad?"

Ilya stared at the bucket of weeds next to his knee. "You know I'm weak for him. It's the opposite of what he wants for me."

I bit back a laugh. "I know that's what both of you want to believe, but you're lying to yourselves, and each other."

"Lying?"

"Well, you're not being entirely truthful with yourselves. He enjoys bossing you around and doing what he wants, and I think he blames you for making him want you."

"No. He doesn't really want me. I'm just convenient. I can't stand up to him."

"You can't or you don't want to?"

"What kind of man would want another man to take him roughly every night?"

"A kinky bisexual man?"

He pulled up another weed and flicked it into the bucket. "What does that mean?"

Crap. How much did he not know? Where did I even start my explanation?

"Not everyone wants polite, regular sex. You know—one man and one woman, the lights off, the man lying on top of the woman, without touching her much with his hands or mouth, other than kissing."

"When it's just a man and a woman...who holds the belt? Who punishes who?"

"When it's vanilla sex, there is no belt, and no one punishes anyone. You know what that's like. There isn't always a belt when we fool around."

"True, but I like when Bron is rough with me. It makes me feel..."
He threw another weed in the bucket. "Alive."

"It's probably more fun than weeding the garden."

He frowned. "I love working out here, but it's different."

"I should hope so."

He met my gaze, pointedly throwing another weed into his bucket.
"This garden and the livestock feed us most of the year."

"That's impressive, considering how cold it seems to be here all the
time."

"It's not cold, you're just not carrying enough weight," he declared.
"You'll see. We'll fatten you up."

"Like a Thanksgiving turkey?"

His brows rose, and he paused. "That is your harvest festival?"

"I...guess so? Although it's in November, so it's probably too late
in the year to be harvesting much of anything by then." I shrugged.
"People get together with their families and have a big turkey dinner."

"We used to have something like that here, when I was a boy. Yana
and our *nyanya* would make a large meal at the end of summer."

"Would your father come?"

"No." He chuckled. "Once a year, in spring, we took the trip to the
house in Moscow, but traveling there takes a long time."

"How on earth would you get there? If there were nine of you, you
must have needed a bus!"

"No, no. Maybe they did when the older ones were small, but by
the time I remember going, many of the older ones were gone to live
at the main house. My father wanted a hand in raising them, but only
after they stopped being annoying. Maybe twelve or fourteen years
old? Whenever Vas noticed you were grown, you went."

"But you never went."

He shrugged. "No."

"He never noticed you were grown? It would be hard to miss."

"I...was never a favorite. I don't have the same steel in me that my father admires in my brothers, which reminds him of himself. My mother was also his much younger third wife. I was told he chose her for her looks, not her strength of character."

I noticed the past tense he was using. "Did they divorce?"

"No."

"Did she...disappear the same way Yana disappeared?"

"No, no. My mother is dead. I should feel sad but I didn't know her," he admitted. "I think Yana was married off to someone. She was an odd one—always with her head in the clouds." He chuckled, smiling to himself. "She raised me, along with our *nyanya*. After our father took Oleg and Dmitry to live with him, it was only the three of us for a few years until Yana disappeared. They taught me to cook, garden, knit—those kinds of things. It made Vas angry when he found out, but what were they supposed to teach me? I needed to learn how to be useful. I followed the handyman around when he came, but there were no other men here."

"After Yana was gone, he dismissed your nanny?"

He nodded. "Yes. The day I turned eighteen, the boat that came to take her away dropped off Bronislav to teach me to be a man."

I shivered at the thought of him being left to Bron's tender mercies at such a young age. At eighteen, I'd been through a lot, but it sounded like poor Ilya had been sheltered until that day. Then again, who knew how rough his older siblings had been on him? He rarely spoke of them except for Yana.

"What did you think of Bron when he got here?" I glanced casually at the man, who was now working on fixing a piece of equipment at the other end of the extensive garden.

"I was terrified of him and impressed, too. He was so big and angry when he came. He told me often that he didn't want to play nanny to a boy-man."

"Why was he sent here?"

"I'm not sure. Once, he said it was because he had laughed when he heard I liked to knit, so Vas sent him here to deal with me. I doubt that's true. If he had stayed with Vas, though, he might already be dead—working security for my father is dangerous. You've seen his scars."

"Why does he call you Ilyusha sometimes? Is that the long form of your name?"

His eyes widened and he sent a furtive glance Bron's way. "No. It's a..." He gave a half shrug. "It's a cute nickname for my name. I don't know why he calls me that sometimes. It's not what men call other men—it's too sweet. Too affectionate. Like a mother...or maybe a lover would say." A blush reddened his cheeks. "He would never say it where someone might hear."

He stood and stretched. Dirt streaked his skin, but that only made him sexier. He pushed back his hair and looked at me. He must have noticed the lust in my gaze because his automatic, friendly smile turned cocky. Yum.

"Do you want something from me, woman?" he asked, arching a dark brow suggestively.

I enjoyed the way he flirted—direct rather than manipulative. The only issue was Bron, who was likely to step in and start directing things. Why was he trying to stop us from fooling around without him? It had to be jealousy.

"When don't I want something from you?"

"My little wife is so demanding."

I grimaced at him. "I'm not your wife. I'm not going to be your wife."

He pressed his lips together.

"You'll have to pretend that's where your relationship is heading," Bron said, surprising me. I hadn't heard him approaching. "At least until the end of your contract."

"Pretending to be someone's girlfriend is one thing, but pretending to be his fiancée is something else entirely. Is his family going to be content with a staged break-up?"

"There will have to be more proof than that."

"Like what? A ring I can give back?"

Bron rubbed a forearm across his face, leaving a smear of dirt. "Maybe a wedding."

"What?!" My involuntary shout was so loud that Verni squawked and launched herself into the air.

"Bron," Ilya snapped. "It's too soon."

"We're out of time for delicacy. We should have told her from the beginning."

"I—I don't understand. I thought you brought me here to make Ilya tougher, not to marry him!"

"It probably won't be necessary, but if it is, you'll marry Ilya, then you can go home as soon as his family is satisfied. We'll pay extra for your trouble."

"I can't get married and go home like it's no big deal. How do we get *un*married?"

"There's this thing we have in Russia called divorce," Bron said dryly. "There's no need to have female hysterics. We're not planning to keep you here against your will."

"Good. Then send me home now." I thought about all the time I'd already spent with the two of them. I couldn't afford to walk away from the money they owed me, and I cared what happened to Ilya, but this was nonsensical.

"We should be able to send you home after we meet with my family," Ilya promised, his dark gaze wide and reassuring. "There isn't time for us to find another woman to pose as my fiancée—not one who would be convincing enough."

"Convincing how?"

"You know me—know enough about me. You look at me as if..." he shrugged. "As if you might love me."

What?

"I know it's only because you're kind," he rushed on, "and because you're being paid. But it's convincing enough for my family. Most of my brothers are married to women who don't even like them, but you?" He smiled, and the charming flash of white teeth weakened my resolve.

"Why do you need a fiancée to bring home, anyway?" I said, scowling.

"You'll do it?" Ilya's smile turned even more hopeful.

"I...it's a lot to ask."

"I know."

"Maybe if you explain, I might have more of a reason to consider it."

"I told you, if I don't prove to my father that I'm a real man by the time I turn thirty, he will cut me off financially and send me away from here."

"And pretending I'll marry you will prove you're a 'real man'? That doesn't make sense. I'm not going to marry you temporarily out of some misguided—"

Bron seized the back of my neck and squeezed, making me cringe.

"Ow!"

"You agreed to our terms when you came here, *De-li-lah*. It's too late to wring your hands and wail for mercy. You trusted us enough to come here when we could have easily planned to skin and eat you. You'll have to trust Ilya enough to divorce you and let you go if it comes to that."

"I agreed to CNC—to rough sex with two sexy, scary rich guys—not to marrying one of them to...what? Impress his family? Grow up. No one makes their parents proud."

"You thought I was scary?" Ilya crowded me from the front as Bron continued to hold the back of my neck.

"That was back on the Island. You never spoke, and you're so tall—and there are the muscles—and the beard."

"Ilya? Scary?" Bron guffawed rudely. "He didn't know where to look when we were there. He hid in our room most of the time."

"You didn't sleep with any of the women there either."

"We were there for you to learn. What help would it have been for me to womanize and leave you to sulk?"

"I didn't sulk."

They were arguing over my head, but I was getting used to that.

"An island of women to fuck, and you watched television."

"An island of women to fuck, and you fucked me!" Ilya snapped. "I am starting to think maybe you don't like pussy at all. Maybe it's all talk."

"You've seen me fuck the woman."

"Yes, yes, and you've had two wives, and now you have none. Why is that, Bron? Maybe it's always been men that drew you?"

Bron's fist shot out, aimed over me to get at Ilya, but Ilya had been expecting as much and deflected it.

"You wouldn't be so upset if it wasn't true."

"What's between us is different. It's about you learning."

"I see the way you watch me, Bron. It's not all about teaching me."

They were bumping up against me to shove at each other, and I tried to slide out from between them, but Bron was still squeezing the back of my neck and wouldn't allow it.

"You see what you want to see. You're too fanciful, and you'll break your own heart."

Bron steered me back toward the house, but he jerked, then let go of me and spun back.

"Did you throw dirt at me? Are you a child?"

"You're the one stomping away from this conversation, and you kicked over my bucket of weeds."

"I'll kick more than that, you stupid cunt!"

Fuck this. If they were going to pound the shit out of each other, they could do it without a spectator.

I backed away, hoping they wouldn't notice I was missing until I was long gone. They were toe to toe, shouting insults at each other, like a New York road rage incident posted to YouTube.

Realizing I was in the clear, I fucked off.

Verni perched in a tree not far off, watching the humans being absurd. I passed her tree and kept going.

I wandered into the forest, planning to go for a brisk walk to clear my head. There'd been no sign of the wolves I'd heard when the guys had hunted for me the one time, and I was starting to suspect it had been the two of them trying to freak me out.

There was no giant mythical wolf living out here, or I would have seen paw prints by now, and they'd at least have dogs or better pens to protect the goats and chickens.

For a long time, I could hear their raised voices. At some point, when they were sounding far away, they cut off suddenly. Knowing the two of them, Bron probably had Ilya pinned on the ground and was fucking him by now. It seemed to be how they sorted things out between them.

They didn't need me—they needed a fucking therapist. Maybe a separate one for each of them. It was painfully obvious that as much as Ilya thought his love was unrequited, it wasn't. But what Bron was bringing to the table was toxic as fuck.

Maybe for Bron it was only lust?

I walked for a long time, the lush green of the leaves and under-growth smelling damp and chill now that I was away from the full strength of the sun. I shivered, wishing I'd brought a sweater. When I thought of Yana's cozy room and a cup of tea, I regretted not going straight into the house instead of taking a walk.

They expected me to agree to the possibility of marrying Ilya. Of all the things men had done to me over the past few years, this one felt like a hard limit. Sure, it was transactional and didn't need to mean anything, but even as a kid, I'd never thought about growing up and getting married. I'd already done enough traditional women's work—cooked and cleaned and raised children. I looked forward to successfully launching my siblings into the world and avoiding any-thing that resembled being a wife.

My dream for the future had involved not having to worry about where the kids were or what they were doing, whether they'd done their homework, or what to make for their school lunches or supper.

Even when I was younger, marrying someone had seemed like agreeing to take on extra work—yet another person to look after. Forget a wedding and a party centered around me and my new spouse. I wanted to sit down after work and eat popcorn for supper and watch Netflix. Read books all weekend.

Although...a wedding to Ilya would be fake. Not the real thing. It wasn't as though marrying a man who didn't love me would ruin my dream, and Bron had mentioned extra money.

But what if it gave the two of them more power over me? What if I went through with it and Ilya refused to divorce me? I couldn't afford a lawyer, let alone one who knew how to dissolve an international marriage.

Even if they let me go home, it would be like an invisible tether linking me back to them and this place.

Not that I hated it here.

Other than Bron stomping around occasionally, being Bron, I couldn't remember ever being so relaxed in my life. Everything moved slower here. There was no Wi-Fi. The guys had phones they rarely touched that usually lived on the counter plugged into their chargers, since they had to go to the end of the dock to get a signal. The two of them worked their butts off in the garden and with the animals. There were fields of grain and other crops, too, but when they went out that far, they usually sent me back to the house to twiddle my thumbs.

Poor me.

Easiest money I'd ever fucking made.

I hadn't even realized how much strain I'd been under most of my life until it was gone. I felt quiet inside. Usually, I felt like I was juggling flaming torches in an oil refinery.

Even Bron's occasional man-trums were nothing compared to the guilt trips my parents used to control me.

Here, when I got tired of reading and watching movies, I'd voluntarily done housework, of all things. As the oldest in my family, I'd absolutely despised all the caretaking I'd had to do, but Bron and Ilya weren't used to having someone around to take care of things. They were so tidy that pitching in didn't feel like an insurmountable task.

Ilya enjoyed cooking and was used to doing dishes. Even Bron did his own laundry.

As each of my siblings had gone away to school, it had left me with less work to do around the house, but more shifts at the store. Once my youngest sister was gone, I might as well just move into the back room at the store and sleep on the cot.

Thoughts of going home were like a wet, smothering blanket thrown over my head.

I turned back, then around, not exactly sure where I'd ended up. It was all very green, and the wind rattled the leaves in an ongoing hiss of motion.

Ilya's island was probably almost as big as the one with the hunt, but it was no tropical paradise. I shivered, then headed back in the direction I was pretty sure I'd come from.

Like some sort of ghost, a man materialized before me.

Ilya?

It looked like him, but the eyes—they were narrowed. Sinister.

"Why did you leave us, little wife?"

Even his voice sounded unfamiliar. It was lower, gruffer.

I swallowed and took a step back, and the predator's eyes caught my involuntary reaction.

"The two of you were busy, so I thought I would take a walk."

"You weren't thinking of trying to run away, were you?"

"Run away?" My hand crept up to my neck, as though to protect it from predator teeth. "Where would I go? We're on an island, and I don't know how to row a boat, let alone start a motor."

"That's right," he said, giving me a quiet smile that would have been fine in the house, but creeped me out here in the forest. "If you want anything in this place, you have to ask."

"You've been very generous."

"You're a guest."

"I'm an employee."

He shrugged. "If that's how you want to see things."

"You really expect me to pretend we're engaged...or maybe even marry you?"

"Would it be so bad? Even after—you wouldn't need to go home right away. If you wanted, you could stay awhile." He stepped closer to me, and my heart rate increased, sensing danger. The thrill of it zinged through my body. A muscle in his bare chest twitched, and I gasped, sure he was going to make a grab for me.

I took another involuntary step backward and bumped into a suspiciously muscular tree. I jumped sideways, getting them both in my field of vision.

"I was only taking a walk. The two of you were busy arguing, so I didn't even think you'd notice."

"We notice everything," Bron said. "We saw you wander into the forest, just like we know when you're awake reading in your room, and how you stand on the stairs listening every night while I punish Ilya."

My face burned, and I switched my gaze to Ilya, who didn't look at all surprised.

"If you don't want me listening, you should try to keep it down."

Bron hummed a short piece of a song I didn't recognize. It was eerie rather than comforting.

"I think... I think I'll head back to the house and take a bath. It's cold out here."

"You will need a bath when we're finished with you," Bron agreed.

I didn't like the hungry look on their faces. Hadn't they had sex? Maybe they hadn't. Maybe they'd stopped arguing to look for me. That didn't bode well. Neither of them looked like they were in a good mood.

"You'd never forgive yourselves if you took your frustrations out on an innocent bystander."

"I think I could live with it. Could you, Ilya?"

"Right now, I don't think I could live without it." His gaze traveled from the modest neckline of my shirt down my long skirt to my booted feet. Nothing about what I was wearing was sexy, but that didn't matter to men who knew what was underneath.

I tried to lunge away as Ilya took a swipe at me, but Bron caught me while I was distracted. How could I run from hordes of men on the Island and yet couldn't avoid the two of them here?

"How is this fair?"

"If we planned to fight you, two against one would be rude, but we only want a little fun." He thrust me at Ilya. "Hold this for me, would you?"

Ilya caught me and turned me toward Bron, holding my upper arms.

"Very nice." Bron cocked his head, considering me.

Unable to help myself, I jutted my chin at him. He got off on people fearing him, and if I could give him a little less satisfaction, that would suit me fine.

"Such a tough girl. You're not scared of us at all. A little nervous, maybe, but never truly afraid." Before I could open my mouth to reply, Bron tugged the axe out of the sheath on his belt.

"Why do you have an axe?" I asked suspiciously.

"What kind of man goes anywhere without an axe?"

"Most men!"

"Not any I would care to know."

Ilya chuckled. "A man never knows when he might need his axe."

Bron turned the axe haft and pushed the burnished wood between my thighs, the thin fabric of my skirt not doing a lot to impede it. I frowned as the long edge of the handle pushed against my pussy.

"This is rude."

He slid the handle back and forth, forcing the cotton of my underwear up into my cleft. The wood was completely unyielding against my clit, which felt annoyingly enjoyable.

"An axe feels good in a man's hands. Does it feel good between your legs, pressing against that stiff little bud I like to suck?" Ilya's voice was like honey. "Does it feel like a big, eager cock?"

"You should rub yourself against it," Bron said gruffly. "Show us what a slut you are for a man's axe."

This was...odd, but both men were wild-eyed and already hard. Well, I'd done weirder things for guys I didn't like half as much.

I rolled my hips, and Bron's lips parted as he took in the motion of my body.

Ilya pulled the neckline of my sloppy T-shirt off my shoulder and kissed my neck as he watched over my shoulder. He groaned in approval. "God, the way you move makes me want to rut you like an animal."

His hands shifted from my arms to my breasts. He tried to tug the T-shirt out of the waistband of my skirt, but it briefly caught on something. Impatiently, he grasped the neckline in both hands and jerked it apart, baring my breasts. I gasped in surprise. He'd torn the fabric without effort.

They both swore.

"Where is your bra?" Ilya demanded.

"I only have one that fits, and it's in the wash!" I had stopped moving my hips, so Bron had taken it upon himself to move the axe handle back and forth, making me a bit delirious. "It's not my fault."

The motion of the axe handle was frustrating—not hitting quite right—and then I started moving again, unable to resist.

I guess it was no different from giving a guy a lap dance, except in this situation there were two guys and an axe...

Okay, maybe not so much like giving a guy a lap dance.

Getting lost in the sensations, I allowed my head to fall back against Ilya's chest and let my body take over, using the smooth piece of wood in a way the manufacturer never could have foreseen.

I was close, my hips moving faster, my legs trembling with the need to give out, when Bron pulled away the axe.

"Such a hot little slut," he said with an amused sneer. "Is there anything you won't fuck?"

"I don't know. At one point I would have said you, but here we are."

He twirled the axe in his hand, and I cringed back against Ilya. He brought the axe up and ran it along the mound of my breast, turning the blade sideways to rub the flat of the metal against my nipple. He inched the axe head over, touching the pebbled tip of my breast with the blade's wickedly keen edge.

"Careful, Bron." Ilya was watching, rapt. "If you slice off her nipple, it's a long way to a hospital."

"There's no such thing as safe axe play," I said. If it wasn't an adage in the kink community, it should have been.

Bron pulled the weapon away, letting me take a full, giddy breath. "Axes are very useful tools in the right hands." He pulled at the waistband of my skirt and set the edge against the elastic. It parted as though the fabric had been nothing more than half rotten rags. The skirt fell to pool around my feet, then something stung my thigh.

"Did you cut me?" I asked incredulously.

"A little." He smirked, then brought the axe blade to his lips and licked the edge. My pussy clenched—why was it such an idiot sometimes? This was not hot. At all.

"How does she taste?" Ilya demanded.

"See for yourself."

What?

Ilya got down on his knees and turned me toward him. He licked the scratch on my thigh, his tongue lingering.

What the fuck? "Let me go, you fucking cannibals!" I tried to pull away, but Ilya regained his feet and grabbed my arms again.

"Admit it—you secretly hope to be eaten." Bron chuckled. "But only your needy little pussy."

He brought the axe back upward, not stopping until he pressed the back of the axe's head between my thighs. The metal was ice cold against my hot, liquid core. He rubbed it there, turning it slightly so that one of the hard edges slotted between my pussy lips where my underwear was already molded to me. I whimpered with frustrated arousal. The cold felt terrible and delicious, and I couldn't help but use it to try to take the edge off my suffering. He pulled it away then returned it, blade side up, hovering there but not touching.

"Bron, don't." I stood still, my entire body prickling with terror. "What are you going to do?"

"Don't you trust me yet, Delilah?"

"Have you given me any reason to trust you?"

The corner of his mouth crept up slightly. "If you wanted a man you could trust completely, you never would have gone to that other island."

"That's not true."

Maybe it was a little true, but this was too much, even for me.

Metal skimmed my inner thigh.

"So now the question is, am I going to cut your panties, or will I cut you?"

"I'd be more than happy to take my panties off for you."

"Where would the fun be in that?"

"I think our definitions of fun are at two very different ends of the spectrum."

"Shh. Don't move, pretty Delilah." He plucked the fabric away from my damp skin. His brow creased in concentration—at least I hoped that was concentration and not the effort to hold himself back from doing something I would definitely regret. There was a tugging sensation, and I swore I could feel the sharp blade touching me. Adrenaline rushed impatiently through my veins.

"See? You lived through it."

He moved the axe away, and I sagged in Ilya's grip. He had held me very still, which I'd appreciated.

Ilya stripped my ruined T-shirt off my shoulders and used it to bind my elbows together behind my back. I shivered from the cold. Rather than take pity on me, he pushed me to my knees and pressed my face into the grass and dried leaves. It was dewy and chill, and I meant to complain, but he got down behind me so quickly it startled me. He thrust his cock into the gaping hole in my panties and—once he got the angle right—into me. Covering me with his body, he sheathed his hot length deep inside my pussy, and I groaned in appreciation. It was exactly what I needed—a hot, flesh-and-blood cock, not Bron's axe.

As soon as he was inside me, he froze. I thought he was trying not to come, but when I turned my head to look back at him, I saw Bron kneeling behind him, spitting into his hand and slicking his hard length.

"Do you think you can concentrate on fucking the girl while I'm fucking you?"

"I thought we were ganging up on her," Ilya complained.

"Poor Ilya, never getting what he wants. So, what's it going to be? Are you going to come because of how it feels to have your dick in her hot little pussy, or from the feel of my dick buried deep in your tight ass?"

Ilya's answer was only a gasp. His cock spasmed fretfully inside me as Bron worked his way into his ass.

He was so distracted by what Bron was doing, he'd almost pulled all the way out of me. I backed up the best I could with no arms to use as leverage, and his cock slid all the way back in.

"Fuck, Delilah—please don't move."

"I want more," I complained.

"The only way you get more is to be patient for a moment," he said through gritted teeth.

Bron hummed in appreciation. "Now tell me, Ilyusha, which of us feels better?"

"Both—god! But to have them both at once is too much for one man to bear."

"Did you already come?"

"No! Now shut up or I might."

I could feel Bron start to move again, jarring Ilya into me. "Do you think telling me to shut up is wise?"

Ilya whispered a curse. Each of Bron's thrusts made Ilya thrust into me in a delayed chain reaction. Trapped between us, Ilya was a gasping, trembling mess.

"Please stop. Please stop," he begged.

"Never. I'll never stop fucking you, you little cunt." He was grunting with each thrust, and Ilya was gasping. Ilya's cock was so impossibly hard, and my breath sounded loud in my ears. "Even if you leave here and marry some woman, you'll never know when I'll show up.

I'll make you kneel for me. You'll suck me down your greedy throat because you know who owns this body."

"Yes, Bron." His voice sounded strained, and I looked back again to see Bron had pulled the axe haft across Ilya's throat and was choking him with it. Ilya's face was scarlet.

"No pussy is ever going to make you as hard as having my dick in your ass."

Ilya had stopped moving again—probably concentrating on breathing and taking Bron's cock and temper. I tipped my hips and fucked myself on Ilya's painfully hard dick, using him like I'd seen girls in porn fuck themselves with dildos that were suction-cupped to the shower wall.

His hips stuttered, and he cried out in tortured ecstasy, his cock bucking deep inside me, filling me with jets of hot cum. Bron tossed the axe aside. My orgasm had been close enough to taste, but my clit needed attention.

"Fuck," Ilya groaned. His hands fisted in the dirt as he shook above me.

Bron was swearing, and he leaned in to bite Ilya's shoulder, making Ilya's cock twitch deliciously.

I wriggled out from beneath them, right before they collapsed, and sat in the grass watching them together. They were both beautiful male specimens that made me sigh in frustration.

The bindings on my arms had come loose and I stripped them off.

"Didn't you make her come?" Bron grumbled. "She's sulking."

"I'm not sulking."

"I didn't have a free hand to play with her while the barbarian on my back was choking me." He brought his hand up to his throat and rubbed at the red mark there.

"Always with the excuses."

Ilya grabbed my ankle and dragged me back to him with no regard for the twigs and stones that dug into my bare flesh.

"Leave me alone," I grumbled.

"No, wifey. It's my job to keep your little pussy happy."

"I'm fine."

"If a woman ever says she's fine, she's certainly not fine," Bron said, heaving himself up and yanking up his jeans. The sight of them slowly sliding down his hips had been damned erotic. What was it about a man's lower stomach vee and his hipbones that made me weak at the knees? "Don't let her go until you've seen to her." He left, heading toward the shore, which I suddenly realized didn't sound far off.

Ilya slid his arms under my legs and wrapped them around my thighs so he could spread me open.

"Poor little neglected clit," he murmured.

"You don't have to—"

His tongue hit with deadly accuracy. I sobbed in distressed pleasure. If the man hadn't been hanging onto my thighs, I might have busted his lip with my pelvic bone.

Unperturbed, he held on tightly and caressed and sucked until I was begging, my fingers hooked into his long hair, the scrape of his beard interfering and overwhelming. The unholy tension in my lower belly and thighs made me arch under his too-clever tongue. Every muscle seized, holding me frozen in the moment as the pleasure crested then skated over the edge. I keened helplessly as I came in a violent series of shattering, delirious tremors.

Bron came up the hill, his hair and chest dripping, hurriedly trying to zip up his jeans.

"Fuck. I thought you killed her."

Ilya ran the flat of his tongue over my now too-sensitive clit, and he reluctantly allowed me to push his head away.

Looking like a sleepy, contented cat, Ilya threw himself on the ground next to me and pulled me into the crook of his arm. "Why would you think that?"

"She screamed loud enough to wake the neighbors."

"There are neighbors?" I demanded blearily.

"Only if you count the small cemetery."

"Yes, those ones," Bron said. "You may have started the zombie apocalypse with all of your screaming."

"It's not my fault. Blame Ilya's tongue."

Bron nudged Ilya's back with his toe. He headed away from us, yanking a long blade of grass from the ground and sticking the end in his mouth before grabbing up his axe and wandering off entirely.

"Why does he always run off like that?" I murmured.

"He got what he wanted. He doesn't need affection." He pulled me closer but dozed off moments later, twitching now and again like a dog dreaming of rabbits.

Chapter Eleven

We started the trip first thing in the morning by taking a boat to the mainland. From there we'd traveled in a small plane that rattled alarmingly. I'd assumed we'd be shopping where we landed, in what Ilya told me was Arkhangelsk, but almost as soon as we were on the ground, we boarded a larger flight to Saint Petersburg, which both Bron and Ilya simply referred to as Peter.

Traveling like a passenger rather than being treated like cargo made this a very different journey. I couldn't say I missed being drugged and black-bagged the way I'd been when traveling with them the last time, but the heated looks Ilya sent my way made me wish we had more privacy.

In Saint Petersburg, the two of them dressed like they had money, in casual clothes tailored to fit perfectly, the way my own clothes never had. Paired with their expensive clothing, their beards made them look more like big city hipsters rather than men who spent most of their time farming. I'd done my best to put together some of the more timeless pieces of Yana's clothing so I wouldn't look so out of place, but there was only so much I could do.

I'd never had money to travel, so doing this was exciting for me, although not being able to read most of the signage was strange and unnerving. The buildings we passed on the way to the hotel were far grander than I would have expected. Most things I'd seen on television about Russia had suggested it was a drab place, but the architecture in Saint Petersburg was stunning, and I spent most of our ride from the airport to the hotel glued to the hired car's window.

When we arrived at the hotel, it was difficult not to stand on the street and gape up at it. The place looked like a palace. It was pale yellow, with white columns and stone lions, and if Ilya hadn't grabbed my hand and tugged me across the sidewalk, I might have stood outside staring at it all day.

The lobby was just as intimidating, and I had to stop myself from openly admiring every minor detail.

Ilya stood with me and manned our shared luggage as Bron checked us in.

Some of the judgmental looks I received from other women reminded me of high school, and I automatically drew myself up to my full height and acted like I owned the place, ignoring them. So what if Yana's clothes were old and out of style, and didn't fit me well?

"Your manner is a disguise you put on," Ilya observed. "Like armor."

He'd noticed, of course. The man noticed everything.

"Do women always dress so nicely here?" I asked quietly, wondering if it was safe for me to speak English. I'd heard other people speaking English, but they didn't have to worry about the police finding out they were in the country illegally.

Almost every woman I'd seen had been wearing makeup and heels, and had dressed like she was on her way to a job interview or a first date. The town I was from was far more casual.

He shrugged. "I don't spend much time in cities. Most of the women in my family dress well, though."

Bron rejoined us, so I asked him.

"Yes, women always dress nicely here."

I fell silent again, still worried about traveling around Russia with no ID. Bron had said they'd gotten some for me, but I assumed it must be fake, and therefore was living in fear of being discovered and thrown in jail.

The suite we were shown to was large, with high ceilings, and the furniture was tastefully ornate. There was even a dining area with a table for eight, and because it was a corner suite, there were windows on two sides of the building. Instead of having one bathroom, there were two, and the main one was almost entirely marble.

"There are two bedrooms," Bron pointed out.

"Who gets their own room?" I asked, letting myself explore without masking my reactions now that we were alone. I didn't care if these two laughed at me.

When Bron didn't answer, I looked at him. His jaw was flexing.

"Should I take the spare room?"

"I'm too hungry to think this through right now. We need to eat, and we need to get you clothing. The plane leaves early tomorrow."

"Why are we staying in such a beautiful hotel?"

They both looked baffled.

"Where else would we stay?"

"Somewhere more anonymous and less expensive? This place feels very exclusive."

Bron shrugged. "If you're not used to rich living, it's good that we came here first. When we go to visit Ilya's family, you can't spend your time looking around in awe."

"There's no problem there, as long as I know to expect it ahead of time."

"Good."

We had lunch at a small café down the street, then took a car about ten minutes away to an upscale shopping area. It was beautiful and bustling, and I was enjoying sightseeing and people watching before we even shopped.

Buying a new piece of clothing had always been a big deal for me, considering we had very little in the way of spending money. My siblings and I wore hand-me-downs from our cousins, mostly, or shopped at thrift stores. Meanwhile, Ilya and Bron spent money like it was meaningless and shopped with all the patience in the world. Most of the stores they brought me into were the fancy kind that only offered a small number of pieces.

Rather than trying to rush me through the process, they browsed through the clothing with me and chose things for me at different shops, waiting patiently as I tried them on. We shopped for the guys, too, and I didn't miss how the blushing saleswomen fluttered around them.

When we stopped for a break at a café with a wide window, Bron sent our packages back to the hotel.

The server who brought our tea practically simpered at the guys. I could tell Bron enjoyed all the fussing female attention, but he didn't flirt back. Ilya seemed to chalk it up to the women being polite.

"That one would suck your dick if you smiled at her the right way," Bron said to Ilya, sipping at his tea.

"Why would she do that?" Ilya's brows rose in disbelief. He glanced over his shoulder at the woman, who was taking someone else's order. She must have felt him looking, because she glanced up at him, met his gaze, then smiled flirtatiously. "She doesn't know me."

"Sometimes women only want sex," Bron informed him. "You're a good-looking boy, and she likes what she sees."

"He's almost thirty. He's not a boy," I pointed out.

Bron made a dismissive sound and took a bite of his pastry.

"It's true. Maybe he was a boy when you met him, but he's a man now."

Ilya was watching us talk about him, eyes flicking between us as though we were discussing a subject he had no stake in.

"If he were a man, he would refuse to obey me."

"He can be a man and still be submissive to you. You've spent years training him to obey you."

Bron's gaze rested on Ilya, who had gone from paying attention to our conversation to trying to make it look like he was watching the foot traffic outside the window we sat next to.

"Or maybe he's weak." He pulled out his phone and fiddled with it.

"Maybe your idea of strength is outdated."

Bron glared at me.

"It's true. Do you think someone weak could take what you do to him and not break? Where I'm from, most submissives are given aftercare, at least."

"If he doesn't like what I do, he shouldn't allow it." Bron looked down at his phone and held it like the glare from the window was making it hard to read, but I knew the look of a man taking a sneaky picture. I glanced casually in the direction he'd been aiming it, but there were no women or interesting buildings in sight—but there *was* Ilya looking handsome in the sunshine, watching the busy street.

Poor Bron. He was a bully, but he had a weakness he wouldn't even admit to himself.

"If he likes what you do, it doesn't make him weak."

Bron chomped down on another bite of pastry like it had done him wrong.

Ilya took that opening to lean forward and touch my hand where it rested on the handle of my teacup. "Are you wearing underwear?" he asked quietly.

Bron coughed like he'd inhaled a crumb.

My cheeks were burning. From any other man I'd slept with, it wouldn't seem like such a scandalous question, but from Ilya it was astonishing.

"No," I admitted. If I was expecting a sly grin from him, I didn't get one. "The two of you ruined my last pair yesterday. It's a good thing you only want me in dresses—I couldn't have tried on pants today."

"How did you know she wasn't wearing panties?" Bron demanded, brows suddenly lowered. Jealous much?

"I've spoken to her about what clothing she needed," Ilya said, his dark eyes guileless. "You can hardly blame her for not wanting to borrow Yana's old ones. We need to find a store that sells them."

Leave it to Ilya to ask a woman if she was wearing panties out of thoughtful concern.

When we got to the lingerie store, Ilya hesitated outside. For an awkward moment, he tried to hand me his wallet.

"Go on," Bron teased. "The panties won't eat you."

"This is a place for women," Ilya objected. "It would be best if we went to that bookshop there and waited for her to be done. The women won't want us in there." A fierce blush had crept up his neck.

"In."

Bron turned him toward the door and chivied him inside. The women who were working didn't appear shocked to see men in their store, but Ilya couldn't seem to find a safe place to rest his eyes, so he looked at the floor.

There was a wide selection of pretty things, and I felt almost as lost as Ilya seemed to be. Bron, however, browsed through the store with the level of comfort I would have had at a library.

The women working at the store struck up a conversation with Bron, and soon they were chatting with him and grinning, their demeanor teasing.

"Everywhere we go, it is like this," Ilya murmured. "They always love him."

"He can turn on the charm when he wants to. He just never bothers using it with us."

"I think they smell the danger on him."

"It could be the same for you. I've watched the two of you spar."

He shrugged. "I don't have the same...air of command."

"You're supposed to be practicing that with me."

"Every time we speak, I feel him frown. Am I so bad at conversing with women?"

"Not at all." I touched his hand, and he smiled at me. "He's possessive."

"Yes, maybe. He is very attracted to you. I could tell even before we took you from the Island. Both of us agreed you were the loveliest woman we'd ever seen."

"I'm not the one he's jealous about."

"What do you mean?"

"He's jealous about you, Ilya."

He snorted, but his half-smile faded as he searched my face and realized I wasn't joking.

"No. He is only worried Vas will blame him for not teaching me properly. He wants to make sure I don't learn bad habits with women, so he wants to supervise us when we are together."

"That's what he keeps telling you, but if that was the only thing bothering him, why does he get so angry when I smile at you and laugh at your jokes?"

"Because he wants you for himself, Delilah. You can't blame the man. I think it grates on him that when we go to visit my family, they will see you as mine and not his."

I sighed. This was probably too big of a discussion to have in a lingerie boutique.

"Why don't you practice taking command now? Show me what you'd like to see me wearing, the way you did when we were shopping for dresses."

He cleared his throat. "This is different."

"Not really. You've seen me naked, so what's the big deal? These are just bits of cloth."

His gaze drifted over to the displays and mannequins, lingering.

Bron approached us, gesturing to the selection. "Don't you like any of these? The quality seems good."

Aware of the fact the women were watching, I browsed through the underwear, feeling fabrics and taking stock of what they had available. Considering I usually bought my underwear in a pack of ten from a department store, it felt like I had far too many options here.

Eventually, the salespeople went back to work, chatting with each other in Russian and not paying us much attention.

"You're almost as bad as he is," Bron said, tsking. "Here." He started handing me things, aware of what size I needed without me needing to tell him. Bras were trickier, and he asked me rather than guessing. If I hadn't been measured by professionals on the Island, I would still be shopping for the wrong size.

"What are these for?" Ilya asked, looking at some less practical lingerie.

"They're for women to wear so men want to fuck them."

"They're for unattractive women?"

"No," Bron chuckled. "They're for any woman."

"Why does a woman need clothing like this to make a man want to fuck her?"

Bron dragged a hand down his face. "It's like wrapping on a gift," he finally said.

"Women put it on so men can rip it off?" His eyes glinted, and he looked at me speculatively.

The words drove a spike of arousal through me.

"If that's what the man likes to do," Bron conceded. "I think Delilah might like that, but usually it's to make women look more beautiful."

"They're already too beautiful. Are they trying to blind a man with lust?"

"Maybe."

"I can't imagine her being more beautiful than she is when she's naked and covered in dirt." He shook his head in disbelief. "If I saw her in something like this, it would be the most exquisite torture."

Laughing quietly, Bron perused the selection of lingerie and handed a succession of little hangers to Ilya, who looked at it all, mystified.

"I'm never going to wear all of this," I complained. "You shouldn't waste your money."

"You think I'm too *skupoy* to buy nice things for my fiancée?" Ilya said almost haughtily, arching a brow at me.

Had I hurt his pride? It seemed wasteful, buying so much. "There are only so many things I can wear."

"Bron says we can rip them off you," he pointed out. "If we don't buy much now, soon you'll have none left."

I swallowed at the earnestness of that declaration. I looked to Bron for help, but his grin was wolfish.

"He has a point."

The total when the woman rang us through made her eyes go wide. If they got paid commission, the two of them could close early.

From there, they outfitted me with cosmetics that didn't come from a drugstore, then brought me for a mani-pedi, then waxing.

After a nice dinner at the restaurant in our hotel, during which I realized both had good manners if they cared to use them, I was ready to fall into bed.

Bron had other plans. As soon as we got back to our room, he'd pulled out his phone and started texting someone. I almost fainted.

"You use your phone for more than getting directions?"

"Rarely."

"Not as rarely as Ilya."

"Ilya doesn't know many people. He also had no video games as a child, so he doesn't crave it," Bron explained. "Then again, neither do I. When I moved to the island twelve years ago, the technology wasn't so good, and since it's difficult to get a signal there..." He shrugged. "We could get a signal booster, but phones waste your life if you let them."

I felt my fingers twitch, wanting to yank the phone out of Bron's hand. It was a portal to a world I hadn't had access to for months now. I wasn't as addicted to social media as some of my siblings, but it had been weird learning how to fill empty moments with only my thoughts rather than with perpetual entertainment.

Was going without a phone a bad thing, though?

I felt so much calmer without one, now that I was used to it. The effect Ilya's island had on me would be hard to explain to other people—as though the trees and working in the dirt were a magical cure for the constant pressure I'd felt back home. There were different stressors here, but I only had two people to cater to. I should have missed my family, but the only person I missed, if I was being honest, was Lane.

Bron shoved his phone back in his pocket. "We're going to a club tonight."

"A night club?" Ilya asked, incredulous. "I don't know how to dance."

"Thankfully, it's not that kind of club," Bron said, eyes twinkling. "I've seen you dance."

Ilya flipped him off. "I doubt you can dance, either."

"Of course I can dance. I wasn't raised by wolves, like you."

"What kind of club is it?" I tried to think of what to wear. They'd bought me so much clothing I'd abandoned the work of hanging things up in the closet after a while, my arms like noodles. Despite how tired I was, going out sounded like fun. I hadn't gone to clubs much back home, because I was always working, running the house, taking care of the kids, and low on cash.

"A kink club."

Both Ilya and I looked at him. I was shocked, but Ilya looked confused.

"There's a kink club here?" I asked.

"The one we're going to is exclusive. The kind where you have to sign an NDA."

"Oh."

"Kink?" Ilya asked.

"It's a sex club," Bron explained.

It was so strange that Ilya had no experience with vanilla sex, other than seeing it in movies. There was no porn at the house that I knew of, and they didn't have the internet.

"People have sex there? Right in the club?"

"Yes."

"Why would we go to a sex club when everyone we have sex with is here?"

"It will be good for you to see how domination works for other people. It will also be good for Delilah to remember how to act more submissive."

I didn't miss the glance he sent my way.

"I'm not really a submissive," I pointed out.

"No, you're a whore. For Ilya's sake, you'll have to fake being submissive to him when we visit his family."

Hearing him call me a whore stung. Sure, I'd been called one before multiple times, but it was usually just dirty talk. This was personal.

Ilya got up from the couch and towered over Bron. "Don't call her that."

"Such a great defender of women, and yet you can't defend yourself."

"She's sacrificing herself for her family."

"Whore is a job description, *suka*. I'm not passing judgment on your little wifey." He pinched Ilya's cheek.

"Apologize to her."

"Or what?" Bron's laugh was disbelieving and aggressive.

"It's fine," I said quickly, springing to my feet and pushing between them.

"It's not fine," Ilya said, not taking his angry gaze from Bron. "It's fucking rude, and Bron is going to apologize."

"Am I?"

I put my hand on Ilya's arm and tried to urge him away.

There were a few tense moments where his muscles corded under my fingers and I thought he would throw a punch, but he gradually allowed me to urge him back. He let me guide him onto a chair, then I sat on his lap to keep him there.

"You're letting a woman tell you what to do now?" Bron sneered.

"She was the one you offended, not me. She wants me to stop, so I've stopped."

"So much fuss over a woman," Bron grumbled. He headed into the main bedroom with his luggage.

"Delilah is mine," Ilya called after him. "I will always defend her."

"Delilah is Delilah's," I reminded him teasingly, trying to lighten the mood. At least Ilya didn't look like he was holding a grudge.

I tried to get up, but he had wrapped his arms around my waist, like a flesh and blood seatbelt, determined not to let me up.

"I like you here."

"If we're going out, I need to go get ready."

Ilya sighed but let me go. As I rose, I was shocked to feel him grab my ass. When I glanced at him over my shoulder, he winked at me.

"You grabbed my butt!"

"It looked lonely." The mischievous twist of his lips made me smile back.

"What are you going to wear?" I asked as I entered the bedroom, Ilya on my heels. I'd put my clothes in the main bedroom's closet since there wouldn't have been enough room in the spare bedroom's closet.

Bron threw a T-shirt and jeans on the bed.

"Can I wear the same thing?" I asked, hopefully.

"No," they replied in unison.

Groaning, I browsed through my new clothes.

Bron handed me a dress I didn't remember trying on. It was a strange, iridescent black, and the fabric felt like metallic water in my hands. Of course, it was short.

"Should I wear some of my new underwear with this?"

"No panties." His dark gaze bore into mine, and I couldn't help but shrink back. "Don't interfere between us again, woman, or I'll blister your ass."

"I think stopping the two of you from having a fistfight in a fancy hotel room was a good decision. There's too much breakable furniture in here. And if someone calls the police, they might find out I'm here illegally. Maybe try to act civilized while we're here."

I hadn't meant to snap at him, but he let it go. The look he gave me, however, before I stepped into the shower, made me cringe at what he would do to get even.

Chapter Twelve

I was expecting the club to be in someone's basement, but it was the top floor of a tall office building that probably didn't suspect what it hosted late at night on weekends.

The dress draped over my body showed off every curve, making my braless breasts look almost obscene. It was the kind of dress where I kept finding Ilya watching me out of the corner of his eye.

The security guards acted as though they didn't see us as we passed their desk, but they were alert, and I doubted they missed much.

We got into the elevator, and as the doors slid closed, Bron tugged up the back of my dress and ogled my bare ass in the mirror behind me.

"What?"

"Just making sure you didn't ruin this outfit by wearing panties."

"You can tell she isn't wearing panties by looking at her," Ilya said, frowning. "You could have just asked."

"True, but then we would have had a boring elevator ride."

Ilya smiled. "Smart."

Bron swatted my ass, leaving a delicious sting, then dropped my dress back into place. The cowl neckline dipped all the way to my navel, and a small chain held it together under my breasts. It was probably the sexiest dress I'd ever worn, and it felt delicious on my skin. Unfortunately, the slightest movement of it also made my nipples hard, which was all too obvious thanks to the drape of the fabric.

It was like being more naked than naked.

"You should see if she's wet."

"She dried her hair thoroughly. I don't think she'll catch a cold."

Bron sighed, grabbed Ilya's hand, then put it between my legs.

"Oh." Ilya tried to check, but my legs were too close together for him to get his big hand all the way to its target. "Spread your legs for me, Lilah." His voice had dropped to a husky whisper, and the order felt more like seduction than force.

I widened my stance, and his fingers brushed my pussy.

"So smooth," he murmured.

"Do you like it?" I held his shoulder because I felt a bit off balance, gazing up at him. My shoes were tall, but even with them on, he was taller. It was strange not having to wear flats so I didn't tower over the men I was with.

"I like both. This is...interesting." He drew away his hand and showed his glistening fingers to Bron.

The anticipation of coming here had turned me on, but so had the short skirt and the knowledge that I was naked underneath, and with two men who enjoyed touching me.

Bron grabbed Ilya's wrist and sucked my flavor from his fingers. Ilya gasped, his cheeks turning pink. When Bron let go of him, Ilya held his hand against his chest, as though he'd cherish that finger forever.

"Show me how you can master her tonight, Ilyusha. People will be watching."

"I don't know how."

"Pretend you're me. We have to see Vas and the rest of your family soon, so I expect you to impress me."

The elevator door dinged and slid open. We stepped out into a foyer. There was a cloak room off to the right with no attendant, and Bron pulled us aside.

"I'm not good at being submissive," I objected.

"If you misbehave in there, you'll be shaming the boy...the *man* who has tried his best to shield you from me. It's your choice whether or not to be a good girl."

I glared at him. "I think we're here because you take perverse pleasure in making us uncomfortable."

He didn't answer, but his eyes did. He fucking loved making us uncomfortable, and we all knew it.

Bron reached into his pocket and withdrew what looked like a dog's choke collar, except the links were more delicate and probably not stainless steel. There was a matching leash.

I growled as he handed them to Ilya.

"Your puppy isn't very well trained," Bron observed.

"You'd better hope this puppy doesn't piddle on your boots," I grumbled.

Ilya frowned at the mess of chain in his hand. "What is this for?"

"To collar your woman."

"Are you afraid she'll wander into the street?" Ilya said, chuckling.

"It shows people I'm yours," I explained. "That you own me."

His brow creased. "But I don't own you. You're my fiancée, not my dog."

"You're paying her, so it's close enough to owning her," Bron said. "You're paying rent on her pussy. It's not time to get sentimental about what collars can mean."

Ilya still looked displeased as Bron showed him how the choke collar worked. He slipped it over my head, watching my expression. It tightened, but not uncomfortably, and it was still warm from Bron's pocket.

I shivered, and not only because Ilya's gaze was intense. What was he looking for?

"You like it," he observed.

My belly fluttered. He was holding the chain under my chin, and it was snug around my neck without hurting me. His grip on it was firm rather than hesitant. I'd been on a leash before—it had done nothing for me. This however...

He kissed me. "Are you going to be good, little wife?"

My cheeks prickled and burned. "I'm not your wife, Ilya."

"You're all mine until I let you go." His gaze roved over my face.

God, his expression was so earnest. It wasn't hard to understand why he didn't realize he was handsome, considering he spent most of his time with Bron. Our own personal terrorist wasn't exactly free with his compliments.

I swallowed, not sure what to say to him.

"Come on. We're not here to stand around in the closet." Bron's brows were dark slashes as he ushered us out.

Rather than a series of offices, which was what I'd expected, the space was set up like an actual club. High ceilings and dim lighting, a four-sided bar in the middle of the main room, comfortable seating, and a sea of people. It reminded me of the Island they'd taken me from, except here many of the women were on leashes and in varying states of undress.

"It's not the same when they're not screaming and running from us," Ilya mused.

Bron shook his head. "We'll turn you into a pervert yet."

Ilya's chuckle made me smile. "I already have a beautiful woman on a leash."

"It's a good start."

Would there be people they knew here? I didn't know how far Moscow was, but then again, I had only the vaguest idea of what Russia looked like on a map. Ninth grade geography had been ages ago and had included memorizing the names and locations of every US state, and a segment about global warming. There had been a few world maps to color. Russia over to the right of Europe, but aside from that, I'd had no interest in studying places I'd never get to see.

I drew myself up, raising my chin and walking with confidence. Bron had selected everything I was wearing, right down to my collar, but it was Ilya holding the leash.

Tonight, I felt like money.

I walked beside Ilya, with Bron at our backs, feeling delicate and pretty in the company of two large, hot men.

Bron found us an empty spot to sit—a semi-circular leather couch. They claimed it, taking up an aggressive amount of space, looking dangerous and delicious. Ilya swatted my ass and pulled me into his lap, as though it were the most natural thing in the world. The two of them had started a conversation in Russian, and with the throb of the music in my ears, even their occasional English words were mostly drowned out.

A man came by and Bron said something to him. Moments later, drinks came with a topless female server who froze like a wild bunny when Bron glanced her way. She gave her head a brief shake and rushed on with her almost full tray.

I surveyed the room as I sipped at my drink, the strength of the unfamiliar liquor making me wince. The people who filled the space lounged and talked. Groups of people danced or made out. There were different flavors and levels of kink out in the open, and people wandered upstairs where there seemed to be private rooms. I recognized the occasional actor or musician.

"There's a reason we had to sign those NDAs," Bron said in my ear, catching me watching a female actor who had a man kneeling at her feet.

"That is not that woman's husband," I informed him.

"No, it is not." He smiled devilishly, our faces so close that when his gaze shifted to mine, we were within kissing distance. His focus dropped to my mouth, and the feel of his breath on my lips made me want him to close the inches between us.

Casually, he straightened, taking away the temptation of initiating a kiss with a man I didn't even like most days.

A pair of men came over, each with a beautifully dressed woman on a leash. The size of the rocks on their fingers suggested they weren't paid company.

Bron made introductions, excluding us women.

"Go dance, woman," Ilya said, unclipping my leash and urging me up. "There are some things we need to discuss."

That weren't for my ears? He knew I didn't understand Russian, but okay...

I rose and headed to the dance floor, feeling awkward. The two women came with me, apparently given the same directive by their fiancés? Husbands?

Rather than ditching me or leaving me out, when they started to dance, they took my hands and encouraged me to dance with them—at least I assumed that was what they were saying. The tail of my choke collar swayed between my breasts, reminding me the man with the leash was watching.

The two women were gorgeous and about my age—one blonde and one brunette. They seemed to know each other, and when they occasionally kissed or slapped each other's asses, I wasn't surprised. It quickly became obvious they were performing for their men, going out of their way to face them and throw seductive looks their way.

The men sat together, looking deep in discussion about something relatively important, even though their eyes kept drifting to us.

I danced with them for a while, smiling suggestively at Ilya and meeting any attention from Bron with snobby hostility, enjoying how it made each of them react.

After a second drink, I got bored with the game and headed for the restroom.

When I came out, rough hands grabbed me and slammed me against the wall, stealing my breath.

Fuck.

But it was Bron, looking unhinged and angry as hell.

"What the fuck do you think you're doing?"

"I just used the restroom," I said, glaring up at him.

"You don't leave my sight—understand me, you stupid bitch?"

"What's the big deal?" I asked. "I didn't realize I needed a hall pass to pee."

"You can't walk around looking like this and not expect trouble. You stay where I can see you. If you need to piss, you take me with you."

"The club is full of security. There are guards—cameras. What do you think is going to happen?"

"Anything could happen. You could get kidnapped."

"Maybe my new kidnapper won't be such a jerk."

His hand came to my throat, squeezing as he looked down into my face, his eyes snapping with anger.

"This isn't a game, *De-li-lah*."

Every time he said my name like that, between the accent and the mocking enunciation, I couldn't figure out if I wanted to slap him or fuck him.

Both. Probably both.

"It's not a game, and yet you still want to play with me, *Bron-i-slav*."

He flashed his teeth at me, but it was more snarl than smile.

"Most of the people in this club want to fuck you. If you don't stay where I can see you, anything might happen."

"I'm used to being on the Island, playing dangerous games with dangerous men. Maybe having access to only two men is boring me." I said it to rile him, and I wasn't disappointed.

There was a dangerous gleam in his eye, and my adrenaline rushed to meet the challenge I saw there.

"I'm trying to help Ilya get to know a few people who know his father, so that word will get back to him that Ilya's not a man-child anymore. I don't have time to deal with your petulant, slutty behavior." He squeezed my neck harder, and my head swam. Scowling at me, he leaned in and dragged his tongue up my lips. "Stop looking for trouble." He gave my neck another warning squeeze, then let go.

I opened my mouth to say something, but he grabbed my arm and slapped my face hard enough to sting.

"Don't speak unless someone asks you a question. Understand me?"

A hot buzzing sensation filled me. I really wished I wouldn't get turned on when he roughed me up.

"Open your mouth."

Confused, I obeyed.

He spat in my mouth, then pushed up on my chin, closing my jaw. He waited for me to swallow, and I did, ignoring the way my body was begging for more disrespect. I was going to need some serious therapy when I went home.

"You look very beautiful tonight."

A compliment? Had hell frozen over?

"You don't look half bad yourself," I admitted.

"We'll need to make a mess of you before we bring you back to the hotel."

"What?"

He dragged me back through the club, not stopping until we reached the couch where Ilya sat. Ilya's face had taken on a strange hardness as he spoke to these men. Even his voice had changed. It was lower now, his words more measured. It reminded me of Bron.

Now that I got a better look at them, the men looked like rich thugs. Like Bron, they were heavily tattooed. My men were in jeans and T-shirts, but the other two were in dress pants and button-down shirts.

My men?

Had I really just thought that?

Ilya reached for me as we got to them, and I settled in his lap again, as though I always sat there.

Bron sat beside him, and they had a brief, murmured conversation before he shifted farther away. Ilya's brow arched, and his gaze came to me. I flushed, realizing I'd been the subject of their discussion.

"Making trouble?" Ilya snapped. "I thought I told you to behave."

I stared at him, wide-eyed. It sounded like Bron coming out of his mouth.

"I'm sorry. I didn't mean to," I said, putting my hand on his chest and gazing up at him adoringly, knowing full well the strange men were watching. If this was supposed to prove to Vas that Ilya was

'manly,' I could act submissive for a few hours. "I went to the restroom."

"You don't leave my sight, understand me?"

"Yes, Ilya."

"If you're so bored that you need to go wandering around, maybe
we'll make your evening more interesting."

"That's not necessary. I—"

He spoke to the half-naked server who arrived with more drinks,
and she flashed him a smile, then sauntered away, the sway of her hips
an invitation Ilya paid no attention to.

I wanted to ask what he was planning, but he was shooting the shit
with the men again, and I didn't want to interrupt and look pushy.
They called another friend over and introduced him as Ty.

"You're American?" he asked, speaking directly to me.

Both Bron and Ilya stiffened, as though a man speaking directly to
me was borderline unacceptable.

"Yes."

"What's your name?"

"Delilah."

He smiled. "A beautiful name for a beautiful woman."

I smiled awkwardly, never sure how to respond when men said
things like that.

"I heard you met her on an island vacation," Ty said to Ilya.

"We did."

Ty's gaze sharpened, as though he knew exactly what that meant.
"Not Reverie."

"What's Reverie?"

Ty gave a nod and a mysterious smile. "That's what I thought."

"You ask a lot of fucking questions." Ilya's tone held a thinly veiled
threat.

The man held Ilya's gaze for a few moments, then inclined his head. "Information is a passion of mine."

"I suggest you move along, friend," Bron said. "He's not a patient man."

Ty got to his feet. "It was a pleasure to meet the two of you," he said to Ilya.

Ilya ignored him, as though the man was of no consequence.

I gave him an apologetic smile, and he winked at me before wandering off.

"Why were you so rude?"

He put his lips to my ear. "The man buys and sells women."

I swallowed. It had never crossed my mind that men like that would be here.

"How do you know he does that?"

"Bron told me when he spotted him earlier."

Well, that explained why Bron was so pissed off when I'd disappeared earlier to go to the washroom. Just what kind of family did Ilya belong to where being seen here would be considered a good thing?

The server finally returned and handed Ilya a folded dark cloth. He negligently dropped a wad of cash on her tray. He missed her pleased grin, but I didn't. The way she kept looking at him annoyed me, and I scowled when she turned her back.

He unfolded the cloth, running it through his hands.

"What's that for?" I quietly asked.

"To keep my little wifey from getting bored."

"I'm not bored."

He shushed me and brought the length of fabric up to my face and fastened it around my eyes. The knot he made pulled my hair, and I fussed with it a moment before he pushed my hands away and attached my leash to my collar again. He said something to Bron in Russian, and

I was plucked from his lap and carried what felt like partway across the club.

Whoever carried me put me down and attached the leash to something over my head.

"What are you doing?"

"Shut your fucking hole," Bron growled.

He unhooked the dress's closure between my breasts and pushed the fabric off my shoulders. Without any hesitation, he stripped me, leaving me in nothing but my heels. Shocked, I froze, scrambling to throw up the mental walls that had protected me on the Island. I'd almost expected one or both of them to fuck me here tonight, but putting me on display like this hadn't crossed my mind.

"Put your hands behind your head and leave them there," Ilya said.

I opened my mouth to object and could almost feel Bron's glare right through the blindfold.

Right.

Tonight, I was being a good submissive and not arguing with my 'owner' or his...underling?

A nervous laugh tried to work its way out—it was funny thinking of Bron as the underling, considering how things were between the three of us in private.

Gingerly, I laced my fingers behind my neck, trying to stand as proudly as I could, even though everything inside me cringed. Being naked in public and not being able to see what was coming made me anxious and not in the fun way.

A rough male voice said something in Russian, and I realized we weren't alone. Ilya's new friends had followed us over.

Fucking great.

In my head, I tried to picture Lane rolling her eyes and grimacing at me from across the room. I missed her with a savage ache. I hadn't realized how much I'd been leaning on her emotionally during my most recent tour on the Island. Here, there was Ilya, but when he put on his Bron mask, I was all alone.

How many people were near me? It was impossible to know.

Something stroked my breast—the back of a knuckle, maybe? It happened again. Who was it? Ilya or Bron?

Warm breath tickled the back of my neck, making my nipples harder.

I shivered, feeling as though I might lose my balance.

"Widen your stance before you fall over, woman," Ilya ordered.

Reluctantly, I obeyed, knowing damned well it left me wide open to almost anything he wanted to do to me.

The island I'd worked on for tuition had felt so far away. I'd gotten used to Ilya and Bron, and their kinks. This was like starting back at zero, not knowing what would happen. Being around strangers again was strange enough, but being touched in front of them like this was humiliating.

Would it look bad for Ilya if I begged to go home?

My breasts got prodded, pinched at. Someone stroked and slapped me. Two hands became four, then there were hands everywhere. The murmurs and chuckles of men.

They're letting other men touch me?

Worse, do I like it?

A woman giggled, and soft lips brushed mine—a woman's perfume and warmth. It had been years since a girl had kissed me. I let her open my mouth under her own. If Ilya and Bron wanted this to stop, they would stop it.

I heard Ilya swear quietly under his breath.

Fuck. How were there so many hands?

It wasn't just Bron, Ilya, and their new friends touching me—complete strangers had joined in. Fingers tickled me, stroking my skin, groping my breasts, touching my pussy, spreading my ass cheeks.

I held onto my disgust as long as I could, but it eroded under the onslaught, leaving arousal in its wake. Someone took off my shoes and touched my freshly pedicured feet, making me cringe.

Thick fingers worked their way into my pussy, and I was already embarrassingly slick. Soft mouths dragged over my skin, zeroing in on my nipples and sucking there in rhythms that didn't match. Someone bearded kissed my nape, below my hands, then nibbled on my fingers with sharp teeth. Hands skated over my back, making me quiver almost as deliciously as the other small torments. Something—a tongue?—flicked my clit, and I cried out.

There was too much, too many, and they were everywhere. There wasn't enough of me to have six, eight, ten people exploring my body. Someone's tongue delved between my lower cheeks, investigating my asshole. The fingers inside me stroked in a distracted rhythm. A man kissed me, his beard scraping my face. Someone lifted my foot, then sucked a toe into their mouth. Someone folded one of my legs and pulled it wide, giving mouths and fingers greater access to my pussy. I almost lost my balance, but someone steadied me, chuckling. The collar choked me just enough to remember I was caught there, as though the hands and mouths weren't enough to remind me.

I panted, wanting it to go on forever, wanting it to stop, wanting to come.

"Please," I begged.

I meant to say Ilya's name, but knew Bron was still in charge, no matter what it looked like to these strangers.

I was crying behind my blindfold, and then I was remembering the hands and mouths and dicks of the boys who'd taken what they wanted from me at that party in high school, and the years after when the word slut had been whispered about me and shouted at me and written on my locker. The pictures and videos that had circulated. The police watching the footage I'd gotten my hands on, groping me with their lecherous gazes, not caring that I'd been drugged, their questions always implying I'd secretly enjoyed it.

"Please what, wifey?" Ilya whispered in my ear.

"Please stop," I begged. "No more."

He said something in Russian, and people moved back.

I dropped my arms from behind my head, shaking, hoping I wouldn't be in trouble for moving out of position.

My feet were cold, and the floor was gritty underfoot.

"You're a mess," Bron said quietly.

I nodded. He probably didn't realize how much of a mess I was.

"You like kissing girls," he observed.

"Who doesn't?" I asked, shakily.

When the blindfold came off, I was looking at Ilya's beard.

"She's trembling," Ilya said, tipping my face up so he could study me.

"She needs dick. Come on, beautiful." Bron detached my leash from the hook above my head and handed it to Ilya.

Naked, I turned, looking for my shoes and my dress. Only then did it compute that I was naked in the middle of a club full of people without so much as a mask to disguise who I was. Sure, there was an NDA, and I wasn't exactly a celebrity, but there was no saying there weren't cameras here.

Only a few people were looking our way now that the action was over, but I was sure we'd been the center of attention for a while.

Ilya found my dress and helped me slip it back on, while Bron tracked down my shoes and set them down the right way so I could slip them on my feet. I leaned on Ilya as we went back to the couch. I felt like an over-tightened violin string about to snap and take out someone's eyeball.

"Can't we go back to the hotel room?" I asked, not wanting to face the people who'd been touching me. When I glanced over at the couch, though, the four of them had moved elsewhere and were in the middle of a private orgy.

"Did you come when they were touching you?" Ilya demanded.

"No." Without my permission, a whimper crawled out of my throat.

He glowered at me. "I almost did."

A hysterical giggle escaped me.

"You should fuck her here and now. Let people know you're a man."

"I let other people touch her because you said it would make me look worldly," Ilya growled. "Now I want to take her home and wash their smell off her. Sharing her with you makes sense, but I'm not doing this again."

"Letting people see she matters to you is showing weakness."

"I'm aware." He strode for the door, with me staggering after him, trying not to overbalance on my high heels and wobbling legs.

Chapter Thirteen

The three of us got into the elevator, and as soon as the doors closed, Ilya scooped me up. I wrapped my arms around his neck.

"I'm sorry for walking so quickly. I had to make it look like we were leaving because I was angry with you. I shouldn't have agreed to that."

"Okay."

Bron grumbled.

"What?" Ilya demanded.

"She's not some delicate little flower. She's a tough girl."

"Shut up, Bron."

The elevator went deathly silent and stayed that way. The ding when we got to the bottom floor felt excessive.

Rather than put me down, Ilya strode through the foyer and out the sliding door. Bron kept up but stayed a pace behind.

The wind had picked up, and I huddled against Ilya for warmth. Several blocks from the party, Ilya cut through a park.

"Are we going to walk all the way back to the hotel?" Bron demanded, still sounding pissed off.

"We walk everywhere at home. Why is walking a big deal?"

"There are cars here."

"There are cars here. People dress nicely here. Men share women here," Ilya said in a falsetto, as though that was what Bron sounded like, when both had voices low enough to make the floor shake at home.

Ilya whipped around so suddenly my stomach lurched.

They glared at each other over my head.

"You're turning into a mouthy little shit," Bron said between clenched teeth.

"Then I should fit right in when we go visit my family."

Bron's face was a mask. "I won't tolerate disrespect."

"When we're not at home, you're my bodyguard, Bron. I'm not your bitch."

"No matter where we are, you're still my bitch. You know it in the pit of your stomach. Act like a big man out here in the world, sure, but if you disrespect me when I can't do anything about it, be sure that we'll discuss it later."

"I'm not a boy for you to raise anymore."

"You stick your dick in one woman and suddenly you think correcting your behavior isn't my business? That's one magic pussy you think she's got there." Bron shoved him, and Ilya staggered back.

He set me down, absently handing me the end of the leash.

"You've gotten things all twisted. It was never supposed to be like this between us."

Bron raised his fists in the universal gesture of I'm-going-to-kick-your-ass. Rather than trying to talk him out of it, Ilya gave him an aggressive chin jerk. I'd seen them sparring a lot, but this didn't seem like a game.

"If you two are going to pound the crap out of each other, I'm going back to the hotel," I declared loudly, hoping to derail them.

Bron took a swing, and I turned my back and strode away the best I could in impractical heels. There was no way I was standing around to watch this nonsense. It was stupid enough when men fought each other when they were young and drunk, but they were hovering around thirty, and neither of them had drank enough tonight to be this stupid.

I headed in what I hoped was the right direction, wishing I had money for a taxi. Realizing I was holding my leash, I dropped it down the front of my dress to dangle down my body. Lord knew I didn't have any pockets in this dress.

The sounds of their scuffle got more distant, then got entirely carried away on the wind.

Was I headed in the right direction? I'd been walking for a few minutes, and the buildings I could see in the distance looked unfamiliar. Had I gotten turned around in the trees?

I bit the inside of my cheek and stopped, turning in a full circle. There was nothing to see except the shadows of trees and dark rolling lawns, along with a web of pale, meandering pathways. There were benches and flowerbeds, but even if there'd been signage I couldn't have read it in the dark...or in Russian.

As much as I didn't want to watch them fight, being this far away from them was seeming incredibly stupid now that the buzzing in my head had quieted and I'd calmed down a bit.

Which way had I come from? Why were there so many paths in this park?

A figure moved toward me.

Ilya?

The man came closer. Not Ilya. It was a stranger. His trajectory was far too certain to make me comfortable, so I walked away, headed into a treed area. If he was trying to get from A to B, he wouldn't follow me down the dimly lit path.

He said something in Russian. It was hard to tell if it was friendly.

Fear trickled through my veins, and I walked faster. The scuff of the steps behind me increased speed to match me.

Fucking hell.

Quickly, I stepped out of my shoes and picked them up, then left the path, heading into the trees and underbrush. My heart tripped along, mirroring my clumsy steps.

Get it together, Lilah. You've played this game so many times. You know how to hide.

But *did* I remember how to hide? I'd tried doing what Lane did on my first tour on the Island, but I'd quickly learned I wasn't great at it. The suspense killed me. It had been easier to get the bad parts over with.

This situation was different. This man might not only assault me—he might traffic me. He might kill me.

I drew a shaky breath and tried to calm down enough to think. Maybe if he got close enough, I could jump out and garrote him with my leash. No. It was probably thin enough to just break, and all I would do was piss him off.

So stupid! Why had I left Ilya and Bron? Was making a point worth putting myself at risk like this?

I could hear him pacing on the path, gravel crunching under his shoes.

Rustling. A Snap.

My dress was dark enough to help me hide, but I couldn't tell how visible the rest of me was. I felt like all the blood had drained from my face.

The man said something I didn't understand and laughed quietly to himself. Shards of ice skated through my veins.

I crouched between a bush and a small tree, finding a hollow where a small animal had frequently made space for itself. I was too big to fit, but between the darkness and how small I could fold myself, maybe he wouldn't be able to see me.

How long would it take for him to lose interest and leave? The grove of trees wasn't large. Would he search it or assume I'd headed out the other side?

I closed my eyelids most of the way but peeked through my lashes, not wanting him to spot the whites of my eyes.

He swore—that much Russian I understood now. Sounding frustrated, he stomped around, beating at the bushes with a stick as though I were stupid enough to let that flush me out of hiding.

Grumbling to himself, he staggered closer, and I caught a strong whiff of alcohol.

The asshole was drunk? That changed things. Maybe I could outrun him, even with bare feet. As long as my ankle held up, I should be fine.

Shit, he was getting too close. When he turned his head for a moment, I made a desperate decision and burst from my hiding place, headed back for the path. He swung around and flailed with the stick. The end of it licked my skin with fire, catching my cheekbone. I suppressed a shriek and ran as he swore and ran after me.

How did a woman even yell 'fire!' in Russian?

I wanted to shout for Ilya and Bron, but they were so far away there was no way they'd hear.

The man caught at the back of my hair, ripped out a few strands, then got a better hold of it, jerking me back. My feet went out from under me, and I hit the ground right where the dirt met the cement path.

I tried to catch myself, and broke my fall with my hands, although a nasty ache ran through my wrist. I'd scraped flesh, but it was the vicious hand in my hair that made me screech. I tried to pull the hand closer to my scalp, trying to force him to release my hair, but either I sucked at self-defense, or he was too drunk to register that I was hurting him.

He hauled back a fist and launched it at my face, and I braced for it, turning my face away at the last moment.

The blow never landed.

There was a cacophony of growling shouts, and the man let go of me. A body hurled past me, and I scrambled to my feet, not sure what was going on, but willing to use it to my advantage.

Everything hurt.

In the dim light of the not-so-nearby park streetlight, I saw one figure beating the crap out of my attacker.

Holy shit. The man was cold-blooded. My attacker was on the ground begging for mercy, but the beating continued until the concrete path was black with what I assumed was blood. He was babbling, begging, spitting teeth.

When I tried to put some space between me and the carnage, the small rocks that littered the path were sharp against my soles.

A large hand caught my arm, and I gasped.

"No one touches you without our permission," the man said simply. Coldly.

Ilya?

I looked up at him, not sure I was right. In the filtered lamplight he looked far more sinister, his eyes twin shadows.

When I tried to yank my arm away, he took a firmer grip.

"Did he harm you?" He sounded more like himself that time, but still not quite right.

"He hit me with a branch, and pulled my hair, but nothing earth shattering. You found me in time."

Ilya said something to what I assumed had to be Bron, who stopped beating the man. They had a brief discussion, and it didn't sound like Bron was happy.

"What?" I asked.

"We are deciding if we should kill him."

Oh god, is he serious?

The moment felt surreal.

The man was mewling, trying his best to crawl away but not going far. His noises and movements sounded wet.

"I think he's drunk," I said.

"I should care?"

Normally, I would have said no, but I couldn't let Bron kill a man in front of me and not try to stop him.

"Why not call the police instead?"

"Why call police to fix a problem we can fix ourselves?"

"Does she want him dead?" Bron asked, like he was going on a coffee run and wanted to know my order.

Did he think I'd lost the ability to speak?

"No, she doesn't," I snapped.

He grunted.

Was that the sound of a zipper?

Bron pissed on the man as Ilya held me where I was. He didn't make me watch, but I did anyway.

"You guys rough me up all the time—so what if he did the same thing?"

"You agreed to rough handling from us. He will think again before trying this with another woman."

I grimaced. "If he can ever walk again." I shuddered in sympathy. There was no way the angle of his right leg was natural.

Ilya found my shoes and helped me balance while I put them on. He picked me up, not listening when I told him I could walk. I should have left my shoes off and held on to them because now I was trying not to let them fall off.

"Why did you leave us?" he demanded.

"I didn't want to watch you pound the shit out of each other."

"So you left and put yourself in danger. You've been a woman long enough that you should know not to wander alone in a park at night."

He had a point, but I bristled anyway.

"I—my nerves were all jangled from the club. I wasn't thinking."

"It isn't right that women have to think about danger before walking alone in a park, but I still expect you to be more careful with yourself."

He grumbled for a while in Russian, and I caught several swear words. When Bron fell into step behind us, he said something to Ilya in Russian, too. I had the urge to tell them they were being rude by not letting me in on the conversation, but maybe I didn't want to know. After so many weeks with them, I should probably understand more, but I didn't have a great ear for languages.

"Aren't you going to call an ambulance for that guy?"

"If he dies, he dies," Ilya said stonily.

"The two of you can't be judge, jury, and executioner!"

"Who will stop us?"

"I don't know...maybe the law?"

Behind us, Bron spat emphatically. "The law can come for me if they like."

Wow. Maybe the law really didn't apply to rich people. They didn't seem at all concerned.

Chapter Fourteen

B ron made a call, then another, and when we got to the street, a car met us there. The ride back to the hotel was silent.

We avoided the front desk and made our way to our suite. Thankfully, Ilya let me walk to our room rather than continuing to carry me, but he held my hand the entire way, as though I might take off again.

Bron stripped out of his bloody clothes and got into the shower as soon as we entered our suite. Ilya checked me over and tended to my scratches, then sat down on the couch. When I headed for the closet for something to change into, he snapped his fingers at me and patted his knee.

Since when was he all finger-snappy with me?

"What?" I asked, wondering how serious he was.

"Come here, woman."

Woman? We weren't at the club anymore, so this wasn't him playing a role.

Arching a brow at him, I got closer.

"Sit," he ordered, pointing at his lap.

Confused, I perched uncertainly on his lap.

He fished the leash out of my cleavage and pulled the collar over my head, then tossed it onto the side table. Frowning, he traced the burning line on my cheekbone where the attacker had hit me with the stick. "I don't like this mark."

"If it's any consolation, I didn't like it either."

"You need to learn not to wander off."

"I'm not a child, Ilya."

"No, you're not, so I expect more from you."

I swallowed, feeling odd. This wasn't usually how things were between the two of us.

"Twice tonight you left my side without making sure you had Bron with you. It's not as safe here as it is at home."

He said home like it was our home, rather than just his.

"I'm aware."

"It occurs to me now that being so beautiful has probably always brought you trouble."

A ball of emotion clogged my throat.

He wasn't wrong, but no one had ever felt sorry for me because of it before. All of the unwanted, inappropriate attention. The groping and catcalls. The assaults. The women who assumed I was a bitch or that I'd try to steal their man. Back home I'd rarely worn makeup and I'd dressed like a slob, but it still hadn't been enough.

"When we were at the club, didn't I warn you not to stray?"

"Well...yes, but I thought you were acting bossy to impress people. I didn't think you really meant it."

"When I speak, I expect you to obey me."

"Okay."

"Not just okay. You say, 'Yes, Ilya.'"

I swallowed, his tone and disapproval making my cheeks heat. He was usually so mild-mannered with me, but lately he was getting so unexpectedly dominant.

"Yes, Ilya." Okay, the reaction I was having to his bossiness had to be a hold-over from what they'd done to me at the club, right? That and the adrenaline from my narrow escape from the creep in the park.

"I think it's time for me to teach you how serious I am that you listen to me. Things could have been much worse at the club or in the park, but when we go to visit my family, you must listen to me immediately and every time."

"I'm sorry. I didn't realize it was such a big deal."

"Whether the deal is large or small makes no difference. You hear me, and you obey, like a good little pet."

I swallowed, not liking the way my cheeks were burning.

He picked me up and flipped me facedown over his lap, completely blowing my mind. The two of them handled me like I was a little waif, and I still wasn't used to it.

"You don't need to spank me, Ilya," I blurted. "I've already learned my lesson."

"Let's make sure you don't forget." He brushed up the back of my skirt and his warm, rough hand settled on my ass.

God, was he really going to do this? I'd been spanked erotically before, of course, but no one had ever used a spanking to discipline me. I wasn't a child, and I'd never been spanked when I was one.

"Ilya, please. This isn't necessary."

He anchored me to his lap with his free hand while maintaining a firm grasp across my body to my far hip. I felt deliciously trapped. Why couldn't this just be a sex thing? I was too old to be disciplined like this.

"I say what's necessary. You listen." His hand came down and crashed into my ass so hard my teeth rattled. The second smack was lighter but stung more.

"Ow!"

"Quiet. You'll wake the other guests."

Smack.

That actually freaking hurt. I wrinkled my nose and tried to squirm around, frowning so hard my forehead hurt.

Smack. Smack. Smack.

He got into a rhythm, and the back end of my world went red and stinging.

And eventually sore.

Was he even counting? I thought men who were into spanking counted things out. He had to be at twenty or thirty by now, and my ass felt like someone had sat me on a stove element.

I sobbed once, burying my face against the couch cushion, not even caring that a lot of strangers had probably had sex on the damned thing.

"Ilya, please!" I whispered harshly, turning my head enough to get the words out. My whole body felt as if it was blushing, and my feet were kicking involuntarily with each slap of his hand. I struggled, but he held me on his lap, following my slow progress as I tried to wriggle off him.

Eventually, I got trapped, my legs spread over his thigh, my ass a fiery red haze. I wanted to get away, but he ignored my struggles. His thigh was hard and thick between my own, flexing with the minor effort he needed to make to contain me. I slowed my kicking, realizing my movements were rubbing my most tender bits against the rough denim of his jeans. I wasn't enjoying this, and I was angry, but my body was betraying me. My breasts had tumbled out of my dress, and I felt vulnerable and helpless.

The man was still fully dressed, and the disparity was stupidly hot.

This was Ilya, not Bron, damn it! He was supposed to be the sweet one.

Abruptly, he stopped. His rough hand smoothed over the bonfire that was my ass, but I wasn't sure if it was helping or adding more punishment.

Tears of pain and humiliation dampened the cushion under my face. I lay there, trying to catch my breath, far too aware of the tension in my lower belly that made me want to squirm against his stupid leg.

"I hate you," I whispered.

"I know you're upset, but you need to remember disobedience doesn't turn out well. You put yourself in danger. That is unacceptable." One of his fingers drifted to the cleft of my ass and trailed along it as though by accident.

"Don't you think I know that? I was the one who got attacked!"

I shivered as that finger trailed again, this time bumping over my asshole. Was he doing it by accident?

"Your poor round bottom is such a bright red, and so hot under my hand." He patted me, the gentle contact still stinging. "I know you didn't like that, but it needed to be done. It's my job as your future husband to take care of you and make sure you are safe."

Safe? Protected instead of always being the one in charge? The concept brought an overwhelming sense of relief, but none of this was real. I was going home in a few weeks, and I'd probably never see him or Bron again.

"I'm not really going to be your wife, Ilya."

His hand stilled, and that finger of his circled my asshole, brushing lightly enough for it to tickle and make me press my pussy against his leg to get away from the sensation. My clit was enjoying the sensation of the rough denim, and the flames in my ass had left a lingering warmth that made me feel like I'd been a very bad girl.

He grunted and his non-answer set off some alarm bells, but his thigh shifted under me, and his finger prodded at me, not leaving me space to think about anything else.

"What are you doing?" I gasped.

He leaned over me and spat, and the warm wetness slid down the crack of my ass to his questing finger. He coated what felt like maybe his index finger, then coaxed it into my back hole in gentle, exploratory increments. I couldn't help but rock with his motions, needing the pressure between my legs to make up for the burning of my ass cheeks.

When I realized I was basically humping his leg, I stopped, cheeks and ears flaming with mortification.

"Don't stop," he said hoarsely. "I know you must need relief after what we did to you at the club." His finger stirred deeper, retreated. He gathered more spit and pressed inward again, stretching me.

"Why did you let other people touch me?" I asked, sullen.

"You looked so beautiful and helpless. I enjoyed watching the other women kiss you and taste your soft skin," he admitted. "Watching the men touch you was different. That made me want to yank you away from them and reclaim what was mine."

"I'm not yours!"

"That's it—rock your hips for me. Fuck my finger deeper into your ass."

I gasped, both at the sensation and at how bossy the man was getting. He was practically a virgin, for fuck's sake!

He spat again and worked a second finger into me, twisting and spreading them, making my stomach cramp. I whimpered.

"What a good girl you are for me. Don't stop rubbing your hot little pussy against my thigh. I love the feel of you soaking my jeans."

I shivered and couldn't help but obey him. My clit was too hard and uncomfortable, and I was so fucking close to getting off. His fingers in my ass were vibrating, and I caught my breath, grinding against his leg, desperate for relief. He gripped the back of my neck possessively with his free hand, and my eyes fluttered closed. My sore ass throbbed, and his fingers wiggled inside me, and his thigh was flexing against my clit, and his words were low and rapt and coaxing, like I was the best show he'd ever watched.

"Come on, wife. Show me how much you love having my fingers in your tight little hole."

The brutal tightness in my lower belly made a sob catch in my throat, then my body stiffened, and the pleasure crested, and I was going to scream like someone was murdering me.

"Stop." The command was firm, cold, like a bucket of ice water thrown on two cats in heat.

Ilya pulled his fingers from me so fast it made me gasp. I squirmed against his leg, determined to finish, but Bron pulled me off his lap. Strong arms encircled my waist, leaving me no way to escape. My ruined orgasm fluttered disappointingly, and I thrashed in Bron's arms, trying to claw my way back to Ilya.

"Please!" I begged. "I need him."

"He needs to stop spoiling your slutty little cunt." Bron was naked, and from the feel of him, already hard.

Ilya stood, frowning and rearranging his hard-on in his jeans. "I disciplined her and then I prepared her for your use."

"Yes, I can see by the bulge in your jeans that you were just selflessly doing your duty."

"It's my duty to correct my wife when she's not making good choices," he said mulishly

"Don't parrot my words back at me, boy. You were thinking about your dick."

"And are you not thinking about yours when you correct *me*?"

"Ilya, please." I stretched my arms out to him, stupidly hoping he might be frustrated enough to rescue me from Bron. "I need to come."

"He does, too, but he's not stupid enough to cross me to get you back, *De-li-lah.*"

Ugh. I wanted to slap him.

"Why do *you* get to decide who gets to come and when?"

"Because I'm bigger and meaner than the two of you."

"And older. Don't forget older," I said.

"If you're implying I'm not up to controlling you both, you're mistaken." He snorted. "I don't think you spanked her long enough, boy. Did you use your belt?"

"Just my hand."

"I can tell by the mouth on her." He manhandled me over the edge of the fancy couch we'd been using while he was in the shower, knocking the wind out of me. I tried to lever myself up, but he got between my legs and was pushing into my ass before I could even catch my breath. I gritted my teeth and did what I could to assist with the angle, considering he was going in mostly dry. It burned like a son-of-a-bitch, reminding me of my first time.

"I'll get lube." Ilya hovered beside Bron, like quality control.

"If she wanted lube, she shouldn't have run off. This is nicer than what she would have gotten from that predator who followed her into the trees." He pressed his thumbs harder into what felt like the bruises Ilya had left on my ass, spreading my cheeks so he could watch himself bottom out. "Boy, take off your shirt."

Ilya complied.

"Now undo your jeans and push them down. Show me how hard you are from watching me rail your beautiful wife. Hands behind your back so you don't jerk off."

Ilya grumbled something I didn't catch, but obeyed, his cock bobbing straight out in front of him.

Hell, what I wouldn't do for some lube. Coconut oil. Spit. I'd even settle for petroleum jelly. Freaking anything to make this less unpleasant.

All those times I'd warned Lane to lube her ass before going out on a hunt when we'd been on the Island, and here I was, unprepared again. Why hadn't I assumed anal would be part of Bron's plan sometime tonight? There was nothing he liked better than to use his dick to remind us who was the boss.

It must have been unpleasant for him, too, though, because when he pulled out, he spat twice before sliding back in. My insides stung, but the girth of him, and the feel of him deep inside me, was enough to make me arch back to meet him.

"Poor little whore," he murmured. "Thought you could get Ilya to give you the orgasm you don't deserve while I was busy."

"Ilya likes me," I said through my teeth. God, he was big. At least my first time had been with a guy who'd had the decency to be on the smaller side.

"Ilya would like a knothole in a fence if it smiled at him the way you do."

His thrust jarred me, and my toes came off the ground. I tried bracing myself on my hands, but he tipped me more, giving himself better access and forcing me to lean on my elbows. Could there be a more humiliating position? Then again, if I gave the jackass time to think about it, he could probably come up with five more humiliating positions off the top of his head.

"You're jealous because we like each other and no one likes you," I gasped out. Probably not the brightest thing I'd said to a sadist using my ass, but I was sore, and I also had the female equivalent of blueballs.

"Have I ever given you the mistaken impression I care if people like me?" He pushed the rest of the way in, holding still with his balls pressed tight against me. "So much for teaching you a lesson. Your pussy is dripping everywhere." He chuckled, which made me grimace at the feel of his cock jerking along with his mirth.

"Ilya made sure I was ready for you."

"He should have lubed your ass before I got out of the shower. I wonder why he didn't."

Some sort of silent exchange passed between them, but it was too difficult to twist around to see their non-verbals. All I could see were a few shifts in Ilya's expression.

He fucked me in earnest then, his use hard and jarring. It was about as enjoyable as being fucked with a sandpaper-covered crowbar. After a few minutes, he stopped and pulled out.

Oh no. Now what?

He yanked me upright by the hair, then pushed me toward the bathroom. "Go shower. Don't touch yourself and don't use the damned showerhead to get yourself off."

Was he fucking serious?

"You can't expect me to stay like this," I said, turning to glare at him and rubbing at my sore scalp. My ass felt worse, but I doubted rubbing it would help at all.

He brought up his hand, and I cringed back, but he only tugged on a lock of my hair. His dark eyes were stern. "Obey me, woman."

Something stupid inside me fluttered. Ugh. Why was I like this with them?

He arched a brow at me, and I gazed up at him, close to simpering.

Oh, he was looking for an answer.

"Yes, Bron." I entered the still-steamy bathroom, feeling wobbly and more hard-up than I'd ever been before in my life.

I closed the door most of the way but left it slightly ajar. After I turned on the shower, I heard a series of thwacks. Curiosity got the best of me, and I peeked out through the crack I'd left.

Ilya had his hands on the dining table and Bron was behind him, wielding his heavy leather belt. Each stripe he left on Ilya's back looked painful as hell, but Ilya took it without a sound.

"That's right, you keep your pretty mouth shut," Bron was saying, his voice low. "You wouldn't want the hotel staff to hear you crying like a child. Or is it the presence of your little wife shaming you into silence?"

Cry? I'd never heard Ilya cry, per se, but I'd heard him cry out occasionally when Bron had been in a particularly foul mood.

He hit him a few more times, and even as I flinched, the interplay of muscles in Ilya's strong back mesmerized me. He had pulled his jeans back up, but they were riding low on his hips, as though they were still undone. The man had a beautiful body. There was no wonder why Bron had ordered him to take off his shirt.

"Did you enjoy spanking her, *suka*?" Bron demanded, his voice hard.

"Yes, Bron."

"Did you like playing with her ass?"

"Yes."

I was blushing again. It was my fault for eavesdropping when I should be in the shower. Steam was filling the luxurious bathroom, and here I was watching the two of them while straining my ears to hear what they were saying.

Bron gave an ugly chuckle. "You weren't getting her ready for me at all. You did those things because it made your dick hard." He flicked the belt between Ilya's legs, and must have caught him in the balls, because Ilya went up on his toes and hissed. His body twisted as he tried not to react too strongly. "Thank me for letting you keep your jeans on."

"Thank you, Bron." His voice was strained.

Bron stopped hitting him, but they stayed as they were.

"Was there any other reason you spanked her?"

He breathed carefully for a moment before replying. "I was afraid. When we couldn't find her, I thought someone might have taken her. I warned her at the club not to wander off again without protection, but she didn't listen."

"So now you understand why I discipline you."

"Because it makes your dick hard, and you care what happens to me?"

"I *care*?" Bron scoffed. "I've been trying to teach you to be a man for how many years? We've been alone for most of that time. It's more like a hostage situation than anything." Bron folded the belt in his hand, then walked the length of the room and back. Ilya didn't budge.

"If you don't like being with me, you could quit."

"If I quit, your father would probably kill me."

"Why? You've never said why."

Bron sighed and tipped his head back, as though looking for his patience on the ceiling. He squeezed the bridge of his nose. "For disobeying? Who knows? He has big, dangerous men lined up hoping to catch his notice, but *he* came to offer *me* a job, and then eventually gave me to you. I thought he was punishing me for something, but twelve years? I wasn't even with him for long. I didn't sleep with his wife or any of your sisters. I don't understand why he exiled me."

"You still see me as a burden you must bear." Ilya hadn't moved and was still staring down at the table.

"I hate..." He grabbed the back of Ilya's neck and stood there holding it, as though he was planning to bless him or something. "I hate wondering if we are the way we are together because there haven't been any women around. The island is peaceful, and it has become my home, but we're like two men in a free-range prison. Maybe we only fuck because there's no one else around."

"We've both fucked Delilah. Nothing has changed between us."

"Everything has changed. You're in love with her."

"I—maybe I am."

What? He wasn't.

He couldn't possibly be.

"How am I to know what love is?" he continued. "She's a prisoner, too, now, isn't she? Trapped on that island with us."

Bron's jaw set. "She's temporary. We're not keeping her." He let go of the back of Ilya's neck and stroked his hand down his spine. When he got to his jeans, he pushed them down with both hands, his movements sharp with irritation. I hadn't noticed before that Ilya had been going commando all night. It was hot and interestingly naughty from him. Had Bron ordered him not to wear any? That would be even hotter.

He spat on his hand and worked a couple of fingers into Ilya's ass. I cringed for him. The look on Bron's face didn't bode well for his patience. Bron got behind him and forced his way in with short, ruthless strokes, and I could see Ilya wasn't enjoying himself. My ass throbbed in sympathy.

Ilya leaned on his elbows, his teeth bared, and his eyes screwed shut as Bron hummed with pleasure. I shifted, squeezing my thighs together. Did Bron realize I was watching? He'd known about me listening in on them back on their island, but that didn't mean he was thinking of that now. They probably wouldn't talk about emotional things so freely if they thought I was listening. It was strange they hadn't switched to Russian, but they were speaking English so often now that maybe it was habit.

Gradually, Ilya widened his stance and tipped his hips, giving Bron easier access. Bron growled in appreciation, and Ilya's gasps shifted from sounding like pain to pleasure. His cock jutted between his thighs, hard and untouched. It seemed so cruel not to at least touch him. If I was closer, I'd crawl underneath him and...

A tremor of pleasure ran through me, like a spontaneous mini-orgasm. I bit back a gasp and grimaced. I needed to get in the damned shower before I gave myself away.

Thinking about blowing a guy shouldn't make me so hot, but the thought of getting in there while they were together was seriously turning me on. Besides, it was Ilya. The man was pretty much perfect—especially now that he was more experienced and sure of himself.

I withdrew from my spot at the door, planning to get into the shower before someone walked in. I was still completely dry. Well...not completely.

Ilya whimpered, and Bron laughed.

"Did you come all over the floor, stupid boy? You like my dick so much you don't even need to be touched."

I shuddered in guilty arousal, wondering if I could disobey Bron and get myself off quickly before they came in.

"Fuck, I love how you milk my cock when you come." Bron's voice hitched, and he groaned, swore. "Your wife's ass is delightful, but I also couldn't wait to get back into yours."

I tiptoed back to the door to peek out, and sure enough, there was a glistening puddle on the floor. Bron's hips stuttered, and he held still deep inside Ilya's ass, both of them panting, slick, and beautiful. Bron brushed a tender kiss along the back of Ilya's neck, and I felt even guiltier for watching.

He loved Ilya no matter what he'd said about them being trapped together. Maybe they wouldn't have ended up in a sexual relationship without the forced proximity, but life was weird that way. Walk into a club or a class, meet someone new, change your life. Speculating on how things could have been different was interesting, but pointless.

"We could keep her, you know," Ilya murmured so quietly I almost couldn't hear him.

My heart leapt, leaving me confused. Did I really want them to want me to stay? If they asked, would I actually consider it?

"You really think she would agree?" Bron pulled out. "A woman so lovely, so intelligent? Why would she choose us and the way we live?"

Ilya slowly pushed up from the table. "No one knows where she is. She's at our mercy."

Oh god—what? He isn't serious.

Bron laughed and smacked his ass. "Quit pretending you're callous enough to keep her against her will and clean the mess you made all over the floor."

"You think I wouldn't keep her?" Ilya asked, getting down on all fours.

"I think you'll ask her to stay, she'll refuse, and you'll mope around for at least ten years."

Ilya licked his cum off the floor as though it was an everyday occurrence. Knowing them, it probably was.

When he got to his feet, Bron grabbed his beard. "Open."

Ilya opened his mouth and showed Bron his tongue. Bron shoved his finger in, rubbing it over Ilya's teeth, then shoving it deep enough to make him gag.

"Good boy."

Ilya flushed pink. "If she refuses, maybe you'll see a different side of me."

Bron sighed. "I've seen every side of you, Ilyusha. You don't have it in you to be so diabolical. Now stay there. Your ass is leaking."

He headed my way, so I crossed the room and slipped into the shower, standing directly under the spray and hoping my hair got wet fast enough to fool him. The hot water stung my freshly punished ass, making me wince.

He grabbed a facecloth, then glanced over his shoulder at me, his gaze sliding from my face all the way down my body. Rather than walking out, he came to the shower and reached in, catching my nipple between two cruel fingers. I gasped, the twinge like a bolt of pained pleasure arcing directly to my needy pussy.

"Are you being a good girl in here?" he demanded.

"Yes, Bron."

"No touching yourself. We'll be joining you in a moment."

The slight curve to his lips was sexy as hell.

If I played my cards right, maybe he'd let me orgasm before the night was through.

The bastard. He didn't.

Chapter Fifteen

It was strange being alone on the island with Ilya. Just the two of us. No chance of Bron walking in to give us shit if he found us doing something he didn't approve of.

Ilya had bought some new movies when we were in Saint Petersburg, and we'd slowly been working our way through them, sprawled out on the TV room's cozy couches.

"Do you think that man is wearing makeup?"

"Probably." I glanced over at him.

He was leaning forward, studying the actor.

"There's nothing wrong with men wearing makeup if they want to. In America, men do it all the time—they wear nail polish, too. Dresses. High heels."

He glanced my way, grimacing.

"What?"

"I was going to say men don't do that here, but I don't know what people do in the big cities."

We fell silent and kept watching.

There was a cushion between us—he'd put it there when we'd settled in, as though sitting right next to me was too much of a temptation. Did he think the pillow would be enough of a speed bump to slow down what we both knew was bound to happen?

I tried to concentrate on the movie, but being alone with Ilya made me hyperaware of his every shift in position. Eventually, though, I got drawn into the storyline and the real world faded into the background.

Something brushed my finger, and I looked down. My right hand was on the pillow between us as though it were an armrest. Ilya's gaze was riveted to the screen, but he'd moved his hand closer to me, and his pinkie grazed mine.

I tried to pay attention to the movie. Was he initiating something against Bron's rules? I'd thought I would have to seduce him.

We sat that way a long time—him seemingly oblivious to the fact that we were touching, while my entire focus had narrowed to the inch where our pinky fingers touched. His finger flexed against mine, and I thought he would pull away, but the tip of his finger ran over mine so gently, that for a moment I thought I'd imagined it. I glanced down again, making sure not to move my head. In the room's dimness, the glow from the television made our hands look almost spotlighted—his rough hand next to my much smaller one, his finger stroking mine in long, delicate strokes.

Hell, leave it to Ilya to make grade-school-level flirting exciting. My cheeks tingled. No one had made me blush in years, but this stupid island and its two male inhabitants could tie me in knots and make even my thoughts stammer.

I kept waiting for him to make a move. My imagination ran away with me.

We progressed to hand-holding, his hand big and warm, making me feel weirdly safe. Men were dangerous—they'd always been dangerous to me, other than my father who hardly paid attention to me unless he thought I was slacking, and my brothers whom I still didn't think of as grown men. Considering some things Ilya had done to me, and had watched Bron do to me, why did he make me feel safe?

Considering he'd told Bron he might keep me here against my will, I shouldn't feel safe at all. The truth was, we both knew him better than that.

He casually flipped my hand palm up and traced the creases in my palm, the flex lines in my wrist, drew circles in my hand. It tickled, and the sensation made me squirm a little. How was a girl supposed to focus on a movie with a hot guy so patiently seducing her?

I dragged the pillow out from between us and threw it on the floor, then moved closer to him, pressing against his side until he had no choice but to put his arm around me. He sighed in satisfaction, like the true cuddle-slut I knew he was deep down. I rested my hand palm up on his thigh, and he took the hint, continuing his slow stroking. When my hand and arm were almost painfully sensitized right up to the elbow, I pulled off my sloppy old T-shirt, not missing the sharp look he gave me.

Not allowed, Delilah.

I ignored the silent warning, focusing instead on his intent gaze, inspecting every inch he could see, as though he'd never seen it before. I crawled over his lap, settling facedown across it, resting my breasts between his parted thighs.

"What are you doing?" he demanded.

I looked up at him, and his gaze had darted to the door as though Bron might come in and catch us. He shifted under me in apparent discomfort.

"I'm not doing anything he's told us we can't do," I said slyly.

"Your naked breasts are touching my leg."

"You're wearing sweatpants and a T-shirt. Even if I was naked, there would still be a layer of clothing between us."

"I don't think it's enough."

"He's not even here, Ilya. He won't be back until tomorrow."

"But that doesn't mean we should break his rules."

"I'll put my shirt back on if you want me to, but his rules are stupid, and he only made them because he's jealous. The whole reason I'm here is so you learn to act tough to impress your father—that's not going to happen if you squeal in horror and hide your eyes every time a woman is innocently topless." I sat up and grabbed my shirt. "I wanted you to do the thing you were doing to my hand, but on my back instead."

There was a long pause, which included the movie, since he'd scrambled for the remote and was holding it like a comfort object.

"You're half naked."

"There's nothing sexual about my back."

"I...I very much disagree."

"You don't want to touch my back?"

"Of course, I do."

"Then do it. Do you have to obey Bron in every little thing—anticipate everything that might upset him?"

"Well, yes."

"Is he going to come back and beat you whether or not you disobeyed?"

"Yes."

"So, if you disobey, then at least you'll know you've earned it."

He gave a slightly hysterical sounding laugh. Slowly, he pulled my shirt out of my unresisting hands. I settled back onto his lap, and he placed his hand between my shoulder blades.

"We've done a lot more than this."

"I know, but we're so...unsupervised right now."

"We are."

"I suppose if he's going to punish me either way, it makes sense, but then I could do anything—we could do anything."

"Yes. Anything we want to do. He's only in charge of making decisions for you now because you allow it, Ilya."

"So, you think you should make decisions for me instead?"

"I think you should make your own decisions based on what you want. You're too old to listen to a nursemaid, even if he's big and scary and hot."

His grunt of acknowledgement was very Bron-like.

He ran his palm slowly over my back, making me sigh with pleasure. Most men I'd been with never bothered with anything as innocent as a backrub.

"Your skin is so smooth and soft," he mused. "It's like petting a puppy."

I blurted a laugh. "A puppy?"

"That's funny?"

"It's adorable, but most women would probably prefer you say something like 'your skin is like silk.'"

"I've never touched silk. Maybe I should say 'your skin is like a green tree after stripping off the bark'?"

I buried my face in my hands and tried not to laugh, but my body shook with mirth.

"A stripped tree is very smooth," he said defensively. His hands had stopped moving, and I squirmed until he took the hint.

He traced random shapes on my back, and I quivered and sighed, and squeaked when it tickled too much.

"Touching you is making my dick hard," he complained, shifting beneath me.

"You're supposed to pretend it isn't."

"Can't you feel it?"

Well, it was digging into my side.

"Does your cock get hard when you touch a stripped green tree?"

"Trees aren't warm and pretty and have curves that make my teeth ache to bite them."

"Ilya! You wouldn't really bite me, would you?"

"Right here," he murmured, brushing a fingertip along the spot between my neck and my shoulder. I shivered. "And here." He swatted my ass, leaving a delicious sting.

I gasped at his audacity. "You'd bite my ass?"

He drew squiggles on my back, which made me hum with pleasure.

"When I spanked you at the hotel, it was all I could think about. I want to leave teeth marks so people know you're mine."

"Okay, werewolf man."

"Maybe I will gobble you up like the wolf with Red Riding Hood. Bron will have to cut me open with an axe to get you out." He growled and grabbed a handful of my ass.

I laughed. "It's a good thing you don't have Wi-Fi. I can't imagine what your porn searches would look like."

"I only have my mind and my notebooks."

"Let me read one."

"No."

"Where do you keep them?"

"I burned them."

"You did not!" I scrambled off his lap and gave him an evil grin before dashing from the room. My socked feet skidded on the hardwood. He chased me, of course, as I led him directly to his bedroom.

I'd never been in his room before—or Bron's, for that matter. The door wasn't locked, and so I burst in and scanned the room for anything that looked like a journal. Groaning shelves held books and spiral bound notebooks, along with wooden sculptures of animals and screaming faces. A dustless dresser. A tidily made bed.

Where would I even start?

I heard him hesitate at the door. "You shouldn't be in here."

"Why? Is Daddy going to spank you for having a girl in your room?"

He came up behind me and hovered there a moment before opening a drawer and handing me a folded shirt.

"What's this for?"

"To cover yourself."

"It's not cold in here."

"It's for me, not you."

"Why? Is my naked body ugly to you? I know you're used to men's bodies. A naked woman must look strange to you."

He shook his head, looking shy and amused. "I've never seen a woman as beautiful as you."

I turned to face him. He was struggling not to let his gaze drop from my face to my breasts. "You're welcome to look, Ilya. You can even touch if you like. Or bite—just not too hard, okay?"

His hungry gaze lowered, devouring me. He raised a shaking hand and brushed a knuckle over my already pebbled nipple.

"You've seen my breasts several times. What's the big deal?"

"There's no one to stop me. I could do anything to you—make you scream with pleasure or with pain—and no one would hear." He withdrew his hand and gazed into my eyes. "It's too much trust to place in a man. What makes me any better than the one who attacked you in the park?"

"You're not like him. You'd stop if I asked you to." I smiled up at him, watching him struggle with his conscience. "I'm here voluntarily...for whatever you want, short of maiming me or killing me." I put my hands behind my back, offering my breasts to him.

He threw the shirt on his dresser.

"Phew. I thought you were really going to make me put on a shirt."

"Take off the rest." He leaned in and brushed his lips against mine before pulling away.

I turned my back on him and perused his bookshelves. "No."

When he didn't say anything, I peeked over my shoulder. He was frowning, apparently not sure what he should do with my refusal.

Well, if he didn't know, I wasn't going to tell him yet.

I strolled to his bedside table and pulled a notebook from the top of a pile. When I flipped it open, I expected him to pull it from my hand, but he let me do it.

Damn. It was in Russian.

"You didn't tell me you wrote your journals in secret code."

He grinned. "You Americans are always trying to steal our secrets, so I wrote my journals in Russian so you wouldn't understand, years before we even met."

"That was good foresight."

"Thank you. I thought so."

I kept flipping, and he tried to grab the book from my hand, but I danced out of reach. Obviously, if he was still trying to get it away from me, there must be something good in it.

He made a noise of exasperation but let me keep flipping pages.

There were rough sketches of Bron with words underneath I couldn't read. Several were just of his face.

"Does he read these?"

"No. He wouldn't care. It's sentimental drivel."

I flipped through to the back and was about to close it when I caught sight of something else. I'd passed the picture, but when I flipped back a few pages, there was a sketch of me sleeping.

It was lovingly done, making me look like a princess frozen by a spell rather than the messy sleeper I'd always thought I was.

The jig was up.

Arching a brow, I glanced at him.

"When did you do this one?" I asked.

He shrugged. "Maybe three weeks ago?"

"Is this from memory?"

He paused long enough that I could guess his answer. "No."

I...wasn't sure how to feel about that. "You sat in my room and sketched me while I was sleeping?"

"Yes."

"I would have woken up."

I thought I woke up every time they came to my room.

"You sleep deeply."

Had they done things to me that I'd slept through? "No, I don't."

"You do." He said earnestly. "Very, *very* deeply."

Rat.

"And you sneak in and draw me."

"I have."

"And have you done anything else to me?"

He gave me a quiet smile but didn't answer. Instead, he went to the bookcase and absently picked up a carving, turning it over in his hand like a stress ball.

"Did you make those?"

"Yes. I taught myself how when I was a boy. They're not very good, but they were a way to pass the time."

"Were?"

"There's no reason to spend my time carving when there is a beautiful woman here to cheat me at cards."

"Just because you're terrible at cards doesn't mean I cheat." I put my hand out for the carving. He passed it to me, and I examined the unpainted seal and all its minute details. "I guess you'll have time to do more art when I go home."

He shrugged. "If."

Frowning, I handed the seal back. "What do you mean?"

"If you go back. You could choose to stay."

I blinked at him. "Stay here?"

"Yes. With us."

Thoughts of my family crowded in. The kids were older now and didn't really need me, but my parents still expected me to help at the store, and they needed me to take care of the house. I couldn't simply call them and tell them I wasn't coming back—walk away from my whole life. And what about school? I'd had plans, vague as they were.

Besides, he didn't really mean it. Or if he did now, he'd change his mind once he stopped living in the middle of nowhere with no women around. Just because I was convenient, and he found me attractive, didn't mean he was in love with me.

And I couldn't possibly be in love with him.

We froze in place, staring at each other. What was going on behind those dark eyes?

"If you impress your father, you'll be out in the real world. There'll be a lot of women to choose from. You shouldn't settle for me because I'm convenient."

His brows knit. "Why would I care about other women?"

"You only think you like me as much as you do because you don't know other women. You haven't been out meeting people. Did you see how women reacted to you when we were at the club in Saint Petersburg? Or even when we were out shopping? You could have your choice of women."

"I had my choice of an island full of beautiful, intelligent women. You were the one I wanted."

"You didn't even know me then."

"I watched you with your friend, Lane. I saw when you went to visit Clover. You have a good heart, Delilah. A kind heart." He put down the carving and grabbed my hand. His was warm and firm. I liked how it felt, and that was a damned dangerous thing. "How many women would have been so patient with me?"

I stared at him, stunned. They hadn't chosen me only because they liked how I looked?

Silence fell between us again. He broke eye contact first.

"Think on it. We have time yet."

He left me there.

I stretched out on his bed and leafed through his notebooks.

If anything was going to happen between us today, he would have to initiate it.

He didn't.

Chapter Sixteen

"Let's go for a walk," Ilya suggested, washing the flour off his hands. The bread he'd made was rising. It was less sweet than the bread I was used to back home, but I liked his better.

"Good idea." I got up from the table and stretched, putting down the romance novel I'd been reading aloud to him as he worked.

We grabbed our jackets and put on boots, since last night's rain had left the ground muddy. Yana's boots were big on me, but they were better than none. I had my own beautiful new coat, but for mucking around on the island, I wore one of Ilya's old ones. He chuckled as I zipped it, flipping up the collar to protect my neck from the wind. Ilya had rolled the sleeves back for me the first time I'd worn it, and they had stayed that way.

"My coat is determined to swallow you whole."

"Until I met you two, I'd never felt small before."

He kissed my forehead, and I couldn't help but melt a little on the inside.

"Where are you going?" Bron demanded, startling me.

"For a walk," Ilya replied, eyes narrowed.

"No fucking."

Ilya made a rude gesture and walked out. I expected Bron to stalk out the door after him. He looked torn.

"It's just a walk."

He grunted, hefting a greasy metal gadget in his hand. It was apparently part of a tiller. Although he'd been working on it all day, I couldn't tell if he'd fixed it.

"Don't let him fuck you."

"Why not?"

"Because his dick is mine, and he doesn't use it unless I say so."

I sighed. "Are you going to keep him under your thumb forever?"

He harrumphed and left.

I doubted Ilya had nefarious plans for me, considering he hadn't jumped me when Bron was gone the whole day before.

As soon as I exited the house and caught up with Ilya, he took my hand. Was this a new obsession of his, or was being able to show affection a novelty?

"I hate him," Ilya grumbled.

"We both know that's not true."

We walked for a long time until we reached the shore, then followed along it.

"For a place called the White Sea, it's a pretty blue."

"It depends on the time of year. There is ice for months in the winter."

It wasn't the same blue as the water off the island they'd stolen me from, but the sun glittering on the surface dazzled my eyes. The rocky shore rolled like motionless grey ocean swells. Birds wheeled overhead, darting down from time to time to dive-bomb small fish.

We stopped now and then to throw stones into the ocean. My chest felt looser—lighter. Life was slow here, and although at first I'd felt strangely cut off from the world with no internet access or phone, it was peaceful when Bron wasn't terrorizing us. There was so much time here compared to back home. I had always wondered how people ever had time for hobbies, but Ilya's sketching and carving wasn't so odd.

What else was there to do with no social media? No Netflix?

It was like camping with indoor plumbing.

"Are you going to miss it here when you live on the mainland?" I asked. "Or are you excited to move on with your life?"

Ilya threw another rock, and it skipped along the water's surface so far that it felt like it might go on forever. "If you'd asked me at eighteen, I would have said you were ridiculous for asking such a question. All I've ever wanted was to please my father and move to the mainland. Now? I couldn't say."

He skipped another rock, but this one didn't go as far.

"In the past few years, we started taking trips to the mainland—at first to shop, and then to introduce me to women. When that didn't work, we went all the way to where we met you. I can't say I'm unhappy here, but life never changes. Usually I like our life here—especially when Bron goes a bit soft on me. When he says he resents having to be here, I want to burn the house and the island to ash."

"Is that what you really want?" I doubted it.

His dark eyes narrowed as he looked down at me. "You know what I want."

I shivered. How did he switch so quickly from sweet to dark intensity? If he'd never met Bron, which Ilya would he be? It was so hard to guess.

"What do you want? Honestly." I asked, genuinely curious.

He grabbed me by the upper arms. I gasped. Slowly, he slid his hands down my arms to my hands. He kept the right hand and reached into his pocket, and I didn't understand what was happening until there was a big diamond ring on my finger.

"What is this?" I asked, possibly more flabbergasted than I'd been when they'd kidnapped me.

"A ring."

"For what?"

"It tells men who you belong to." He said it with a churlishness he'd definitely picked up from Bron, but I got the feeling he was embarrassed.

"This is for our pretend engagement?" I asked.

"Of course."

"You didn't need to buy such a big fake ring." It looked obscene on my finger. I was going to take someone's eye out with it—maybe mine. "No one will believe this is real."

"It is real. It was my mother's."

I swallowed. I didn't know a lot about diamonds, but I was pretty sure the one I was now wearing would have paid for this island.

"What happened to her?"

"Vas had her killed." He shrugged. "Officially, it was a car accident."

"I'm so sorry."

He shrugged. "I didn't know her well. She was beautiful. I think she was kind, but maybe that's only how I wish to remember her."

"I'll make sure you get it back after we visit your family. Maybe you should hang onto it until we actually go. It might fall off or something." It fit perfectly, but the idea of wearing something so expensive and sentimental gave me the heebie-jeebies.

"No."

He turned away and threw another rock. Were his cheeks red, or was it the wind?

"Is there a reason you put it on my right hand instead of my left?"

"That's where such rings go when you are Russian. You're in Russia and you will be a Russian wife. If we go to America, you can wear it on your other hand if you wish."

"What do you mean? I only have a few more weeks here and then I'm going home."

He said something in Russian, but between the language and the wind, I couldn't make out his tone, let alone what he was saying.

"What?"

"You're the only thing in the world that's mine, wife. I won't let you go." His expression was unreadable.

Was he...joking?

It didn't sound like a joke.

"I'm a person. You can't just keep me," I said, intending to sound jovial. Instead, it came out worried and weak.

"Why not?" he demanded, the words clipped. "I love you. I will give you a good life."

The words made me happy, and that was a dangerous thing. Did I love him, too? I had feelings for him, but were they love? Attraction, yes. Fondness, yes. Would I miss him when I went home? Absolutely.

"It's not only your decision, Ilya. I get to choose, too."

"Then choose me. Your family is full of terrible, selfish people who don't appreciate the sacrifices you make for them."

"They may not be perfect, but they're still my family. I'm a big girl. I don't need you to rescue me from my old life."

He chewed at his cheek, his brows a surly line. Long strides carried him away from me and he paced the shore, pushing his long hair out of his face with short, impatient movements every time the wind blew it.

"Is it because you want Bron instead?" he asked. "Because what belongs to me belongs to him."

I blinked at him. "So that goes for your actual wife, too, not just the random whore you're banging?"

He grabbed my arm and hauled me against him. I caught my breath at the fury in his gaze. "I don't like that word."

"Which one?"

"Don't call yourself names."

"Why not? Bron does."

"Sometimes Bron says things when he's talking with his dick, but that isn't how he really feels."

"How would you know? Is he writing secret love poetry about me?"

His mouth twisted wryly. "I doubt that, but he wouldn't be so cruel to you unless he felt something for you."

I shook my head. "Love isn't supposed to hurt."

He slid his hand up my arm and held my throat so gently I wasn't sure if it was a threat or a caress. "But my wife enjoys love that hurts."

The roughness of his deep voice made the pit of my stomach drop like the first freefall of a rollercoaster.

"How do you know I don't dream about sweet and gentle lovemaking?"

"I've watched you come for Bron too many times to believe that."

He kissed me, and I melted for him.

"I don't care if you love me or not. You will stay."

Just like that? He thought he could put a ring on my finger and declare ownership? Fuck that.

"What makes you think I'm yours? This isn't a magic ring. It doesn't change reality."

"How can you refuse me?" he said with a cruel laugh. "You don't have any way to get home. You don't even know where you are."

I opened my mouth to argue that I could figure it out, but many steps lay between me and getting home. Just how hard was I willing to fight to get there? He'd get bored with me eventually and send me back. There was no need for me to consider trying to swim to the mainland, right?

Besides, Bron wouldn't really let him keep me, as though I were a stray cat.

And if Bron was also unreasonable?

When we went to visit his family, we'd be on the mainland already. Then I could sneak off and...what? Find a job? I'd probably have to do sex work and hope to make enough to pay for airfare home. Then somehow travel with no passport. Maybe I could find my way to an embassy, but I didn't even have a phone or internet connection to look up where one was.

I had nothing here except Ilya, Bron, and their good will.

"Putting a ring on a woman's finger doesn't mean she's your property."

"No, it means she's going to be my wife." He pulled me close and kissed my neck, not letting go when I struggled. He bit the side of my neck, and I gasped at the unexpected pain. My body was responding to the way he was acting, and I really needed to get out of here before he took my physical responses to mean I was conceding. "Our engagement was supposed to be an act for my father, but now it's not."

He let me pull free. My neck was throbbing, but so were other, more treacherous parts of me.

I backed away from him, stumbling over a rock before righting myself.

"Run from me all you want. Where can you go?"

He had a good point, but I ran anyway, feeling like my boots might fall off between one step and the next. I took the chance of looking back at him once. He hadn't moved, so I slowed to a walk as I got into the relative safety of the trees, trying to sort my thoughts.

I walked for what felt like ages, filling my lungs with the clean, crisp air while I watched the birds. I thought I spotted Ilya's raven a few times.

A small part of me was still afraid of the possibility of wolves. I hadn't heard any since the one time the guys were hunting me, though, and I could almost believe it was them being creepy weirdoes. The memory of the beautiful, deadly sound still made my bones feel hollow. Then again, considering what Bron had done to the man in the park and their complete lack of remorse, maybe wolves should be the least of my concern.

Did he really mean to keep me here forever? Knowing Ilya, he did. He wasn't the kind of guy to say one thing and mean another. I was trying hard to be afraid and worried—to be angry that he thought he could make such a huge decision without at least discussing what I wanted with me.

The only thing I felt was relieved.

I wasn't ready to leave the two of them and go back to playing the full-time Cinderella role in my family. Sure, there was work to do here, too, but it felt fair. More evenly divided. Here I felt like the main character in my life instead of being a servant in the background of everyone else's.

So, the sex was rough. Ilya wasn't wrong about me liking it that way.

What would I miss from my real life? Not much came to mind. I'd miss getting new books, but knowing Ilya, he'd buy them for me if I asked. As for people? Even though I'd raised my siblings, we weren't friends—we'd been more like fellow hostages. They could be cute when they wanted something, but they were all ambitious and competitive, and I found them exhausting. They were also busy with their own lives, which was as it should be.

Being here meant no one could ask me for favors. My parents couldn't guilt trip me into giving up my few plans to work at the store or clean the always immaculate house. I'd thought I loved my family, so why did the idea of living so far away from them and only visiting them occasionally fill me with exhilaration? It tasted like freedom.

The only person I really missed was Lane.

What did that say about me as a person?

Guilt gnawed at me. I needed to go home when my time here was over, but if Ilya kept me here, and it wasn't my fault...

No. This was ridiculous. I had plans to go to school with the money Bron had promised me. I wasn't going to stay here to be a live-in...what? Piece of ass?

I thought about all the different fields of study I could take, but going back to school now felt daunting. I'd graduated from high school at seventeen, but I'd been cleaning and raising kids since I was old enough to hold a rag. I didn't even know who the hell I was, what I liked, or what I was good at. It wasn't as though I had aspirations to become anything in particular—not the way Clover did, with her dream of being a doctor. My big dream had been to escape my role as my parents' unpaid support staff.

But what was I here? Then again, what were they? We worked around the house and in the garden and fields, and with the animals. There was no pressure to *be* anything as permission to exist. There was no mortgage or rent to pay that I knew of, and no bills for the solar and hydro power we used. We grew or made most of our food here other than sugar and some spices.

Something in the environment changed—it wasn't a sound or a smell, just a feeling. I wasn't alone.

I scanned the area and caught sight of him between one tree and another. A flash, and then he was gone again.

Was he spying on me or stalking me?

I kept walking, directionless other than trying to move away from him. Had he been trailing me the whole time? Of course, he had been. It didn't seem to matter what I was doing, Ilya was always paying attention.

"I know you're there!" I called out, trying to calm my nerves. Not knowing what his intentions were, had made me start shaking. This was Ilya, not Bron. He was nowhere near as scary. This possessive edge he'd developed had changed things a bit, but it didn't mean he was suddenly going to skin me alive and wear me as a suit.

I picked up speed, trying not to trip on my boots or hurt my screwed-up ankle.

"Leave me alone! I need time to think, and you're not helping!"

Was that a twig snapping behind me, or was it one breaking under my foot? How could he move so silently when I was still loud enough for them to hear me on the mainland? They didn't need a bell to keep track of me when my feet did an admirable job of letting everyone know where I was.

I slowed to a walk again. Either I had actually lost him this time, or he was only planning to keep an eye on me to make sure I was safe.

I found a strangely shaped tree that seemed familiar, and from there located the wider path that led to the old fisherman's cabin. It seemed as if I kept finding my way there.

A smarter woman would have avoided the place, but the log walls were comforting when it felt like Ilya was watching me from the trees.

Inside, I assessed the work I'd done the last time I was here. The dirt floor was clean of debris now, and I'd also wiped the cobwebs out of the corners. The place could use some intact chairs.

As secret clubhouses went, it wasn't very secret or homey, but it was the closest thing I had to privacy on the island, other than my bedroom, which apparently was public access when I was asleep. With all the fresh air and exercise I got here, no wonder I conked out at night. That they came into my room sometimes while I was asleep should have disgusted me, but it turned me on. I really needed to get a therapist.

I was sitting on the cold hearth when the door slammed open. Startled, I leapt to my feet.

Ilya loomed in the doorway, shadowed and shaggy, blocking the only exit unless I suddenly developed the power to freeze time so I could squeeze out one of the small windows. I didn't even know if they opened.

"Why are you hiding from me?" he demanded.

"I told you I need time to think."

"I already thought for both of us. You only need to cooperate." He entered and shut the door behind him. His gaze took in the work I'd done on my prior visits, but I wasn't sure if he approved.

"I hope you don't mind I cleaned up in here." Maybe trying to have a normal conversation with him would snap him out of this weird, dangerous mood he was in.

He shrugged. "I used to hide here when I was a boy. There wasn't anything worth salvaging."

"Hide?" I asked. "Who were you hiding from? Your nanny?"

"No, from my brothers. I was small for my age—or at least small compared to them."

"They weren't nice to you?"

"They were children hoping to win our father's approval so they could leave this place."

I wrinkled my nose in sympathy. "What did they do to you?"

He shrugged. "What brothers do. Stole my clothes. Tied me to trees. Whipped me and dripped soda on me so the ants would bite."

What the fuck? Was that what kids were like when they grew up without access to the internet—they went full-on *Lord of the Flies*?

"My brothers didn't do things like that."

"Your brothers weren't encouraged to be cruel and competitive?"

I shook my head. "No. Our parents raised us to be useful and obedient. You definitely had it worse."

He toyed with the folded net I'd hung on some nails. It was thick and rustic-looking and felt at least quasi-decorative.

"You only had a few years of peace after they left, and then Bron came and started it all again."

"What Bron does to me isn't the same."

"Maybe it's different because you both like it."

The way he prowled closer didn't make me feel safe.

"After Bron moved here, I was filled with confusion. He stripped me naked every night and beat me and said nothing about how my cock would harden. One day he found me here stroking myself. When I admitted I'd been thinking about him, he took my ass on that table as a punishment for my perversion." His throat bobbed with emotion, his expression contemplative.

"Did he take his time?"

"Not really, but it could have been worse." He unzipped his coat and threw it on the floor.

"What are you doing?"

"You've accepted my ring, so I'm going to explore what's mine."

"I agreed to pose as your fiancée. I haven't agreed to anything else."

"We shall see."

I tried to scoot past him, but he lunged and grabbed me, then stripped me as I struggled to get away, not stopping until I was naked and cold. The cabin's log walls blocked the wind, but that didn't mean it was as warm as the house.

"Kneel and take me in your mouth."

"It's cold!"

"Shut up and do as you're told," he said, voice gruff.

I blinked at him, but his gaze was determined. He grabbed my shoulder and pushed me down. At least his jacket was warm under my knees.

Was refusing worth making him angry? It was just a blowjob.

Slowly, I unbuckled his belt, then unfastened his pants and dragged them down, forgetting how cold I was when I freed his cock. His arousal sparked mine.

"What has you so hard?" I demanded.

"I told you to shut up." He tangled his hand in my hair and jammed his cock between my lips, making them stretch wide around him, then held me where he wanted me as he fucked my mouth.

I pressed my thighs together, liking this far too much. What the hell was going on with him?

"Look at me," he demanded, yanking off his T-shirt with his free hand so he could get an unimpeded view. I gazed up his hard body to the flint of his eyes, gagging, eyes watering, as he took what he wanted. It was fast and rough. I was feeling needy by the time his cock bucked in my mouth, and he sprayed the back of my throat with cum. "Good." He pulled out, and I swallowed and wiped the cum-infused drool from my chin.

My jaw hurt, but I needed relief.

"Lie back."

"What are you—"

He gently smacked my cheek, the warning clear in his gaze. "Do as I say, woman."

I held my cheek, shocked. "You've been spending too much time with Bron. It doesn't have to be like this between two people who care about each other."

"Now!" he barked.

Startled, I did as I was told, not sure where he wanted me. His jacket was already losing the warmth from his body and the cold was creeping up through the thick fabric. He came down over top of me and nibbled and bit his way down my body as I gasped complaints. I was still annoyed with him, but apparently my body didn't care.

He settled between my legs and looped his arms beneath them, then spread me open with his fingers. The warm breath that curled around my pussy made me shiver.

When he lowered his mouth to me, I dug my fingers into the lining of the jacket I lay on, not sure if he'd get offended if I grabbed his hair the way my hands ached to. He attacked me like he was hungry and impatient, and needed my orgasm to survive. It was ruthless and intense. I'd never had a lover who'd gone down on me like they'd die without my pussy. My heart fluttered, so full of adrenaline it felt like it might burst. I whimpered and writhed. A wave of heat washed through me. How had I ever thought it was cold in here?

"Fuck!" I meant to beg for mercy, but he groaned against my clit, and I lost the ability to think.

I whined and writhed beneath him, thrusting against his mouth, not caring about anything but the aching, desperate need. He was huge and controlling on top of me, and there was no stopping him. I pushed at his head with my hands, overwhelmed, but he only tugged me tighter against his mouth, his wicked tongue relentless as it tortured my clit.

The pressure in me exploded. I arched beneath him, shoulders the only part of me touching the ground as he kept going, forcing the pulsing release to go on and on, until I was begging him to stop and trying in vain to push him away.

When he finally relented, my legs shook, and I lay there drifting in a shivery haze.

"Fuck," I said again, my voice ridiculously breathy.

"I love the way you whimper and squeal while I pleasure you."

I flushed.

Oh jeez. Did I really make obnoxious noises?

I pushed to my feet, feeling wobbly. Cold was creeping in. When I reached for my clothes, he tugged them away.

"I'm freezing!" I protested.

"I'm not done with you, wife." His voice was a growl.

"Can't we go back into the house where it's warm?" I tried to jam my foot back into my boot, but without my sock, it got stuck near the top.

"Bron is there." Ilya caught me around the waist and pulled me away from my boots. "As my wife, you must learn obedience."

"I'm not your wife, and obedience isn't my thing."

He sat on the coat and put me facedown over his lap. I tried to get up.

"Stay, woman."

My body went hot all over. I'd dated a few dominants, but they'd only been kind of bossy. This was more like Bron speaking through Ilya—not a bear I wanted to poke.

He fumbled between us and pulled his belt free from his waist.

No way. He wouldn't!

He put the heavy buckle in his hand and wound the belt around it.

"I'm sorry, Ilya."

"You say that as easily as you ignored me. If you were truly sorry, you wouldn't have tried to leave after I forbade it."

The first crack of the belt was loud but not terribly painful, and I almost laughed in relief. It stung, but it wasn't anything I couldn't take. The next was harder, and I hissed in a breath.

Had he said how many he was going to give me? He hadn't when he was spanking me at the hotel, and Bron wasn't going to come by to interrupt and inadvertently save me this time.

The belt hurt far worse than his hand, stinging and making me shift and yelp. The blows came harder and faster as he became more confident.

"Please, Ilya. I'm sorry!"

It went on until I kicked, then eventually went limp, sobbing. When he stopped, my world was a red haze of pain.

He was breathing hard. My ass was on fire and throbbed like it had its own heartbeat.

Why was he so angry? Was trying to leave such a big deal?

"I'm sorry," I whispered again, not sure what I was sorry about.

"Why does hurting you only make me want to hurt you more?" When had he started shaking?

The pain was receding to a more manageable level, but I had the feeling it would take a few days before the ache went away entirely.

He leaned sideways, then started going through his coat pockets as I stared at the glittering ring on my finger. The world felt surreal. I was hot and cold and turned on and calm and angry, and I also felt like I wasn't really in touch with reality.

"What are you looking for?"

"Something most men don't need to carry, just in case."

Band-Aids? Was I bleeding? Between the biting and the belting, I wouldn't be surprised.

A cold packet of something landed on my back.

"What is that?" I couldn't see it well enough to read the label.

"Kindness."

He spread my legs, and I was so tired from the beating that I let him do it.

Was that a lube packet? Damn it.

"Ilya, no!" I tried to snap my legs back together, but he gripped the inside of one thigh with bruising fingers that were a warning not to interfere with his plans.

"Hold still," he said harshly. "If you fight, I'll hurt you more—and damn me, but I'd like to."

Reluctantly, I relaxed my legs, going still and compliant. I wasn't stupid enough to test him now, while I could tell his adrenaline was still running high.

He lowered his mouth to my ass and investigated the damage he'd done by brushing his lips over the marks he'd made. My backside throbbed, but the burning paired with his gentle investigation made my pussy twitch with an orgasmic aftershock. His scalding tongue dipped into the valley of my ass cheeks, and I buried my face in the coat, inhaling the scent of gasoline and wood smoke. I didn't want him to do it, but I didn't stop him as he stroked at my back hole with his tongue, the electric feel of it making me squirm and struggle. His big hand kept me from sliding away.

I heard the click of the lube bottle's cap and then cold liquid slid over my skin.

"Isn't my pussy good enough?" I complained.

"The very thought of your pussy makes my cock ache to be inside you. So hot. So wet. And the grip on my cock..." He groaned.

My legs spread wider, inviting him to take what he wanted. Instead, he coaxed his finger into my ass with patience that made me impatient. I didn't enjoy anal that much, but knowing he'd never done it before and yet bottomed for Bron all the time made me more than willing.

I expected it would be awkward and probably painful because of his inexperience, but at least he was using lube.

A second finger didn't go in any more easily than the first, and he was muttering to himself in Russian. Hopefully, he wasn't expecting me to answer him, because even though I'd learned a little, I didn't recognize what he was saying.

He put me belly down on the coat and hauled me up by the hips.

"Tell me if I do this wrong."

"If I say you're already doing it wrong, will you stop?"

"No." He sounded amused. "But you're welcome to give me advice."

He lined himself up and slowly worked the head of his thick cock into my ass. He swore in Russian, occasionally hissing, but I couldn't tell if it was with pain or pleasure. With my eyes screwed shut and my teeth gritted, I tried to ignore the cramping in my guts.

Unlike Bron, at least he gave me time to adjust. Ilya knew what it was like when Bron did it to him.

When he was balls-deep, he groaned, shuddering.

"This is very...different. I prefer your pussy, but this is—"

He grunted and started to move, as though he couldn't help himself. Why was hearing him enjoy my body so hot? I was used to stoic men who took their pleasure and maybe went as far as breathing differently when they came, but Ilya was vocal in his appreciation. It felt like a compliment even if I wished like hell he was smaller. My skin was covered in goose bumps, and the parade of them over my body made me shudder.

"Fuck, this is good," he mumbled to himself as his hips took up an unsteady rhythm. "So fucking tight."

I was glad one of us didn't feel like we were having our guts stirred with a greased telephone pole.

When an uncomfortable whimper escaped me, he was kind enough to slow down, groaning quietly with each thrust. Soon, my body adjusted, and I rocked back to meet him—enjoying it even though I was still annoyed with him.

Being his first for this, too, was an interesting feeling—as though I were corrupting him one hole at a time, even though he was the one buried in my ass. I reached between my legs and scraped my nails over his balls, making him gasp and his cock flex inside me. I moaned in appreciation, feeling like I might get off even without him paying attention to my clit.

The door banged open.

Of fucking course.

Ilya jerked out of me, on his feet so quickly I didn't have time to react other than to fall flat without the support of his hands.

"The fuck are you two doing?" Bron snarled.

We are so dead.

He caught Ilya by the neck and shook him. Ilya tried to break his hold, but Bron grabbed his hand, twisted his arm behind his back, and forced him to his knees.

"I was fucking her ass," Ilya snapped, trying to swing at Bron with his free hand. He must have connected with something because Bron swore and kneed Ilya in the side of the head. Ilya went down on his side, but grabbed Bron's ankle and jerked, sending him sprawling. As the two of them wrestled, I crept away, snatching up my clothes and doing my best to dress before they noticed.

Once I'd dressed, I skirted the pinwheeling fists and slipped out the door.

There was no point in running when they'd probably be pounding the crap out of each other for a while, so I zipped up Ilya's old coat and headed toward the house. My ass ached from the belting I'd gotten. I'd left my underwear off and tucked them in my coat pocket. The rub of fabric against my ass still hurt, but the memory of what he'd done was hot, even if I'd thought I'd hated it at the time. I was tender inside, too, and the sensation was making me walk more carefully than I had been on my way to the cabin.

Ugh. Men.

The two of them needed to sort out their issues because I was tired of being underfoot when they were butting heads.

If Bron had shown up a bit earlier, then maybe I wouldn't have gotten the cranky end of Ilya's belt.

What had that been about, anyway? Would his family really expect me to be that submissive, or had he given in to his sadistic urges since Bron hadn't been around to stop him?

Why weren't the birds singing?

Hadn't they been a moment ago?

I stopped and looked around me. Trees and more trees. I wasn't even sure I was going the right way to get back to the house, but the island was only so big. Once I found the shore, I'd follow it.

The feeling of being watched nagged at the back of my brain.

Was that a growl?

A twig snapped.

Did wolves snap twigs when they moved through the forest? It seemed unlikely, but still...

I moved faster. Should I climb a tree? Wolves could definitely run faster than I could, but they couldn't climb—not that I'd climbed anything in years. Maybe I couldn't climb either.

Something dropped over my head, falling heavily around me. I tripped and fell to my knees, and a shocked scream escaped me. A net? I turned my head and found both men behind me, grinning evilly.

Their fight had apparently been short-lived. Ilya had a busted lip, and Bron's cheek was bruised, but they both had the same look in their eye—which didn't bode well for me.

I tried to struggle out from under the old net, but there was a lot of it, and I didn't reach the edge before they were on me. One of them scooped my legs out from under me, and they jerked at the net, which closed me in like a bag. I panicked, screaming and struggling, but they both seemed far too at ease with manhandling the thing.

"These old nets are harder to throw," Ilya observed.

"Heavier, too." Bron clucked his tongue. They sounded about as bothered by my struggles as they were when one of the cows got fractious during milking. "It's been a while since we went net fishing."

"Not so long. I'm just used to the new ones now."

"The new ones are so light the woman could throw one. I would have thought you were stronger than her, but first you let her escape, then you could hardly throw the net? Too much sex is making you weak."

"And maybe if a certain twat wasn't always getting in my way, I wouldn't have trouble keeping one small girl in check."

I found an area where the net had disintegrated and had a larger hole, but it was too small for me to escape from. I could probably get my arm out, but that wouldn't help much. There was a swooping sensation as they flipped me around and pulled me into the air. When I could focus and not puke, I realized Bron had thrown the rope at the end of the net over a tree limb and hauled on it until I was suspended. They tied off the rope, leaving me dangling waist high off the ground.

"Do you think that will hold?" Ilya asked skeptically. "It's unraveling in a few spots."

"Am I ever wrong?"

"Well, you probably should have suggested stripping her first."

They laughed at themselves and Bron smacked Ilya on the back.

"At least she's wearing a skirt. It's the panties that will make things more difficult."

I had shifted to more or less a sitting position with my legs crossed under my long skirt. While they were pretending this was a stupid stand-up act, I'd been looking for weaknesses in the net. I needed to get out before they got any bright ideas.

Bron found a place where the net's openings were wider and slipped his hands through, then tugged my long skirt until it reached my waist. I tried to slap his hand away, or squirm around to stop him, but he only laughed.

"Look at that," Ilya said, grinning. "No panties."

"An obvious invitation."

"You're delusional!" I tried to shove away Bron's hand, but he pushed two fingers into my pussy, which was still damningly soaked. It wasn't my fault I'd been turned on when Bron had so rudely interrupted.

"She complains, but do you hear her gasps? Do you hear the liquid sound of her pretty cunt?"

"Her asshole has closed up again. It was so much work to get in. I thought she was going to snap my dick in half," Ilya grumbled.

"You'll get better at it with practice. Just no more fucking her without my permission, or I swear I'll beat your balls until your grandchildren feel it." Bron patted my ass, and I winced. "You took your belt to her?"

"She disobeyed me."

"Did you tell her to run when we were arguing?"

"No."

"Then maybe she didn't learn her lesson." Bron pulled his belt free from his belt loops. The sound struck fear into me, and I tugged at the net, making it sway, not caring if the rope let go and dropped me to the ground. Ilya pulled his belt from his pocket and shook it out.

Oh no.

I shut my eyes and tensed.

There was no gradual warm up this time. They took turns hitting me, the *snap, snap* of the blows turning the net as I writhed inside its confines. Stinging fire licked at me, and I shrieked and begged them to stop.

"That's probably enough." Bron spread my ass cheeks apart. "Now show me what you were doing."

"With her in the net?"

"Your dick will fit through those big holes. It was a net for fish, not bait."

"Wouldn't it be easier if she was on the ground?"

"Lazy. Get to it."

Ilya grumbled but lowered his pants and stroked his cock under Bron's scrutiny. It always annoyed me when they discussed me as if I wasn't there. While Bron watched Ilya, the bulge in his own pants grew. He might think he was straight, but Ilya absolutely turned him on.

When Ilya got into position, I tried to wiggle out of the way, but Bron moved in front of me and caught me by the thighs and held me in place for him. Ilya coaxed a finger into my ass, then two. "At least her body hasn't forgotten about me entirely." He withdrew his fingers and forced the head of his cock into my ass again. It felt stranger than usual in this position, but there was nothing I could do except hang on to the net and angle my hips so it was less uncomfortable.

Bron chuckled. "You like her ass, Ilyusha?"

"She's so hot inside," he mumbled, fucking me with slow thrusts. "I love the way her body grips my cock—how it feels to be sheathed in her, like she was made for me."

Bron slid his fingers over my pussy, his fingers slick with my arousal. I gasped when he stroked my clit, and I shuddered, my body tightening around Ilya's cock. I whimpered.

"When she makes noises, I have to concentrate on not coming," Ilya complained.

Bron dropped to his knees and held my labia wide, watching my empty pussy clench and shudder as Ilya filled the hole I didn't want him in. There was the gentlest of touches on my clit—a tongue? Then more, the pleasure almost sharp. I was still sensitive there after Ilya had gone down on me, and the feel of Bron's mouth and scratchy facial hair was almost too much to bear.

He dipped his tongue into my pussy, exploring, tasting.

"Please!" I whimpered.

Ilya groaned. "What are you doing to her? Her ass is like a fist squeezing my cock."

"I think she wants both holes filled," Bron observed.

"Have you done such a thing before?" Ilya asked, going still inside me. I could feel his dick pulsing. Had he come, or was he just trying to calm down? When I tried to get enough leverage to get him out of me, his fingers clamped down on my hips, keeping him sheathed deep in my guts.

"Who would I have done this with? One of my wives? No." He gave a short laugh. "Besides, why would I choose to be so close to another man's dick? I don't like men that way."

Ilya made a quiet sound I couldn't interpret.

How could he seriously make that declaration to the very man he'd been having sex with for over a decade?

I was about to say as much, but then he distracted me by pushing a thick, slick finger into my pussy. I already felt stuffed.

Double penetration wasn't my favorite, and I'd never done it with two men who were so well hung. It felt overwhelming with two average-sized dicks. I wasn't sure I wanted to die by DP.

From what he'd said, he wouldn't even consider doing it anyway, but the thought of it made me nervous.

Bron withdrew his finger and got to his feet. "You like having two men inside you, Queen of Whores?"

Ilya's hands clamped tighter on my thighs, but I wasn't sure if he was excited at the idea or upset with Bron for calling me a whore again.

"It can be fun, but I think the two of you are too big to make it enjoyable for me."

"What is it you Americans say? Ah yes—sucks to be you." He unzipped his pants and freed his already hard cock.

Damn it.

I would have tried to escape, but there was a big dick jammed deep in my ass, and strong, determined hands holding me still.

"Your dicks might touch," I blurted, hoping to discourage him.

"Chances are low. He's already in your ass." He bared his teeth at me. Was there no empathy in this man?

Duh. I knew him well enough to know there wasn't.

He pushed against my front, which pushed me back harder against Ilya. My crossed legs bent toward me across my belly until I was folded in half.

"Please don't," I begged. "This isn't going to be fun for any of us."

"What man doesn't like a hot, tight hole to use? Ilya got my favorite one, but he deserves to know what it feels like for once."

He slotted his dick through one of the holes in the net and rubbed the head of his cock up and down my pussy, making himself slick. I was so needy that I squirmed against him, hoping he'd hit my clit. Every time he did, it was like an electric shock, and I clenched around Ilya, whose dick was a motionless steel bar.

Slowly, Bron worked his cock into me, needing to hold it to force his way in.

"It would be easier if Ilya pulled out more, or maybe if you let me out of this stupid net," I said, teeth gritted against the mind-blowing size of them trying to make room for themselves inside me at the same time.

"Maybe, but this is fun." Bron's grin was sexy, but considering what he was doing to me, I didn't have time to enjoy it.

Fun for them, maybe. Between this and the extra belt marks they'd given me, I felt like a kinky sex piñata.

They pushed and pulled at me, at the net, grunting, fighting over the angle they needed, fighting for space in my body, until they were both deep inside me. I breathed through the sensation of aching fullness, hoping my body would adjust. It took a few minutes for them to find a rhythm that worked for them both, but unfortunately, neither of them went limp or fell out. When they stopped silently fighting over me, and had a decent rhythm going, Bron slipped his hand between us and found my clit despite the fact that I was being crushed between them.

"There is room for both of us inside you," Ilya rasped. "Your body knows who it belongs to."

Involuntarily, I clenched around them and gasped, but Ilya gasped, too. Bron's gaze burned into me, but strayed to Ilya, although he tried to hide it.

"You might...dislocate my spleen...if you move too fast," I managed to say, not sure I was kidding.

"Shut up, woman," Bron commanded. "Ilya is trying not to come."

If I could get them to come faster, that would be perfect.

"Is it a tight fit, Ilya?" I asked, my voice even huskier than usual.

"Damn it, wife. Shut your mouth." His body quaked behind mine.

"Can you feel the way Bron's cock is rubbing against yours deep inside me?"

Bron's grunt sounded suspiciously like a moan he'd let slip.

"Yesss," Ilya hissed. "I feel everything he's doing. Two swords squeezed into the same scabbard."

"She's between us," Bron insisted, but I felt his hips stutter too. "We're not touching."

"One thin layer of flesh between us. The three of us together."

It wasn't only Ilya who found the idea hot.

The small circles Bron was rubbing on my clit were slippery and relentless and made me squirm on their cocks while wishing I had some leverage to participate. All I could do was hang there and let them use me while my legs cramped up.

Bron's free hand was wrapped in the net by my face. I leaned forward the short distance and bit his finger.

He growled at me, and his dick jerked, making both Ilya and me swear.

Rather than pull away, Bron fucked my mouth with two rough fingers, and I sucked, not caring when I gagged and drooled. Now that my body had adjusted, I could let go and stop panicking. Bron's hand strayed, his thumb taking over the pressure on my clit as his fingers investigated lower, tracing the thin separation between their two cocks. Back and forth, his fingers stroked over the sensitive flesh as he thumbed my clit.

I tried to hold back, worried that an orgasm would be too much for my body to handle, but they were still hard, and it was so good and so nasty. I sucked Bron's fingers like the whore he'd called me, desperate and squirming as their tempos synched and they withdrew and shoved back in simultaneously. Ilya gave a hoarse cry, and his fingers dug into my flesh as the pleasure Bron inflicted on me tightened the coil inside me with brutal intensity.

No, I don't want to.

No, if I came, I'd move the wrong way and die.

Fuck, can I even stop myself?

Bron tortured my clit and thrust viciously into my body.

Ilya's dick throbbed, stinging and hot and deep.

"Can you feel him filling your ass?" Bron asked, his voice harsh. "I'm going to fill your pussy next. How much cum do you think your little cunt can take for me?"

My body was trembling, quaking from the effort of holding myself back, but I could feel his fingers stray from my perineum to Ilya's balls. Ilya choked, pushing deeper and harder into my ass.

Bron stared into my eyes, his dark gaze penetrating, ruthless. "Come on our cocks, Delilah mine. Fucking do it."

No, please.

But it was too late. The pressure inside me snapped, and the orgasm cut through me with an intensity that felt a lot like pain. I screamed and struggled, and my inner muscles clenched and rippled, feeling like too much and not enough, like it would go on forever, like I might die.

Bron held it together while I fell apart on his cock, and Ilya cried out loud enough to make my ears ring.

"That's right. That's my girl," Bron coaxed, pulling his fingers away from my mouth and clit and grabbing my thighs. He stabbed into me deeper than he had been, the violence of it stealing my breath.

"Fuck, your sweet cunt is so hot...so tight." He grunted crudely, and his fingers dug into my flesh hard enough that I knew he was leaving bruises with his fingertips. I couldn't find it in myself to care about bruises as my orgasm went on and on, my pussy feeling like it was sucking his dick dry as it jerked and twitched inside me.

They both stilled, panting, swearing quietly under their breath. Ilya pulled out first and collapsed back into the grass, but Bron took a few moments longer, stirring his hips, enjoying the aftershocks of my orgasm.

"How are you so beautiful?" he murmured so quietly I wasn't sure I was supposed to hear the words. I had collapsed forward, toward him, and my forehead rested against the net. He wiped the spit from the finger blowjob off my chin, then pressed his forehead against mine, still panting like he'd run a marathon. "If the boy wasn't marrying you, I would be sorely tempted to make you my third wife." He chuckled to himself and slapped my ass before pulling out. He lowered himself to the grass, too, not complaining when Ilya shifted over and rested his head on his chest.

I felt my eyes closing, even though I was in an uncomfortable position and the rope was digging into my skin.

When I opened my mouth to complain that I wanted them to free me, I glanced down to see Bron's hand toying with Ilya's hair. I doubted Ilya could tell what he was doing, but I saw the affection in Bron's gaze. I spied shamelessly, feeling warm and fuzzy and satiated, even though I could hear the cum dripping out of me and landing in the dried leaves beneath the net. Watching them together was worth me getting cold and ignored. Eventually, I would go home and maybe the two of them would have a different dynamic by then. Maybe they could be happy.

I vaguely remembered Bron saying something as my orgasm was finishing—something about marrying me if Ilya hadn't planned to? Of course, it had been his dick talking, but I clung to the statement, letting it keep me warm as I waited patiently for them to remember I existed.

Chapter Seventeen

"Don't smile unless there's something to smile about," Bron snapped, tapping my mouth with the switch he held. I'd watched him cut and strip the green stick earlier, and hoped we'd gotten marshmallows in our grocery shipment, but no such luck.

The kitchen was still warm after Ilya and I had spent all day making *pelmeni* for the freezer. Sweat trickled down my spine. I was already tired, but Bron didn't care, and he was determined I needed to practice my 'wife lessons' tonight.

They'd already filled my head with rules and customs, and short phrases I still got mixed up, although my pronunciation wasn't bad. Sometimes I suspected they were rules Bron had made up on the spot.

"How am I supposed to remember not to smile?" I snapped back.

"You smile too much. People will think you're dishonest or stupid."

Do this. Don't do that. Don't speak unless spoken to in case I said something Vas would disapprove of. It was enough to make me want to scream.

"I'm American. Wouldn't they realize there are cultural differences?"

He switched my ass, and I had to force myself not to react, so I didn't dump the soup I was carrying to the table. At least I was wearing clothes. Yesterday, the struggle had been to make ladylike small talk while they'd passed me back and forth, groping and teasing me until I screamed at them in frustration and begged them to fuck me.

"Are you going to make me walk with a book on my head next?" I demanded.

"How would that be a useful skill?"

I made a sound of disgust and put down the soup in front of Ilya a little too hard. Some of it sloshed onto my hand. I sucked at the serving-my-man bullshit Bron was trying to teach me.

My hiss of pain made Bron grumble.

Ilya went to the freezer to get an ice pack that he wrapped in a tea towel. Bron hauled up the back of my dress and switched me three times on the backs of my bare thighs.

"Fuck you!"

Ilya took my hand and held the ice to my burn.

The switch came up to tap my mouth hard enough to sting. I really wanted to hate it—hate him—but his aggressively bossy bullshit was unfortunately turning me on.

"Watch your mouth or you'll go to bed with a needy pussy and more welts than you can count."

"You're impossible!"

"You need to learn. Vas is old-fashioned. He won't tolerate your mouth."

I walked away before I exploded at him. He'd been so on edge as we got closer to leaving. Neither Ilya nor I could understand why, and of course Bron hadn't provided me with an answer when I'd been brash enough to ask.

After I grabbed Ilya's old coat, I stepped out of the house, meaning to let the evening air clear my head. I walked down to the goat shed. They were happy to see me, but I hadn't brought them snacks this time. They milled around me, nibbling at my coat and the hem of my dress.

There was no way to stay angry while standing in a little tidal pool of goats.

The shed door squeaked, and Bron came in. I moved further away, realizing I'd effectively trapped myself.

In the dim light of the shed, I couldn't see his expression, let alone read it.

"I know you don't understand, but I'm doing this for your benefit."

"Just like you fuck Ilya in the ass for his benefit?"

He cleared his throat. "That's— Maybe that's different."

Wow. Progress?

"I'm not really marrying Ilya. It makes no difference if Vas doesn't like me much."

"You need to be a submissive woman he approves of, otherwise you're not proof Ilya is a man."

"That's ridiculous."

"It's the truth."

I scratched the white splotch on one of the goat's heads because I could see it, even in the dimness.

"Do you really consider Moscow your home? Ilya has never lived there, and you haven't lived there in years."

"What would you consider our home, then?" He sounded incredulous. "This godforsaken island?"

"Absolutely. You've built a life here—fixing the house, farming the land, caring for the animals, spending time with Ilya. This isn't a jail. You go to the city when you want to. You're not waiting to be let out on parole."

"Who would choose to live like this if they could do anything else?"

"A lot of people."

"I miss civilization," Bron growled. "I miss..."

I waited for him to finish his statement, but he didn't.

"You miss what?"

"I had a life there—not like here."

"And is that life still there waiting for you? Are you going to call up your ex-wife as soon as we get there? Hook up for old time's sake?" Jealousy twisted.

Why was I feeling so...aggressive?

I had no claim to him and no right to be jealous. I liked them both too much for a woman who was getting paid to have sex with them. Lines were so blurred I wasn't sure if there'd ever been lines in the first place. Meanwhile, all I was to them was their stunt cunt.

"No." He laughed. "Even if she would have me back and didn't have four snotty children with my cousin, her idea of adventurous sex was wearing pretty underwear to bed and shutting off the light. If my cousin didn't put a bullet in my skull for trying to lure her away, I would die of boredom."

"Oh." A bit of my tension eased. "So, what life are you missing?"

He fussed with some of the goats, who were trying to pilfer snacks out of his pockets.

"I don't know." He sounded exasperated rather than angry. "What do you want me to say? You don't understand what this is like for me. This is my job. I shouldn't want to stay here any more than you. Do you consider this island home? Of course not."

"You have a life here with Ilya."

"You have, too, but don't you have aspirations other than crawling around weeding the garden, and spreading your legs for men whenever they have a hard prick?"

A flash of anger caught me off guard. It was probably embarrassment in an ugly coat. "What else am I supposed to want?"

"To go to school? Weren't you doing this to get yourself a scholarship? And what about love? Don't all women want love—a partner? Maybe some snotty brats of your own?"

"I don't even know what I want to do," I admitted sheepishly. "Maybe I'll use the money to start a small business instead, but I'm not good at anything."

"You're good at taking it up the ass."

I blew out an exasperated breath. "Why are you such a fucking jerk?"

"Why do you want a man who's a fucking jerk? Do jerks make your pussy wet?" He grabbed my arm and twisted it behind my back, using the pain to hold me against him.

"I don't want you."

"You always want me."

It wasn't a lie, but sometimes the truth sucked. "Maybe I don't always hate you."

He tsked. "Are you falling in love with me, *De-li-lah*? Do you love this island and its men?"

I drew a shaky breath. Although I wanted to deny it and save face, admitting it was true was braver and possibly necessary at this point. We were going to Vas's the day after tomorrow, and I might lose my chance or my nerve. What if we got there, and they got permission to stay with Vas? Everything would change.

"So what if I do?"

The lack of light felt like it had given him harder edges. His breath caressed my face. "What are you hoping to get from me with this adorable declaration?"

He sounded strange. Amused? Was he laughing at me? Of course, he was.

What had I been thinking?

I tried to headbutt him, but my forehead hit his chest.

"Are you going to weep now and declare your love for me?" His tone was sharp, caustic. "Why aren't you inside, using your wiles to lure Ilya away from me as you always do?"

"That's not what I've been doing!" I protested.

He yanked my arm higher behind my back, and I cried out in pain and stood on my toes, trying to ease the pressure.

"Lies. You tempt men wherever you go, and now he rolls around in bed thinking of this body." Bron pressed me against him, my breasts mashed against his unforgiving chest. He leaned in, burying his face in my hair, his mouth next to my ear. "This siren's face and the voice that makes him lie awake at night and think of his name in your pretty mouth."

He groaned, and I realized he was hard.

What?

His lips came down on mine, ruthless and demanding. He took what he wanted, not waiting for me to reciprocate, plundering my mouth and turning my bones to water. I let him kiss me, not trying to escape, even though his grip on my arm fell away. I curled my fingers into his shirt and kissed him back, barely registering the goats and their curiosity.

The kiss turned sensual—mingled breaths and the sliding of tongues. I twined my arms around his neck and stretched up the length of him, running my fingers through his long hair.

"Why are you so angry with me?" I asked when we stopped, panting. His arms had slowly crept around me, and he hadn't let me go.

"You're going to be Ilya's wife." He swallowed, but his eyes were in shadow and unreadable.

"We're fake engaged. It's not real."

"Yes, yes. Tell yourself it's all a game, but I can see how things are progressing. The two of you will be together, and I'll be what? Your bodyguard. Will the two of you pity me and sneak me into your bed?"

"You're jealous?"

"Jealous. Such a childish word." He exhaled, the breeze of it ruffling my hair. "Yes, I'm jealous. Is that what you want me to say? I don't want you touching him, and I don't want him touching you. You're both mine, not each other's, and yet I feel like there's an axe waiting to fall on my neck." He shook his head. "I can't go from being everything to Ilya to nothing—from being your tormentor to your father-in-law's thug. If you stay, you'll marry him. If you go home, we'll both lose you. Either way, in two days we're leaving this island, and everything will change. Ilya will impress his father, you'll make your choice, and I'll probably get pulled back into Vas's group of enforcers."

He would? I put my forehead on his chest. "So then why are you saying you're looking forward to getting back to your real life?"

"Because I've always known my life with Ilya would end. I try to convince myself I'm eager to go back to working my way up the ranks in Vas's army."

"You're not?"

"I'm not a child out to prove myself anymore. I'm not angry and self-destructive the way I was. Hurting people—killing people—that's not what I want to do anymore."

Anymore?

He'd killed people.

I shivered. I'd suspected as much, after seeing what he'd done to the man in the park, but hearing him admit it so freely was shocking.

Should it have changed the way I felt about him? Yes. Maybe it did, but not the way it should have. It made me feel safer, which was ridiculous.

"Will Vas let you walk away?"

"I doubt it. And if anyone finds out what I've been doing to his son, he'll put a bullet in my brain." He sighed and rested his chin on my head, his shaggy beard tangling in my hair. "I knew this day was coming. It's why I chose you for him. I thought if I was to lose him to someone, it would hurt less if it was to someone like you. And then you smiled at me for the first time, and I was besotted."

He was making fun of me. This was the Russian idea of a joke, right?

His hand grazed my cheek, then cradled it. He brushed his mouth against mine. "Why is it easier to tell truths in darkness?"

My heart caught, forgetting to beat.

Was he cruel enough to say things like this to me as a prank?

"If you like me so much, why do you hurt me?"

He hummed quietly, the vibration moving from his mouth to mine, my heart picking it up as its rhythm.

"I hurt you because we both enjoy it."

My mind whirled, too full of thoughts to have answers.

"This job destroyed my life, and now it's my job to take the two of you to Moscow and destroy it again." He sighed, then kissed me gently one last time. "Now enough with the womanly petulance. You still have things to learn."

Chapter Eighteen

Taking the scissors to Bron's face would have been much more satisfying if I wasn't just cutting off his beard. As a punishment for teasing them both about needing to shave for the first time in years, they'd ganged up on me and teased me back, but with their hands in their mouths. I was sulking, and Bron's silent amusement was making me feel stabby. It didn't help that I wanted to hump his leg.

"You already did this for the boy?" he asked as I worked at hacking off his beard so he could shave.

"I did."

"What does he look like?" His gaze on me was too intense.

"Why do you want to know?"

"I haven't seen him without a beard since he was about twenty. He must look like such a puppy." He chuckled, but there was no cruelty in it.

"He shooed me out before he shaved, so your guess is as good as mine. He still had a lot of stubble when I left."

"You don't approve?"

Had he really picked that up from my nonverbals? "I don't know yet."

"But you have your doubts."

"I have no doubt the two of you will be attractive without the beards, but I'm used to them, so you're going to feel like strangers. Besides, your beards are sexy."

"You could go fetch a bag to keep mine as a trophy."

"I'll pass, but thanks for your generous offer." I fought down a giggle at the idea of keeping his beard in a Tupperware container like a little coffin. Maybe I could superglue his beard back on when he was sleeping.

"So, you say you have feelings for me—for us—but they don't extend as far as you keeping mementos or thinking romantic thoughts?" His lips flattened in a disapproving line, and he shook his head. "If you really cared about us and wanted to prove how Russian you were becoming, you would need to write our beards some sad poetry."

"When it comes to you and Ilya, I'm pretty sure I'm the beard." I smirked and snipped off more hair. His brows rose in question. Of course, he didn't get the reference. I considered explaining it to him but thought better of it. If he still considered himself straight, he wouldn't welcome jokes about them using me as a disguise for their relationship.

He waited patiently for me to be done. There was something satisfying about taking care of them this way.

"What about your hair?"

He ran his fingers through it, pushing it out of his face. "Should we cut our hair, too?" He shrugged. "We won't have time to go to a barber, but we could cut it ourselves."

"Do you have a pair of clippers here?"

"Of course. How do you think we shear the sheep?"

I choked out a laugh. "I don't know how to use those kinds of shears. I used to cut my brothers' hair back home, so I can do a decent job of it if you want me to try. I just can't do anything fancy."

"You know everything about cooking and getting out stains. You don't complain about crawling around in the dirt planting seeds or helping with the animals. Now you tell me you know how to cut hair? Is there anything you can't do, woman?"

"I haven't learned how to use an axe."

"We can show you that if you really want to learn, but with two strong men here, why would you ever need to?"

"Maybe to fight off the wolves?"

"The only wolves here walk around on two legs."

"That was you and Ilya making those sounds when you were chasing me through the woods?"

"Most men have a beast lurking not far underneath the skin. You, of all women, should know that by now."

I shuddered, trying not to think of all the men who'd chosen to give in to their inner beasts rather than being civil to me. For some reason, it wasn't the same with Bron and Ilya. They were honest about what they wanted and what they planned to do to me. There was no trickery. No subterfuge. If they hid anything from me, it was usually because they were hiding it from themselves first.

When I'd finished and put down the scissors, he handed them back to me and pulled the leather thong from his hair, letting it fall free.

"Are you sure?"

"You're right. I don't think men wear their hair long anymore, considering what I saw in Saint Petersburg. I need to blend in with the other men who work for Ilya's father."

"You don't want it cut down to almost nothing?" I said, aghast.

"I do."

I grimaced, wishing I had clippers but not willing to ask them to bring the ones for sheep shearing up to the house.

I ran my hand through his long, silky mane. Why did men always have the best hair?

"It feels like a crime to cut it."

"Maybe I will grow it back."

"But I won't be around to see it."

He grunted, not agreeing but also not contradicting me.

I sectioned off his hair and cut it, wincing with each snip. The stubbly beard and stubbly hair version of Bron looked more danger-ous—more like the crime family enforcer he apparently was. He had several interesting scars, and I assumed they were from people he'd fought on his boss's behalf.

I stepped away when I was done, then fixed a few places where his hair was uneven. Considering I didn't have clippers, it looked good.

"I'm sure any barber would see the flaws, but it looks decent," I admitted.

"No one in Ilya's family is a barber, so I'm sure they won't notice when we visit. Besides, I'm no one in that house."

I ran my hand over his hair, and he leaned into it, as though it had been a caress rather than me checking my handiwork. I scratched at his scalp, and he groaned in pleasure.

"Do you want me to shave you?"

He gave me a long look with his dark, brooding eyes. "You think I should trust you with a razor near my throat?" he murmured.

How could he make that sound sexy?

"Are you afraid I might take advantage of you?"

His slow, dirty smile turned me on.

"I can still taste your pussy on my tongue." He sucked at his bottom lip like there might be some of me there, too, and I groaned in frus-tration, vividly remembering the feel of his mouth on me from when they held me down and tortured me earlier.

I put down the scissors and straddled his lap, reaching up to play with his hair some more.

"You like my hair short?" He reached between us and slid his fingers along the seam of my leggings, pressing the fabric between my labia and using the seam to torture my still sensitive clit.

"You must feel lighter, between the beard and the hair."

He pulled his hand away from me and ran it through the hair I'd left him. I was relieved it looked good.

"This is probably how the sheep feel." He coaxed me up off his lap and gave my ass an affectionate smack that made me smile on the inside. I managed not to smile on the outside. Trying to remember not to smile was the hardest part of his lessons. "Go. I will be down to see you after I shave."

Without meaning to, I heaved a sigh.

"Is your needy little cunt reminding you to be a good girl?"

I glared at him. "It's encouraging me to be a very bad girl."

"No fucking Ilya, and no touching yourself."

"You suck."

"Your clit? Maybe if you're an obedient little bitch."

Head held high, I grabbed the scissors and walked out of the room with as much dignity as I could muster. Was I fantasizing about going back and begging for an orgasm, or even for the pleasure of sucking his cock? Yes. However, the man was already cocky enough and didn't need me to encourage him.

As soon as I entered the bathroom Ilya was shaving in, I fell back a step. He met my gaze and gave me an uncertain smile. Fuck, he was hot—like runway-model-in-Paris level hot. God, his face.

"You're...beautiful."

He grimaced. "Beautiful? Men aren't supposed to be beautiful." His brow creased. "I should have kept my beard."

"No, Bron was right. You can't show up there looking like you live in the bush."

"But we do. Vas knows that because he left me here." His voice had a growl in it I rarely heard him use outside of sex. I gave a shiver, finally pairing this version of him with the one who'd learned with an almost fanatical enthusiasm how to make me come.

"What happened here?" I reached up and traced the scar that slashed his cheekbone. I'd noticed it before, of course, but I'd never asked.

He touched it, fingers exploring the ridge. It wasn't a terrible scar, but it stood out white against his skin. Come to think of it, it surprised me that although their skin was a bit paler under their beards, it wasn't super obvious.

"One of Vas's rings caught me there when I was small."

"He used to slap you around?" I ran my fingers through his still-long hair.

"Sometimes, if he noticed me. He didn't pay me much attention."

"You weren't his favorite."

He flashed a grin at me, and I blinked at the overwhelming urge to disobey Bron and jump Ilya here and now. That smile with that face? Absolutely devastating. It made me feel suddenly bashful, as though he were someone else now and far too good for someone like me.

"I'm no one's favorite. I'll settle for being your second favorite." He winked at me.

Was swooning an option? Because goddamn, he was *fine*.

"For the sake of marriages everywhere, it's a good thing Vas hid you on this island. You'd tempt too many wives and at least half of the husbands."

He grimaced again, as though he thought I was only being nice.

Noticing the scissors in my hand, he lifted his brows. "Are those to threaten Bron with? You won't die of frustration, you know."

"I figured you were the easier target. Besides, you enjoy giving me orgasms—I'll do you a favor by letting you give me one."

"When was the last time I gave you only one? I prefer you screaming and shaking for me, and all sweaty and limp when I'm done."

I groaned and pressed against him. "Please? Just one? Bron doesn't have to know."

He chuckled and shook his head in mock disapproval. "Such a naughty, needy girl." His gaze warmed, lingering on my face in a way that made my heart sigh in contentment.

Was I in love with him? Probably. How could anyone not be?

These feelings were probably something like Stockholm Syndrome from being trapped here for so long with two hot men who had big sexual appetites. It couldn't get serious, and all three of us knew it, right?

The guys were starting new lives back in civilization, and I'd be going home.

Hell, I didn't even have so much as a visitor's visa to be in the country. I didn't relish the idea of being sent to a prison in Siberia if I got caught, that was for damn sure. I could go home and apply for a visa, but how long did those even take? How long did they last? I knew nothing about traveling legally, let alone how to live in Russian society.

"Hey, you know it's only a joke, right?" He cupped my face in his hands. "You're not naughty at all. You're very good." He tipped my face up so he could study my expression. "You're upset." He kissed my forehead. "Tell me."

Tell him what? That I wanted Vas to leave us alone on this island? That I didn't want him to achieve his dream of being allowed to leave permanently and be close to his family—something he'd been working toward for years?

"I'm just nervous about pretending I'm your fiancée."

He kissed me again, this time on the mouth. Without the beard to scrape my skin, his kiss felt different. When he pulled away, he sighed and rubbed his face on mine like an overgrown cat.

"It feels so different."

"Mmhmm." I threaded my fingers through his hair and scratched his scalp the way I had with Bron. He groaned in contentment.

"Do you think my face would feel good between your thighs?"

I nipped his bottom lip, and he picked me up and perched my ass on the edge of the vanity so he could get between my legs. He kissed me again, trying to get me to open my mouth, but I playfully refused. His tongue slid along the seam of my lips, coaxing me, making me think of him sinking to his knees and doing the same to my needy, aching pussy. He could push down my leggings, push aside my panties...

It was impossible not to part my lips, to let him in. Our tongues slid together, and I was so wound up, the wicked sensation sent an orgasmic shudder through my entire body. There was something magical about a man who loved making out like a teenager—who did it for the pleasure of it, instead of as a box that needed to be checked so he could put his dick in me.

His dick was straining at his jeans, and I pulled off my leggings and hooked my legs around his, putting my feet on the backs of his calves so I had leverage to rub against him. My panties didn't do much to protect me from the denim he wore, but I was so frustrated I didn't care.

He slid his hand up my shirt and cupped my bare breast, pinching my nipple hard enough to make me squirm against his cock. There were too many layers of cloth between us. What were the chances he'd agree to fuck me before Bron came in and pitched a fit?

Ilya groaned into my mouth, and the sound shot straight to my brain, making me feel like I'd risk anything—do anything to hear it again.

"What the fuck are you two doing?" Bron's growl at the door made me jerk back. Ilya only looked at him. I expected him to be flustered and apologetic, but he only narrowed his eyes.

"What does it look like we're doing?" Ilya's brows dipped.

"The rule is the two of you aren't allowed to paw at each other behind my back."

"And why should I obey you?"

Bron invaded Ilya's personal space, trying to intimidate him with his body. "Just because you grew into a man while hiding under that beard doesn't mean anything has changed between us. Obey me or I'll punish you."

Ilya turned to face him but leaned a hip casually against the counter between my thighs and wrapped an arm around my waist.

"Tomorrow, we go to see Vas. This arrangement between us is over, Bron. We may choose to be with each other after this, but I will only obey you when it's what I want to do."

Bron grabbed his arm, but Ilya broke the hold as though he'd always known how to counter it. They grappled, bumping into the door and the wall. I drew my legs up and tucked them underneath me, ignoring the urge to try to stop them. They had to sort out their new dynamic without my interference.

Bron was broader and heavier, but Ilya seemed slightly faster. They both had something to lose and a point to make.

Stray elbows and fists flew, and I flattened myself back against the mirror.

After a blur of movement that was too fast and too close for me to follow, Bron got Ilya into a headlock. I was disappointed for Ilya, but maybe this struggle between them would need to take time, anyway.

Ilya grabbed between Bron's legs.

The fight stopped. An angry, rapid discussion in Russian ensued, and I only caught a few words—most of them swears Ilya had taught me.

"Let go of my balls, *suka*."

"Let go of my head, *suka blyat*."

Slowly, they let go of each other and straightened.

"Bedtime. Both of you go to your rooms," Bron snarled.

"Seriously?" My outburst earned me a raised eyebrow. He was a whole different type of scary without the beard. I'd expected him to have a rugged, homely face, but the man was irritatingly hot. No wonder he had two ex-wives—he was definitely handsome enough to attract women by the busload and then keep them wondering if he'd ever be faithful. Other women would always throw themselves at him.

Keeping these two men trapped on a remote island should have been tried as a crime against humanity.

Under Bron's hard gaze, I felt a little less brave.

I couldn't let the man win without sassing him at least a little.

"Fine."

He grunted his annoyance before turning to face Ilya, who hadn't agreed or moved. Instead, Ilya had folded his big arms across his chest and cocked his head in challenge.

"No. No more treating me like a child."

"Then get to your room, and I'll beat you like a man."

"Then fuck me like a man? No. If you want anything from me from now on, you will ask as though I'm an actual human being with free will."

"Why should I change my ways now when you and I both know I can take what I want, and you like it that way?"

Ilya swallowed. "There are many times I do enjoy it, but also times you should have honored my wishes when I told you to stop."

"I'm not here to be your boyfriend."

"And yet..."

Bron stormed off, but apparently Ilya wasn't done. He followed, and I slid off the counter and trailed after them, feeling like I was intruding but also wanting to mediate if I could.

We ended up at Bron's room, where he was pacing in the space at the foot of his bed. Ilya stood, blocking the door, as though he thought Bron might take off again.

"Why are you so angry?" Ilya demanded.

Bron ran his fingers over his newly shortened hair, as though he would be pulling at it if he could get a grip on it. "I don't know!"

"It's not because I won't submit to you tonight."

"No," Bron admitted. "I should kick your ass for your disobedience, but I don't have it in me right now."

"Going home tomorrow is upsetting you."

"Yes."

"Why?"

"I don't know! Why does the thought of leaving here make me feel this way?"

"Is it because things will change between the two of you?" I interjected. They needed to see what I saw, but I doubted they'd get there on their own at this point. It had been too long.

"What are you saying, woman?" Bron snapped.

"You're worried about losing Ilya."

He stopped pacing and glared at the portion of me he could see past Ilya's muscular body.

"Just because I accepted your dare and kissed him doesn't mean I'm soft for him."

"Give me your phone."

"What? Why?"

"There's no signal here, Delilah. You know that."

"Give me your phone," I demanded again, holding out my hand.

"No."

"Why do you need his phone?"

"Because he's lying to himself. You know how you write poems about him? Well, he takes pictures of you when you're not looking."

"He does?" Ilya asked, incredulous.

"I like photography," Bron said stubbornly. "You're only imagining it means more than it does."

"Let me see," Ilya demanded.

"My phone is none of your business."

Ilya eyed the phone where it lay on the dresser but jammed his hands into his pockets.

"Fine, then tell me this—why did you start fucking me if you don't like men that way?"

He grumbled, scrubbing a hand over his face. "What were we supposed to do here alone, two grown men?" he said defensively. "Were we supposed to stay celibate? Sleep every night with our cocks in our fists, wishing there was a woman here to be a receptacle for our baser desires?"

"If satisfying your baser desires was your only reason for fucking me, there had to be other options. It's not like money is short."

"Of course, I considered bringing a whore or two here to see to our needs."

"But you decided against it."

"I did."

"Why?"

"I'd developed a taste for you and your suffering and didn't want to stop. I couldn't have you if there were whores here to gossip."

"You're not worried Delilah will gossip?"

"Delilah is different. She was on that damned island. She understands how it is between us—and Americans aren't as shocked by men choosing to fuck other men." He glanced my way, then back to Ilya. "If Vas hadn't finally summoned you home, I would have happily tormented you for the next few decades until one of us died."

Ilya pressed his lips together. "Hurting me was enough for you? You never wanted more? You never wanted a relationship? Someone to love?"

"Love is a fantasy made up by women," Bron protested, his clean-shaven face doing nothing to hide the red blush that stained his neck and cheeks. "Relationships only burn hot and bright until the newness singes off. If they last, they mature into companionship, shared jokes, and some affection. Haven't I given you all that?"

"You don't always have to make it hurt."

Bron put his hands on his hips and looked at the ceiling as though it might provide them both with answers. "I knew this thing between us would have to be temporary. It was easier to leave it the way it was and not let feelings grow. I'm not a man who ever thought about men the way I think about you, so it was always easier to hide behind the lie I told myself—that I was only teaching you a lesson."

"You've always resented being sent to take care of me."

"At first, but not for a long time. How could I resent you after I got to know you? You're my life." He looked uncomfortable and hooked his thumbs into his belt loops.

"Tomorrow, we go to the mainland and back to the real world," Ilya said with forced joviality. "You're being set free from your prison. You can find a woman. Get remarried. Have a family."

Bron grunted, but he didn't look pleased at the prospect. "What about you?"

"What about me?"

"What do you want from life now that you'll have choices for the first time?"

"I should want to be part of my family, but they're strangers to me." Ilya's mouth twisted. "I would rather we stay here."

"He would never allow it." Bron pulled off his shirt, and Ilya paused, his lips parted with a response that never made it out. It was like a wave of lust erased thoughts written in sand.

"Why are you getting undressed?" Ilya asked uneasily as Bron unbuckled his belt. He shivered.

"I'm done talking."

Bron's pants dropped, leaving him in only boxer briefs. His body was hard. Glorious. Covered in scars.

Now both Ilya and I were staring from the doorway.

"Take your fucking clothes off."

"Both of us?" Ilya asked, incredulous.

Bron's lips curled into a hard smile. He crossed the room to us and grabbed our hands, then led us in. In all the time I'd been here, Bron's room had been completely off limits.

He stood us in the middle of the room, then turned one of the chairs by the fireplace and sat down. Although he was wearing a lot less than we were, I felt naked.

"Undress each other."

Ilya frowned at him. "Why do I feel as though you're trying to distract us from the conversation?"

"We cannot solve anything tonight. We need to visit Vas, see what happens, then decide from there."

"If Ilya doesn't care if he gets sent back here, then there's no need for me to go, right? He doesn't need a fake fiancée."

"You're coming. You'll be Ilya's elegant, appropriately affectionate future bride. Proving he's a man is important if he wants to make his own choices."

"And what if this man doesn't want to strip at your whim?" Ilya folded his arms.

"You'd really refuse me one last night before I become nothing more than a hired thug again?" Bron's face was impassive, the way it often was, but his eyes filled with...what? Regret? "I could beat you first if you want to keep pretending you don't want me."

I turned to Ilya and toyed with the hem of his T-shirt. He looked down at me and sighed.

"Fine." Ilya moved his hands to the buttons on my shirt. I expected him to rush through the task in irritation, but he unfastened them slowly, dragging it out. The occasional brush of his fingers against my skin sent sensual jolts through me. I studied his shaven face, feeling like he was a strangely familiar stranger and not the shy, eager, almost-virgin I'd met twelve or so weeks ago.

"Kiss," Bron commanded.

Ilya sent him a sour look.

"Don't be ill-tempered. It's what you were doing before I interrupted."

"You want us to do it for your gratification?" Ilya grumbled.

"Why not? Entertain me."

"If we aren't entertaining enough, are you going to give us a thumbs-down and feed us to your lions?" I asked, suppressing a grin. It was hard to hide my feelings the way they did, but I was getting better at it if I remembered to try.

Bron rose and opened a drawer. He sifted through its contents and withdrew a leather strap the length of his forearm. It had a forked tongue. Idly, he swished it back and forth in front of him. "If you're not entertaining enough, maybe my tawse can give you some inspiration."

"So, if we don't perform, you'll beat us?"

"It was a child's punishment in some places not long ago. I'm sure you'll survive. I won't even need to use it on you if you cooperate."

Frowning, I grabbed Ilya by the shirt and tugged him closer. "Kiss me before he beats us both."

"You know he'll do it anyway. Hurting us makes his dick hard."

I slid my hands further up, wrapping them around the back of his neck and urging him down to me.

He brushed his lips against mine and pushed my shirt off my shoulders, letting it slide off to the floor. Briefly, he pulled away and stripped off his T-shirt. It wasn't what Bron had asked us to do, but he didn't object.

Ilya kissed me again, and I sucked his tongue into my mouth. His hands explored my bare skin and eventually tangled with the back of my bra as he struggled to unfasten it. Bron's chuckle didn't deter him, and he worked at it for a few moments until it loosened around me. He stripped it off, eyes gleaming with wicked delight. I loved seeing him so proud of himself.

"Aren't her breasts perfect?" Ilya covered them with his hands, squeezing.

"As perfect as her ass, although both could use some bite marks."

"No biting! I don't want to meet your family covered in bite marks. This isn't high school, you know."

"I never got to go to high school, so you'll have to forgive my fascination."

"With biting?"

"With everything to do with you." He bit my neck, not hard enough to leave a mark, but I could feel the desire to mark me trembling in his mouth.

He lifted me into his arms and coaxed my legs around his body, devouring my mouth as he walked us slowly toward the wall and pinned me against it. His mouth was everywhere, hot and demanding, his tongue exploring my mouth, my neck, his teeth catching at my earlobes, my jaw. I slid my feet down to his calves and braced them there, grinding my pussy against his thick cock and the frustrating amount of clothing between us. Still two layers, if my panties counted.

I slid my hands over his muscular back, his shoulders, his neck, up into his hair, grabbing handfuls of the silky length. If he was looking to impress his father, we probably needed to cut it, but it was so pretty it would be a shame to chop off.

Bron made a rumbling sound. "You could bite places her clothes cover," he suggested. "No one will see except us."

Ilya's evil laugh made me squeal, and I struggled to get away. He turned from the wall and took me down to the floor and pinned me there, watching me struggle like a trophy butterfly.

"I love it when you fight me. Your cheeks are red, and your eyes and hair are wild."

"Don't you dare bite me."

He straddled my waist and kept my arms pinned. "My pretty wife doesn't get to give me orders."

I struggled, loving how immovable he was. Before these two, no one had made me feel the way poor Lane probably felt all the time. Tiny. Delicate. Helpless.

He shifted downward, biting a trail along my skin, harder where no one would see. I gasped and shuddered, meaning to fight or push him away, but so turned on I had to swallow a moan.

"Every bite of you belongs to us," he whispered against my stomach, sinking his teeth into me there, too. His hair trailed over my skin, soft and tickling, the pads of his callused fingers scraping, the heat of his mouth intoxicating. I forgot about fighting him off and melted into a puddle on the floor. Why not let the man work?

He tugged down the waistband of my panties, then sucked the sensitive flesh next to my hipbone. The tension in my stomach twisted almost painfully, flooding me with more warmth. When he forced his way between my thighs, I realized he'd left an ugly purple mark next to my hip. He ran possessive fingers over that mark, looking pleased with himself. Slowly, he bit his way down to my pelvis, and bit me there harder, leaving teeth marks. My clit throbbed with reckless envy. He wouldn't bite me there, too, would he?

"You'd better hold her down if you're going to suck her clit," Bron observed. "She's so ready for you, she'll probably buck. You may also want to take those panties off her first."

Ilya ignored him and slid his arms under my thighs and looped them around. What was he planning to do?

His hands caught at the crotch of my panties, and with a hard jerk, the stitches gave away, opening a rent large enough to do whatever he wanted to me.

"You ruined my underwear!"

"We bought you a million pair of panties, woman," Bron grumbled. "They are meant to tempt men and get ripped off."

"No, they aren't! There's nothing wrong with wearing pretty panties."

"I never said there was anything wrong with wearing them," he assured me. "You should just be prepared for what happens if you do."

I sputtered a protest, but Ilya used his fingers to spread my labia wide, distracting me from the argument. He inhaled deeply, like I was his favorite dessert, and I shut my eyes in mortification.

"You always smell like something I want to sink my teeth into," he murmured to me.

"Don't bite me there! That part of me is too delicate to be rough with."

He tsked. "Maybe no one has bitten you the right way then." He lowered his head, and I tried to grab his hair but it slid through my fingers in a beautiful dark cascade.

"Ilya, no!"

At the last minute, he turned his head and bit the inside of my thigh. I squealed in surprise, then in pain as he closed his teeth harder over the spot. I hissed in a breath and clutched convulsively at his head.

As I was about to scream, he released the spot and turned his head so he could give me a twin bite on the other thigh. I smacked his face, but I couldn't yank away. It felt like he might bite the chunk of flesh right off if I moved too quickly.

I couldn't decide which side hurt worse, and I was sobbing by the time he stopped, but he was still holding me wide open for whatever attack came next. I tried to curl in on myself, but the best I could do was slap a protective hand over my clit.

"No more! No more, please! If you bite me there, my clit will come right off."

He pried my hand away.

"No! Please, Ilya!"

"Don't you want to feel my teeth on the tenderest parts of this beautiful body?" He bared his teeth in a feral grin, and it surprised me they weren't covered in blood. He'd bitten my thighs so hard my head was still swimming from the pain.

"No!"

"No? That's too bad." He pushed his face between my legs and bit down on one of my labia, but nowhere near as hard as he'd done to my thigh. I shrieked and smacked the top of his head, trying to push him away, but he was undeterred. He bit again and again, making me think of vampires or maybe werewolves devouring me.

I struggled in his arms but could only do so much for fear of the damage I might do trying to tear delicate parts of me out from between his teeth. When his mouth came down over my clit, I shrieked in fear, bucking, catching him in the chin with my pubic bone. His mouth fastened down over me, and he sucked, his tongue doing devilish things, his teeth sharp, not biting, but too close. A layer of sweat covered my skin—fear and arousal and confusion buzzing between my ears. Did I trust this man?

His curious fingers investigated, learning how turned on I was despite my anxiety. He plunged a finger into me, then a second, thrusting in and out of my hot, needy pussy.

I clenched my teeth against his onslaught, the delicious tugging pressure of his mouth, his fingers curved upward, searching. He found my g-spot, damn him, and I felt as if my tongue was going to fall down the back of my throat, as he hummed in delight, the vibration so perfect that all I could do was whimper. Stubbornly, I fought the orgasm, but he was winning no matter what I did.

I opened my mouth to scream, and my back bucked, arching. A cock slammed into my mouth, muffling my scream, and then someone was fucking it—Bron? It had to be him because the torture between my legs didn't stop. I squirmed on Ilya's tongue and choked on Bron's dick, surrounded and trapped by hard male bodies. I could feel Bron's cock swelling, but he jerked away at the last moment. Our gazes met, and he gave me a wolfish grin, backing away even though his cock was so hard it was bobbing in protest. I didn't have time to think about what his expression meant because Ilya had stilled above me, letting my impending orgasm ebb.

I screamed incoherently, trying to kick him into action, but more than willing to finish myself off if he wanted to play games. He laughed aloud, then the sound cut off abruptly.

"Bron, no!" Ilya gasped.

"I told the two of you to strip, but one of you is still wearing pants."

I heard Ilya's belt buckle hit the floor and Bron forcibly shucked off Ilya's pants and tossed them aside.

Bron spat, and Ilya's gaze widened. He looked at me like there was something I could do about what was about to happen to him.

I could feel Ilya bracing himself, and I watched his expressions with a mixture of arousal and sympathy as Bron pushed into his ass.

I slid out from underneath him, wanting to watch, but feeling guilty about it. Then again, Bron's victim had just deprived me of a spectacular orgasm, so I hardened my heart to his suffering.

He grimaced in discomfort, teeth gritted, breath labored. The tendons in his neck stood out with the strain of accommodating his tormentor's obnoxiously large cock.

"That's a good boy. Stop fighting me."

"Bron, it's not supposed to be like this anymore." He gasped.

"It will always be like this, Ilyusha. You will always belong to me, no matter who belongs to you. Even if we part ways—even if you get married and have ten brats running around—one day you will see me on the street and you will follow me wherever I lead. You will let me into your body because you know who you belong to."

Ilya's fists were curled as though he were angry, but a tear trickled from his eye and slid over the bridge of his nose.

When Bron was deep inside him, hips flush with Ilya's ass, he folded over him, skin to skin, mouth brushing his ear with infinite tenderness. His expression was so full of regret and pain it broke my heart. He loved Ilya and wouldn't admit it to himself, let alone to the man who knew him better than anyone.

How could Vas rip this away from them? It wasn't fair.

I crawled closer, ducking under Ilya to run my tongue along his cock. He gasped, and Bron's hand came down to block what I was doing. I dodged him, licking his fingers almost as often as I reached Ilya's cock, and eventually he wrapped his hand around it to keep me away. Ilya gasped in surprise and shuddered above me. For a moment, the hand stalled as though Bron had abruptly realized what he'd done, but then he stroked him with sure, unhurried movements. I licked the head of Ilya's cock, then managed to get it into my mouth, vying with Bron for real estate, sucking until Ilya gave a ragged cry and flooded my mouth with cum. I sucked and swallowed until he was empty, then crawled out from underneath him to watch as Bron kept stroking his cock, making him twitch and swear, bucking under him until Bron groaned, and his hips lost their rhythm. I watched as he came, and my body shuddering with jealous need. They were absolutely gorgeous together, and I wished I dared to grab Bron's phone and take some pictures for myself for later.

As Bron slowed to a stop, they stayed locked together, Bron's body surrounding Ilya's, the layers of muscle pressed together almost baffling to the eye. I crawled closer and kissed Bron. I half expected him to pull away at the taste Ilya had left in my mouth, but his tongue invaded, exploring and curious.

"Did we leave you desperate, *De-li-lah*?"

I nodded sulkily.

He pulled out of Ilya and flipped him over, then moved me over Ilya's face.

Without hesitation, Ilya growled and pulled me down tighter against his mouth.

"No, I—" My words stalled as Ilya shamelessly devoured my pussy.

Before I fell over, Bron moved up behind me and lowered me to brace on my hands, my thighs spread so wide that Ilya could get at anything he wanted with his wicked mouth. Fingers explored me from behind, groping my ass, pushed deep into my pussy. Bron ran his lips down my spine, following that track to the cleft of my ass. His tongue darted out, stroking between my pussy and asshole, bumping into Ilya's fingers. I trembled, my orgasm already so close, the pressure inside me so intense I could cry. The fingers in my pussy found a ragged rhythm, and Bron's tongue drifted upward, exploring my ass cleft and bumping over my back hole.

Their hands and mouths were everywhere, reminding me of being blindfolded at the club. Bron's hand rested on my mid-back, his thumb on my spine, and my belly quivered with the possessive feel of it.

Bron pulled away and bit my ass cheek, then spread me apart and blew a cool stream of air over my damp flesh. His gaze was invasive. I felt inspected. It was hot as hell.

"Are you going to come on his tongue, my little whore? I want to watch your holes clench when you come."

I rocked against Ilya's mouth, torturing myself, forcing my orgasm down, edging myself with his tongue. My miserable whimpers filled the room, and the tightness in my belly had spread to all my muscles.

Bron's tongue swept over my asshole once more and I stopped moving, unable to do anything but feel their mouths and attention completely focused on me. The first flutter of my orgasm was so tight it hurt in the most delicious way, followed by a long pause before an earth-shattering convulsion. Ilya groaned in satisfaction, the vibration making me squeal in protest as I got off so hard it felt like I was turning inside out.

"Good girl," Bron crooned, his fingers exploring where my muscles twitched and shuddered. "Fuck, that's hot."

When my orgasm and the worst of the aftershocks finally abated, Bron picked me up and laid me on top of Ilya, then lowered himself to lie beside us on the carpet. Both men were looking at me, but I was too limp and tired to feel self-conscious.

Ilya's cock twitched, and I realized he was hard again.

"Ilya, no."

The sound he made was almost a purr. "Wifey, yes."

Men.

*

I woke in the night, naked, needing to pee and surrounded by mounds of muscle. Quietly, I slid over Ilya and made my way down the hall to the bathroom.

When I came out, a dark shadow waited for me.

"Bron?" I guessed.

The shadow didn't say anything.

"This isn't funny." This was a scene from every second horror movie I'd ever seen.

Adrenaline tried to convince me to run.

He grabbed my wrist and pulled me to him. Bare skin brushed against bare skin. I put my hand to his chest and gazed up at him.

Definitely Bron.

"What's wrong?"

"Can't sleep," he admitted. He slid his hand into my hair and gripped it gently at the scalp, hard enough to make me feel trapped in the shivery kind of way.

He used his grip on my hair to tip my head back, then kissed me leisurely. His hum of pleasure had me wrapping my arms around him, too, grazing his back with my nails. "Woman, you'll be the death of me."

I could feel his interest growing, digging into my stomach.

"What's keeping you awake?"

He shrugged. "Go back to bed before he realizes we're missing. He'll think we abandoned him." Rather than let me go, he stole one last kiss.

"Where are you going?"

"I need to add a few more things to the note for Lev." The 'note' for the man who took care of the farm when they were gone read more like a book at this point.

"About the new goat?"

"Yes, she's not getting along well with the others. It was a bad time to bring her over."

He gazed out the window to the kitchen garden like a father who was leaving his newborn with a stranger.

Bron kissed me on the forehead, and let me go. "Go on, my Queen of Whores. Don't let me keep you up." He slapped my ass. I went.

If none of us were going to live here anymore, nothing about the farm mattered, did it? And yet both men were still talking like they were moving back to Moscow and never looking back.

Sighing, I crawled back in beside Ilya, buried my face in his chest, and tried to dismiss all the uncertainty from my mind.

Chapter Nineteen

When Bron had mentioned a private plane, I'd assumed it would be something just big enough for us, our luggage, and a pilot. Instead, the plane that Vas sent for us was a living room with wings. Waiting for takeoff, I felt like an agent on *Criminal Minds*. No one asked to see my fake ID, and no one rifled through our bags. There was something to be said for traveling with people who had money.

"Better than our last trip?" Ilya asked, looking amused.

"Yes, and a million times better than the trip before that."

Bron snorted. "You're saying you didn't enjoy being drugged and fucked while you were helpless? You were so wet for me—you must be lying."

I shuddered in revulsion. "No, it's not my thing. Never has been."

"I suppose you had it done to you a few times on the Island." Ilya stretched his legs out in front of him.

"Yeah. There, too."

"It happened to you before that?" Bron asked, not sounding pleased.

"High school, except I didn't get paid for it that time. The entire soccer team had a piece of me."

Ilya growled. "And their names?"

The information lodged behind my teeth, but I wasn't about to spit it out. "Why?"

"Because you're ours, and a wrong has been done to you."

"We were teenagers. I hope they've already learned their lesson."

"They went to jail?"

"No." I thought of the video, the police station, the hours of questioning. The lost evidence.

They were both staring at me with murderous gleams in their eyes.

"Why be mad at them but not angry at yourselves?"

"Like you said, you volunteered for such treatment when you went to the Island. It's different than being taken unaware by people you trust." Bron's eyes were terrifying. I couldn't help but think about how satisfying it would be to watch them beat my bully assailants to a pulp, the way Bron had with the man who'd attacked me in the park in Saint Petersburg.

"I didn't volunteer to be kidnapped by you," I pointed out.

"A technicality." Bron flicked his fingers, as if what he'd done to me then, and since then, had been of little to no consequence.

The plane taxied, and we buckled in for takeoff.

"You came on my dick often enough. I knew you liked it despite yourself."

"Orgasms aren't consent."

He flashed me a wicked smile.

"I'm serious, Bron."

"And I don't care, *De-li-lah*. You were bought and paid for."

"I only agreed to take a contract from you after you kidnapped me."

"First you were under contract from the Island, then to us. You didn't seem to mind having me breed your sexy ass."

"You can't breed someone's ass." I glared at him.

"Obviously, you're mistaken," Ilya said dryly. "It's the only way to explain how Bron came into being."

"If anyone is a piece of shit on this plane, it's you."

"I also suppose if it was possible to breed an ass, you and I would have a million little bastards running around the island," Ilya said quietly. His eyes gleamed with amusement, but he was smart enough to turn his gaze out the window rather than keep teasing the man who enjoyed beating him.

"I can only imagine how much you'd love that. Brats everywhere."

"I think I'm safe," Ilya whispered. "Two ex-wives and now me, and still no children? You must not have strong enough spunk in that little prick of yours."

Bron unbuckled and lunged for Ilya, even though we hadn't finished our ascent.

"Sit down," Ilya snapped, then lowered his voice. "My father pays the pilot and flight attendant. You think they won't talk?" The attendant hadn't come out of the cockpit at all, but there was nothing saying he wouldn't pop out at a moment's notice.

Bron's fists curled at his sides, but he lowered himself back into his seat. "Tonight, we will see what you think of my little prick as I rearrange your fucking guts."

"After all these years, I think you have permanently rearranged them."

The silence that fell was tense, but both men had been acting strangely since we'd woken this morning.

Time to change the subject.

"How did you end up working for Vas?"

He shrugged. "I was quiet, big. I got into a lot of fights. Older boys. Teachers. It seemed like the right work for me."

"But how did you cross paths with him in the first place? Did he go to schools looking for boys to recruit?" I suddenly had visions of Vas having a band of little pickpockets, like Fagin from *Oliver Twist*.

"No, no. My mother was one of Vas's cooks. She got me a job washing dishes, and it helped us get by. He noticed me—probably because I was so big. Everyone is afraid of Vas, but he was usually good to me." His eyes strayed to Ilya, as though the statement made him feel guilty.

"You were probably what he wished his own sons were like," Ilya grumbled.

"Why? The two of you are similar sizes."

"Not when we met," Bron said, looking amused. "He was long and lean, like a swimmer."

"I meant his attitude—his expression, and the way he walked," Ilya said.

"He intimidated you?"

"I—" His eyes darted to Bron, then back to me. "Yes. I wanted to be him, but maybe it wasn't only that. He was the first man I'd spent much time with, and I found him fascinating."

"You still find me fascinating," Bron said smugly.

How could he think he was straight and then still flirt with Ilya the way he did? The man was either confused or a jerk. Maybe both.

"If that's what you choose to believe."

The plane banked, and I watched out the window as the sea gradually disappeared from view. I studied the landscape, feeling like I hadn't had a long enough vacation from my life, even though it had been months since I'd been home.

Home. Such a strange word. For me, home was a room in my parents' house that I used to share with one of my sisters. I thought longingly of what I was leaving, even though it would never look as pretty and well-kept as my parents' house.

When we eventually arrived at Vas's gate it was difficult not to look impressed. Our car was buzzed through by security, and our driver followed the long driveway that terminated in a circular garden around a white marble fountain. The pale blue building was large and ostentatious, with white columns and a carving in the peak of the roof. A second floor balcony extended across the entire front of the massive building. It looked like a museum, or maybe a palace.

I tried to picture myself going back to work at my parents' store, stocking shelves, heading off shoplifters. That reality was so far removed from walking up the stairs of a mansion while wearing couture clothing. I was also on the arm of a hot guy while his secret lover trailed behind us. It felt like one or the other of my lives had to be a dream.

If I'd expected Ilya's family to meet us at the door, I would have been disappointed. A servant greeted us, and more servants led us to a suite of rooms. It was a beautifully decorated suite that reminded me of our stay in Saint Petersburg, but nothing about it said Ilya.

"Where are all your things?" I ran my fingers over a marble bust of a man I didn't recognize.

"My things?" he asked after he finished thanking the servants who'd brought our luggage in, then closed the door behind him.

"Your books or toys or whatever? Nothing in here reminds me of you."

"These rooms were never his." Bron dropped into an armchair. I still wasn't used to his short hair and their cleanly shaven faces. I kept feeling as if I was traveling with strangers.

"I've never had a room here. When I visit, the housekeeper puts me in one of the guest rooms."

"Oh."

He cupped the side of my face and rubbed his thumb over my cheek. "Don't look so sad. I liked my life running wild on the island. Here, my father expected perfect manners from us all the time. A dropped spoon was grounds to be banished to my room for the rest of the visit."

I frowned, feeling sorry for the boy he'd been. "But children are clumsy by nature."

"Your parents sound more patient than my father."

"My parents weren't around much. I raised their children for them."

Bron's brows rose. "Is that why you went to the Island so many times? Because you felt responsible for their education?"

"I knew my parents would never agree to pay for school. Sometimes, I think they only had us to help them run the store." I opened my bag and hunted down my makeup. I'd need to touch it up before we met his family. "I didn't want them to be trapped in that life, with no hope of ever making their own decisions."

Ilya led me into the main bedroom which was large enough to be a classroom, and showed me the lavish washroom. The shower had multiple heads, and there was a generously proportioned tub.

I decided to take a quick shower and start getting ready from scratch. By the time I got out, dried my hair, and did my makeup, the two of them had unpacked our things.

"We're dining with the family," Ilya told me. "It's formal. I got our clothes ready."

"Oh. Thank you." Although I hadn't put on much makeup, it would have to do. He'd remembered what shoes went with the dress he'd selected, which made me smile. He always noticed minor details that made me feel important to him.

Bron had unpacked his things in the spare room, but he got ready with us. He even did up my gown and kissed my nape when he was done. When I'd tried on the dress at the boutique, it had made me feel like a Hollywood starlet from the 1920s. Ilya had loved it on me so much he'd insisted on buying it despite the staggering price tag.

The two of them looked strangely dangerous in their suits—as though they both had a side-hustle as either hitmen or movie mobsters, since their muscles were too defined to make them suit models.

We walked through the echoing hallways, our footsteps loud in the house's silence. Ilya had a casual arm draped around my waist, but he stared straight ahead, apparently lost in thought. Bron was behind us, playing the part of bodyguard.

"You okay?" I whispered.

Ilya nodded but didn't say anything. He was wearing his Bron mask, which was hot, but also disheartening. I already missed his more animated expressions, and the affectionate look he always had in his eyes, but it made sense that this was the Ilya who would meet with his family.

We entered a space that was too classy to be called a living room but brought the word salon to mind. Impeccably dressed, lovely people stood in small groups chatting and sipping at drinks. It looked like I imagined intermission would at an opera, with quiet, intelligent conversation and hushed voices. Most of them appeared to be in their mid-thirties to early forties, which made me feel like a baby.

"I thought this was just going to be dinner with your family." I looked up at Ilya, and his gaze was sympathetic.

"This is only my father, my six brothers, and their wives. You know about Yana, and my other sister doesn't spend much time with the family. She's married to a friend of my father's and he's old and unwell."

Hopefully, she'd married the man voluntarily. And six brothers? I'd thought *I* had a big family.

Everyone looked over as we entered, and I straightened my shoulders and raised my chin, knowing exactly how to play this game. The expressions turned our way weren't friendly or pleasant. Most of the men regarded us gravely, the women coldly, except for one or two who had turned up their noses. The women were all chic and lovely.

"There you are." The one who had spoken was a man who must have been in his sixties. He was leanly muscled, like a long-distance runner. If he'd bothered to color his white hair, he would have passed for much younger, other than his dark, soulless eyes.

When his gaze landed on me, it was all I could do to not cringe away.

"My apologies," Ilya replied. "Although I'm not sure the guests of honor can be late."

I expected them to hug or shake hands, but no one moved other than to sip at their drinks and continue their conversations. Considering Ilya hadn't seen his family in close to five years, it seemed ridiculous that we'd come all this way to be snubbed.

The others were casually taking our measure in between socializing with each other. This wasn't a family—it was some sort of stupid high school clique.

"Vas, this is my fiancée, Delilah. Delilah, this is my father, Vas."

Ilya's father looked me over with an almost rude intensity.

"An American?"

"Yes," I agreed, not sure whether he considered that a good or a bad thing.

He sniffed, which still wasn't an answer either way. "She's pretty enough to be seen with the family. Good bones. Good bearing."

What the fuck? Was he going to check my teeth next? Kick my tires?

"Does she speak Russian?"

"Not yet."

His dark eyes met mine and narrowed. "If you're going to be part of this family, girl, remember your place."

He walked away, leaving me wishing I had a drink to throw at him.

I turned to Ilya. "Is he always so charming?"

"He must like you. He didn't throw you out of the house," Bron murmured.

"He would do that?"

"The man wouldn't hesitate."

Ilya's brows rose.

"You were never allowed to eat with the adults, Ilya. If one of your brothers brought home a woman your father didn't want to look at, they were out on their asses."

A server came and asked what we wanted to drink, and we waited for her to move away before continuing the conversation.

"That's ridiculous. The last time he visited, they made him eat by himself? He would have been what? Twenty-four or twenty-five?"

"I've always been shunned here." Ilya shrugged with about as much concern as a bookworm discussing rain in the forecast.

"But that doesn't make sense." I tried not to show my anger.

"I am not my father's favorite." His tone was bland. "It has never mattered to me."

This version of him that didn't care about anything hurt my heart. On his island, he'd been bright and enthusiastic. Here, a shadow lurked in his dark eyes.

A couple drifted over, and Bron moved behind us again, keeping a respectful distance.

"You've grown taller," the man said in English. He had broad shoulders and shrewd eyes.

"You haven't seen me in a long time, Alexander. Not since I was a boy."

"Business keeps me busy, and Alina hates it here."

Wow. Candid much? I managed not to show my surprise.

"Things are going well?" Ilya asked politely.

His brother inclined his head. "I can't complain."

The server arrived with our drinks, and I gratefully accepted my glass of wine.

"This is my fiancée, Delilah."

"Nice to meet you. Congratulations."

Congratulations? Oh right, on our engagement.

"Thank you." I smiled slightly, not sure how much emotion to show.

His wife, Alina, looked like she'd swallowed a live goldfish—disgusted and maybe a bit green. She nodded once, then turned to gaze at a piece of artwork near the door while she sipped at her champagne as though it might wash the unpleasant taste from her mouth.

Wow. The woman didn't even know me. Why the hostility? Had my smile been too much? Or maybe my dress wasn't up to her standards?

I focused my attention on Ilya's conversation with Alexander, which was difficult to do considering they had switched to Russian now that the introductions were over.

A servant opened the door and made an announcement in Russian. Everyone set aside their drinks and filed out of the room and down the hall, two by two, as though it was how things were always done.

"Time for dinner?" I asked Ilya.

He smiled tightly, then glanced over at Bron and said something in quiet, rapid Russian. The pat on my arm felt distracted, but he dropped a kiss on my forehead, which was apparently safe since no one else was around. I'd been lectured about public displays of affection before we'd arrived.

"Soon, wife."

I really hated not being able to understand Russian. I'd catch a few words I understood here and there, but Bron and Ilya spoke so much English that when they switched to Russian, it felt like they were keeping secrets from me.

Sighing at my paranoia, I gave my wine glass to a server. I took Ilya's arm and let him lead me down the broad, marble-floored hall where his family members were entering a room where double-oak doors stood open.

The room was slightly bigger than the last one. A man who hadn't been with us earlier stood at the front of the room. He was older than Vas. Was he Ilya's grandfather or something?

A glance around the room showed me religious icons and rows of chairs.

The family was so religious they had their own chapel? Religion hadn't really figured into our lives on the island, so Ilya coming from such a religious family hadn't even crossed my mind.

Ilya led me down the aisle toward where the others were sitting. Had Vas summoned us here for some sort of religious service he hadn't mentioned? A funeral? I definitely wasn't dressed for one. Why were men so bad at giving a girl a heads-up ahead of time?

Ilya bypassed the chairs and led me right up to the man at the front. I didn't know anything about their religion. Maybe I needed to be welcomed into the family as Ilya's fiancée? Or maybe there was some sort of church service for getting engaged?

The weight of our fake engagement felt suddenly heavier.

I made eye contact with who I assumed was the priest. He was wearing a suit, not robes, but I didn't know what was usual for their religion. My family was Catholic, but only vaguely—I'd only been to church maybe three times as an adult, and it had been for family weddings and a baptism, not regular services.

He watched us as we approached, and when we stopped in front of him, he spoke in Russian. The rest of the family murmured some sort of response, and I glanced up at Ilya, trying my best to look like everything was cool and I was happy to be there. He would explain later, I was sure.

The service went on for a while, with Bron whispering in my ear anytime I was expected to nod.

Suspicion made my ears buzz. I felt faint.

Surely, he wouldn't—*they* wouldn't...

At some point, the man seated us at a table and put documents in front of us. My eyes swam, trying to decipher the Cyrillic.

"What am I signing?" I whispered to Ilya.

"I'll explain later," he whispered back. The family was talking among themselves and barely paying us any attention.

The pen shook in my hand. Everything about this said it was a wedding, but Ilya wouldn't do that to me, right? The ceremony—if that's what it was—had only taken about seven minutes. A rich family like this would make more of a fuss for a real wedding.

Wouldn't they?

When I glanced up at Bron, he nodded at me in covert encouragement.

A panicked feeling writhed in the pit of my stomach.

My mind kept screaming at me that two plus two equaled four—the expensive, albeit pale blue dress he'd insisted on buying me, the religious service, the family gathering, the congratulations.

No rings had been exchanged, but that was a technicality.

I slid my gaze to Ilya, but he was looking down at where his scarred hands rested on the table, still clutching his pen. His neck was red, but his expression was impassive.

I signed, forcing my expression to remain demure and my hand not to shake.

If this was what I thought it was, we'd sort it out later.

We rose. The man gave a brief speech, and the service was over.

The family filed out of the room and crossed the hall to a large, formal dining room.

"I need to talk to you," I whispered to Ilya. I clutched at his arm to let him know I was serious, and it wasn't some whim.

"Not now, wife. I'm sorry, but it will have to wait."

Had the way he'd called me wife sounded different?

Were we really married? What if he'd arranged a wedding without telling me and I was standing here, legally his wife?

I didn't even know what his last name was.

Maybe Bron would do something underhanded like that, but Ilya would never, right?

I thought about all the times we had fallen into a sweet, comfortable rhythm around each other—baking bread, working in the garden, taking care of the animals.

Would being married to him be so bad?

But that wasn't the point! Getting married was a two-way street. He couldn't just trick me into doing it. I was supposed to be willing. I was too young to get married and didn't even know if I wanted to, let alone to a man who had paid me for sex.

The couples wandered over two at a time and spoke to us in Russian. Either no one had told them I could only speak English, or they didn't feel the need to speak to me directly. Maybe they couldn't speak English?

As the fourth set of them went back to socializing, I glanced up at Ilya again and pulled on his arm.

"I know you are confused. I will explain everything later. Be yourself and pretend you're happy, okay?" Eyes I would have expected to be pleading were hard and unyielding. Tonight, he wasn't interested in placating me. Or was this part of the Bron disguise for his family?

Well, no matter what had happened in the other room, there was no fixing it right then.

I beamed at him, then remembered to tone it down for Russian consumption.

After my third glass of alcohol, I made my way down the hall to where a servant indicated there was a washroom.

I made use of the facilities, but everything had a weird, dreamlike feel to it. I checked my hair and makeup in the mirror, feeling different than I had when I left our room. Was that the face of a married woman? Did I have a husband?

I washed my hands, and when I opened the door, someone grabbed my arm and pulled me around the corner.

Alina?

"Stupid girl." She gave my arm a shake.

"Excuse me?"

Her eyes were wild, but her blonde hair was impeccable above her improbably smooth face.

"You may be new and shiny in this family, but I'm the *first* daughter-in-law. Never forget that."

She dropped my arm and stalked off, her designer pumps clicking in annoyance as she made her way back to the dining room.

I wanted to call her back to see if she would tell me whether I was married. Considering her outburst, I assumed I was.

I *was* married. To Ilya.

With my mind in a weird haze, I retraced my steps to the dining room and made my way to his side. His gaze was soft when he noticed me, but he shuttered that quickly.

Bron's face was like stone. He lurked nearby, not speaking directly to either of us. It felt so unnatural to be in a place where Bron was supposed to be nothing to us, and he wasn't swinging his dick and temper around to keep us in line.

We sat down to a nice dinner, complete with what sounded like rehearsed and insincere toasts. I kept a small, vague smile plastered on my face.

I was married, and my family wasn't here. Lane wasn't next to me, teasing me about being in love with a predator I'd met on the Island.

I was married, and I was in love with my husband.

I was married, but both of us were also in love with the man who, according to society, was nothing more than his tutor/bodyguard.

What the hell was I going to do?

Chapter Twenty

Eventually, when the drinking had gone on long enough, Ilya excused us from the salon where we had moved to after supper. We made our way back to our suite, trailed by Bron.

As soon as the door closed behind the three of us, I rounded on them both.

"What the hell is going on?" I whispered, the anger and betrayal I'd felt all evening welling up in my throat.

"Calm down, woman," Bron grumbled. "It isn't the end of the world. You could do worse than the boy. Besides, people get divorced all the time. If you can hold your peace and stay married for a year or so, then quietly file for divorce, you will be a rich woman."

"What do you mean?"

"If you divorce, you'll get a settlement of some sort. Be patient."

I rounded on Ilya. "This is the kind of bullshit I would have expected from Bron, but from you? Why the hell didn't you tell me you were bringing me here to marry me?"

"I wasn't sure if you would agree, and it needed to happen as soon as possible."

"Why? Did I get you pregnant?"

Bron snorted, but Ilya didn't seem to find it as funny.

"Your contract with me is finished soon. I didn't have time to convince you."

"If I march right back to that dining room and tell the priest I didn't know what was going on, he would rip up those papers."

"Considering he's one of my father's closest friends, you may be mistaken, but I assumed we meant enough to each other that you would do me one small favor."

"A small favor is lending you gas money or picking you up from the airport. Marrying you to prove a point to your father is not a small favor."

"I'm sorry you're angry, but I won't lie and say I'm sorry we're married." His grin and shining eyes took the wind out of my wrath-filled sails.

"I just—" I shrugged irritably. "I never imagined being in the position where I wouldn't know I was getting married until halfway through the ceremony. Call me old-fashioned."

"I love you," Ilya said, approaching me slowly, as though I might bite.

The idea of biting him wasn't off the table.

"If you love me, why would you do something like this? Why wouldn't you tell me what was going on ahead of time and trust that I would cooperate?"

"It's a piece of paper. It's no big deal." Bron made a dismissive gesture. "Don't tell me you're one of those women who has fantasized about her wedding since she was a little girl."

I glared at him. "No, but don't tell me this meant nothing to you. I could tell how upset you were."

"I'm not upset. Your delusions about how I feel are cute, but you are mistaken."

"I'm not mistaken at all, but I guess your feelings on the matter don't really factor into this. The two of you decided what the best course of action was and didn't even bother letting me in on the plan."

Bron sighed and scooped me into his arms even as I struggled and tried to get him to put me down. Unfortunately, when the man got an idea in his head, there wasn't much I could do about it.

"You'd better be quiet," he whispered. "This house has good soundproofing, but it's not magic."

"Put me down!" I whispered back, scowling.

"Nonsense. It's our wedding night," Ilya reminded me, his smile feral. "We need to consummate our union."

"That would sound old-fashioned, except your bodyguard is here," I pointed out, in case he'd failed to notice the man carrying me toward the bedroom. "If you think I'm having sex with either of you tonight, get ready to be disappointed."

"Oh, we're both ready, but not to be disappointed. Now we'll make sure you're ready too."

I struggled in Bron's arms, but his chest vibrated with something that sounded suspiciously like a cross between a chuckle and a growl.

"I can't believe you would treat me this way, after everything the three of us have been through together over the past few months. I need time to process this, and I don't think I'm ever going to forgive you."

"What makes you think we care if you forgive us?" Bron handed me to Ilya.

"Ilya cares. I know he does." I looked at my husband—my husband!—and frowned, wanting him to grovel and tell me how sorry he was for doing something so heartless to me. I never would have expected him to do something so underhanded.

"I'm supposed to be sorry for making you my wife? I told you I loved you. I've been calling you my wife for weeks, and you've hardly complained."

"I thought it was a joke because of our fake engagement!"

"Americans have a strange sense of humor," Ilya said to Bron, shaking his head.

"Marriage is supposed to be voluntary. You're not supposed to ambush a woman with a wedding when she doesn't even understand the language."

"Different cultures have different customs," Bron said with a shrug.

"You can't tell me that Russian men always trick women into marrying them. I don't believe that for a second."

"Who said anything about Russians?" Ilya's grin was completely evil. This time, it didn't look anything like one of Bron's expressions—it was something all his own. "Our island has its own culture, or hadn't you noticed?"

"Toxic relationships aren't a culture," I snapped.

He threw me onto the bed and they both descended on me as I tried to fight them off. Their hands were everywhere, unzipping my dress, stealing my shoes, shucking me like an ear of corn. I was naked except for my panties, in about ten seconds flat.

Both men looked cocky, and sexy as hell.

"You can't do this to me. If you try to have sex with me right now, I'll scream bloody murder, and your brothers will either save me or call the police on you."

Bron hooked his fingers under one side of my underwear and yanked a knife out of his pocket, slicing the fabric with a quick, lethal slash that made me gasp. He cut through the other side, too, then wadded up the fabric and stuffed it in my mouth. The satin, or whatever it was, immediately grew soggy, and I could taste myself on them.

"No problems, only solutions."

I tried to shriek at him, but the fabric deadened the sound.

Ilya tapped me on the nose. "This house is very well soundproofed, so I'm not concerned. When I was small and would come to visit,

I could scream and run around and jump on the bed as much as I wanted to. As long as the door was closed, no one would hear."

"She looks pretty with her mouth stuffed full, so I'm leaving that in." As I tried to yank out the fabric, Bron removed his belt and wrapped it around my head twice, the leather holding the fabric in place and keeping my teeth apart. As he tightened it, I tried to smack his hands away, but Ilya caught my wrists.

"So, what would you like to do with your wife on your wedding night?" Bron asked. "According to tradition, I should probably go to my room and leave the two of you alone."

"In public, we have to say she's my wife, but we both know she's *our* wife." Ilya's eyes shone with an almost unholy glee. "What should we do to claim her officially as ours?"

Bron's face went dangerously bland. I didn't trust that expression for a moment.

"In this situation, maybe we should go for something traditional."

"Taking turns?" Ilya asked. "Who goes first?"

"No, not that. I think we could both fit in her pussy, if we're careful."

"At the same time?" Ilya raised his brows, looking scandalized.

I tried to kick Bron for his suggestion, since they'd taken away any chance I had of using my words to object. He grabbed my ankle and held it casually. The feel of his big hand wrapped around my ankle shouldn't have made me shiver, but they both had a way of making me feel small and helpless.

"I don't think she likes that idea."

Bron squeezed my ankle—thankfully it was my good one. "We'll make her come, and she'll forget her objection."

I shook my head and struggled, but they didn't let me go.

Were they seriously considering fucking the same hole at the same time? It wasn't something I'd ever wanted to try, but guessed I wasn't going to get a choice in the matter.

"Is it even possible for both of us to fuck her pussy at the same time?" Ilya asked uneasily.

If he thought he was uneasy, he should try being me.

"I've seen it on pornography, so it should be possible."

Oh my god, what?

I gasped and almost choked on the fabric of my impromptu gag.

Of course, it was possible, but that didn't mean I wanted to do it.

"If a woman can birth a baby, or take a man's fist, she can probably fit two dicks at once," Bron assured him.

"Won't it hurt her?"

"We'll go slow to start. Besides, a woman's wedding night is supposed to hurt at least a little." Bron wound a lock of my hair around his finger and gave it a tug. "Have you done this before?"

I shook my head in dismay. I'd always assumed if it ever came up, the men would be less well-endowed.

"A first time for all of us," Bron said with a satisfaction I didn't share.

Was he serious? He needed to give his head a shake.

No one had ever fisted me, either, but the idea had never held an attraction for me. There was no way I was going to cooperate, and I doubted Ilya had the self-discipline it would probably require.

The idea of the two of them sliding against each other inside of me sent prickles of heat through my body. The idea was sexy, even if the reality would be unpleasant.

With his grip on my ankle, Bron yanked me partway across the bed and tipped me backward so I was lying flat. He pushed my thighs apart even though I tried not to let him.

How were his arms stronger than my legs? It wasn't fair that these men were so huge and could do whatever they wanted whenever they wanted. I struggled, but Bron settled between my legs and Ilya grabbed my wrists, holding me down. Ilya kissed me, trying to distract me from what they were planning, but it was Bron sliding down my body to get between my thighs that made me forget everything, including my own name.

Ilya had become a finely tuned lethal oral machine—he always took my subtle hints, but also made me wait for it, meaning the ultimate orgasm he gave me would make me need to muffle my screams.

With Bron, it was all about him. He went too fast and was too intense, making me feel as though I would crawl out of my skin. My back arched up off the bed and I gasped for breath around the gag, feeling like I wasn't getting enough air. I cried out, writhing in the trap of their hands, Ilya kissing my face, neck, and breasts, and coaching me to keep quiet. When that didn't work, he clapped a hand over my mouth, cutting off the excess sound I couldn't seem to hold back. By the time Bron had me teetering on the edge, I felt like somebody had run a metal rasp over my clit, and I was making horrific begging noises that would have embarrassed the hell out of me if I wasn't so desperate to come.

Bron crawled up my body, undid the belt holding my gag in place, then fished my ruined underwear from my mouth.

I gasped, clinging to Ilya, trying to push Bron away from me with my free hand, too angry and overwhelmed to even process what I was doing.

"You didn't like that, Queenie?"

I lashed out, raking his cheek with my nails, but he only gave me a wolfish grin. Someone stroked between my legs, then speared two fingers into me, stretching my pussy, but not giving my clit the attention it needed to get me off. I ached there, everything sore and sensitive.

"Leave me alone!" I smacked Bron's shoulder, trying to push him away with my legs.

He groaned, kneeling between my legs while fisting his cock.

"I can't wait anymore. I need to get my cock into your little wife."

It occurred to me that I'd had a safeword at one point, but I couldn't remember it. "I don't belong to either of you. Ilya has my signature on a piece of paper I can't even read, and what do you have? His blessing?"

"You signed a contract," Bron reminded me. "Technically, we can do anything we like."

"Marrying me wasn't part of that contract."

"No, but it wasn't a hard limit, either. Neither was using your pussy."

"Well, no, but the two of you will never fit into me together." I shouldn't let them distract me from being pissed about the wedding, but I couldn't do anything about that now. My priority had to be dissuading them from trying this.

"Women push out babies all the time. How is this any different?"

"They don't do that for fun!"

He picked me up.

"Lie down," he told Ilya.

My husband was a good boy and did as he was told. His cock was hard and bobbed against his stomach. Damn it. I was hoping the idea would freak him out, but as usual, his cock was all too happy to obey Bron.

"It won't work. I'll snap your dicks off."

"Some risks are worth taking." He put me face down on top of Ilya and shifted me down his body. He grabbed the back of my neck and whispered in my ear, "Cooperate, or this might do some damage."

"Please no," I whimpered.

"I love when you beg us not to fuck you when I can see how wet you are for us. Unlike your mouth, your pussy doesn't lie."

"My pussy is a needy, shallow bitch!"

He laughed, which wasn't the response I'd been aiming for.

Ilya's dick was already at my entrance, hot and thick and eager, and it was all I could do not to wriggle down onto that cock and take what I wanted from him.

"Give her some cock, and I'll try to figure out how to make this work."

My legs had automatically fallen to either side of Ilya's body, and when he pushed into me, I couldn't deny it to myself. Both of us groaned, and my head dropped to his shoulder.

"Is this what my little wife needed?" Ilya asked. Bastard.

I squirmed on top of him, rocking my hips, taking him deeper into my body. He blinked rapidly and then his eyes rolled back for a moment. He groaned, and his enjoyment made me shudder. I loved hearing how much he loved being inside me.

I fucked him, grabbing onto his wrists and holding them down on either side of his head.

He chuckled, and his cock bucked inside me. I whimpered, wishing I had more dominant tendencies, but the feel of him made me all hot and empty-headed. He thrust his hips hard and slow, and I heard myself sob helplessly even though I was supposedly the one in control. I squirmed down his body, impaling myself deeper, taking him until it hurt. There was no way anything else would fit inside me, let alone something as big as what Bron was planning on.

From the angle Bron was at, he should have been able to assess the matter better, but I felt the bed dip behind me, and he was at my back, looming over me.

"I don't know if this will work," Ilya said, going still beneath me. I made it sound of frustration and tried to coax him into moving again, but he wrapped his arms around my upper body, pinning my arms below the shoulders. "Hold still, wife."

"Pull her up further. You can't be so deep, or I won't be able to squeeze in with you."

Ilya's eyes widened and his lips parted. "But if you do this, we will... I mean, our cocks will..." His heart was drumming so hard it was shaking us both.

"So?"

"I thought you didn't want us to touch that way." He bit his lips together as though he had said too much, and the glance he sent Bron was shy.

"I know what I said before—what I used to say. I didn't want to think of myself that way, but what can be so bad about it if we want to do it? It's not like we have to announce it to the world."

"I won't tell anyone."

Bron sighed and ruffled Ilya's hair. "I am not ashamed of what we do, at least not anymore. I just think a lot of people won't understand."

Ilya's smile was small and sweet. Both men were so repressed when it came to their feelings for one another, and keeping me between them felt like they were using me as a universal adapter on a trip to a foreign land.

"The two of you seem like you have some things to talk about. Let me go take a shower and give you some privacy."

I tried to unskewer myself, but Ilya and Bron both held me in place.

"See what happens? We take our attention off her for a moment, and she gets her feelings hurt."

"Poor Delilah," Ilya said, his tone mocking. The jerk. He had been hanging out with Bron too long. "Nice try. You're not getting away now, woman."

There was the telltale click of a lube bottle's cap snapping open.

"Lube? Wow. We're moving up in the world, Ilya. Usually all we get is spit."

"If we're lucky."

We grinned at each other, and Bron swatted my ass.

"Why am I the only one in trouble?" I complained. "He agreed with me."

"Shut up and take my cock." Bron pressed a hand down on the back of my neck, trapping me against Ilya's warm bulk. Part of me thought it might be a good idea to try to get away, but I was curious, even though I doubted it would be pleasant. It would hardly be the worst thing a man had done to me. Maybe my adventure-seeking was unhealthy, but if they were really hurting me, I trusted them to stop.

Bron's cock slid against me, looking for a way in. Slowly, he urged my body to take him, too. I grunted, gritting my teeth and breathing through it. It wasn't a nightmare, but it also wasn't my favorite sensation.

"Is it too much, my Queen?" Bron's breath was warm on my back, and I shivered.

At least he gave a damn about whether he was splitting me open.

"It's...a lot." I gasped. "At least I don't feel like it might kill me."

"Good." He pulled out.

That was it? Had he changed his mind?

"Since my finger wasn't too bad, let's try my cock."

"That was only your finger?"

He tsked in my ear. "It's a sad day when a woman can't tell the difference between your finger and your cock."

"That's what we get for choosing such an innocent woman," Ilya said with a sly smile.

"Yes. Poor thing. Such a shame she fell into our evil clutches."

He lined himself up behind me and forced his way in a bit at a time, realizing exactly how wrong I had been before the head of his cock was even all the way inside me. Ilya's awed expression as Bron's cock slid along his was so raw I hoped Bron wasn't missing it.

"That's our good girl," Bron encouraged. "You can take us both, can't you? Such a brave girl."

Their hands were all over me, making my skin buzz with awareness and stealing some of my attention from the ache they were causing. My pussy felt like it was being forced wider than it should be, the sensation overwhelming. It reminded me of how it had felt the first time I'd done anal, except somehow worse, knowing my body was being forced to take an unnatural amount of dick.

I breathed through it, probably sounding like I was in labor, but I focused on Ilya's expression. He winced a few times, but mostly his eyes were wide with wonder and shining like his heart might burst. Bron worked his lube-slicked cock into me with slow, determined pressure. When they were both in, they held still. Bron nipped the back of my ear.

"That's a lot of cock in one little girl," he observed. You feel—" His breath hitched. "You feel like a fist forcing us together." His hips stirred, and he slowly moved. I could only imagine how it felt to them, tight and slick, sliding against one another inside my pussy. Ilya's short panting breaths made it sound as though he was struggling hard not to come.

"Ilya, look at me," Bron demanded.

The younger man's tortured gaze slid from my eyes, over my shoulder to Bron.

"Try not to think about how it feels yet. I don't want this to be over."

"Yes, Bron." His gaze fastened on Bron, and they figured out a rhythm that stole my breath. I clawed at the pillow under my hands because it was either the pillow or Ilya's shoulders, and I didn't want to draw blood. It wasn't that it was excruciating, it was just a lot to manage.

My breath came in quiet sobs that were half discomfort and half grudging pleasure, and my clit rubbed against Ilya, my hips crushed between theirs. The hand on the back of my neck had shifted to my hip, and Bron had a firm hold of me there, keeping me still while the two of them rocked above and below me. They picked up speed and the liquid sound of our movements made me wince. Bron groaned in my ear, and I shuddered, trying to ignore the pain and the tight knot of desire building.

"You are ours, Queenie. You may be married to him, but you belong to both of us now, and we are never letting you go."

I whimpered, wanting to argue, but my thoughts were too jumbled to form words. Time seemed to still, leaving me in a never-ending loop of thrusting and retreating, three people in one body, breathing each other's air, sweat mingling. A soft body pinned between two that were impossibly hard, nailed in place by two massive cocks vying for space inside me.

My eyes closed against the intensity of the orgasm that was building, the rolling hips, the roving hands, the grazing teeth. I hated them for knowing my body so well and using it against me. I hated this, yet never wanted it to end.

"I can't hold back anymore," Ilya gasped.

"Wait," Bron growled.

"I can't."

Bron bit the back of my neck, and my racking shudder pushed my orgasm past the point of no return. I teetered on the edge for a long, awful moment, making me feel like I was in freefall, and yet I couldn't be more trapped. I fought them, suddenly needing to escape, but two sets of hands grabbed a hold of me, their fingers not gentle.

"Oh, fuuuck," Bron groaned, as though he'd been defeated. Ilya's helpless sob was the last thing I heard before my orgasm crashed into me. Someone swore bitterly, and then their cocks jerked hard inside me, sliding against each other as I writhed between them, trapped and so deliciously helpless. My vision blurred, went white, my ears ringing, but I didn't care about anything more than the pleasure they were wringing from me—how much it hurt, how good and awful it felt, as my body trembled and spasmed around them.

My body shook long after the storm passed, aftershocks rocking me, making both men groan and curse.

They kissed me, fighting over my mouth, my head turned to the side to accommodate them, not satisfied with only owning my pussy.

"I love you," Ilya said, kissing me, then pulling Bron's head down to get him, too.

Bron stiffened but then gave in, kissing him back with a passion that surprised me, but seemed to surprise them even more. Bron held the back of Ilya's head, and then, somehow, they were kissing me too, all of us a mess of emotion, sated and a little shell-shocked. He gazed down at Ilya, his expression frank. "I love you, Ilyusha." His voice caught, as though saying the words aloud hurt. "I don't know how any of this is going to turn out, but I love you. I've loved you for a long time." He kissed my temple. "I love you, too, little troublemaker."

I wanted to argue, but I knew in that moment there was no fighting this. I loved them, too. How would I ever convince myself to go back to my family when I could have Ilya and Bron as my own?

Ilya kissed me passionately, his eyes red with tears. He stroked my hair away from my temple. "I love you, wife, and I hope you choose to stay with us. I know it's not what most women want, but if you choose to stay, we'll try to give you a good life."

My fried brain was too stunned argue with them or to even argue with myself, so I laid my head against his shoulder and let myself drown in all the feelings that welled up in me.

It had been a long day, and sleep dragged me down into its clutches.

Much later, my growling stomach woke me. I tried to lever myself up from between the two big, warm bodies pressed against me, but the arm around my waist kept me pinned down and the hand on my breast tightened in disapproval. It never would have occurred to me that Bron was a cuddler, but he hung onto me like I was his stuffed animal, and he was a seven-year-old with nightmares. His other arm pillowed his head and stretched over me, his fingers buried in Ilya's hair. Our legs were a tangle.

I would have gone back to sleep, contented and warm and sore, but my bladder also wanted to be emptied.

I couldn't remember being this sore even after some of the more hardcore hunts on the Island. We'd finished the night with a shower, thank god, and after what Bron had done to Ilya, I wouldn't be the only one still dripping cum at brunch.

Ilya grumbled and shifted, his dark eyes opening slowly and taking a moment to focus.

When had he gotten so sexy? I traced his lips with my finger, and he nipped it playfully.

"Good morning, wife."

The sound of that made my toes curl with pleasure. My reaction to it was stupid, but could it really be terrible when it felt so good?

"Good morning, husband."

"Good morning, bodyguard who only wanted ten more minutes of sleep," Bron grumbled from behind me.

"I think he feels left out," I said in a playful whisper. "We're going to have to make sure we call him husband, too."

"Yes."

Bron let go of me and rolled to his other side, stealing most of Ilya's blankets. Ilya yanked them back. The room wasn't freezing, but without the heat of Bron at my back, I felt bereft.

Ilya's gaze was soft, content. "You're going to stay with us," he said, as though predicting the future. "You're not going to go back to those horrible people."

"Those 'horrible people' are my family members. And they're not horrible—they just take me for granted."

"Well, maybe I can send them money to hire someone. It doesn't need to be you helping them. You belong here with us."

"First, you trick me into marrying you, and now you're trying to get bossy with me about staying? What if I want to leave?"

His jaw flexed, and his eyes narrowed. He rolled me over onto my back and lay on top of me, pinning my arms and pushing between my thighs until his morning wood threatened to make me even more sore.

"If you refuse to stay, I'll hold you captive on that island for the rest of your life. If you stay voluntarily, I'll let you visit your family once in a while, when you can convince me to let you out of our bed."

"Will you bickering puppies keep it down?"

"Is he always this much of a grump in the morning?"

"You've been around long enough. You should know he's like this all day."

Bron turned back toward us and propped his head on his hand, glaring at us both. "The two of you are going to need to learn respect for your elders if this is going to work."

"It's time to get up for breakfast, anyway. Do you want me to fetch your cane, old man?" Ilya teased.

"Absolutely. Get me a cane and we'll see how much you like me using it on you."

Bron grabbed Ilya's hair and pulled him close, biting his bottom lip and then kissing him ferociously. Ilya smiled against his mouth and kissed him back.

"If I'm not needed for the next few minutes, may I be excused? I really need to pee." I smacked at Ilya's chest, and he slowly slid off me and onto Bron. The sight of the two of them together, making out in bed, naked and tangled in our sheets, slowed me down on the way to the bathroom. Watching them together could definitely become my new favorite pastime. I wished I had a phone so I could take pictures or maybe a video I could save for later.

Then again, that might not be a safe idea in Russia. I'd have to ask them what the actual laws were.

I padded into the bathroom and used the facilities, then checked out the bruises I'd acquired during our long, entertaining night together. Sure, I'd had threesomes before, but most of the time the guys tried not to touch each other. I enjoyed this way of doing things much better.

By the time I returned to the bedroom, the two of them were lying side by side in bed with enough space between them for me to crawl back in, and they were talking about trying new feed for the chickens, of all things. It was sweet as it was, but then I spotted the fact that they were holding hands.

Ugh. My heart.

I started sorting through my clothes, trying to decide what to wear.

"Where are you going?"

"I'm going to see if there's food. I'm starving."

"You didn't eat very much at supper last night," Ilya said.

"The surprise wedding made it hard for me to appreciate the cuisine."

"It was good," Bron said helpfully. "I think I'm still full."

"That doesn't help me now."

"That sounds like poor planning. You should always eat if you have a chance to eat."

"Quit lecturing me and get dressed."

I chose a dress that was brunch appropriate and threw it on the bed, which meant it was also half on Bron.

"Is this for me?" He slid it up his body and held it in place. It was like a little clothing mohawk down the middle of his torso that ended at the top of his thighs.

"Absolutely. I figure since I'm the only wife in this relationship, I'd better pick out everyone's clothes from now on."

"I have excellent taste in clothing," Bron said, sounding slightly affronted.

"Who told you that? Probably some girl who was trying to get into your pants."

He frowned at me, and I could tell he wasn't sure whether to take me seriously. That someone like him might care what other people thought of his fashion sense made it difficult to hold back a laugh. Teasing him was too much fun sometimes.

Without warning, he tugged me sideways over his lap and sat up long enough to swat my ass a few times, then let me go. The casual spanking had done just enough to wake everything in the lower half of my body, and my nipples really hadn't minded being chafed on his leg hair.

"I can see spanking her will not achieve the desired effect," he mused.

Ilya shrugged. "That effect seemed like fun."

I snatched my dress off Bron's legs and shot them both a sassy glare, then went to dig through my mountain of new undergarments. The dress had a low back, which meant I would either need a very specific bra or I was going to have to go braless.

Both men rolled out of bed and started browsing through their own clothes.

"So, are there any more surprises today, or is this a simple breakfast?"

Ilya shrugged. "As far as I know, it is only breakfast. I don't even know if anyone else will be around. Some of them might have gone home already."

"Can *we* go home already?"

"Don't you want to look around? We could go sightseeing this afternoon."

"Sightseeing?"

"It's traditional for newlyweds to tour the city. We spared you that last night since we had just arrived, and everything was a surprise."

"You wanted to give me time to get used to being tricked into marriage, so I wouldn't scream at strangers on the street to rescue me."

He stopped buttoning his shirt and leveled his gaze on me. "You really hate it so much?"

"You're not serious about staying married, are you? I mean, I know it would make things easier for the two of you to be together if you had me posing as your wife, but you're not going to want me here all the time. If I go back to the States, you guys could travel wherever you wanted to and say you were coming to see me."

He dropped his hands from the shirt and grabbed my wrist fast enough to make me gasp. He pulled me against him and kissed me long and hard. At first, I stiffened at the unexpectedness of it, but it was impossible not to respond to him. My heart performed a little funny somersault, and I groaned inwardly, knowing damn well I was already hopelessly in love with both of them and hating that the whole situation was still making me feel off balance.

Living over, under, and around each other had sort of sped up what a normal dating process would be like. I'd had a friend who'd gotten married after dating a guy for six months and she still seemed happy enough. We'd only been together for about three, but we had been alone for most of it. Just us, living and working together and having a hell of a lot of sex—not to mention all the conversations and movies, as well as the games we'd played in the evenings. As soon as I'd arrived on their island, they'd incorporated me into their life.

"We haven't even known each other very long."

"What does time mean? The deed is already done. Now you must only decide whether you will give your husbands a chance, or if you will run away like a coward." Bron patted my shoulder, but I staggered with the weight of it. He righted me and fixed my dress, as though he hadn't realized his own strength.

"You should write greeting cards," I said wryly. He looked at me in confusion, and I shook my head. "It's a joke. I'm saying you're not very romantic."

"You want romance?" He snorted. "What is more romantic than us sharing your pussy last night?"

"Should we have gotten you flowers?" Ilya asked, brow creased in concern.

"Bron's version of romance is...unusual."

"And since you didn't marry any of those other men before you met us, I have to assume those other kinds of romance are inferior." He gave a satisfied nod and then clapped Ilya's shoulder. No wonder I'd almost fallen over. He was used to someone Ilya's size, not mine.

"Shall we go see what my family is plotting?" Ilya asked. With that, we finished getting ready and left the room.

Chapter Twenty-One

The family was gathered around the table, eating. Only a few of them looked up as we entered. Ilya and I found spots to sit next to each other, and Bron stood by the door.

"Sit, Bronislav." Vas gestured to an empty chair.

Bron looked astounded.

"There is plenty of food, and there is family business to discuss. You might as well sit."

Shoulders stiff, Bron lowered himself into the chair to my right.

Servers brought trays for us to select food from. There were things I didn't recognize, but I was adventurous enough that I took some of everything that looked interesting and hoped my eyes weren't bigger than my stomach.

As we were finishing up, Vas got to his feet.

"I know most of you have been wondering why I called you to the house. Of course, Ilya's wedding was a decent excuse, but as most of you no doubt suspect, there is more than that." He lifted his glass to his lips. I doubted the clear liquid was water.

When everyone fell silent, he gestured for the servers to leave the room. I could tell Bron wasn't sure if he should go, but Vas stepped behind him and briefly put a hand on his shoulder before moving on to refill his glass from the sideboard.

"I plan to retire."

His sons turned their gazes to him in shock.

"I've worked long enough, and I'm ready to choose a successor. Although I won't step aside for another few years, whoever takes over will need time to learn his role before I move somewhere warm with my new wife, whoever she may be."

He toasted the unknown woman, then chuckled and slapped one of the twins on the back. I still didn't know Oleg from Dmitry.

I would have expected Alexander to be the center of attention, but no one was looking his way. In fact, Alexander looked puzzled at the news.

"I know some of you have no interest in running things." He gestured to Alexander. "Others have qualities that make them unsuitable." He didn't center out anyone, but Yuri and Andrey looked away.

Oh god, Ilya wasn't in the running for this, was he?

What if he was? None of the other sons had been centered out for toughening up. Vas had no idea that Ilya's new attitude was all a sham, and I doubted Bron would betray him to his father. I didn't want to live here—especially not if Vas was running some sort of criminal empire. If he planned to choose Ilya and train him for the position, I was absolutely going back to my family.

That was if Vas would allow it. I had no idea whether this family would tolerate a woman divorcing them and leaving. Bron had said divorces were no big deal, but Bron wasn't Vas.

My new father-in-law put his hand on the back of Ilya's chair and moved to stand behind him.

Oh no.

"As you know, my role comes with a certain amount of risk. It was my hope one of my elder sons would prove they could deal with those uncertainties." He gave a few of them a hard look. "I waited. I even banished my most promising son to a remote island in the hope one of you would spare me the embarrassment of needing to choose him."

Most of Ilya's brothers kept their expressions neutral and their gazes fixed on Vas, but a few of them looked at Ilya, disgruntled.

Ilya *wasn't* the least favorite? Why would Vas be so brutal with the son he'd felt was the most promising? He'd been left there and made to work hard for over a decade, all to give his older brothers a chance to prove they were the better choice?

"Unfortunately, all you have shown me is that you like your allowances to be on time, and that you have good taste in women." His large hands tightened on the back of Ilya's chair.

I wanted to shout at Vas not to be ridiculous—that Ilya was the most soft-hearted of his sons and that he was only pretending to be hard, but I held my peace.

Had this been Ilya's goal all along? It made sense, but it didn't mean I was happy about it. Sure, he was tougher than he'd been when I first met him, but there was still a soft soul under the hard exterior he was presenting here. I doubted he would be happy as a mob boss, or whatever the hell Vas did for a living.

I braced myself for the words I knew were coming.

"That is why, beginning tomorrow, I will train Bronislav as my successor."

I opened my mouth to correct him. What a time to say the wrong name! But then Vas slapped Bron on the shoulder and gave it a squeeze.

Bron glanced up at Vas, his expression blank.

What the fuck?

My mind scrambled to catch up.

If he was Vas's son...

Ilya staggered to his feet and strode out of the room.

I felt rooted to my chair.

God... They were *brothers*?

How could Bron be cruel enough to make his little brother fall in love with him?

I thought of Ilya's poetry journals and the quiet, desperate love he'd harbored for Bron for so long, and how he'd finally gotten everything he wanted.

Had it all been a sick game?

"But he's a bastard!" Yuri shouted. "You can't mean to pass the business to the son of your dead cook!"

Bron sipped at his drink, looking calculating and unflappable. Hard.

My gaze shifted between him and his father, hating that now I could absolutely see the resemblance. I felt like I might puke.

"What difference does being a bastard make? I gave every one of you the opportunity to obey me and to show your worth, but he is the only one who's ever obeyed me without question. He's done everything I've asked. He even made a man of a failure, which I never thought I would live to see. Why shouldn't I entrust all of my hard work to someone who won't fuck it up, gamble it away, or spend it on a fleet of speedboats?"

The conversation wasn't as loud and obnoxious as I would have expected. If nothing else, Vas had trained his sons to be in firm control of their emotions—all except Ilya.

I got up to sneak out, but Vas caught me by the arm. His grip hurt. "If that boy thought he was in line to be heir, maybe he's not as grown as I thought. You and I will have a discussion later about the allowance he gets and which of you should manage it."

I grunted something noncommittal and pulled my arm away, not missing how he tried to control me until he was ready to let go.

A slow grin crossed his face.

"I see my son chose a woman with a spine, at least."

I walked away, and Bron's gaze met mine as I passed him. Disgusted, all I could do was glare.

How could he have done this to Ilya? How could he fuck him for twelve years, pretending he was Vas's lackey, when he was Ilya's half-brother?

I walked as fast as I could back to our suite of rooms, suddenly chilled at the thought of what Ilya might do in his shock. It felt like I wasn't completely in control of my body—like I was on autopilot. My hand trembled when I turned the doorknob, afraid of what might be on the other side.

I burst into the room and slammed the door behind me, my shoes clacking obnoxiously on the floor.

"Did you know?" Ilya was on me as soon as the door was closed. He grabbed my upper arms and yanked me against him, his face wild and desperate.

"Of course I didn't know!" I assured him, my voice sounding and feeling like someone was strangling me.

I wrapped my arms around his waist and put my head against his chest. He hugged me. His body shook with the ugly emotions that had to be running through him.

How could Bron tell us he loved us last night, under their father's roof, knowing the truth would come out today?

He let me go and headed for the bathroom.

"What are you doing?"

He went in and locked the door behind him. The water started running, but it wasn't loud enough to cover his strangled sobs.

I knocked.

No response.

I tried the door, even knowing he'd locked it.

He shouldn't be alone right now.

My cheeks were wet, and my eyes hurt, and the lump in my throat felt like it was choking me. I wiped my face with the back of my hand. I was so cold my teeth started to chatter.

Less than an hour ago, I'd thought the three of us were happy.

Two of us had meant what we'd said to each other.

One of us was a brother-fucking liar.

I sat outside the bathroom door with my back pressed against it, trying to feel him on the other side.

"I love you, Ilya."

Nothing.

"Please open the door? Let me in so we can talk about this."

I imagined the things he might say in reply, but he didn't say anything at all. He had invested more than a third of his life into his relationship with Bron, only to find out everything had been a lie.

How had I never seen it?

At some point, the water turned off, but he still wouldn't respond.

I was still sitting there when Bron stormed in maybe an hour later.

"He's in there?"

I got to my feet and threw my shoes at him one at a time. Both of them connected with his chest. He hadn't attempted to bat them away. He reached past me and tried the doorknob.

"Do you think I haven't tried that?"

"You should have come for me."

"And how would I explain that to your family? Why the hell do you care anyway?"

He pulled a knife from his pocket and stuck it in the keyhole, then gave it a vicious twist. I heard something snap.

"What are you going to do?" I tried to push him away from the door. The knife in his hand scared me. Surely, he wouldn't try to hurt him? He folded the knife and stuffed it back in his pocket.

"Stop being hysterical. We deliberately chose a woman who could keep her head in a crisis."

He opened the door, looking like he was ready to fight his way in, but Ilya didn't try to push it closed. The lack of response made my heart go cold.

I rushed in after him, but Ilya was only sitting on the floor, leaning against the vanity, looking dazed.

"Am I a fucking joke to you?" Ilya said so quietly it killed me.

"Of course not!"

"I'm having a hard time believing that!" Ilya snapped, his jaw flexing and his fists balled in his lap.

"After everything... Do you really think I knew? I found out when you did, Ilyusha."

"Don't call me that!"

Bron hauled him up, steadying him on his feet and looking him in the eye.

"I didn't know." His voice was hoarse, and he stood there, staring into Ilya's eyes as though willing him to believe it. "I didn't know! What reason would I have to lie?"

"I don't know. My mind doesn't work the way yours does."

"Even I wouldn't do something this cruel." His fingers curled into Ilya's shirt, and he took a step closer. One of his hands slid up to Ilya's neck and his thumb caressed his jaw.

Ilya leaned into the caress, his eyes closing as he relaxed and let it happen. A moment later, his eyes flew open, and he jerked back. He pushed Bron's hands away.

"Stop."

"Is it really wrong?" Bron stepped back, giving him space. He ran both hands over his short hair and laced his fingers behind his head as though trying to stop himself from touching Ilya again. He retreated further and leaned against the opposite wall.

"What do you mean?" Ilya demanded. "Of course it's wrong!"

"We didn't know, so there's nothing wrong with what we did." His throat bobbed as he searched Ilya's face.

"You really didn't know?" I couldn't help but ask.

Bron grimaced. "Both of you believed that of me? I suppose I deserve that. I'm not the easiest man to live with."

Ilya's face was mottled, and his eyes were red, but he kept his head up. "Neither of us knew, so I suppose there is no point in being ashamed. Someone should have told us."

"My mother always told me that my father was a stranger she'd met at a club. I never thought to doubt her." Bron shrugged helplessly. "I came here all the time growing up, and no one said a word."

"Our family likes its secrets and its exclusivity. Even as the son of Vas's last wife, they always treated me as an outsider. I'm not surprised they did the same to you." Ilya smiled tremulously. "So how does it feel to be our father's favorite?"

"I would rather have you than know who my father is."

"But now you will be rich." Ilya clapped his hands once. "Rich, and in charge of managing the rest of us."

Bron scrubbed his eyes with his palms. "If you don't want me to take over from Vas, I won't. I don't know why he would pick me over the rest of you, anyway. I don't know anything about business."

"Vas will make sure you have people to help you with that."

Bron made a dismissive gesture. "We can talk about that later. I want to know what this means for the three of us."

Ilya frowned. "I'll go back to the island. Delilah can spend half her time with me and half with you."

"You're going to ship me back and forth like a kid with divorced parents?" I snorted. "No. I don't think so."

"You're not still thinking of leaving us."

Ilya made a sound of frustration. "There *is* no us anymore. If having us by turns isn't good enough for her, then she should be allowed to make that decision."

"How would we explain why I'm here half the time with Bron while you stay home?"

"Considering the secrets this family keeps, I doubt anyone will care. I'm still the rejected brother, and no one will question Bron taking what he wants. My father always takes what he wants, and no one tells him no."

"What if..." Bron chewed on his bottom lip. He blew out a breath. "What if we don't let this change anything? What if the three of us continue our relationship? No one has to know."

"We share the same father!"

"We weren't raised as brothers. We don't have brotherly feelings for each other, and we never have. So what if we share a father? It's not like I can get you pregnant. What we do together is no one's business and won't affect anyone else."

"But *we* will know! I can't believe you're suggesting this."

"Why not? Why can't we have this?" Bron cried, his voice desperate. "I can't give you up. The two of you are the only people who matter to me in this world. I don't care about Vas or his money, and I don't care about the rest of his family. I can't live without you."

"No."

"Ilya, please."

"There is nothing more to say."

"Ilya," his voice was low, panicked. "I need you more than I need the blood under my skin."

"Bron—"

"I can refuse to take over, and we can go back to the island. It will be like before."

"So, the three of us will hide there forever and be ashamed?"

"I know you wanted to have the option to re-join the family, but do you really care about any of these people, Ilya? They turned their backs on you. They left you there to rot. No one cared what we were doing before, so why would they care now?"

"I don't care about them. Winning Vas's approval was hollow. I wish we could go back to our old life, but we can't erase what we've learned." Tears leaked from Ilya's eyes again, and I went to him, wrapping my arms around his waist. He rested his cheek against the top of my head, and I let my tears soak into his shirt.

Bron was looking at us from the other side of the bathroom. He wiped a tear away before Ilya saw it. He'd been raised to hide his emotions, but even he wasn't heartless.

"It would be wrong," Ilya insisted.

Bron held up his hands, as though to stop Ilya from saying more. "Don't decide now. Think for a few days. Even if you don't give me an answer for months, I don't care. I'll wait for you forever if that's what you need."

"And what about when Vas insists you find a wife?" Ilya said miserably. "What then? I won't sneak around behind your wife's back. That isn't fair to us or to her."

"You're going to end everything between us over a theoretical wife?" Bron demanded, incredulous.

"No. Everything has to end because we are *brothers*, Bron."

"When I got to our island, we were strangers. Everything that has happened since? We've earned that. We've earned everything that led up to that damned breakfast this morning, and I'm not willing to let it all go because Vas tumbled my mother thirty-four years ago. What about me? What about you? Why can't we take what we want? We took Delilah for ourselves, so why can't we have each other?"

He approached us slowly. Was he worried we would bolt from the room? When he was in front of Ilya, he brought his hand up to his face, wiping away his tears with the pad of his thumb. Ilya shoved away his hand, but Bron growled in disapproval.

"I take what I want, too. The two of you are mine, and I don't care if they drag me into the street and shoot me, I'm not giving you up." He wrapped his arms around us and pressed us back against the vanity. We had no way to slide out from under his arms, but I didn't try. Ilya put up a brief struggle, but Bron's lips came down onto his, subduing him. They had spent so much time together before this, with Ilya submitting to whatever Bron wanted, that maybe standing up to him was an insurmountable task.

Maybe I should have been disgusted by them kissing, but how could I blame them for not being able to shut off their feelings? This new information didn't erase their past. It was weird and upsetting that they were related, but maybe Bron was right. Did it have to change everything? Their staying together wouldn't have ramifications for anyone. They deserved to be happy, and maybe letting Vas ruin everything would be the real crime.

Bron broke the kiss and brought his lips to mine. They tasted like Ilya's tears and mine.

I didn't want to lose either of them, but until they settled things between them, all I could do was wait.

We stood there long after the kiss broke off, clinging to each other.

I wished we could go back to bed and wake up to find all of this was all a bad dream.

Chapter Twenty-Two

Vas took up all of Bron's time.

For days, Ilya sat in the dark in the bedroom we'd all shared, the blinds drawn. He'd been mostly silent, not willing to discuss much of anything, although I got him talking about his plans to rebuild the chicken coop.

At night, they slept separately. I would comfort and have sex with one, then get sent to take care of the other. Although I alternated who I slept with, Bron rarely even shut his eyes, obsessing over the pictures on his camera, so miserable he didn't care that I saw his entire camera roll was full of beautiful candid shots of Ilya and me.

I hated seeing them apart like this, but I didn't know what the solution was any more than they did.

"I'm not being very good company for my new bride," Ilya said one day.

"I'm okay."

"You're not. Neither of us are, but we can't stop living forever."

"No. It doesn't help anything, does it?"

"I'm taking you out for the day."

The two of us showered together and got ready to go out, but it felt strange and sad for Bron to be absent.

Ilya arranged for a car, and although we ran into a few of his siblings and their wives on our way to the front door, they only nodded to us politely or completely ignored us.

When we were safely ensconced in the car, with the divider up between us and the driver, Ilya scowled up at the house we'd just left.

"I wish we could go home today." He leaned back against the seat. "Why did I work so hard for this? Why did I change who I was to suit these people? I don't even like them."

"Maybe they're shy."

"I kidnapped you away from your friend—away from your life—and you have always been nicer to me than these people." We rode in silence for a few minutes and then he added, "Bron is such an asshole, I should have guessed he was my brother."

He gave a sad laugh, and I smiled at his attempt at a joke.

"Maybe they're like him—slow to let themselves be vulnerable?"

"No. No one is like him." He pointed his gaze out the window. His hand sought mine, and I laced our fingers together. "I won't die from losing him, but I almost wish I would."

His throat bobbed and his nostrils flared as he struggled to master his emotions.

"I have no idea how you're managing."

"It's even harder knowing he wants me even now. I feel like I'm denying myself air. Seeing him..." He swiped at his cheek, then turned back to me and leaned in, kissing my nose. "You're enough on your own. I just miss him." His voice broke on the word 'miss' and the nightmarish wave of despair swamped me all over again.

He squeezed my hand. "I wonder how Lev is dealing with the goats. I hope he's remembering to put them in the shed at night."

"And I hope Nayda isn't being difficult." My favorite goat was a pain in the ass and had a big attitude that always made me laugh.

I'd wondered about them so many times since we'd left our island. If anyone had told me a few months ago that I would be worried about the welfare of my goats, I would have wondered about their grasp on reality.

"I'm sure Lev is doing fine. He managed well the other times he took care of the farm for us. We had everything organized when we left, and the schedule should be easy enough to follow."

I nodded, but still wished there was better cell reception on the island so we could check in.

When it came to phone calls, I really needed to call my family, too. I hadn't spoken to them in months. And what wouldn't I give for Lane's phone number so I could call her, and tell her what was going on so I could vent about it?

"While we shop, maybe we can find a place that sells different varieties of seeds," Ilya mused.

"That sounds like fun." Had I really said that? Shopping for shoes was fun. Shopping for seeds shouldn't be.

"We should get you some rubber boots that fit better, too, and maybe some steel-toed boots in case we do heavy work. We should have thought of it the last time we were shopping, but I was focused on the trip here."

"At that point, I don't think you were planning to go back to the island at all."

He turned his head and looked at me, his dark eyes showing golden flecks in the bright sunlight. God, he was gorgeous. I missed his beard, but he didn't need one to hide his handsome face. I ran a fingertip over his smooth cheek. He leaned in and kissed me, long and sweet. His hand slid into my hair and cradled the back of my head.

"When we go back, I'll do everything in my power to keep you happy."

"You always make me happy. I'm not worried about that."

"I know it's not the same as having Bron with us, but maybe we could still have a good life there—maybe we could learn to live without him."

"Maybe he can visit us."

Ilya shook his head, but not at me, more at his own thoughts. I couldn't imagine what it would be like to find out the man I'd been pining for loved me back, and then to have that ripped away hours later. It had been a rollercoaster for everyone involved, but unfortunately, we were at the end of the ride.

Moscow was beautiful.

Ilya didn't know it as well as he did Saint Petersburg, so it was more like being on a honeymoon rather than him showing me around his old haunts. We had lowered the privacy screen between us and the driver, and the man did his best to play tour guide. Ilya was an attentive sightseeing partner, and it might have been a fun day if I didn't keep catching glimpses of my sadness mirrored in his gaze.

We had dinner out, rather than with his family. It was a relief not having to make small talk with people who didn't like us and who I often didn't understand. Ilya assured me they didn't talk about me when we were sitting right there, but maybe he just didn't want to hurt my feelings.

When we returned to the house, it was late, and I was tipsy from the wine. I was leaning on Ilya's arm and laughing at a joke he'd made when I looked up and found Bron watching us from only feet away.

"The two of you look like you had a pleasant day." His deep voice held an odd note that sounded a lot like jealousy.

"We went sightseeing, then had a nice dinner," I replied, aiming for nonchalance.

Ilya stared at him like a dog who'd missed his master but wasn't allowed to greet him.

"We bought some seeds for the garden. Maybe they'll grow well on the island."

Bron's smile was faint and wistful. "Show them to me later?" He fell into step with us as we headed toward our suite.

"I could show them to you now."

"I wish I wasn't on my way out, but Vas has me running an errand. I should be back in a few hours."

"Oh."

Bron closed the suite's door behind us and turned to look at Ilya, but Ilya jerked his gaze away and went into the bathroom, shutting us out.

"How is he?" Bron demanded, eyeing the door closed between them.

"Melancholy."

He shook his head. "I don't know that word."

"He's very sad, but he's trying to hide it."

"And you?"

"I'm sad, too."

He sighed and pulled me close. The kiss was welcome, but it didn't fix the weirdness between them or how often Bron was gone. Even if I traveled back and forth between them, when I was here with Bron, would I ever see him?

"How can I live if he never allows me to touch him again?" Bron asked, voice rough.

"Maybe he'll change his mind." I doubted he would, but I felt compelled to give him hope to hold on to.

"I don't think I can stay here, wife," he whispered to me. "Even if he never touches me again, I need to be near him."

"But you wanted off the island so much. And what about Vas? He's counting on you to take over."

"The longer we're here, the more I realize this isn't what I want. And Vas? I knew he was involved in some shady shit, but it's worse than I thought."

"Oh?" I tried to look surprised, but after meeting the man, I really wasn't. A man like him didn't get rich by legitimate means. Considering he'd left Ilya in exile for no reason, and that he'd made Yana disappear, I assumed all this money came from something I wouldn't find palatable.

"I'm not sure he'll let me leave, but for now he doesn't have much to hold over me, except he knows I care about my little brother. If I don't cooperate, he might cut off Ilya's support, or sell the island out from under the two of you." He sighed. "Shit. I almost forgot—Vas wants to meet with you. I told him I would walk you to his office when you came back, if I hadn't left by then. Five minutes later and I would have missed you entirely."

"He mentioned something about me managing Ilya's allowance, but I assumed he was joking."

"Probably not. I've been managing it all these years."

"He can't manage it himself?"

"I don't know. No one has ever let him try." He gave me a rueful smile. "You can't tell the man you work for how to run his family. I didn't know at the time I could speak for him as a big brother."

I could tell he'd meant it as a joke, but it fell flat, and both of us stared at each other awkwardly for a long moment.

"Let me tell Ilya I'm going."

Hopefully, he'd be able to hear me over the fan. "Ilya? Vas wants to speak to me. I'll be back in a few minutes."

He didn't respond, but that wasn't unexpected. Being around Bron still hurt him.

I found a piece of paper and a pen and scribbled a note, then left it on the coffee table, hoping he'd see it if he came out in the next few minutes. I doubted the meeting would last long.

Bron walked me through the mansion, taking me on a twisting path I had to work on remembering. It was strange walking with him and yet knowing I couldn't touch him in case someone came around the corner and saw us together. The last thing I wanted to do was embarrass Ilya in front of his family, especially since they still weren't treating him with much respect. If I did travel back and forth to visit Bron, though, it would only be a matter of time before their family pieced together my relationship with him.

By the time we reached the office, I was completely turned around. If worse came to worse, I could stop a servant and ask for directions back.

Bron rapped on an ornately carved door and waited for permission before opening it. Vas's office was large and modern, and he sat at a sleek, steel-and-glass desk that faced the door. He closed a file in front of him and slid it aside, then rose to greet us.

"Dominika, was it?"

"Delilah." I smiled politely.

"Yes, Delilah. Lovely name." I could tell he didn't give a rat's ass what my name was and wouldn't bother remembering. "You may go, Bron. Make sure you tell Sergei I expect to hear from him tomorrow."

Bron nodded and pulled the door shut behind him.

"Please, have a seat."

He gestured to the visitor chair, leaving the desk between us. When I sat, the chair's leather was still warm from its previous occupant.

"I make a point of meeting with all of my sons' wives. Usually, my first meeting with them is before the nuptials, but I can understand why Ilya was in such a hurry. I'm sure he wanted to get a ring on your finger before you had time to come to your senses."

I narrowed my eyes. "I'm happy with my choice of husband."

"You didn't look happy at your wedding."

"Ilya surprised me. I don't know if surprise weddings are common in Russia, but they're not in America."

"Weddings usually take place over several days here—at least two." He shrugged. "What does it matter? The end result is the same."

I smoothed my skirt and waited for him to get to the point. If this was a social visit, I'd be surprised.

He moved to the side of his desk and sat on the edge, scrutinizing my face as I examined the painting of a storm at sea that hung behind his desk. It looked like an original, but I didn't know enough about art to recognize it or the signature. Considering Vas's house, I assumed it was probably expensive.

"This isn't really about Ilya's allowance, is it?"

"It is." He got up and poured himself a drink from the sideboard. I declined politely when offered one. He moved behind his desk and sat again, then sipped at his drink before elaborating.

"I'll put this bluntly. My children are lazy. The only one who's ever shown grit is Bronislav, and that is only because he wasn't spoiled by his mother. I did my best with them, but I'm a busy man." He shrugged and drained his glass. "It's too easy to get distracted by a pretty face. It's a woman's character a man should consider before he breeds her."

He turned his dark gaze to me. The man that gave me the willies. Sure, Bron was dangerous, but there was something in Vas's eyes that I recognized all too well from the Island, where rich men hunted us for sport. There were rules there, but there were always men who were looking to circumvent them. Vas was that type of man. Dangerous. It wasn't a question of whether he'd killed people or had them killed, it was only a question of how many and how recently.

I straightened my spine and tried to look as dignified as I could. Being the object of his scrutiny was making me wish I'd stopped long enough to use the bathroom because I suddenly needed to pee. I waited, not knowing what he was looking for in my eyes. Guilelessness or calculation? I had a feeling this man didn't have a lot of respect for anyone naïve enough to be guileless.

"You understand that in this family, I am in charge. I decide which of my children are in favor and which of them get an increase in their allowance."

"Of course."

"Bronislav has told me that Ilya is very fond of his little island and expects that he may choose to return rather than stay here."

Slowly, I nodded.

"A woman like you never wants a weak man unless he has money."

"I can assure you I don't want Ilya's money, and he's not weak at all—he's only different from you."

He raised an eyebrow at me.

"So, you understand who will pay all of your bills?"

"Yes," I said hesitantly. Once Bron took over, I supposed it would be him, but maybe the money would be tied to Vas until he died?

"Everyone in this family knows it's in their best interest to stay on my good side."

I didn't like where this seemed to be going. "That makes sense."

"Good. I'm glad you understand your place in the family and my expectations of you."

We stared at each other across the desk.

"What do you mean?"

"I expect the same thing from you that I expect from the rest of my daughters-in-law." He toyed with his empty glass. "You will come to my office when I summon you and you will do everything I say without exception or hesitation."

I felt like an eel had invaded my stomach and was slithering around in there. "As in, you expect me to..."

His smile was nasty. "If you're a good lay, I may even increase your husband's allowance."

What in the actual fuck?

Needing to stall for time, I got up and poured myself the drink he'd offered me. He'd already indirectly paid for me to be here, through the money he'd put in Bron or Ilya's wallet, but this was fucking creepy. Could I bring myself to do this to help Ilya keep his island and his stipend?

I felt ill.

How could he be so disgusting?

Aside from the ick factor of sleeping with a man who was sleeping with all my sisters-in-law, and the chance of catching an STI, I didn't want to earn our livelihood by doing sexual favors for my father-in-law. There was no way my men would want me to.

My brain felt like it was short-circuiting.

If Vas had been hunting me on the Island, I wouldn't have thought twice, but things were different now. I wasn't single anymore.

I didn't want Ilya to lose his island, but he and Bron would help me figure things out without having to resort to this.

"I...don't think that's a good idea." How could a woman politely reject the sexual advances of her tyrannical father-in-law without pissing him off?

"I think you should remember who has all the power in this room. Besides, I doubt a woman like you came to your marriage a virgin. What difference does it make if a man plows a field that has already been plowed?"

He got up so suddenly I jumped to my feet. As he strode to me, I backed away, and was about to turn when he crashed into me. With a cruel grip on my hair, he yanked my head back and he shoved his tongue into my mouth, half choking me with it.

"Stop! Let go of me!" I beat at his chest, but I doubted anyone could hear us, considering how soundproofed this whole house seemed to be. I tried to fight him off, but his hands were everywhere, groping, pinching. He let go of my hair long enough to grab the neckline of my dress and tear it open. I slapped him hard across the face.

"No!"

Trying to shove him off me wasn't working. I hoped someone would burst in and save me, but Bron had gone out on business—I doubted Vas sending him away was a coincidence. Ilya wouldn't come looking for me yet, even if he'd already come out of the bathroom.

I screamed and kicked as he groped my breasts and then tore off my panties. When I tried to slap him again, he caught my wrist and twisted my arm behind my back, using the leverage and the pain he caused to hold me still while he ran his free hand over my near nakedness.

"I'll have to thank Ilya for marrying a woman with a bit of spirit. I don't think any of the others ever fought me this hard." He chuckled and pushed a finger into my pussy. "See? You're making such a fuss, but your body wants me. A woman's body always wants the strongest man in the room—it's nature's way of ensuring the species stays strong."

What he was interpreting as my interest was only what two of his sons had left behind the night before. His breath smelled like alcohol.

Despite how much he drank, he'd unfortunately kept himself in good shape.

"Maybe you'll be lucky, and I'll breed you."

"I'm your son's wife! Why would you do this?"

"Because I can. Because it's my job to ensure the family line is strong. My weak sons shouldn't be the ones impregnating their pretty wives."

He tried to kiss me again, but I snapped my teeth, narrowly missing his nose.

"Oh, Delilah. Breeding this body is going to be so sweet for me. You might not like it much, but I'll like that even better." He chuckled. "Don't worry, my sons know some of the children they are raise are mine. It's not betraying your husband. He knows why you're in here. He knows the price of having my support."

Betrayal flared in my chest.

But no, the adrenaline was confusing me, making me believe his lies.

"There's no way Ilya would allow this." I tried to force his finger out of me, but instead he added another one. It only felt rough and invasive, and I tried not to let myself get upset about it. This was just any guy. Men had pawed at me uninvited often enough, even before I went to the Island. Hopefully, no matter what happened in here I could shake it off.

He pulled his fingers out of me and fumbled with his belt. It stuck on something, and his focus shifted to the task. I was half leaned back against his arm where he still had mine wrenched behind my back. He had trapped my legs between his so I couldn't kick him. I let myself go lax, as though I'd given up on fighting him, still wondering if I should let him do it—wondering if I would fuck up Ilya's future if I didn't.

His buckle popped open, and everything in me rebelled.

Hell no.

I twisted my hip and jerked my leg up, kneeing him squarely in the balls. It hit home hard.

He opened his mouth in a silent scream and went down, letting go of my arm. I unlocked the door and bolted from the room, not caring that the shreds of my dress were flapping behind me, still trapped to my shoulders. I turned the wrong way a few times, expecting to hear him coming for me.

What was I going to do? I'd kneed a very dangerous man in the balls.

Somewhere along the way, I'd lost a shoe. I kicked the other one off so I could run faster. My bad ankle was making me limp by the time I got to our suite and burst in. Maybe I should have run down the drive and away from the house—maybe gone to the police station or gone into hiding?

As soon as Vas recovered, he would kill me and make Bron dispose of my body.

I closed the door behind me and realized the sound in my ears was my own shriek of rage. The bathroom door ripped open and bounced off the tile. Ilya came charging out, his gaze horrified when it landed on me. He was naked and his hair was wet.

"What happened? Who did this to you?"

"Did you send me to your father's office knowing he would try to rape me?"

His face flooded with rage.

"My father did this to you?" His voice was so quiet I barely heard him.

"Yes. I hurt him and got away. I shouldn't have come back to our suite. I need to hide."

His gaze went cold. "He won't hurt you again."

"He said he'll cut off your income. All the daughters-in-law have to do it. I'm sorry. I couldn't let him. He's going to get even with me—with us. I need to go."

He wrapped his hand around the back of my neck and pulled me close. The kiss he gave me was careful, as though he thought he might break me.

"I'll deal with him." He went back to the bathroom and grabbed his jeans, pulling them up and buckling his belt. Without bothering to put on anything else, he went to our luggage and unzipped the large back pocket of his suitcase.

"What are you doing? Those are empty."

"Mine is not." He reached in and pulled out a wooden handle which made no sense until the axe's head came out.

"You brought an axe to Moscow? What did you think you were going to be doing here?"

He propped the tool-turned-weapon by the door. "A man never knows when he might need his axe."

Grimly, he retrieved a throw from the back of the couch and wrapped it tight around me, then sat me down and handed me the TV remote. "Find something loud to watch. I'll be back in a few minutes."

"Ilya, you can't threaten him. He's a dangerous man. You have to get me out of here—I have to hide."

He grabbed my chin and kissed me. "Stay here, woman." The command was still ringing in the air as he took up his axe and went out the door. He shut it behind him.

I sat motionless on the couch until he opened the door again, startling me. "Lock the door, wife."

As soon as he closed the door again, I crossed the room and locked it. I heard him tap on it from the other side, showing me he hadn't left until he was sure I'd obeyed him.

My teeth were chattering. It was ridiculous. I'd been assaulted so many times in my life, so why on earth was this freaking me out? Whatever Ilya thought he was doing wasn't going to work—Vas was a hardened criminal.

Was he seriously going to threaten his mob boss father with an axe? The man probably had a dozen guns in his desk, loaded and ready.

God, what if he kills Ilya.

I unlocked the door again and fled after him, getting the twists and turns right this time, but even my frightened run was no match for Ilya's angry strides. At one turn, I saw him bump into a maid who almost went sprawling, but he caught her arm and patted her.

"So sorry."

The woman gave him a frightened smile, and she shrank back as he turned away and kept walking. It was only then that she saw the axe in his hand and she squeaked and ran past me the other way.

"Ilya!" I almost stage-whispered, but he didn't slow down. Had he not heard me? Maybe I'd said it too quietly, or maybe he was too angry to hear me.

When he got to the office, the door was closed. Ilya tried the knob and when it wouldn't turn, he backed a few steps and kicked it open.

Vas rose from the visitor chair nearest the door. He stood and turned, still clutching where I'd kneed him. Rage burned in his eyes.

"Don't even think about trying to save that little bitch from me—"

A chill slid across my skin, and my belly churned. Vas really was going to kill me. Threatening him would put Ilya's life in danger.

I was three steps away from the door when Ilya brought the axe up and smashed it into Vas's head.

There was a sound—a scream? Was it me or Vas?

My limbs wouldn't move.

The second blow came before the man even hit the floor.

Ilya hit him again once he was down, then stopped, chest heaving.

Oh god. Was he alive?

He couldn't be. His head wasn't anything close to head-shaped anymore. It was open. Oozing. Blood and chunks of pulpy flesh had splattered Ilya, the carpet, the walls. Bits of it were dripping to the floor from the axe's lethal edge.

Bile burned the back of my throat, but I swallowed it down.

My husband stood with his back to me.

"Ilya?" I whispered. It seemed loud in the silence.

I reached out to touch him, but hesitated inches away.

He blew out a breath, then turned to look at me, hair wild, gore dripping from his handsome face.

He looked unhinged. Ferocious.

He shook the axe with a quick twitch, shaking off the worst of the gore.

"Why?" I whispered.

"No one hurts my wife."

He looked like a marauding Viking from a movie, covered in blood, with an axe in his hand. The stench of death filled my nostrils.

"You were supposed to stay in our room."

"I was afraid he'd kill you."

He grunted and stalked past me. "Follow me."

I stayed close, watching behind us, ready to warn him if a guard or one of his brothers showed up.

I did my best not to step in the blood that still dripped from him. He was leaving a noticeable trail.

"Where are we going?"

"To speak to my brothers."

"Ilya, no. They're going to call the police. We need to leave."

"I'm not going to run. You have another husband to keep you warm while I'm in jail."

God, my heart couldn't take any more of this. "Stop and think, Ilya."

He turned to face me. I should have cringed from him, but I didn't.

"I've thought all I need to." He kept walking. We were in the family wing now, going through the hall outside the family suites. "Family meeting! Now!" He pounded on the doors as he passed them. He shouted in Russian as he kept going, then walked down the stairs, his bare feet silent against the marble.

"Are you going to kill them, too?" I whispered, eyeing the axe in his hand.

He turned an incredulous look my way. "Why would I kill them?"

"You're still holding your axe."

"The axe will be in my hand until I'm satisfied you're out of danger."

Confused family members wandered into the dining room, freezing as soon as they saw the condition Ilya was in, and the weapon in his hand.

I was still holding the throw tightly around me, but even so, I felt naked, knowing the state my dress was in.

"What did you do?" Alexander demanded.

"You knew Vas would prey on my woman, and you said nothing to me?"

"What did you do?" Alexander said again.

"I dealt with it." He took my hand and looked like he would pull me close, but then glanced down at himself and only squeezed it. "Why did no one warn us?"

"How did you not know?" Yuri spat. "All of us have been aware of Father's proclivities since we were children."

"Did you kill him?" Andrey asked, his face its usual controlled mask.

The wives whispered among themselves, their worried gazes on Ilya.

"He's dead. One of you should have done this years ago if you knew he was using your wives against their will." He spat on the floor.

"You really didn't know," Alexander mused.

"No, I didn't." Ilya waited, but nobody made a move. "Who will call the police?"

Everyone in the room looked to their spouses and then the brothers began whispering amongst themselves in Russian.

"No one is calling the police—at least not yet," Alexander finally said. "Go clean the blood off yourself, and we'll discuss this when Bron is back."

Nodding, we left the room, Ilya's hand firm on my lower back.

Chapter Twenty-Three

I lya stood in the middle of our suite's living room, looking for somewhere to lay down his gory axe.

The door opened behind me, and I whirled, ready to fight whichever brother was planning to attack Ilya. Bron entered and met my gaze, then dropped his focus to where my fists were up and ready. He was chewing something and had a takeout bag in his hand.

"Am I already in the doghouse?" he said as he closed the door behind him. "I didn't even stop for a beer on the way back. I brought you two some *ponchinki*."

From the gleam in his eye, I could tell he was amused, but when he saw my expression, he took in the rest of me. He touched the blanket I had wrapped around me. "What happened to your dress?"

His attention flicked from me to where Ilya stood behind me, partially shielded from view.

"Jesus, what happened?" He pulled me to him and practically dragged me across the room to where Ilya stood. The blood on him had mostly congealed. It had to be itchy.

"Ilya, look at me," his voice was sharp. "What happened?"

"I had no other choice."

"No other choice? What do you mean?"

Ilya didn't respond, so Bron turned to me.

"Who did this to you?" He took me by the arm and looked me over as though he might identify my attacker by examining the damage he'd done.

"Vas."

"What did that bastard do?" Bron demanded, eyes flashing.

I looked from him to Ilya.

"He tried—" I swallowed, but I couldn't finish saying it. "I got away."

Ilya clarified, "She kneed him in the balls."

"And then?"

"I went to talk to him."

"Talk to him?" I said, probably too shrilly.

"I only meant to threaten him."

"You didn't *say* anything. That wasn't a threat—that was retribution."

"He deserved it." He narrowed his eyes at me. "And I would do it again."

Bron paled. "Ilyusha—you can't hurt a man like Vas and expect him not to retaliate."

Did he seriously think Ilya only hurt him? There was so much blood. It was hard to believe it all came from one person.

"Vas is dead."

"Dead?" He shook himself. "Are either of you hurt? Is any of that blood yours?" Carefully, he took the axe from Ilya. "We need to wash you off and get you out of here before the police come."

"The police aren't coming unless you call them. The others won't do it. I've spoken to them."

"You trust them?"

"They seem relieved he's dead," Ilya muttered.

"Go wash."

Their stare-down was silent and left me wondering what they were saying to each other.

Ilya turned and went back into the bathroom, and as the water started, Bron picked up the axe and hefted it.

I had sunk onto the couch, and I eyed him suspiciously.

"Where are you going with that?"

"Stay here and lock the door behind me."

"Bron!"

He scowled at me. "For once in your life, woman, do what I say. If anyone tries to come through, go tell Ilya."

Despite his stern tone, his eyes were worried. Did he think their brothers would attack Ilya as soon as he was out of the room?

"Don't kill anybody," I recommended.

"I'll kill every last person in this fucking house if it means keeping the two of you safe." He leaned down and kissed me, holding the bloody axe away from me. "Now be a good girl."

He left.

Once he'd gone, I did as he'd instructed and locked the door.

I stripped the rags from my body and slipped on a dress that didn't make me look like a scarecrow. In the sudden quiet, there was time to notice I was sore from when Vas had violated me with his fingers.

Those fingers were attached to what was now a dead man.

I shuddered in revulsion, trying to think of the encounter as something a stranger had done on the Island where I'd met my husbands. I missed it there. It was a brutal, painful place, but at least it was honest. No one there had taken me by surprise the way Vas had. In a place like that, a woman knew what to expect.

It wasn't like I'd trusted Vas—I'd barely known the man, but I also hadn't expected him to assault me.

Now he was dead.

Ilya had worked so hard to win Vas's approval, and all he'd gotten was betrayal and possibly a twenty-year sentence if Russian law was anything like American law.

I wandered into the bathroom, not in the mood to be alone with my thoughts. Steam filled the room, and I turned on the fan. Ilya wiped the water from his eyes and turned to look at me.

"Are you okay?" He planted his hands on the glass shower surround. He'd been in long enough that the water running off him was clear rather than pink with blood.

I shrugged.

"I'm sorry I listened to Bron and came to shower instead of checking on you."

"I'm fine."

"You're not fine."

"You know damn well this isn't the first time something like this has happened to me—it's the only time anyone has cared enough to make sure it never happens again." I kissed the glass where his palm rested against it.

"You're not afraid of me or angry that I lost control of my temper?"

"Hell, no. Are you upset you killed your father to keep me safe?"

"He tried to rape you," he said, as though the only logical response had been violent axe murder. I imagined him murdering the entire soccer team from my high school, but at the time, him being seven years older than me would have been creepy.

"You saw what Bron did to the man who attacked you in the park. I expected more from the man I've been trying to impress for most of my life."

His mouth twisted. Rivulets of water followed the hard grooves and bulges of his arms, torso, and legs. He was so beautiful, and not just on the outside. It wasn't fair that no one in his family except Bron loved him the way he deserved.

The civilized part of my brain was telling me I should be repulsed. Instead, I felt safe. I felt valued.

"I don't understand why my brothers allowed him to do that to their wives. What kind of men am I related to? They are all cowards, except for Bron." He scrubbed himself down with soap, then scraped under his short nails. "I'm sure I'm not the man you thought you were marrying. If you want a divorce, I won't blame you."

"You protected me without worrying about what would happen to you afterward. That's exactly who I thought you were, although I didn't think you'd go so far—or ever need to."

He rinsed away the soap and shut off the water. Rather than getting out, he stood there and watched the water running down the drain. I grabbed a clean towel and opened the shower door to hand it to him.

"I'm a murderer."

"You don't think he was, too?"

"I know he was."

I helped him dry off. He leaned on me, and I hugged him. The dampness of his skin seeped through my clean dress, but I needed the contact as much as he seemed to.

It was hard to say which one of us was more of a mess. Ilya was doing his best to keep his emotions masked, but I could tell he was a bundle of nerves under that.

"I'm sorry I told you what he did. I'm sorry you felt like you had to defend me like that."

He hugged me tighter. "Don't be sorry. If you can't even rely on me to protect you, then what kind of husband would I be? As much as we like to play rough with you, that doesn't mean your safety isn't important to us. You belong to us, and any other man who tries to harm you will get what he deserves."

"I could have cooperated. I didn't need to make a fuss."

"And he could have chosen not to be a treacherous piece of shit. He's been coercing women and forcing them to service him. Bron and his mother struggled for every mouthful of food she earned working in his kitchen, and he let that happen. He probably exiled me just because he didn't like my mother." He buried his face in my hair and inhaled. "My father wasn't a good man."

We had just left the bathroom when Bron came in. There was blood on his clothes.

"What happened out there? Are you hurt?" Ilya demanded.

"I dismembered Vas. Oleg will dispose of him." Bron had said Vas was into some criminal shit, but he'd had his sons disposing of bodies for him?

"Wouldn't it be easier to move a body that was intact?" Ilya asked.

Bron shrugged. "Probably."

The satisfaction on his face as he went to take his turn in the shower was enough of an explanation.

Chapter Twenty-Four

By the time we got back to the rest of the group, they were sitting around the ridiculously long dinner table. It now smelled like a distillery. The loud talk died down as soon as we walked in.

No one looked angry, but they all watched Ilya and Bron with wary eyes.

Bron sat at the head of the table in the spot Vas usually occupied. It was a statement that raised no objections. Ilya helped me into the seat next to Bron, then stood between and behind us, like a bodyguard. He'd left the axe back in our room, but when he'd gotten dressed, he'd strapped his sheathed hunting knife to his belt.

"I know it's getting late, but I thought we should discuss this as a family before going to bed," Bron said.

A few of the older ones nodded.

"Since none of you called the police, I'm assuming you won't?"

There was a general agreement to that.

"I take it our father wasn't well liked in the family?"

The brothers and their wives stared at him, not answering, although Dmitry snorted.

"We only want to know if you plan to cut off our allowances," Kirill admitted.

His wife, a petite brunette, leaned closer to him. "And what you expect to receive from us in return."

I cleared my throat. "So you acknowledge that either Bron or Ilya, or both, are heads of the family now?"

Yuri stood. "Ilya can't be head of the family. He's nothing to us."

What the fuck?

"What?" Bron demanded.

Several people at the table looked at Bron, incredulous.

"You have two eyes—look at him," Kirill said, gesturing at Ilya as though we might not have seen him before. "Everyone knows Ilya's mother was having an affair with her bodyguard. Vas had been in Portugal for six months when she got pregnant with Ilya. None of us were to speak of it, but we all knew."

"Vas wasn't my father?" Ilya looked more terrifying than when he'd been covered in blood.

"No," Alexander confirmed. "Vas didn't want anyone to know. He claimed you as his own and then quietly got rid of your mother and her guard. They were stupid to think Vas wouldn't take revenge."

Ilya isn't Bron's brother.

Neither of them reacted. I had to fight down a sob of relief. I got to my feet with all the dignity I could muster and left the room.

There was so much emotion trapped in my throat, it felt clogged. I swallowed, and then swallowed again, trying to calm down and willing the tears away. Ilya came out, too, and walked past me, putting his hands on his hips and looking steadfastly at the ceiling. All I wanted to do was wrap my arms around him, but I knew if I did, the tears he was trying to hold back would come. It wasn't the time.

"I'm so sorry about your parents."

He turned back to me and pressed his lips together. "I wish I could say I missed my mother, but I barely remember her." He brushed a lock of hair behind my ear.

Bron came around the corner a moment later. His lips were trembling just enough for me to notice. He caught Ilya by the cheeks and kissed him hard on the mouth, then on the forehead before letting him go. He kissed me, too, then turned and wordlessly went back into the dining room.

"None of you will challenge me being head of this family?" I heard Bron demand.

Both Ilya and I moved back into the room, not about to leave him to deal with these people alone. I took my seat again, but Bron and Ilya stood to either side of Vas's chair.

Alexander held up his hands. "There's a reason none of us challenged his decision when he named you as his successor. None of us want it. We just don't want our incomes to vanish."

"Good."

"So, it's business as usual then?" Alexander asked. "Oleg and Dmitry will clean up the mess and get rid of the body."

"Vas didn't have people for that?" Ilya asked.

"No. We take care of most things in-house. We were all raised to fill certain roles. I do the accounting."

Bron grunted. "It's not going to be business as usual. As far as I'm concerned, Vas's business died with him. My plan is to liquidate his assets and divide them equally between us. If any of you want to keep things running, you can do it with your own portion of the money."

The silence that fell around the table seemed stunned rather than angry at the idea. They all stared at Bron.

Kirill got to his feet and opened his mouth, then closed it, gestured, then opened it again. "So...you're saying that as the new head of this family, you're choosing to set us free?"

Alexander shook himself like a dog who'd come in from a downpour. "It may take some time to liquidate everything."

"I could go to music school," Dmitry said under his breath.

"What? Your dream wasn't to run the crematorium with me?" Oleg said, his voice laced with sarcasm.

"I want a divorce," Alexander's wife, Alina, declared.

"Good. I'll give you half my share, and I never want to see your face again." Alexander threw back the rest of his drink and slammed his glass down on the table. She walked out of the room and didn't look back.

"I know he's not blood, but I think Ilya deserves a share of the money," Andrey said from his spot further down the table. "He may not be our brother by blood, but he's the one who had the balls to get rid of our problem."

"He also has an axe back in his room," Oleg pointed out. "I think giving him a share is the logical choice."

"I want the island," Ilya said without hesitation.

The rest of the brothers looked disgusted.

"That pile of rock? You can have it," Kirill said. "I doubt it's worth much. I know *I* never want to see the place again."

"Why do you want it?" Alexander asked, brows pinched.

Ilya shrugged. "It's my home."

"It can be your bonus for solving our problem. The rest of us will fight over the properties that are actually worth something."

Oleg and Dmitry started acting out how they imagined Vas's murder went down, complete with their impressions of the face Vas probably made as he died.

Alexander and Bron agreed to look over the books together the next day, and we left what was rapidly becoming a drunken celebration.

"They're all so fucked up," Bron said as soon as our suite door was closed and locked behind us.

"I think they're just letting off steam," I replied. "Your father controlled their lives. He even said several of your brothers' children were actually his."

"I think most of them are going to either run through their inheritance filling the pockets of their therapists or they'll drink themselves to death."

"Not our problem." Ilya's face was stoic.

Bron grabbed the front of Ilya's shirt and pulled him close. "Such a coldhearted little brother."

"Don't call me that."

"Oh, now that we know we're not related, I think I'll always call you that. It's funny as fuck."

"I don't know how you can call days of hell funny."

"Did you miss me so much, Ilyusha?"

"I thought I might die." He said it so earnestly, with his heart in his eyes. I held my breath, worried Bron would make a joke of it.

Instead, Bron's expression softened, and he kissed him, long and sweet. I collapsed onto the couch and watched them, more than happy to play voyeur and give myself a minute to breathe.

"I'm sorry we were right about your mother being dead."

"Well, if they were in love with each other, I'm glad my parents died together. If something ever happened to you or Delilah, that's what I would want."

"Ridiculous, romantic boy." He grabbed Ilya's hand and kissed his knuckles.

Eventually, they let go of each other, and Bron led him to the couch where I sat. Bron picked me up and then sat down, holding me on his lap. Ilya cozied up next to him and pulled my legs over his.

"Will you still stay with us, wife?" Ilya's hand was warm on my knee.

"I don't know. Maybe Alina had the right idea," I teased. "Seriously, though—you kidnapped me, used me, married me without even asking me. How am I supposed to trust two men who don't understand the concept of consent?"

Bron bit my bottom lip hard enough to make me whimper, and then he kissed me long and thoroughly.

"Do you think our wife is in a temper because she misses having both of us in her bed at the same time?" Ilya's hand closed over my ankle and squeezed.

Bron removed his tongue from my mouth and let me breathe. "I think she's tired. It's been a long day."

"It has."

"You're a murderer."

"I am."

"It doesn't bother you?"

"It should. Maybe it will tomorrow." Ilya shrugged.

Bron pressed his forehead to mine. "I'm sorry I trusted him with you and that I wasn't here to protect you."

"He sent you away on purpose."

A growling sound came from low in his chest. "Probably. I wish I had been the one to kill him, but I'll have to be satisfied with helping my brothers dispose of him." He cleared his throat, looking uncomfortable. "Do you want to see a doctor or a therapist?"

I rested my cheek against his shoulder. The clean, familiar smell of him calmed me.

"No. I think I'll be okay," I murmured. "He's dead. He can't hurt me again."

"If you change your mind later, you tell me." Between Bron stroking my hair and Ilya rubbing my feet, I started to nod off.

"Shutting down the business might take a while. We may not be able to go home for weeks or even months," Bron said.

"I don't like keeping her here," Ilya said. "Maybe our brothers really are happy to be rid of him, but they were raised in a treacherous house. Who knows what their plans truly are?"

"I agree. I think you should take Delilah home and keep her safe there. I'll come to you as soon as things are more settled."

"I don't like leaving you alone here, either."

"She's the priority."

I drifted off. Later, I half woke when someone moved me, but I burrowed into my spot between two warm, muscular bodies and fell right back to sleep.

Chapter Twenty-Five

The house was modern and stylish, with clean, elegant lines. It looked nothing like our ramshackle monstrosity on the island. A normal woman would have been envious of this beautiful home, but the landscaping looked like a bitch to maintain. I'd rather have goats than topiaries.

When we went home again next week, Ilya and I planned to ambush Bron with some puppies, too.

I couldn't believe we were actually here. Ilya's arm was solid and comforting under my fingers as we walked up the steps to the front door. As we reached it, it swung open.

"Delilah!" Calder exclaimed, a wide grin on his handsome face. He looked more or less the same as when I'd seen him last, but maybe a little more relaxed. It made sense. I don't think any of us had relaxed much on Prey Island.

"Thank you so much for tracking us down," I said, grinning. "I didn't know where to start searching for her. You know Ilya and Bron?"

The men shook hands and there was the obvious air of the three of them sizing each other up. I rolled my eyes.

Of course, my husbands knew I'd slept with Calder and Ajax before I'd even met them. They weren't jealous, but they also weren't *not* jealous if their subtle body language was accurate. I was just happy they were willing to do this with me rather than sending me off on my own or insisting Lane come to us.

After my first phone call with Lanie, I'd discovered Bron had never followed through on making sure she'd been told where I was. Supposedly, he hadn't realized it was a big deal, but I was still pissed. Poor Lane had gone through months of unnecessary worry because of it.

"No offense, but where is she?"

Calder laughed. "I know, I know. You're not here to see me. I'll try my best not to take it personally."

He led us into the foyer and took our coats. He had tracked us down a couple of months ago, but we'd been in the middle of harvest, so we'd had to delay our visit.

"She's upstairs. Ajax is fussing with her, and he won't let her come down until he's decided she's ready."

He had just shown us into a living room the size of a dance hall when Lane came running into the room, cheeks pink and eyes shining.

"Delilah!" She flew at me, and I barely had time to catch her. We almost toppled over together, but Bron steadied me and kept us upright.

I clung to her and found myself crying even though I'd sworn to myself I wouldn't. Until Calder had tracked me down, I'd started to despair I would never get to see my best friend again. Maybe we hadn't spent that much time together—it had only been a month—but I'd never clicked with another woman like that before, let alone had time for a friend.

I kissed her cheeks, and she laughed and let me go. She wiped at my tears and then at her own.

She looked radiant. There was a little velvet choker around her neck with a silver bell. It was cute and definitely looked like a collar.

"I'm still mad at you!" she grumbled, pointing at Bron.

"I know." Bron's face was solemn but his eyes twinkled. "But I'm a man. Men forget things."

"You forgot to tell Island management to tell me she wasn't dead. You owe me like...four months of my life back. You gave me grey hair!"

"I'll buy you some hair dye. What color would you like?"

"No hair dye," Ajax interrupted, pulling Lane back so she didn't actually poke Bron's chest. "Knowing the brat, it'll be technicolor by tomorrow."

She pretended to consider it. Ajax sighed and pulled her in for a kiss before swatting her ass and sending her my way.

"Let's let the boys make awkward conversation for an hour or so. I'll show you around so we can have some privacy and talk."

"Behave yourself, Half-Pint," Ajax warned, but his mouth twisted wryly.

"What on earth do you think we're going to do?"

He chuckled, and I noticed both he and Calder ogled her as we walked away. Apparently, they weren't tired of each other yet either.

The house looked like it belonged on a reality TV show. I couldn't help but compare it to the small apartment she'd described as where she used to live with her sister and aunt.

"We're both moving up in the world," she said with a short laugh.

"When I signed up for that place, finding husbands was the last thing on my mind."

"You're really staying married to them after they tricked you?"

I grimaced. "It wasn't super romantic, but I can't complain about being married to them."

"Men." Lane rolled her eyes. "Originally, mine offered me a contract for a year, but they've already thrown that out the window. Ajax already has our vacations booked for the next three years." Her face was flushed.

"I'm guessing it's not only future vacation plans between the three of you."

She sighed, looking amused and embarrassed. She pulled down the neckline of her dress and showed me a little bird-shaped scar over her heart.

"It was supposed to be a fee-for-service arrangement, but apparently now they're keeping me." She grinned and waggled her eyebrows. "I'm even allowed to sleep on the bed now."

"Oh my god, you kinky weirdo. Where the hell did they have you sleeping before that?"

She swung open a door to reveal a large room with the biggest bed I'd ever seen. It was way bigger than a king-size. She swept up the bed skirt to reveal bars that went all the way around the base of the bed.

"They made you sleep under the bed?"

"Hot, right?"

I laughed and gave her a hug. "Jesus, Lane. When you got to Prey Island, you were so new to kink, and now look at you—brands and under-bed cages."

She caught my hand and brought it up to eye level. "Nice rock on the engagement ring."

"It belonged to Ilya's mother."

"That's so sweet! And the double, entwined wedding band? Nice touch."

We'd picked it out together, later, and I loved it.

"They're both my husbands—at least as far as we're concerned."

"That's the way things are here, too, except everyone is Ajax's bitch."

"Everyone is Bron's bitch at our house."

She led me into another living room and flopped onto an elegant couch, then patted the seat beside her. I sank down and leaned my head against the back of it, considering the modern art sculpture that stood on the other side of the room.

I grabbed her hand and squeezed it. "So...did you choose to move here, or did you get kidnapped too?"

"They gave me a choice, but only after they stalked me and broke into my apartment." She groaned as though the memory was embarrassing. "Is there anything toxic men won't do to get their way?"

"Speaking of which, have you had any new leads on Clover?"

"The guys have been looking, but they haven't had any luck yet. The poor kid has nothing. Did you know she aged out of foster care? She never mentioned that to me. Did she mention it to you?"

"No. She talked about her parents as though she lived with them. You haven't found any family?"

Lane frowned. "Calder found out her parents are dead—her father when she was still a baby, and her mother when she was fourteen. She lived in a group home after that and then got her own apartment. From what the guys have been able to piece together, after her tour on the Island finished, she never came home. Her landlord sold off her stuff to pay back rent, and moved in new tenants. The neighbors say they haven't seen her."

"Oh god. Where could she be?"

"Ajax has been reaching out to other people he knows—the kind of people you and I don't want to know." She shivered. "One of them said he met you and your men briefly at a club in Saint Petersburg. It's how they tracked you down."

I felt my cheeks grow hot, and I looked away.

"So, what happened at this club?"

"Nothing compared to what you've been doing here!"

Lane bit her bottom lip and was clearly trying to hold back a laugh.

"You know you can tell me anything. I mean, who am I going to tell? I would never tell the guys because they might get ideas I don't want them to have."

Of course, I told her everything.

For the week we stayed, it was like we had never left Prey Island, except there were no organized games and there was a hell of a lot more privacy. Lane and I got to hang out, and Ajax gave Bron instructions on how to get internet on our island so Lane and I could keep in touch.

As for Clover, Calder and Ajax promised us they would keep looking, but there was no way to know where one small, helpless girl could have gone.

Chapter Twenty-Six

"The two of you are like small children masquerading as adults." Bron came in with an armload of firewood. "You would think everyone we know was coming to visit for a week."

"Okay, Mr. Grumpy. I don't see that stopping you from sneaking bits of dessert every time you think we can't see you."

He'd left the dogs outside, thank goodness. They were mostly obedient, but they could be opportunists when it came to food, and they weren't tiny puppies anymore. They could reach things on the table without any trouble.

He shrugged. "There's no reason to deprive myself of the spoils, considering how much of your attention is being taken up by these silly preparations."

Ilya grinned. "I think he is jealous of the time we spend together baking."

"Is that true, Bron? Are you jealous of this chocolate chip cookie?" I waved it at him, and he snatched it out of my hand and shoved it into his mouth.

"Not anymore," he said with his mouth full.

We both watched his mouth move as he chewed.

"Maybe I'm the one jealous of the cookie now," Ilya admitted.

"Is that so?" Bron walked Ilya backward until he was bent at an uncomfortable angle backward over the counter. In the year and a bit since we'd taken full ownership of our island, the two of them had regrown their beards, and Bron's hair was back to being shaggy.

They were both more delicious than anything I could make in this kitchen.

"If you two are going to start wrestling, you need to get the hell out of the kitchen before you wreck all our hard work."

"No sex." Ilya pushed Bron back with a hand on his chest.

Seeing Bron get shot down was probably the funniest thing I'd seen all week. He looked so confused—almost wounded.

"You can't say no to me," Bron complained.

"Sure I can. The only question is whether you will respect my wishes."

Bron growled. "I'll *respect* any part of you I please, anytime I want to."

I wedged myself between them and pointed at Bron.

"If you keep being grouchy, Santa will bring you coal for Christmas."

He caught me around the waist and swung me in a circle, then bit my neck, making me squeal.

"Quick, I've got him distracted!" I said to Ilya. "Get those cookies out of the oven before they burn."

Ilya tugged on my new floral oven mitts, which looked adorable on him and were much more civilized than grabbing things out of the oven with a towel. Even once the cookies were safely on top of the stove, Bron kept chewing on my neck, sending flashes of heat through me.

"It's pretty bad that one of us has to keep him distracted so we can get anything done around here."

"I don't know how people manage with only two people in a relationship. Who distracts the horny man while the work gets done?"

Bron raised his head from his vampiric endeavors and made a sound of annoyance.

"I do plenty of work around here!"

"And yet you haven't made one cookie for Christmas."

"Who are we baking all these cookies for?" he exclaimed. "There are only three of us!"

"I'm packing them up and mailing them to Lane, my family, and all of your brothers and sisters."

"You can't mail cookies to people."

"Why? Does Russia have a 'no mailing cookies' law I should know about?"

"I've had to suffer through all the baking—I deserve to get fat from them." He turned me in his arms and kissed me.

A lock of hair had escaped his ponytail, and he looked both mischievous and freaking hot. I tucked the rogue strands behind his ear.

He picked me up and tossed me over his shoulder.

"We're not done baking!" I was dangling so far down his back that I smacked his sexy ass but stopped when he gave me a warning retaliatory smack.

"You are, for now," Bron growled. "Come, Ilyusha."

"You two go fuck. I'll finish in here."

Bron turned, and I heard Ilya gasp. When I craned my neck, I saw he'd grabbed Ilya by the hair.

"That wasn't a request."

"You don't need us both!" I laughed and pounded on our Neanderthal's back. "Let one of us finish up."

"If you don't behave, I won't let either of you finish in bed either."

"Hey! Threatening to withhold our orgasms is playing dirty."

"You like it when I'm dirty." He didn't stop until he'd gotten us into his old room, which we now shared.

"You can let go of me," Ilya said. "My dick has decided the cookies can wait."

Rather than put me down, someone tugged down the back of my leggings and bit my ass.

"I wish I'd had some warning before I married a couple of cannibals."

"Brace yourself, woman," Ilya warned.

Bron threw me onto the bed and pulled out his pocketknife.

"Exactly what do you need a knife for?" I asked with completely called-for suspicion.

"The rope."

"What do you need rope for?"

"So you don't wriggle away from us while we give you more orgasms than you want."

"Bron, no!"

"*De-li-lah*, yes." His chuckle was warm and dark, and made me want to roll in it, like a dog with a rotting animal carcass.

Lord. Living here was making me as weird as they were.

I struggled, not even trying to hide how much I enjoyed the fight.

They never played fair with sex or with love.

It was absolutely, toxically perfect.

More from Sorcha Black

Rough Romance

Prey Island: An MMF Bisexual Rough Romance

Cruel Idols: An Enemies to Lovers MMF Bisexual Romance

The Sharp Edge of Bliss: An Enemies to Lovers MMF Bisexual Romance

The Severin Duology

Feral King: An MFM Bisexual Romance

Tragic King: An MMF Bisexual Romance

Valentine: Dark Superhero Romance Boxset

Ein: A Dark Fantasy MFFM Romance

DD/lg Romance

Protecting His Brat: A DD/lg Romance

MFF BDSM Romance

*The Badass Brats Series
with Cari Silverwood and Leia Shaw*

The Dom with a Safeword

The Dom on the Naughty List

The Dom with the Perfect Brats

The Dom with the Clever Tongue

The Dom with the Kink Monsters (this title is MMFF)

The Dom with the Deviant Kittens

M/F BDSM written as Sparrow Beckett
(cowritten with Leia Shaw)

All titles also available or coming soon as

Chapters Interactive Stories

Masters Unleashed Series
Finding Master Right
Playing Hard to Master
To Have and to Master
Master in Shining Armor
All's Fair in Love and Mastery

Masters of Adrenaline Series
Stealing His Thunder
Fueling His Hunger
Pushing Her Limits

Made in the USA
Las Vegas, NV
15 March 2025

19606003R00197